XEI   300

D1145372

THE RUNNING THREAD

The
RUNNING THREAD

BY

Drayton Mayrant

APPLETON-CENTURY-CROFTS, INC.

New York

Copyright, MCMXLIX, By

APPLETON-CENTURY-CROFTS, INC.

All rights reserved. This book, or parts thereof, must not be reproduced in any form without permission of the publisher.

ALL NAMES, CHARACTERS, AND EVENTS IN THIS BOOK ARE FICTIONAL, AND ANY RESEMBLANCE WHICH MAY SEEM TO EXIST TO REAL PERSONS IS PURELY COINCIDENTAL

The quoted lines from "Weavers" have been reprinted by permission of The Poetry Society of South Carolina.

PRINTED IN THE UNITED STATES OF AMERICA

For

Mamie and Godmother

the little daughter of two and the baby the soldier grabbed

FOREWORD

Although told against a background of history, this story is pure fiction. With the exception of Colonel Bond'Ion, General Sherman and a few others whose names are briefly mentioned, all characters are fictional. Lieutenant W. T. Sherman was actually at Fort Moultrie about ten years previous to the time I use. But his friendship with Colonel Bond'Ion and events in Columbia are unwritten history from family records.

D. M.

For, better far a man should have been dead
Than he should break or soil the running thread.

"WEAVERS"

THE RUNNING THREAD

I

LOOKING SOUTHEAST from the Glassin Rocks, Dinah saw Inishmaan across Gregory's Sound. But the cliffs of that middle island blocked her view of the Foul Sound and of Inisheer beyond it. Inisheer had been her mother's home. It was the most remote of the Arans. Distance and love for her mother had vested it with enchantment. Besides, she knew the stories of its Altar of Love.

There was white water off Glassin Rocks where the rollers broke on stone. In between the islands it was deep and still. Less than a mile away she saw currachs at anchor and fishing. She thought to herself that they looked like flies which crawled slowly on a dark mirror, a mirror cracked and clouded with age, the only kind of mirror she owned.

Her mind had a way of turning so to things within the cottage. Ever since her mother's death she had been its only woman, and she had done her best to care for a father and five brothers. Work was lighter since the young men had gone, but she missed them in spite of their roughness. They were horsemen rather than fishermen, and they had scattered to stud farms and race tracks throughout West Ireland. For old Corley was not of Aran as are the Aran-folk whose fathers, and fathers' fathers, have been there for a thousand years. He was North of Ireland Protestant and, in his early youth, had moved to Connach and broken a farm from its surly soil. The same love of horses which his sons inherited had made him attend every county fair from Sligo down to Tralee. It was in Clare, in a rare moment of human weakness, that he had seen and fallen in love with Una O'Laune. She could walk under his outstretched arm without rumpling her blond-brown curls, and she believed in love and hard work and the fairies and the saints.

She was probably the reason why Angus Corley, although he quarreled as an Ulsterman with his neighbors in Connach, took up Irish cudgels against the landlords with them. During The

Troubles of the eighteen-forties he left his farm and moved to Inishmore in Galway Bay.

But Dinah remembered nothing of that and knew nothing of politics. The quiet stream of her life ran between her father's cottage and the various affairs necessary to its keeping. She was domestic by nature, and a woman's duties had fallen on her curly head while she was yet a child. She accepted it and loved it, but she longed for the affection which her mother had never been ashamed to show. Her brothers cared for her in their way but would have died rather than admit it. Her father considered harshness good for the immortal soul.

In the small, strong, lovely body of his youngest child and only daughter, had fused the romance of the islands with his northern steadfastness. More than one husky Aran lad cast his eye upon her as she followed the donkey laden with straddle and baskets of seaweed. The creature was not along with her this afternoon. Dinah Corley had walked, in her short time of leisure, down to the rocky south shore. And in a cleft of those rocks she had spied a small deposit of clay. It would be only large enough to fill her two cupped hands, but it was worth its weight in gold for a tiny Aran farm. That of her father had been made, patiently and through long years, by spreading seaweed on terraces of limestone walled from the wind. Upon this layer of rich fertilizer was deposited, day by day, every handful of soil that a Corley found. It was slow labor and dangerous; for the small clumps of earth built themselves, grain by grain, in crevices of the cliffs. But, once they were made, those island gardens resembled jewel-green handkerchiefs tossed here and there on gray stone, and they repaid their makers with the crops they bore.

Dinah was unknotting the woolen scarf from her hair. Walking the beach or climbing the cliffs, she never wore her mother's shawl, the shawl woven on Inisheer by a great-great-grandmother and blest at Saint Kevin's Altar of Love. She kept that for Sundays, and on weekdays caught her curls with the small, gray-black, well-worn square that she was now untying. As she loosed it, her hair blew free and the sunlight touched it. A mile away and a hundred feet above her, Danny Moloney saw and recognized her. Riding bareback, he urged his shaggy young mare downhill toward the place.

Dinah had not even seen him. She was too intent upon getting the little clump of earth to help root the next year's potato slips. She knew that she needed both hands to climb, so the shawl must serve as a basket. She slipped a corner of it through the criss around her waist, tied it, and then, footsure in her small pampooties, began climbing the face of the cliff.

Danny had no fear of her falling. He knew that the island women were agile and strong, and that they were safe on steeper slopes than the one she was ascending. But he saw a chance for a talk with her alone, and the sunlight was making dark honey of her loose hair. So, heels in the mare's ribs, he leapt intervening boreen walls and, arriving at the beach, dismounted and dropped his lines as signal for her to stand.

He was a tall lad, lean and dark and with a certain rawboned grace. He strode to the foot of the rock and began to ascend it by the twisting ledge that was scarcely wide enough for a foot at a time. As it took him around on the sea side he saw the girl above him.

With careful hands she was lifting the precious deposit of earth. She dug its last grain with her fingers from the limestone crevice where some freakish updraft had carried its nucleus. Leaning her weight against the cliff side to balance, she tied it in her shawl, crossed the four ends so that nothing might spill, and again looped it through her woolen girdle. Only then did she turn and look down, and see Danny climbing below her.

She gave him the smile that always encouraged him anew, although he knew in his heart that she gave the same smile to all Aran. But he was young, and hope loves to walk hand in hand with youth.

"So ye've got it yourself," he said. "I was coming to help you, Dinah."

"My thanks to ye, Danny, all the same. But the path is easy here."

He did not try to lead her, because he knew that a person's own two hands are the surest help in climbing. When he jumped to the beach from the last rock, he reached up and lifted her down. She pushed back her hair and looked up at him with big, dark-lashed gray eyes.

"Tis rich earth, and me father will be glad of it. Already it has a small sprout of green from some seed of grass or flower."

"I am glad for that," he replied. But he was thinking that her father had never been known to show gladness about anything.

"I will set it in the new garden, west of the boreen. I must be on me way back, for Roddy and Betsy are coming."

"They have come ashore already. I was watching the Galway bowt from above when I saw you down here on the strand."

He picked up the white mare's bridle rein and looped it over an arm. "I saw Roddy and Betsy and the Donovans and O'Leary. There was a redcoat sojer along with Tim and Mary."

"Oh, Danny," she begged, "let us hurry then. Mary Donovan is me best friend. I was hoping that she and Tim would be coming for the horse lepping."

They walked uphill together, with the white mare following. Dinah knew that Danny was going to ride her in the next day's wild race, which was called "horse leaping" on Aran. She said, "Datheen Costello and Rory Coola told me you would surely win the prize for first in the lepping."

He turned and put a hand on the mare's flat, hard, white cheek, and the animal blew softly in response.

"Rory and Datheen say she sails over the top of the walls as easy as a gannet sails the waves in Gregory's Sound. They say, too, that you are the lad to ride her, Danny."

He knew he could ride, but it was sweet to hear it from her lips. He flushed and muttered: "I will be after doing me best."

They were walking north and inland now and, as they made the next turn, saw three people coming toward them. One was a tall, slim girl with hair that glinted like copper. Upon one side of her walked a tall young man who had a possessive arm around her. Upon the other, smart and trim in his vivid uniform, was the redcoat soldier of whom Danny had spoken.

The two girls shrieked with joy and rushed to meet each other. When the young men reached them they were still hugging and kissing. Dinah, although overjoyed, was gentle in demonstration. But Mary Donovan's voice rose with her excitement.

"Me Da brought us in the herring bowt, and Roddy and Betsy came with us. Roddy says Muldoon is shipping horses to America. They are for hunting; but the good God knows where is the place they are going! Muldoon wants Roddy to go along and care for them on the voyage. Betsy says she is going too. She is wicked as ever. Tim says he would hate to be Roddy, because— Oh, Danny! Oh, Dinah! I had clean forgot that ye had not met. Tis one of Tim's friends, Mr. Croft."

Laughing at her, Tim caught her arm and pulled her close to him.

"Will ye give Dinah a chance to breathe and meself a chance to talk? Tis me friend John Croft from the barracks. Croft, step up and meet Dinah Corley and Danny Moloney."

The soldier took a step forward and made a stiff little bow. He was a frank-faced young Englishman, medium tall, erect and slim, and the brilliant uniform gave him a transient distinction. His dark eyes lingered on Dinah's face with open admiration. It was a small and provocative face with its slightly tip-tilted nose, and with the bright-brown, windblown curls showing its white brow and small ears. So intent was his gaze that the curved lips parted slightly, deep red flooded the rose-tan cheeks, dark lashes fell and hid eyes not yet ready to meet it.

Danny Moloney's blue gaze narrowed as he watched. But the soldier did not see him; he saw nobody but Dinah.

Mary Donovan said, "I promised Judy Costello to stay with her this time. Father always stays with the Meekins. Rory Coola said there was room at his house for Timmy and John."

Disappointment was in Dinah's voice. "Ah, but Mary, I was hoping that ye would stay with me as ye always do."

"I promised Judy," said Mary. She loved Dinah but did not love old Corley. She added: "Roddy and Betsy will be with ye. It is enough."

Croft heard Dinah sigh very softly and he watched the color, which had come swiftly, drain from her face.

"We must be walking," said Mary. "Tis two miles to the Costellos'. I have no wish to be climbing your ledges of stone in the night."

Timmy pulled her closer and whispered audibly: "Would not myself be there and climbing with you, Moireen?"

Their loud and innocent laughter grated on John Croft's ears. He had suddenly discovered that he liked small, soft-voiced girls. He forgot his admiration for vivacious, red-haired Mary. He remembered, with uncalled-for loathing, a plump lass with bright black eyes who had seemed desirable enough to cause several fights in his regiment.

"Climbing with me or not," said Mary, "it is time we were off. Are ye coming along, John Croft, or are ye stuck where ye stand?"

"I'm coming," he said, but he was not looking at her. He was looking Dinah straight in the eyes, and this time he held her gaze. His voice, as well as his look, was urgent. "I must see you again. Will you be at the race tomorrow?"

She nodded—tried to speak and failed—then turned and laid a hand upon Danny's sleeve. "Danny is riding in it. He has the best lepper on Aran."

Croft's eyes went to the mare. He was horseman enough to detect her fine points beneath an unkempt coat. "She has good legs and plenty of bone. I wish you luck, Moloney."

Danny did not answer as the three of them walked away. He was looking down at Dinah, and his eyes were dark with anger. "I want no luck from a redcoat," he said resentfully. "Why would Tim O'Leary be bringing him to Aran?"

She was wise enough not even to attempt an answer. She said simply: "I must be on me road."

They walked the short way without speaking. Except for the wind, the only sound was the striking of the mare's hoofs on rock as she followed. At the boreen gate they stopped, and Danny took down the higher bar. He had recovered himself when he turned to face her.

"Would you want me to set the clod in the west garden for you?"

In the slow northern twilight he saw her shake her head. He remembered the soldier's eyes fixed on the glint of her loosened hair.

"I wish to show it first to me Da." Her voice dropped to a wistful note. "It may be that the sight of it will put him in a good humor."

She stepped over the lower rail and turned to face him across it. He was already replacing the second bar. With the gate now between them, they looked wordlessly at each other. Then he stepped back, adjusted his lines and vaulted to the mare's back.

Dinah was vaguely troubled. "Have I done aught to make you angry, Danny?"

He reined the mare closer and frowned down at her. "Why would ye be planning to meet the redcoat tomorrow?"

"It was only—only that he asked if I would be there."

"And ye told him ready enough." Danny's young voice was hard.

"I told him truth. I always go. I go to see you ride, Danny."

With his off knee he moved the mare closer. She was young and powerful, but gentle as a kitten. He was close to Dinah now, looking down in her upturned face.

"Do ye mean that ye wish me to win in the lepping, Dinah?"

"That I do, Danny. Ye know it well enough."

He asked her eagerly: "Why do you wish I should win?"

"Because ye are me true friend. And the way ye ride is a wonder. I have great fear of the beasts, meself. I would not get on the back of one."

He gave a short exclamation of impatience. "It is not *that* I wish to know. I wish to know if ye care for me. I—I care for you. You must know it, Dinah."

She was gripping the top rail with both hands and, in the faint but glass-pale light, he saw her lips part for the indrawn breath and her eyes go wider. But his words and his look lacked impact to make her lashes fall in the shy surrender she had shown to another man.

"You must marry some day. It is hard for a woman to live alone on Aran."

"I like you well enough, Danny; but I cannot leave me Da. What would he do without me? And I am not yet eighteen."

"Most island girls are married by the time they are eighteen. Your father is not too old to work or too poor to pay a helper. Willie's wife wanted to stay with him, but he ran her off. If you married me, you would not go far. You could see him and tend him every day."

"I know," she said. "I know." But her voice was again troubled.

"Are you going to let him keep you from getting married at all?"

"I would not be knowing that. I had not thought of the matter, Danny, until—until—"

Her voice faltered and, leaning close, he asked very softly: "Do you mean you had not thought of it until I asked you, Dinah?"

But she would not lie to him. "It was not that I was meaning."
He said roughly: "Then it was the sojer made you think it."
She stepped backward and away from him. "What are you saying, Danny?"

"It is not what I am saying, but what you said yourself. You said you were not thinking of marriage with me. But you thought of it the minute you clapped eyes on a swaggering redcoat!"

He wheeled the horse away from the gate and drove both heels in her ribs. She plunged like a swimmer into the cool sea of twilight. Dinah lost sight of them at once. She stood and heard hoofs ringing on rock, until the sound died in the distance. Then she turned in the narrow lane and began to walk uphill. She felt sad for Danny's anger and hurt and yet strangely elated. Tomorrow, at the horse leaping, she would see the young Englishman. He had wished to see her enough to ask if she would be there. She wondered if his features were as clean-cut as she remembered.

She had reached the door of the cottage. Loud voices came from within it. A parallelogram of light streamed out and yellowed the dusk. Just to one side of its beam she stopped and untied the shawl from her criss. Its small bundle was damp and cold through the cloth. She hoped it would please her father. She heard Betsy's voice, sharp and fretful, and then Roddy's deeper tones. He seemed to be insisting. . . .

She sighed at the thought that the two of them would have irritated Corley. Then she moved on and put a foot upon the step.

The shark-oil lamp was lighted in the middle of the table, and the blue china she had laid was visible around it. In the chimney the turf burned slowly and, on his bench beside it, her father sat with ash stick in hand and with fury on his face. Roddy, hulking but indecisive even in his anger, stood before him as if on trial. She heard him repeating doggedly: "Ye do not understand."

Old Corley raised the ash and roared: "Too well I understand! I understand that me own son is no better than a vagabond. He will leave his home and leave his Da to go with the scum to America!"

2

THE ARGUMENT BETWEEN the two men became so acrimonious that Dinah had no chance to display the prize in her shawl. She heated the stew and brewed the tea and set it and the bread on the table, while Roddy was trying to get his father to let him explain. Matty Muldoon, for whom he worked as a trainer at the farm in Clare, had offered to pay the fare for both Roddy and Betsy, if Roddy went on the cattle boat to care for the hunters on the voyage. Besides that, the American who was buying them offered big wages if he would stay with them as groom until they were used to the climate and settled in their new home.

"And where in the States will be this place ye think ye are going?"

"Tis a city by name of Charleston in a state called Carolina."

Old Corley took exception even to the name. "Tis no seaport of the Irish. I never heard of it. The lads who have gone to America went to Boston or New York."

"Tis a city smaller and farther south," Roddy told him placatingly. "But it has a race track and its people ride and hunt. I tell you it is the chance of me lifetime, father."

"Muldoon thinks more of you than I do if he pays your ticket just to have you look after the beasts. What is the name of the man fool enough to wish to hire you over there?"

"His name is Bull, and the wages he offers are not twice but three times what Muldoon is paying me."

"Tis a Sassennach name," said Corley. "No good can come of your going."

Dinah finished washing and drying the supper china, picked up the earth in her shawl and went out to the new garden. She set it carefully upon its foundation of seaweed, packed it tight, and straightened up as she heard a noise behind her. Her sister-in-law's gaunt figure took shape out of the darkness.

"Why did ye follow me, Betsy? What is it that ye are wanting?"

"I wanted to see," said Betsy, "which one of the island lads you might be sneaking outdoors to meet."

"I came to set the sod I had found and not to meet any lad. But why would you spy upon me? Did you never meet Roddy before you and he were married?"

Betsy denied it sharply. "Never in all me life."

Dinah remembered the cattle fair where a thin, no-longer-young woman had made all the advances to an easily influenced and not-too-bright young man. She shook the last grains of earth from the shawl into the garden and started back to the house, saying over her shoulder: "Then, if ye never met him, ye must have overtook him."

Such plain speaking did not sweeten the older woman's temper. She made up her mind to keep an eye on her young sister-in-law. She knew that her father-in-law expected her to do her share of the work while she was staying in his house, so she helped Dinah with dishes and sweeping next morning. Then she put on her best clothes and started for the plateau where the people of Aran were gathering.

Dinah had not waited for her. She had hurried on ahead by a little path she knew as shorter but steeper than the main road. The larks went up all around her into the misty sky, and she knew she was almost there when she saw the great rock at the turn. As she came around it, she came face to face with the British soldier in well-brushed coat and boots bright black from shining.

She stopped short and gasped her surprise. "But, how did you know—"

In dismay, she choked on the words. Suppose he had only been walking that way? Suppose he had not come to meet her?

He saw her distress and spoke at once. "Mary Donovan told me that this path was the shortest way from your home to the plateau." He looked at her intently. "I shall be on the island only until day after tomorrow. I wanted to see you, and I was afraid I might not find you at once in the crowd."

She looked back at him gratefully. She had been eager to see him, but she was too much of a woman to wish him to know it yet.

He said: "It's not time for the start. I've never been to Aran before. I thought you might show me some of the ruins for which it is famous. I've heard of Dun Angus and the Valley of the Seven Churches."

She pointed west. "The fort is there—across from Kilmurvy

Bay. Tis a climb of miles and twould take us the day to get there and back. The churches—"

She turned to show him and saw him laughing at her.

"It would suit me as well, Miss Corley," he said, "to walk that little lane with you. In fact I'd prefer it to either Dun Angus or the Seven Churches."

They walked from lane to lane, through the stone-walled boreens of Aran which connect farm with farm or with the main roads to towns. The sun was nearly at zenith, and they stopped in a clump of thorn trees. They were smaller than those on Ireland and were warped and sheared by the wind.

He said: "Away from England, it's the trees that I miss the most. There's a grove of yews not far from my house, and there are tall oaks and beeches."

She looked at him with sympathy. "I'm thinking ye'd often be homesick. Tis the wandering life that a sojer must lead, far off from the people he loves."

"The people I loved are dead. They were only my mother and father. I had no brothers or sisters. In a way it was loneliness that made me take the Queen's shilling."

He thought it was easy to talk to her. She kept her gray eyes on his face, but she did not interrupt with too many comments or questions.

"I still own the cottage and a small farm." He was looking hard at her. "I've wondered more than once why I was keeping them."

She said in perfect innocence: "Do ye mean ye like barracks life? Would ye rather be a sojer than to live in your own home?"

"I thought so once, but I've changed my mind. With the wife to make me happy, I would not re-enlist at the New Year. I'd go home a married man."

She could not misunderstand his eyes, even if she chose to ignore his words. Suddenly she was frightened. She had only met him yesterday. She had never seen England or been farther than Galway. The Aran rock, with its wild fuchsia trailing from crevices, and the stunted thorn in the boreens were the only home she knew. He was going too fast for her. She said a little breathlessly, "Tis time we turned back, Mr. Croft. Mary and Tim will think it strange if we are not there when the race begins."

He knew that Mary and Tim were too much in love with each

other to notice whether or not they came to the race at all. He realized that their interest in him, shown by telling him of the path that Mary and Dinah had often walked, was only the overflow from the happy current of their joy. But he did not wish to frighten this girl who was shy and gentle, but strong. He took her arm as she turned, and he spoke gravely. "After the race, will you show me the churches down in the valley?"

She nodded, and they did not speak as they hurried the short way back. As they reached the crowd on the height, they saw they were just in time. A yell of "Are you ready?" made them look off to the post. Roddy Corley was acting as starter. He had lined up before him a dozen shaggy, heavily built island horses, and he was endeavoring to keep them in line and prevent nosing-out and false starts. Then he stepped quickly to one side, and the wind brought them his shout of "GO!"

At the signal the clumsy-looking animals plunged forward with startling agility. They crossed the narrow beach in a bunch and, at the road, fanned out to take paths or cut across fields toward their common objective.

Croft threw an arm around Dinah and pulled her to one side. "Stay close to me. Any one of those brutes may bolt. It's rough riding and devil take the hindmost."

The race went by them to the accompaniment of mad yells from gallery and jockeys. Most of the latter rode bareback, guiding with crude bridles or homemade hackamores. They leaned well forward to take weight off their mounts' hindquarters and encouraged them with shouts, oaths and shillelaghs on their ribs. In their lead was a wicked-looking, moon-eyed horse of dirty dun. Foam was flying from its lips, and its ungainly legs moved as swiftly and surely as the piston rods of an engine.

They saw that the big brute was headed directly for a boreen where the four-and-a-half-foot walls were no more than twelve feet apart. Horses behind him were swerving right and left, but he thundered toward it as if he did not even see its double barrier.

Dinah heard John Croft cry aloud: "He'll never make it!"

But, as he spoke, the big dun horse rose like a running gull. When he took the first wall he was still rising, and he was in descent from the same heroic leap when he cleared the second. His hind legs unbuckled from beneath his belly, his forefeet reached for the uneven sod, and he was away at the head of a frantic pursuit.

Watching that spectacular feat, they did not at first see the thin young jockey wheel his white mare and head her straight at the same place. But yells went up from the Aranmen.

"Nay, Danny! Do not be tryin'!"

"Take her away to the left, by Mullen's pigsty!"

"Are ye crazy entirely, lad?"

"She'll knock the wall!"

She knocked the wall. Her rider had turned too close to give her a fair take-off. But he was determined to take the lead given by the dun, and he was putting her at it in spite of that handicap.

John Croft realized, and in apprehension pulled the girl against him as if to shelter her from the disaster that he saw must come.

The white mare was strong of heart and she did her best. She rose bravely, but she was too near the wall. A jagged projection of limestone caught her hoof and turned her completely over, catapulting her rider across the lane, and clear.

John Croft left Dinah and ran with the other men. As he dropped into the boreen the mare was struggling to her feet. Her slate-gray muzzle was wrinkled with pain; she was trembling violently; a jet of red was gushing from the inside of her near thigh.

He turned to a decrepit old man who, in spite of infirmity, had clambered over the wall as quickly as he had. "Whose horse is she?"

"She is the horse of Dan Moloney, Sassennach," said the old man. "She would have finished second had she not knocked the wall. And, had the big devil which won the race and my money," he added bitterly, "not been towed here from Inishmaan behind his master's currach, she would have won the entire race herself."

Croft's eyes went back to the injured mare. He recognized young Moloney, who with help from others, was trying in vain to staunch the jetting blood. He heard the word "Bleeder" going from tongue to tongue, and he saw that a half-grown boy had started downhill in a run. He moved nearer. "A bad job. The artery's cut, isn't it?"

The Aranman who stood at the mare's head nodded. "Yon jagged bit of limestone took her. Limestone is sharp as a butcher knife. It cut a vein, and there is naught can save her but the Bleeder now."

Croft put a hand on the soft muzzle. It was cold from fear and pain. She blew her breath out gustily. He asked curiously: "The Bleeder?"

"Mikkel the Bleeder," the Aranman said, in a tone no more than casual. "It is me lad who has gone for him. His spell can stop the blood."

John Croft drew his hand away and stared at the other man. But just then Danny Moloney emerged from beneath the horse. His hands were smeared with crimson and it streaked his face. "My sorrow," he grieved. "She's dying—and she like a sister to me! She's dying before me eyes, and I can do naught to save her." He rubbed a sleeve across his face, and the blood ran down his cheeks with tears. "Is Mikkel the Bleeder dead, himself, that he takes so long to come?"

Another man had taken his place, and was pressing against the wound with rags and raw sheep wool. But the mare's life trickled in a bright stream between his fingers, and her tired head drooped lower.

A shout from the onlookers went up at sight of Mikkel the Bleeder. He was being brought up the hill on the back of a strong young boy. When set on his feet he had to be supported on either side, because he was so frail and small, and so full of years. But he cried imperiously in a shrill cracked voice: "Let me be at the crayture!"

And, as they helped him forward, the mare turned her head weakly and rolled her great soft eyes imploringly toward him.

Croft stood staring, wondering whether to believe his eyes and ears. He saw the strange little old man squatting underneath the horse and reaching up to touch the wound with his clawlike hands. Then the bystanders, who had been talking loudly, some in Gaelic and some in English, fell suddenly silent as he began to sing.

It was more of a chant than a song; eerily high, in some dead, lost tongue. And he seemed to be repeating its few words over and over. But, when he withdrew his reddened hands and a man leaned and lifted him out, Croft heard the islanders release a hissing breath of relief.

The Englishman stepped forward and stooped to look. Thunderstruck, he saw that the blood on the mare's soiled legs was already drying, and that no more came from the wound.

Moloney stepped close and caught the shriveled fingers in his strong ones. "The saints of the Seven Churches send you more power, Mikkel the Bleeder! Tomorrow morn I'll be bringing you the whole half of a young sheep; for you've saved the life of the grand mare that is like a sister to me."

It was a gift of magnificence in that time of famine. Men nodded and smiled and muttered their approval. Croft turned to look for Dinah and found her close behind him. She did not show the least surprise at what had taken place. She said gently: "The pitiful thing! I feared that the Bleeder would not be in time."

"The old man must have some drug that clots the blood."

She shook her head. "Tis a charm come down from the Druids."

The white mare's owner had thrown his sheepskin coat across her withers. The wind was cold on the limestone peak, and he began to lead her away. Most of the crowd was following him. Mary and Tim had disappeared.

Dinah spoke shyly. "Would you like to be seeing the Seven Churches?"

He drew her arm through his and held it close against his side. She could feel his heart beat through his tight scarlet tunic. As they went down the path she thought with regret of Danny. But he had not once looked her way or given her a chance to express sorrow for his accident and loss of the race he had hoped to win. With every step now, he seemed more of a stranger than did this quiet-voiced but capable young man.

When they reached the valley he drew her down to sit beside him on a toppled slab of stone, and he listened while she told him about churches and saints.

Time went by and the sun moved on toward daybreak in America. Dinah looked up, and blushed rose-red as she met his eyes fixed on her face. But he had no longer any doubts. Her hand—small, square, and hard from work—lay on the stone between them. He covered it with his own and leaned closer to her. "Dinah?"

He had never called her name before and it was sweet in his English voice. Her eyes fell again, but she did not try to withdraw her hand.

He took her by the shoulders and turned her, gently but firmly, until she was obliged to look him in the eyes. "Dinah—I love you. Is there a chance you might care for me, my lass?"

The lovely color in her cheeks grew even deeper, and her eyes grew wider and darker gray. She had no coquetry, and he saw his answer while she was trying for words to frame it. He caught her into his arms, and her face lifted toward his mouth.

"My own lass," he whispered. "My own—of all the world!"

3

DINAH'S HEART SANG at her work that evening and next morning. Mary arrived promptly after breakfast.

"'Tis me last day on Aran, Mr. Corley. Will ye let Dinah go with me for a picnic on Straw Island?"

He looked at her under lowered brows. He considered her forward and unwomanly. But she was his daughter's friend, and he loved his daughter in his hard way.

"Dinah may go, so long as she does not leave her day's work undone."

Betsy had come forward. The day before she had seen Dinah and the soldier at the race. She had inquired and found out his name, that he had come with O'Leary and was staying at Coola's. Watching from a safe distance, she had seen John and Dinah go down to the Valley of the Churches. It had been night when Dinah came home, but that made no case against her. Of all places in the world, the Aran Islands are safest for a lone woman, dark or day. If she—Betsy—spoke without proof and Dinah had been with Mary, her father-in-law would turn the rough edge of his tongue upon her instead of on Dinah.

She asked Mary Donovan: "Will you and Dinah sail the bowt by yerselves?"

Mary looked back at her contemptuously. She loved Dinah and knew Betsy's spite and jealousy of her. "'Tis Datheen Costello's bowt, and he will do the sailing. His sister Judy is going, and Tim." She made no mention of Croft.

"Father," said Dinah eagerly, "I have done all me morning's work. I got up early to do it because I wished to be with Mary today. I have fed the sick pigeen and cleaned the house. I do me scrubbing tomorrow."

"Ye may go," he repeated shortly. He looked at Betsy. "Me son's wife should be able to cook the dinner for him and for me."

Loss of that first round made Betsy even more dangerous. But she dared not say any more until she was sure of her facts. She made up her mind to spend the morning calling on the Costellos, the Coolas and the Moloneys. From those three families she should be able to discover the history of the only soldier on Aran. When she came back she would give her father-in-law an account that would make his dinner disagree with him. She would be able to tell him of Croft's origin, reputation, religion and probable destination. Also, she hoped to break to him the news that the man in question had been with Dinah the evening before, and was now spending the day with her on Straw Island.

She watched the two girls from the door as they went away, happy and laughing. Tim O'Leary was waiting outside, but she saw no sign of the soldier. She guessed he would be on the Cockle Strand, but she dared not follow them now.

On the strand Judy sat on a stone, beside her a big willow basket of lunch. She was a merry, red-cheeked girl, and she called out as she saw them: "My curse on you, Dinah and Mary; for the each of you have a lad. Here I sit alone on the beach with nowt but a picnic basket!"

Mary laughed and Dinah blushed. Her secret seemed to be secret no more. She saw no sign of a red coat. Two men wearing fishermen's boots were working the sailboat into shallow water. One turned and waded toward them. She saw it was John Croft dressed in Jacky Costello's fishing jacket and pants and boots. Tim turned and picked up both Judy and the basket.

"I will first of all get the food safe on board. Tis more valuable than the three of you girls." As he waded out in the surf he called: "I will be back for you, Mary!"

Croft was coming toward Dinah with purposeful steps in his long hip boots. There was only Mary to see, and she giggled and turned her back.

"I told her last night," he said. "You don't mind her knowing it, Dinah?"

She shook her head. She minded nothing in all the world as he caught her up and bent his head for a quick kiss. She lay still, head on his shoulder and arms around his neck, as he waded out with her to Costello's sailboat.

Straw Island is small, but not too small for a couple to find themselves alone. Mary helped them all she could, and Judy's comments were broad but kind. The lonely beach, strewn with seaweed and straw and other flotsam, was not a romantic setting. But John and Dinah walked hand in hand and saw only rose-colored clouds ahead, although the wind was chilly and strong and the gray skies threatened rain.

"I go at daybreak tomorrow," he said. "I must talk with your father before I go."

He had said the same thing the night before, but she had persuaded him to wait and to leave her outside the cottage door. Now her face was troubled. "Can we not wait a while to be telling him?"

"No," he said slowly but positively. "The matter should be settled."

"Will you not come back to Aran soon? If we waited, twould not be so sudden. Twould, at least, give him time to hear about you from others."

Croft shook his head. He knew he was right, and he would not let her persuade him. "I will come back whenever I can. But I must tell him, myself and now. We have a right to marry. I wish to be honest about it. Your father should hear it first from me, before he hears it from others."

She nodded and sighed. She knew he was right. But she knew her father too.

"I would like to marry you now, and take you to live in Galway. I'm a careful man. I've put by my pay. I can take care of you, lass."

She would like that too, but her tender heart went out to an old man left all alone. "It is only that if we waited, I could see that me father was cared for. I would write to me youngest brother. It may be that he and his wife. . ."

Her voice trailed off as she recalled the eviction of Katie and

Willie. Croft was disappointed, but he took a fair view of it all.

"My regiment will be in Galway for several months longer. Of course there is always the chance that trouble may call us away. Can you arrange things in a few weeks? I get another leave next month. I could come back and marry you then."

She was grateful to him for understanding. She loved him quietly and calmly. She wanted tempestuous wooing no more than he wanted to give it. They sat on the rough and pebbly shore, with their arms around each other. The Arans loomed like the mountains of stone that they are. The wind roared and the sky was black. But he told her about the English farm and the cottage with its small garden.

"There are daisies and roses and hollyhocks. The wallflower scent comes out at dusk."

He stopped to kiss her upturned face as she listened. "Will you be happy there?"

"I will be happy there, me John, and I will make you happy too."

She thought of the flowers. She loved them, but not many grew on the Aran rock.

"I am so happy that I can wait until me father is cared for. Then we will be married and I will try to make you happy always."

"You'll make me happy always, my own dear girl," he said.

He caught her tight in his arms. He kissed her mouth, her face, her throat.

With his mouth against her mouth he said: "Dinah, I'll wait —but it's hard to wait!"

Tim's voice, shouting for them to come and eat, made them draw apart. He grinned good-naturedly. "Mary and I used to be that way at first. But you will get over it before long, and you will remember the mealtimes."

The wind was changing, so they sailed back to Corra Strand not long after noon. Datheen anchored his boat safely, and they paused on the beach to make their plans. But it was still broad daylight and they were not too far from the valley. Croft caught Dinah by the hand.

"Good-by to the rest of you! You may go wherever you please. But the churches brought luck to me yesterday, so Dinah and I will walk that way."

The wind was less strong in the valley, but the sky was still black overhead. They found the same stone upon which they had sat, but there was no sunset to mark the time. It went by on wings, as they talked softly or sat in a silence that needed no words. The change in the wind did not trouble them. They were both made of too sturdy stuff to imagine portents in a stormy sky. There were so many plans to make, and there was such joy in the planning. They went over it all again, and he gave in to a month's delay. He admired her all the more because she cared for her family. In return she had agreed, letting her happiness quiet her fears, that he was right to speak to her father when they went back that very night.

"If he is angry, be soft with him, John. Since me mother died, I have tended him."

"I will be as soft with him as I can. He had his love time and his marriage."

"Ah," she said, "I know you are right. But he is old—and me father."

"He has five sons and four daughters-in-law. I'm alone, except for you."

She caught his arm in quick sympathy and nestled her head against his sleeve. "Never again will ye be alone. Tis meself will see to that matter."

He said: "I'm Catholic, lass, and I know you're Protestant. But my father was Protestant, and he and my mother were happy."

"Keep your religion, me John," she said. "Keep your religion and I will keep mine." She lifted her rose-sweet face to his, and her smile made it glow in the twilight. "Sure, the good God would never want his churches to make us unhappy."

Croft nodded, relieved upon that score. He knew that his army record was good, and that her father could find nothing against his character. He had heard enough to guess what he would face when he faced Corley. But the directness ingrained in his nature made him more anxious to finish a task that threatened to be hard.

Before he could speak again, she cried: "Ah, but they are lighting the lamps! Tis time for me to be home."

He looked and, along the slanting stone where the village rose from the valley, saw the dim glow of the cottages climbing one after the other. Dun Angus and its mighty cliffs were across the island from them. Peace nestled here with the broken stones, where priest and friar and saint had walked. Seaward they heard the crying gulls and the surge and fall of waves on rock.

He tucked her hand more close in his arm, and they started on the winding road. "There's nought to fear from your father," he said. "The Donovans sail at daybreak. We will settle the matter tonight."

Dinah murmured, as if to herself: "Willie and Katie would come."

Croft looked down at her questioningly, and she explained to him: "Willie is me youngest brother. He married an island girl. He has not the love for the horses that Johnny and Roddy and Torc and Patrick have. He and Katie would gladly live here, and build a few more feet of soil every year, and make a few shillings by gathering the seaweed."

"That's the idea," he told her so confidently that she did not add: If me father will let them!

This joy of first love left no room in her mind for doubts and fears. The pulse in her arm seemed to draw from his side his calm strength and assurance. As they passed the lighted cottages she greeted those on the doorsteps: "God with all here"; and they answered: "God be with you." The road became a path and led to the farm above the Cockle Strand.

As they entered the cottage door they saw old Corley standing as if hewn from Aran rock. Over in the shadows by the supper table Betsy was sitting, and Roddy stood beyond her. But, in spite of the gaze of those three pair of hostile eyes, Croft moved forward undaunted and drew her along with him. Dinah clutched with small, cold fingers at his sleeve.

"Father," she begged with her heart in her voice. "Father, it is me John."

Corley was both tall and big and he towered over them. "So it is 'John' and 'Dinah' on the tongues of the two of ye? Never a mister or missus ye speak for decency's sake. Ye've come to this intimacy by stealth and behind me back."

Croft spoke with dignity. "I do nothing by stealth, Mr. Corley. I love your daughter and I've come to ask her for my wife."

"Ye lie," said Corley, "the two of ye." He was now beyond control. "Ye've been walking the island, and the night upon it."

"Or," said Betsy, "sitting alone in the dark of the ruined

churches. Since they did it last night, it is likely they did it again."

Corley yelled aloud at that and thumped the floor with his ash plant. "That I should live to see the time when me only daughter stravages the roads and hides behind stones in the night with a soldier!"

Dinah burst into tears, and Croft stepped between them and caught her close. Her head went down against his breast and the cloth of his rough jacket muffled her sobs. He looked the old man in the eye across her rumpled curls.

"Say no more, Mr. Corley. I love your daughter, and no man— not even you—shall abuse her."

Dinah took heart and raised a tear-drenched face. "I love me John and he loves me. Why would we not marry each other?"

"Three reasons," said Corley; "and one alone of the three is reason enough. He's Sassennach—redcoat—and Papist! Now let him be gone from me house!"

He raised his stick in menace; but Croft's eyes never wavered and he held Dinah tight. "I love your daughter honorably and wish to marry her. I've come to ask you honestly and decently for her."

"I'll see her lying under the sod before I'll see her the wife of a British sojer and a Romanist besides."

"I've done nothing to you, Mr. Corley. Can't you forget old wrongs? Must differences in the politics of our countries and the faith of our families interfere with our happiness?"

"Aye," said the old man grimly. "That they must."

Croft was provoked beyond his British stolidity. "I've asked you for her fairly, and I warn you now—"

He paused and his opponent spoke warily. "Aye?"

"I warn you I'll marry her, with or without your consent."

"Out of me house now, redcoat," said Corley in cold rage. "Ye'll never marry Dinah, and ye'll never see her more."

Croft looked down into Dinah's face.

She said softly: "Go, me John."

"You'll wait for me?" he asked her.

"I will wait. But—go now."

He released her and crossed slowly to the door. On its threshold he turned and stood, looking back at her.

She took a step toward him, then caught herself and stopped. But she spoke clearly, for them all to hear.

"Wherever it be—and however long it be—you will find me waiting for you, me John!"

4

DINAH CAME DOWN to cook breakfast before dawn of the next day. The turf had been banked. Its fire was not allowed to go out from September to June. She blew its smoldering spark to flame and set fresh blocks upon it. Using a long paper spill, she carried a light to the shark-oil lamp, and set it under its china shade in the middle of the table. Old Corley appeared then and took his seat in grim silence.

She gave him his bowl of porridge and his first cup of strong tea from the pot that sat brewing on the hearth. He spoke harshly. "Surprised I am that ye take time to tend your old father."

Roddy and Betsy were descending the stair from the loft. The latter heard and added spitefully: "It's time, I'm thinking, for Father Corley to send for Willie and Katie."

He turned his anger upon her. "You're a meddlesome woman, Betsy! When I want Willie and Katie I'll do the sending for them."

Roddy said impatiently: "Give me me vittals, Betsy. I have to go clear to Bungowla—maybe to Brannach Island."

His wife, having served him ungraciously, seated herself and began to eat. Dinah lifted the teapot and refilled his cup. The meal continued in silence until she spoke again. "Would ye wish more porridge, Roddy? There is some yet left in the pot."

He accepted it and cut another thick slice from the dark, heavy loaf of bread.

Betsy cast a malicious look at Dinah. "The Donovans will be about leaving now. Are ye going down to Killeany to see them, Roddy?"

"I am not," he told her shortly. "Donovan knows that you and I are not sailing with him."

Dinah blinked back hot tears as she leaned over the teapot. John

Croft would be rowing out in a currach to the herring boat. But, he had asked her to wait for him. . . .

Roddy took his coat of off-white, unbleached Connemara wool from its peg on the wall and struggled into its well-worn warmth. "Muldoon asked me to see a man named O'Dwyer, who lives between Bungowla and Brannach Sound. He has a chestnut filly that might one day be making a hunter."

Nobody answered him or evinced the slightest interest in the filly's prospects; so he clumped in his heavy boots to the door and went out in the mist.

Corley rose more slowly than his son had done. "It's nigh on time for sunrise. I must feed the creatures and milk."

"I'll get the swill, father," Dinah told him.

She hurried into the background, thick with shadows, and returned with a bucket so large she could hardly carry it. He took it without acknowledgment and started for the door.

She followed him a few steps. "Is the sick pigeen better?"

He did not turn. "I've things more heavy on me mind than the health of a runt pig."

She followed him still, entreating kindness. "When I've finished me work in the house I'll carry him out in the boreen. He may find a green blade or a tender root under the leaves."

He turned then. "Ye'll not leave the house until I can be sure ye will act like a decent woman."

"But father, I have to carry a dress and two shirts to Missus O'Flaherty. I've sewed by candlelight in me room because she must have them today."

"Betsy will take the sewing to Moira O'Flaherty and will bring back the money she owes you for the making."

"That I will," said Betsy, still eating at the table.

Dinah pleaded. "It is me day for the washing and scrubbing. How will I do the work if I cannot draw the water?"

He spoke to Betsy across her head. "See that Dinah goes no other place than the well."

Then he turned and went outdoors, carrying the garbage, while Dinah walked sadly back to the fireplace.

Betsy was finishing the last crumb of the long loaf. She was one of those women who eat hugely yet remain skinny and rawboned. She was lazy too, and she now saw a chance to escape the chores.

"Since I'm walking the miles to the O'Flaherty farm for you, you can do the housework by yourself, I take it."

"I can do that," said Dinah. "Work helps me not to think."

Betsy started to rise from her chair and caught her shawl on a nailhead. "Me only shawl to me back," she exclaimed, examining it in anger. "With money as scarce as it is, and things hard to buy as they are!"

Dinah, always forgiving, crossed the room to her. "Oh, Betsy, I'm sorry! But I can mend it for you. I can mend it so no one will ever see that it has been torn."

"Ye would do well," said her sister-in-law ungratefully, "to be mending your ways instead of mending the shawls."

Dinah drew back, and seeing that she had gone too far, Betsy held out the torn garment. "Take it then. It is one thing ye do well. I will say for you, Dinah Corley, that you could any day make your keep by the fine needlework."

Grateful for any small kindness, Dinah took the shawl. "Me mother learned me the sewing when I was a child. She and her people always had the gift of the making hands. One of them wove the shawl I wear a hundred years gone, on Inisheer."

It lay like a quilt across the unused cot in the corner, and the other woman looked at it enviously. It was larger and warmer than her own, and its deep rose-reds and greens had only softened with age instead of fading. But she was not generous enough to show her admiration.

Dinah's voice grew tender. "I can remember me mother wearing it to church. Me mother loved the pretty things. And she always loved the laughter. . . ."

"I'm thinking you take after her," said Betsy sourly. "She would have been just as likely to run after any redcoat."

Dinah threw the torn shawl on a chair and stooped to the hearth for a weapon. "One more word out of you about me mother, and you'll get the skillet with its hot grease in your wicked mouth, Betsy O'Toole!"

Betsy retreated from her hostile gesture. "I'm saying nothing. But you would do well to clean the house before you start the mending. If the old man comes back and finds work undone, he will be after us both."

In silence Dinah set down the iron frying pan, went over to the wall and took two pails from the pegs on which they hung. She was on her way to the door when Betsy spoke.

"Where is the sewing I am to take to the O'Flahertys'? And how much will I ask from the woman of the house?"

Dinah turned. "Tis on me bed, ready and wrapped in a bundle. I make two shirts for a shilling, but the dress is a shilling alone."

"Two whole shillings?" said Betsy enviously. "She pays you well."

"And she's kind," said Dinah, "is Missus O'Flaherty. She could get the sewing done for less, but she told me she'd rather be paying me more because me stitches was smaller."

"Well, don't let kind words turn your head. Get on and draw the water now. I will be gone when ye come back, and ye can get after the cleaning."

Dinah opened the door upon a milky fog shot through with pale opal rays of dawn. "Day is breaking," she called back over her shoulder. "Before ye go, will ye put out the lamp so as to save the oil?"

Betsy did not trouble herself to reply. She blew out the lamp and started up the stair.

A moment after she disappeared John Croft stepped in through the open door. He stopped there and looked around the big room in the half light. Its turf flame threw twisting shadows and its windows were pallid rectangles. "Dinah?" he questioned softly. And when there was no reply, he came to the fire and stood with his back to it, still looking around him and frowning.

From the loft above, Betsy had heard. She stole noiselessly a few steps down and, from above and behind him, leaned over the stair rail and saw the back of his red coat. As if sensing her presence he turned, but she was too quick for him. She darted back, and as she did, Dinah came in with a pail in each hand.

She dropped them both and the water sloshed across the boards of the rough, bare floor. "John! Me John!" she whispered.

And, with two jumps, he had her in his arms.

"But I thought ye had gone," she told him, unable to think him real. "Ye said ye were sailing at daybreak, and Betsy said—"

He laughed and caught her closer and kissed her again and again.

"I told Timmy about us last night and he and Mary fixed it.

Tim went out and found the lad who makes the best poteen on Aran, and the two of them are taking Mr. Donovan over to get a keg from where it's hid in the rocks. He'll not sail for Galway until he has that keg aboard."

He pressed her head into the hollow of his shoulder and let his cheek rest on the soft, thick curls. "Didn't you know I'd come?" he asked reproachfully. "No matter when it is or where you are, I'll always come back for you, Dinah."

She nestled even closer. "Will ye that, me John?"

"I will, my lass." He looked all around. "But, where are your people?"

"They are gone entirely," she told him securely. "Roddy to Bungowla, which is clean across the island, me father to feeding and milking, and Betsy down to Kilronan."

He drew a long breath of relief. "Lucky for us, I call it! Because I've plans to make with you, my girl."

He drew her over to the trestle bench, and they sat side by side. "You must marry me at once, Dinah."

She dropped her head compliantly back on his shoulder. "There is nowt in the world I want more than that."

"I've asked your father properly, but he can't be made to see reason. It's his fault now if we go ahead and get married without his consent."

"But, could we do that?" she asked him anxiously.

"We could. This very next Saturday. Mary Donovan says you'll be eighteen years old then."

She nodded and he continued: "Besides, I've been talking to Father Sweeney. I went straight to him when your governor turned me out last evening."

Dinah asked doubtfully: "But—but would Father Sweeney help you to marry a Protestant?"

He took her by both shoulders and gave her a little shake, then held her off at arms' length and laughed at her. "Father Sweeney is a Catholic priest, but he is an Irishman too. Do you know what he said to me last night?"

Her voice was eager. "What did he say then?"

"He gave me a long lecture first, reminding me of the rules of the church and all the dangers of mixed marriages. When he got through with that he said: 'My son, I've been talking to you as your priest. If you harken to what I've just said, you'll let that old devil Corley scare you off from your colleen entirely. But—talking to you as man to man and this man an Irishman—only a fool would let himself be scared off from marrying an Aran lass as sweet and wholesome as Dinah Corley.' "

She threw her arms around his neck. "Oh, the old, fat darling he is, your Father Sweeney!"

He put a hand under her chin, lifted her face and kissed her. "Save your 'darlings' for me, my girl. I grudge them to any man."

"Ah, me John," she said earnestly, "you cannot ever use up the love or the love words. I have enough for you and for Father Sweeney and—" She stopped and cast a troubled look around the empty room. "And for me own people too, if they will but let me give them."

He tried to reassure her. "Once we are man and wife, they'll have to give in and forgive you. That's what I came to tell you, so listen to me, Dinah. We can be married next Saturday by my regimental chaplain. He'll do it with less delay, and since he's Church of England, your father will have to accept it as legal. Then, if you're willing, Father Sweeney will publish the banns and marry us too."

She said gently: "I'd like that. I'd like to be married both in your church and in mine."

"Then we'll be married in both, my lass," he said exultantly.

"But, how will I ever get to Galway this Saturday?"

"Mary Donovan has already written you a letter asking you to come over on Friday with Roddy and Betsy, see them sail for America and then spend the night with her."

Dinah gazed up at him with eyes in which fear struggled with happiness. "Mary is me friend and I've stayed in her house. If me father will but let me go . . ."

"He can hardly refuse to let you go with your brother to see him off." Optimism carried him on. "I'll find out from Chaplain Holmes at just what hour on Saturday he'll splice us. Then I'll tell Mary and she'll tell you."

Unable to contain himself, he rose and picked her up and took several steps with her in his arms. The cot stood, like a long bench under the shawl's bright cover. He crossed and sat upon it, holding her on his knees. "A hug and a kiss, and then I must go. They'll be down at the beach with the poteen."

But she had bounced from his lap and he saw that her cheeks were scarlet rather than rosy. "Tis a bed, and we must not sit upon it."

He rose quickly, embarrassed; and he loved her more for her modesty and quaint propriety. A soldier got his fill of bold women in the garrison towns. Before he could speak, she added: "And, too, tis Saint Kevin's shawl."

He looked down at it, then raised his eyes in question to her face.

"Me great-great-grandmother wove it on the island of Inisheer. In her day 'twas the custom for the girls to take their shawls to the Altar of Love for Saint Kevin's blessing."

He knew that the altars of South Aran were in some cases so ancient that they had served pagan gods before Christian saints.

She lifted the shawl and held it up. It was the size of a small blanket and its lower edge dragged on the floor. She said earnestly: "Tis a love spell, the blessing of Saint Kevin. When it is once given, no matter how long ago, the girl who wears that blessed shawl can always be sure that the man she loves will come back to her, from no matter how far away."

He caught both her and the big homespun woolen square in his arms. "Even without a spell, Dinah, I'll come—wherever you are. But I must go now. The Donovans will be waiting."

Red as a rose and breathless, she emerged from his embrace. He disentangled himself from the shawl and threw it back on the cot.

"I'm so full of happiness," she gasped, "that I must be working it off." She looked around her. "I'll scrub the house. And I'll scrub everything in it!"

He laughed as he went toward the door. "Scrub your father's house while you may. Soon you'll have your own house, in England, to keep in order."

Then, at the threshold, he wheeled and saluted her smartly. "Good day to you, Missus Croft! I'll see you in time for the wedding."

Misty-eyed with joy, she watched him as he went, then turned and looked in dismay at the disorder around her. She cried aloud: "I've the father and mother of a morning's work to do before me father or Betsy comes back and catches me!"

She rushed to the table and removed the cups and plates which

Betsy had left, then snatched her empty pails from the floor and dashed out to the well for more water.

As she disappeared, Betsy appeared at the top of the ladderlike stair and began to descend it slowly. Her eyes were bright with triumph and her mouth was hard. She spied the cot with the rumpled shawl, stopped short and stood, smiling evilly. Then a step caused her to turn toward the door.

Old Corley came through it, a bucket of milk in his hand. He stood on the threshold while his glare moved around and then rested on her.

"Are both me daughter and me son's wife such lazy sluts that they do not wash dirty dishes or wipe up water spilled?"

"Will ye leave me out of it?" she demanded angrily. "Talk of your own daughter. It is likely the words may suit her."

He came forward and set the milk on the table, still glowering. "And why will the words not suit you too when you leave work undone?"

"Did ye not tell me with your own mouth to carry the shirts to O'Flaherty's?"

"If ye did the errand," he parried, uncompromising, "ye walked fast, Betsy O'Toole."

She started furiously: "I did not do it, because—"

"I know ye did not do it," he interrupted her.

She gave him a look of pure malice. She had the proof she needed now. "If you'll listen to me, you'll hear a pretty story! I went up in the loft to get Dinah's needlework and, before I got down again, Dinah's Englishman walked in. She thought I was gone to O'Flaherty's, and she told him so. But I was there on the ladder, watching their cuddling and kissing."

"In me house?" he shouted. "Do ye mean to tell me Dinah—"

It was her turn to cut him off. "Aye," she said with spite in her voice. "I mean your precious Dinah. All the long time I crouched, hid on the ladder yonder."

She turned and gestured toward it, as if proud of her sneaking. "It was up there I was all the time, watching their love-making and listening to their plans."

She went a step nearer to him and spoke more forcefully. "I watched and I listened *and this is what I heard.* . . ."

5

THE THREE DAYS that intervened between the horse leaping and the date of Roddy's departure passed swiftly for Dinah. She was alternately radiant and depressed, balancing between smiles and tears. Mary's letter of invitation was brought by Judy Costello. Old Corley did not comment when his daughter showed it to him; but, to Dinah's surprise, Betsy took her part.

"I had the mind to be asking her to travel to Galway with Roddy and me. Tis well she should see the great bowt upon which we will cross the ocean."

Dinah could only say, "Tis kind that ye are to me, Betsy," and feel herself wicked and traitorous as she thought of their innocence. Everything about the place became doubly dear to her. She went three times a day to the west potato garden to look at the clod of earth she had brought from the Glassin Rocks. She carried skimmed milk to the undersized pig, which was runt of a late litter and likely to be starved by his stronger brothers and sisters. She patted the old donkey as he cropped dry grass in the lane, and ran her fingers along the dark cross on his back. She gathered lovingly every wild flower she saw, lingering to listen to the larks and the shrilly-sweet blackbirds. She stopped to watch the island boys as they ran rabbits with their dogs. Her memory went back to days when her own brothers had killed them with thrown sticks and brought them home to be cooked. Of all the five, Willie had been gentlest to her. He had made her a doll, roughly carved of a prized bit of driftwood; and after her mother's death, he had helped her with the heavier work.

She knew in her heart that Willie and Katie would come back gladly, and she knew that her father would let them come if he had nobody else. She tried to comfort herself with the thought, for she needed comfort in spite of the fact that her love for John Croft did not waver. He was never out of her mind. Although the year was at autumn, he held her with the spell of spring and the first love she had ever known. She seemed at times to hear his English voice so distinctly that she glanced over her shoulder more than once in the foolish fear that the others might hear it too. More than once she caught them looking at her, and they always averted their eyes quickly. Her secret made her feel a guilty tension in the air. She took the full blame for that guilt, but John Croft outweighed it all.

On that last afternoon she walked again to the Glassin Rocks, but this time it was to look directly east toward England. John Croft had told her about his home, which was to be her home. He had spoken of roses and hollyhocks and wallflowers in the garden. His time of enlistment would be up before the New Year. Before he met her he had intended to re-enlist and go to the Far East with his regiment. But, although soldiering was his trade, it would hold him no longer. At the New Year he would take her home . . . to an English cottage with flowers in bloom. . . . For her the Aran life was ending with the end of the day.

"God give me peace forever," she whispered as she turned west.

She looked with wistful eyes around the house as she entered. Corley and Roddy sat at one end of the table, mending the donkey's harness by light of the shark-oil lamp. Betsy was descending the railed ladder. She was the type of person who is more often seen out of the corner of an eye than with honest full gaze. Although awkward to the point of jerkiness, at times she gave the impression of sliding.

She smiled now at Dinah, showing discolored teeth. "Ye will not forget to be taking your shawl to Galway?"

It lay, smoothly disposed again, on the benchlike cot by the wall. Dinah looked at it, then looked back to Betsy's face in surprise. "Tis all I have to warm me, so I'll take it on me back." She added, feeling as she spoke the shame of hypocrisy, "The things I will be needing for the night at Mary's house I will carry in me small shawl here."

She took it from her head and hung it on one of the wooden pegs. Fully a score of these pegs were driven in the wall, and from them hung the family shawls and bauneens, cowhides to be cut for pampooties, bundles of herbs from the garden and bunches of dried eels. Turf, brought down from the store in the loft, was stacked on each side of the chimney. On shelves and upon the big low chest were jugs and mugs and cups and plates which her mother had brought as a bride. Dinah had no idea of their real value. She knew they had come long ago from China in ships upon which men of Inisheer had sailed around the world. But she loved each piece because it had been her mother's, and she handled it carefully and seldom broke anything. She wondered how she would ever keep house without that beloved and accustomed blue glaze. Her eyes blurred until the slow dance of the turf flames ran together.

But, in spite of all this, she slept the sleep of youth and health and hard work that night. Roddy called her at four o'clock, and she found Betsy already downstairs.

"I've started the porridge and wet the tea," her sister-in-law told her, without the usual reproaches for tardiness.

Her kindness made Dinah happy. She had longed to be friendly, but the thin, sharp woman had before this rebuffed her. "Go you on with Roddy," she said, "and take all with you you can carry. He has the creature outside the door, saddled with straddle and baskets."

Dinah went to stand in front of her father, hoping that he would offer to kiss her good-by. But his mouth was a thin line above his thick gray beard. "The Corleys have always been decent people," he charged her. "Wherever ye be, remember it, if ye call yourself my daughter."

She threw her arms around him and, although he turned his head, managed to bring her lips in touch with a leathery cheek. Then she ran outside, where Roddy was loading the donkey, so that the lamplight might not betray her tears.

The heavier bundles went into the straddle baskets. A boy had been engaged to lead the animal back to the farm from the beach. Betsy had said she would follow, so Dinah and Roddy walked slowly through the cold fog down to Killeany.

The lad who waited to row them out and to lead back the donkey turned out to be the youngest Moloney. Dinah managed to whisper to him: "Peadar, will ye tell Danny that I said good-by, and God between him and all harm?"

Then he and Roddy had loaded her and most of the luggage into the currach, and they were on their way through the surf to the hooker. It was a black boat of ten tons, built to serve either for fishing or carrying freight. Dinah stood forlornly on deck, holding her bundle with one hand and her shawl around her with the other, until a second currach trip delivered Roddy and Betsy. It seemed to Dinah that the latter had accumulated even more luggage. She said admiringly: "Ye will be traveling in style, Betsy, with the small trunk ye have and all the other bundles."

"I'm thinking it will be needed in the new land," Betsy told her.

After an hour of sailing the fog lifted from the water. Dinah enjoyed it, for her outings had been infrequent. She sat on Betsy's trunk and watched the rocky coast of Clare and the lower, greener shore of Connemara converge as the bay narrowed and they approached Galway. It was midafternoon and tide running fast to flood when the hooker brought them to the Claddach pier.

The cattle boat was easy to find: a tubby vessel with three bare masts. It seemed enormous to Dinah. She gazed with parted lips. "Are ye going on board now?"

Betsy took her by an arm. "We are, as soon as Roddy talks with the captain. He must see, first of all, if the horses are safely loaded."

Waiting, they watched groups of strange-looking people who walked on the pier or on and off the ship. They were talking together, throatily, in a foreign tongue. After a while Roddy came back with two of Muldoon's trainers who had seen to the loading before he arrived.

He said briefly: "Larry and Pat will help us carry this stuff aboard." Then he added: "'Tis me wife and me sister, boys."

Larry swung the trunk up on a broad shoulder and grinned down at Dinah. "So ye will be going to the States?"

She smiled and shook her head as she followed him up the gangplank. "I have but come to see the great bowt in which me brother is going. I spend the night in Galway with me friends the Donovans."

In a large, bare stateroom with three bunks attached to its walls, Larry set the trunk down hard and grinned at her even more boldly. "It may be I'll see yourself then. The Donovans are me own friends."

For some reason Roddy seemed annoyed. "Ye would do well to get back to Muldoon's. And tell him all I told ye about the beasts in the hold."

Still talking about the horses, he managed to get the two young men outside and to shut the cabin door after them and

himself. Dinah was relieved, for she dreaded interference with her
plan to go direct to Mary after the boat sailed. She heard the
men's footsteps receding along the corridor, and she looked curiously around her. Parcels were strewn untidily on the narrow beds
and on a bench and two chairs. The floor rocked slightly under
her. The beams overhead were heavy and dark. Even here in
officers' quarters, the air was dank with the unclean smell of cattle
and human steerage.

Betsy said importantly: "The captain's room is next door. Himself is housed no better than we are."

Dinah looked around again in wonder and admiration. A ship's
lantern, unlighted, hung by a chain from a beam. Two portholes
furnished afternoon light from starboard. "The windys are
round," she cried in delight, "and they have glass in them, Betsy.
If it is raining or if the wind blows, ye can shut them yet twill not
be dark."

"It has the conveniences, it has," agreed Betsy, highly pleased.
"But ye should be seeing the steerage, in the bottom of the bowt."

"What is it then?" asked Dinah, wide-eyed with all the new
sights.

"Tis a way that some folks travel, and tis no better than the
beasts. They are crowded together like pigs, eating and sleeping
on the floor."

Roddy came in just then. He looked troubled and embarrassed.
The raw smell of poteen came with him and flooded the cabin.

His wife remarked: "So you're at it again? Could you not wait
the few hours?"

He scowled at her. "Hold your noise! God knows I need the
heartening for the job ahead of me."

Betsy wheeled on him fiercely, but Dinah was speaking gently.
"Twill be uncommon hard, I know, to tend the horses aboard the
bowt. But I would like well to see them in the place they are
traveling."

Betsy approved. "Take her along and show her while I wet the
tea."

The corridor was narrow and barefooted sailors ran through
it, past them and toward the deck. Roddy guided her down two
stairs that were merely railed ladders. There, in a big, windowless
enclosure, four stalls had been built by making three sides with

rails against the hull. In them stood the Irish hunters: three chest-nut geldings and the bay mare Kathleen Avourneen. They were beautiful and proud, and bright-eyed with fear. More nervous than the geldings, the mare's satin coat was twitching. She shifted her weight from foot to foot and whickered when she saw Roddy. Her stall was largest and farthest aft, where the hull curved into the stern. Beyond its aft rails was left a small space, almost as narrow as a bed.

"Why did ye rail it off, Roddy? Twould give the creature more room."

He shook his head. "She would hurt herself against the curve of strakes and beams. She is nervous enough already. She will yet be giving me trouble."

Dinah shivered. Although the air in the hold was close, it was cold. She drew her shawl tighter around her. "There is sadness in her eyes, Roddy. I fear that she knows she is going away, and she wishes someone whom she loves with her. God be helping the creatures. To journey in such a place!"

Roddy said shortly: "The humans are journeying here with them."

She turned then and looked. The hold was beginning to fill with the same strange-looking people whom she had seen on the pier. They were coming by the narrow way that she and Roddy had come, disposing themselves in corners, spreading blankets and shawls on the floor. Their guttural voices rose loud and harsh. Only the horses kept proud silence.

She put a hand on her brother's arm. "Take me away from here, Roddy!"

As they climbed the ladders, other emigrants met them and squeezed by. Roddy left her in the cabin with Betsy. She had the tea boiling and handed Dinah a large cup of the steaming black liquid. "I have brought along a jug of the cream. And do not be sparing the sugar."

Embarrassed by that unaccustomed kindness, Dinah sat on the edge of a chair and sipped her tea. "Where did Roddy go?"

"God knows that," said Betsy. She frowned. "He's been after the poteen."

Dinah shook her head sadly over her empty teacup. "It is the saying good-by that is tearing the heart in his breast."

Betsy took no such charitable view. "Roddy gets after the poteen without any saying good-by."

She walked over and refilled Dinah's cup, and the younger woman smiled up at her. "Betsy, let us forget ill will. It was kind of you to ask me to come and drink your tea and see this great bowt."

Betsy was pouring more water from a jug into the teapot. There were sounds of running feet and shouts on deck. She froze suddenly. Then she spoke quickly and loudly to hold Dinah's attention. "It is a grand bowt, it is. I am proud to be crossing the wide sea in it."

Dinah had risen, startled, and set her cup on the bench. She started toward the nearest port, but Betsy managed to block her way. "Sit you down and drink your tea. Roddy will be coming to say good-by."

Dinah exclaimed with pleasure as her cup was filled a third time. "It is a fair treat! But, have you enough for yourself?"

"Eight pounds of India," said Betsy greedily. "I'm taking it because Annie O'Rourke said Barry Sullivan told her the Americans cannot make tea at all at all."

Roddy appeared in the doorway and, as he did, the ship lurched and he caught with both hands to steady himself. He stood shamefaced and miserable and looking at his sister.

"Roddy asthore," she asked anxiously, "what is the trouble now?"

Betsy, hard-eyed, did not answer.

Dinah persisted. "I hear men running and yelling. Is there trouble with the horses?"

He shook his head miserably.

"Have you no sense at all?" his wife demanded angrily. "Tis a cattle bowt and, for all you know, the cows may be loose and rampaging it from end to end."

That roused him from shame and poteen. He said roughly: "Are you fool enough, woman, to think Ireland has cattle to ship? The bowt goes over empty save for the horses and the humans down in its hold. Coming back from America twill bring cattle, please God!"

"Yourself is the fool to talk that way before her," Betsy warned.

Dinah said gently: "Likely he's sad at leaving. I'm thinking my heart would break with sorrow entirely if it was me sailing away to a strange land."

Roddy raised a hand to his face. "Oh, me soul! I can't do it!"

"Give him a drop of the tea, Betsy," Dinah urged. "There is nowt like good strong tea when your heart is hurting inside you."

Roddy collapsed in a sitting position on the edge of the nearest bunk. Betsy poured a cup of tea and Dinah carried it to him. He drank it in gulps, never taking his eyes from her face.

She smiled farewell at them both as she picked up her shawl from the bench. "You are sad with the leaving, Roddy, and I shall be sad without you. But my love will go with the two of ye across the sea to America."

Then she saw her sister-in-law filling her cup again, and she cried aloud: "Ah, but it is too much, Betsy! Never in all me life have I had four cups of the tea at one time."

"Sit you down and drink it then," Betsy told her shortly.

Smiling with pleasure she sat on the bench and looked at them over the rim of the cup. "I will think of you, Betsy, with all your fine luggage. And of Roddy drawing a rich man's wages."

Roddy rose to his feet, saying desperately: "It is time I was going back to see after the horses."

"Go, then," said Betsy between her teeth. "And the quicker the better."

Dinah rose too, and set down her empty cup. "I must be going, meself; so let us say good-by, Roddy."

He stood, uncertain and agonized, but she smiled tenderly at him. "Will ye show me which way I'll take to get back to the quay?"

The cattle boat wallowed heavily and threw her against her brother. He put his arms around her and looked over her head at Betsy. But his wife had no mercy. She caught at a bunk to steady herself and, as she looked back at him, her laughter was cruel. "Ye'll walk on water, whichever way ye go now, Dinah Corley!"

Still holding onto Roddy, Dinah turned a frightened face. "Betsy! Betsy! What do ye mean?" she implored.

"If ye will look out yon windy," said Betsy with relish, "ye will see for yourself what I mean."

The shawl slid to the floor from Dinah's shoulders. She flew to the porthole, took one look, and screamed aloud.

"The bowt is clean gone from the pier! We are sailing the wild western ocean!"

6

BETSY, A HEAD TALLER, looked over her shoulder. "We are not yet that," she corrected. "Yonder is Connemara's coast, and we have not passed the islands."

Dinah turned and cast herself upon her brother. "Roddy! Roddy!" She hammered his chest with small fists. "Roddy, make the captain stop the bowt and set me ashore! I'll walk the weary miles alone, from Connemara to Galway! Roddy, make him set me ashore! I must get back to me John!"

Roddy tried clumsily to put his arms around her, but Betsy seized her shoulder and jerked her away from him. "Walk back to your John, ye would? Ye little fool! Your John is the reason your Da is putting the sea between you and Ireland."

Dinah cried hysterically: "No! No!" She turned back to her brother. "Roddy?"

But he had dropped again on the bunk and dropped his face in his hands.

"I am going to the captain, meself," cried Dinah wildly. "I will ask him to stop the bowt! I will ask him to set me ashore!"

She started again for the door, but Betsy held her fast.

"I would not be doing that, me fine lady. The captain has already been told about you. He knows that your father is sending you away from home, in care of your brother and your brother's wife, because a soldier is trying to ruin you. He knows you are not yet eighteen years of age. He knows that your family are doing what is best for you."

"Ah, but I will tell him different! I will make him understand. I will tell him that tomorrow I will be eighteen years old!"

"Today is today," said Betsy. "Tomorrow has not yet come."

"How could you be so wicked? *You* did it, Betsy O'Toole! I do not believe that me father knows! I will tell the captain that."

"The captain has a letter wrote by your father's hand. Roddy took it to him while we stood upon the pier."

She wheeled then on her brother again. "Roddy, did you do it?" He refused to meet her eyes. She saw that he would not help her. She jerked away from Betsy's clutch. "I will tell the captain all! When he knows that I will be eighteen tomorrow and that I was going to—"

She stopped, and Betsy laughed aloud. "I know about that too. Go on and talk to the captain, and see what he says to you."

She saw that they had laid their plans and set everyone against her. In a last appeal, she turned back to her brother. "Roddy! Take me to the captain quick! Tell him that it was all a mistake!"

But poteen only made him weaker than nature had made him. "It is already too late for that. It may be—if I had thought. . ."

"Leave off with your excuses," his wife shrilled at him. "If there is blaming, you are as much to blame as your Da or me."

"You made me do it," he told her bitterly.

Being a bully, she shrank from him and turned on Dinah, who was standing white, silent and hopeless.

"You will never set eyes on your John again, the plotting, sneaking redcoat! Did I not hear the two of ye planning to marry behind your Da's back? Was I not there, on the ladder, when he came three days ago?"

Dinah drew away from her as from an unclean thing. "You were hid? And you listened?"

"I listened," said Betsy. "And I watched. And I told your Da."

Dinah had been shocked into quietness. Now she faced her sister-in-law and spoke steadily. "You are a mean woman, and a cruel one. You never loved my father. You never gave him kindness. You did not do this to help him. You did it to hurt me."

"Will ye listen, Roddy," shrieked Betsy, "to the words she lays on your wife?"

He dropped his hands from his face. "Aye, and I was thinking she took the very words out of me mouth."

"I did it for your own help," she blustered to Dinah. "What good would a British sojer mean with an island girl like yourself? Before ye could count the pigs in Biddy O'Hara's house, he would be off and leaving you."

Dinah looked her in the eyes. "My John loves me and I love

him. Nobody else in all the world has been as kind and gentle to me. It is a wicked thing you did."

Betsy began stridently: "If that is the way you feel—"

But Roddy rose to his feet. "Hold your clatter!" He turned to his sister and his voice softened and pleaded with her. "It is done now, Dinah. Can you not forgive us? You will find work in Charleston, and you will be happy again."

Betsy lifted a bundle, broke its string and scattered its contents on a bunk. "When you left the cottage with Roddy, I went and got your clothes. Here is the dress of blue wool that you wear to church on Sunday."

Roddy added: "Twas why I asked the mate of the ship for a three-bed room. I wished you to be living with us on the way."

Dinah shook her head. Her brown curls were damp and tumbled and her soft mouth was set. "I will not be with you and Betsy—never again. Not on the wide sea nor in the wild land that ye are taking me to by force."

She stooped, picked up her mother's shawl and, crossing to the bunk, began to gather her small possessions. With them knotted in it, she turned toward the door.

Roddy cried out: "You cannot go! There is no place else but the steerage!"

"I would rather the steerage than to stay with you—and her."

"They are foreigners, and living no better than the beasts. You saw the rats running among them, and the filth that soils the floor."

Dinah looked back at them from the cabin door. Never before had her level gray eyes reflected scorn.

"The beasts are not as cruel as the human beings," she said.

Outside, she leaned against the wall, courage and strength draining from her. The wind roared through the open hatch, bringing with it all the unaccustomed sounds of creaking canvas and straining beams. Through the stout partition she still heard Betsy's voice belaboring Roddy. She knew that he would follow her as soon as he could escape it, so she took a few steps in the semidarkness of the narrow passage. In front of her dropped suddenly the railed iron ladder down which Roddy had guided her when they went to look at the horses.

Step by step she descended, stiff with misery, gripping her bundle with one hand and the cold rail with the other.

After a short flight the ladder came out on another passage. It was dimly lighted by a swaying lantern. Behind the stair she had just descended, she saw a second going still farther down. When following her brother she had not noticed landmarks, but she felt sure that she was on her way to the hold. The ship was pitching and she was trying to keep her footing when a man came around the turn of the corridor. He was broad-shouldered and red-faced and wore oilskins and sou'wester, and he seized her shoulders with both hands to steady her.

"Be careful or you'll fall down the hatch! What are you doing above steerage?"

She did not know it, but he was the mate who, with two others, had been displaced from the cabin for Roddy's passage. He looked hard at her, and she shrank against the skeleton stair. "I'm trying to find me way to the steerage now," she whispered.

He stared harder. "Aren't you Corley's sister? I saw you come aboard with him, and he asked for the large cabin."

She had slipped by him and reached the top of the second ladder. The ship rolled so heavily that she had to stop and catch its rail as she was starting down. He leaned from above and grasped her shoulder. "You're Corley's sister," he said again. "You belong with him and his wife."

She clung to the rail, already giddy with her first seasickness. But she looked up in his face and spoke with dignity. "Take your hand off me shoulder, or I will roar for the captain."

He removed his hand but followed her down into the vessel's hold. The ladder came out suddenly into the horror of the steerage. Men and women now lay on the floor in further stages of disarray. Others were eating supper, talking or gambling. Dirt and disorder were revealed by two lanterns swung from a long, low beam.

Appalled by the sight she stopped, and the mate caught up with her. He did not touch her and he spoke respectfully. "It's no place for a young woman like you. Are you not looking for your brother?"

She shook her head, standing alone with the bundled shawl clasped to her breast. She had no longer anyone for whom to look.

The man she loved was leagues behind, and her brother had betrayed her. She was so numb with misery that she could not think. Her eyes took in the sprawled figures, her nose the unclean smells, her ears the gutteral northern speech that she did not understand. But her brain refused to accept the fact that she was part of the pattern, on a lonely ocean, headed for an unknown land.

Then, in the far corner where the horses' stalls had been built, the bay thoroughbred threw up her head and pawed and struck out with her front feet. There may have come to her delicate nose, through the fetid smell that offended her, some faint whiff of her trainer's scent brought by Dinah from Roddy. Or her sixth sense may have recognized, in the brave, forlorn little figure, a comrade as helpless and alone and gallant as herself. Whatever it was, it caused her to throw her weight against the stout bars and point her soft ears forward and whinny loudly and shrilly.

For a few seconds the emigrants were quiet with surprise, and the girl and the bay mare looked silently at each other.

Then Dinah moved slowly forward, picking her way in and out among the groups, and the husky mate, Mr. Kincannon, followed her foot to foot. By the mare's stall she halted. She was afraid of horses. But she was friendless now except for this other exile, this proud, lovely creature who had called to her.

Before Mr. Kincannon could intervene, the sculptured head had darted to the length of its long neck and given the girl one of those pushes which are nudges of love to a horse, but which can easily knock a grown person down. This one shoved Dinah back and aside, directly into the narrow space between the last stall and the stern of the ship. She brought up clutching the bars to keep from falling, and the mare swung round and nuzzled her hair with fawn-pale, tender lips.

While Kincannon looked, Dinah lowered herself to the floor in complete exhaustion. She sat leaning back against the ship's hull, with her feet stuck out before her, and he saw the pallor of distress and illness on her face. He tried again. "You can't stay here. You'll have a good bed in the cabin. Let me take you back to your brother and his wife."

She was past words now. She closed her eyes and shook her head.

"This deck is damp and cold and hard. I'll get you a sleeping sack of some kind."

The gray eyes opened. "I would like well an armful of the horses' hay. Tis soft and clean, and it smells sweet. I will spread me shawl upon it."

He brought the fragrant grass hay from a broken bale beyond the stalls. When he had made the couch for her he asked again: "Won't you change your mind?"

But she only shook her head, and he saw she was trying not to weep.

Seth Kincannon turned and faced the crowd in the steerage. Some were watching him openly, some furtively as they talked. He stooped and picked up a broken bar which Larry and Pat had discarded. It was a four-by-four and was nearly five feet long. He balanced it from hand to hand as, without a word, his eyes went from one man's face to the other. They understood his warning. The talking died to quiet. Still without speaking, he turned and placed the bar diagonally from the lower rail of the mare's stall across the girl's narrow housing. Then he turned, and without looking at them as he strode among them, went above to take the night watch.

Twice a day the steerage passengers came up on the cattle boat's uncovered deck for air and exercise. Roddy and Betsy were the only cabin passengers and, whatever their faults, they had no objection to sharing the open space with less fortunate travelers. The captain, a kindly Dane, and his competent Yankee mate were humane and allowed them all possible privileges. Upon the planking in the thin autumn sunlight, they huddled together for warmth or walked up and down, commenting in various Scandinavian tongues.

Dinah always went with them, and never at other times, although given the freedom of the ship by Kincannon and Roddy. She refused the food that Betsy brought from the officers' table. She bought dark bread, honey, onions and cheese from fellow travelers who carried more than they needed. In Dinah's bundle of clothes Betsy Corley had put her cloth purse containing the savings of her life. Its few gold coins jingled against shillings and pennies earned by long hours of needlework for the Aran housewives.

She slept at night, untroubled. If any ideas entered the practical

heads of the North Europeans around her, they were dispelled by
memory of the brawny mate, feet set well apart and a five-foot
club in his hand.

Her presence calmed the high-strung mare who had adopted
her. It helped Roddy in the difficult and dangerous task of trans-
porting horses by water. Dinah became used to softly-loud breathing in the night when Kathleen Avourneen stretched her neck over
the side-rails of her stall to reassure herself that the friend she had
chosen was there.

But Roddy's shame and self-reproach made him more surly
than ever. He threatened to beat Betsy when she hid his keg of
poteen, and he shouted at Dinah in his insistence that she should
come back to his cabin. Once, half-drunk, he tried to drag her
there. But Seth Kincannon, without even the assistance of a rail,
soon made him leave her alone and warned him not to try it again.

Attending the horses three times a day, Roddy swore at the dirt
and the smells of the hold. Each day he forked up and threw
overboard the soiled beds of hay in which they stood and broke
new bales to give them clean, dry footing. And, while he did so,
his mind was tortured by the thought that his sister slept alongside
in a space that Muldoon's trainers had left because not spacious
enough for a horse.

A month later, in mid-November, they sighted the pilot boat
waiting off Charleston bar. It was a two-master, about sixty feet
long. Dinah watched it drop a rowboat carrying one of its pilots.

It was late afternoon and the sun seemed to be going down
behind white beaches feathery with a backdrop of palm and pine.
Before them stretched the harbor with its sentinel islands lying
north and south. Mr. Kincannon told Dinah that these two islands
were named "Sullivan" and "Morris." The names, Gaelic and
Galway, warmed her worried heart. The fat pilot had caught a
thrown rope and simply walked up the side of the ship. He was
steering them toward a low fort in midchannel. Mr. Kincannon
said it was called "Sumter" and had been built recently on a small
natural sandbar.

The pilot was moving them toward the Quarantine Station on
Morris Island. From it Dinah saw a second rowboat coming to
meet them. Two black men handled the oars, and three white men

climbed aboard as it was held alongside. The two younger, who wore fashionable riding dress, went directly down to the hold while the third stayed to talk with Mr. Kincannon.

Dinah stood aside while they argued. She heard the mate address him as "Doctor." After a while the other two came back, bringing Roddy along with them. Beside her brother they were slim and exquisite; their voices sounded softly arrogant. They were demanding that the ship should not be held at Quarantine, but should at once proceed and allow them to unload the horses.

All five of them finally went up on the bridge to the captain. A half hour later they were under way again. Standing alone on deck, Dinah watched a steady white beacon to port and aft.

"It's Charleston Light," Mr. Kincannon told her, coming up through the dusk of the deck beside her.

She said irrelevantly: "'Tis warm as the months of summer on Aran."

"Yes. You'll find it warmer here than in West Ireland. My home is on the Maine coast." His eyes were soft on her shawled head that came only up to his shoulder. "I think you would feel more at home there than here in the South."

Ah, she thought, never at home! Never until I find me John! Not at home in the North or the South. Loneliness overwhelmed her. She tried to change the subject by asking about the islands. Faint lights were winking to the right and to the left.

"That's Fort Johnson port, and Fort Moultrie starboard," he said. "We were scheduled to anchor off Quarantine tonight, but these damned young bloods won't wait to have their horses. Bull, and a friend of his named Bay, have come aboard with a doctor from the lazaretto. They are paying to have the pilot take us in to a Cooper dock, and then bring us back to Quarantine when they get the horses off."

He looked down again at that hooded head, lonely but erect. "You are logged as cabin, not steerage, and I intend to get you ashore tonight. I'll not have you subjected to the indignity of the examinations they put these immigrants through. Have your things ready and at hand. While the horses are being unloaded, I'll take you down the gangplank from the bridge and you can meet your brother on the wharf."

7

So DINAH, weary of standing, sat upon a bollard, shivering in the wind and looking fearfully around. The wharf was lighted by fires of lightwood knots built in boxes of deep sand three or four feet square. The yellow flames leapt and licked out and, in their contorted light, figures strange and terrifying to her came and went. Enormous black men, stripped to the waist and sweating in spite of the autumn cold, were mooring the ship and unloading the horses. She had never before seen Negroes and she shrank as they passed her, with bare feet sure on the wharf wood and eyes and teeth flashing white. She could not know that they were slaves brought by Rawlins Bull and Maurice Bay to do the unexpected work in place of the regular dock hands.

Mr. Kincannon had, with the doctor's permission, brought her ashore and exacted from her a promise to wait and talk with her brother. Roddy, in turn, had said he would take her to a lodging house and not force her to go with him and Betsy. Only they three were being released. Yellow fever had come to Charleston more than once upon some ship. The cattle boat would be taken back and tied up at Quarantine until the doctors were sure that none of her passengers carried infection.

Trembling, the girl looked around her—at the shadows leaping against the wharf shed, at the dark harbor pricked by Castle Pinckney's dagger of light, at the skyline of the sleeping city. It was midnight and all quiet, except upon this wharf. Here the ship's strakes and crossbeams groaned against soft palmetto piles. Hatches slammed and gangways thudded. Men shouted and horses plunged and stamped. She distinguished one voice raised in anger above the racket.

"Blast you for a clumsy fool," it shouted furiously. "You have that mare too near the edge. If she goes over I'll break your neck!"

It was Maurice Bay and he was speaking to Roddy Corley. It brought home to Dinah suddenly that coming ashore meant parting with the only living link between her and Ireland. She had grown to love the beautiful creature with a doe's eyes, alongside of whom she had lived for nearly three months on the cattle boat. She got up and walked to the turn of the shed and looked out along the wharfside. The first hunter had been led ashore, the bay mare Kathleen Avourneen. She was rearing crazily while, at each side of her head, Roddy and one of the gentlemen who had come in the rowboat soothed her.

Dinah longed to go forward and speak to her or touch her, but, like the mare, she was by now beside herself with terror. She could only watch with sympathy until the gentleman cried: "Stand clear!" Roddy obeyed the command. The gentleman put his left hand, with gathered lines, on her crest and vaulted to her bare back as her front feet came down on the planking.

His drastic methods diverted her from her attempts to throw herself overboard. The mare reared again and plunged forward and, with hoofs thundering on the wharf, tore past Dinah as she shrank aside, and disappeared into the night.

Dinah stood flat against the shed until her rider brought her back into the wavering orange light. He was talking aloud to her and leaning forward to pat her neck. For several minutes he rode her in a circle at the end of the narrow dirt street that led down to the dock. "Quiet, girl," he was saying. "Steady, Avourneen! Steady!"

Then he spoke to a Negro man who had come out of the shadows and who stood watching him. "Think you can take her now, Hilt?"

The man, small and gray-haired, came forward and spoke with assurance. "I can handle her, Mr. Morry," he said. "I left Buck with the watchman on the cotton wharf."

The young gentleman slid easily from her back and stood holding her bit ring and stroking her cheek. "Take her straight across town to Rutledge Avenue. Turn west on Calhoun and pick up Ashley where it begins. Where Ashley ends at Spring, follow the path to Lowndes Grove. They are looking for you, and Titus can bring you home."

He watched the Negro mount and ride off sitting a fast trot. Then he turned and saw Dinah. "What are you doing there all by yourself?" he asked sharply.

She edged back toward the bollard, too frightened to speak. As he came toward her, his eyes fell on the bundle. "Did you come off the cattle boat?"

"I did," she whispered.

He was medium height and thin, but he towered over her. Although his voice was low, it was commanding. He was frowning down at her. "The docks are no place for a lady. It must be after midnight. Is there nobody with you?"

She managed to say: "I am waiting for me brother. 'Twas he brought the horses."

"Oh, is your brother Muldoon's groom?" he sounded vastly relieved. "In that case you're all right. I'll get back and help with the hunters."

As he went around one side of the shed Betsy appeared from the other. She stopped as she saw her sister-in-law and she spoke angrily. "I have been searching ye ever since the Naygurs tied the bowt to the quay."

Dinah shivered, hugging herself with both arms for that little warmth. "It does ye no good to search for me, Betsy Corley."

Betsy came closer. "Are ye crazy entirely? It is time you came to yourself, me girl, and did as you are told."

Dinah looked straight ahead of her and made no reply. The trampling and shouting had redoubled in the background. Betsy yelled to make herself heard above it. "Roddy has more patience than I would be having with you. Get yourself up now from that post, and help me carry the bundles!"

"I will carry no bundles for you, Betsy Corley."

"And is that the way it is, me fine lady? Ye will have nowt to do with your brother or his wife? What do you think to do then, in this black land we have arrived at?" She pulled her shawl closer and glanced fearfully around. "I am looking, any minute, for a wild red Injun to jump out of the night on me and skelp the hair from me head."

Doubly terrified by this voicing of her own fears, Dinah gazed around big-eyed, but still said nothing.

"You will change your tune when your belly begins to pinch," Betsy prophesied. "You are not feeling the hunger now because of the cheese and onions you had in the pigsty in which you traveled. You, a girl from South Aran, who could have sat like a lady in a room that is called a cabin and been drinking tea every day!"

Dinah was trying desperately to keep back the tears. Roddy saved her from further torment by arriving in a run. "Betsy! Betsy!" he was calling distractedly. "Betsy—do you know where's Dinah?"

Betsy gestured toward the small, disconsolate figure huddled on the bollard in the lightwood's smoky glare. "Here she sits like a seagull on a post on the Claddach quay, and no more words in her mouth than a bird, and no more sense in her head at all."

He came forward and put a hand on his sister's shoulder. "Dinah, will you not let bygones be bygones and come to the plantation with Betsy and me?"

She said quietly: "No, Roddy. I will not go with you."

He took his hand from her shoulder and his face was ashamed and unhappy. "Father and Betsy made me do it. But—it is done, now."

She did not reply.

"Betsy and I will have a fine cottage to ourselves. You can stay with us and get work at the price that will fair make your eyes stick out. I have talked with some of the Irish lads who do the stevedoring. With the pay ye would get for the fine sewing—and with the looks of ye—ye could have your choice of a dozen fellows for husband."

She said: "I will have no husband unless I have me John."

He threw up his arms in despair. "Oh, me God, will ye help me!"

Betsy said angrily: "Didn't I tell ye?"

He wheeled on her. "Hold your uproar!"

But, before he could renew his plea to Dinah, that low, authoritative voice called: "Corley! Corley, where are you?"

"I am here and coming," he shouted. But he stopped to look back at his sister. "Wait for me, Dinah."

One of the Irish dock hands came around the corner of the shed. "Corley, that there bang-tail lepper is about to lep in the sea!"

The two made exit hurriedly toward the wharfhead, where cursing and stamping and smashing of wood was getting louder. Betsy waited until her voice could be heard above it.

"And what do ye think to do if ye will not come with Roddy and me?"

Dinah did not answer her and she continued: "I am washing me hands of ye then. Ye can starve or ye can walk the streets of this Charleston, with your fine ideas and your clothes wrapped up in your shawl."

She flounced herself again around the wharf shed to collect the bundles she had hoped to put upon Dinah. And Dinah, sitting still until she went, turned then and looked after her. . . .

Her eyes widened with terror as she saw, upon every side, darkness beyond the uncertain light of the wharf fires. Her lips quivered. She dropped her face in her hands. She burst into tears, rocking herself back and forth on the bollard. "Oh, me John," she sobbed aloud, "it is weary without ye! I do not know where to be going or what to do at all."

She wept so violently that she did not even hear the horses go by, induced ashore by Roddy and ridden by Rawlins Bull and two of his slaves. The first sound that pierced her grief was a voice sharp with annoyance. It said: "Holy smoke! Are you still here on the bollard? And crying too?"

She cried even louder and could not answer him. He stood beside her, demanding: "What's the matter with you? Isn't your brother coming to take you with him?"

She looked up at him then with enormous, wet gray eyes. "I will turn me face back toward Ireland and jump into the ocean before I will go a step with me brother or his wife."

"That's a pretty how-de-do," he said indignantly. "But"—and he stopped and pulled a handkerchief from the tail pocket of his riding coat—"for heaven's sake, wipe your eyes!"

She took the embroidered and hemstitched square and examined it with interest. "It is too handsome by far for me to wipe me eyes on, sir. Needlework is the one thing I know, and this is master needlework."

He was thankful for the digression. "My mother made it for me. If you like sewing, you and she would get on well together."

Sobs still caught at her words, but she was diverted. "Does she make her living by her needlework then?"

Maurice Bay laughed aloud with delight. "Not exactly. You see, my poor mother is kept so busy that she really hasn't time to make her living."

"Ah, the poor lady," cried Dinah. "I would help her if I could."

"You're a kind little thing to want to help other people when you're alone and homesick on a wharf at night. But"—he put a foot up on the nearest bollard and his voice grew more determined —"you must go with your brother. You can't stay here."

Betsy came into sight just then, with Roddy following her. Both were laden with bundles, and both were weary and cross.

"Here she is," shrilled Betsy. "Stubborn as a Kerry donkey." Then she saw Maurice Bay and stopped short.

He looked them both up and down, without moving his foot from the stanchion. "Are these your people?" he asked Dinah.

"They are me people," she told him truthfully.

Betsy, gathering courage, advanced toward him. "Her people we are—her own brother and her brother's wife. She would do better to come with us, instead of sitting there talking with any stranger like a woman of the docks."

He said softly, and too politely: "I'm just beginning to see why she'd rather jump in the dock than go along with you."

Roddy dropped his bundles and clenched his big fists. "Are ye meaning any impoliteness to me wife?"

"My good man," said Maurice gently, "I always mean what I say."

Roddy looked at him, puzzled, then started toward Dinah. "It is later than I thought it would be when we finished unloading. For this night you will have to come to the lodgings Mr. Bull has engaged for Betsy and me. I have no time to be finding another place for you. In the morning you can decide for yourself."

Betsy advised: "If she will not, just pick her up under your arm. Teach her, the once and for all, to be doing as we say."

Roddy was angry. Both Bull and Bay had blamed him for the conditions under which the horses had traveled. Then he had difficulty in getting them ashore, and had been cursed and shouted at in addition. "I've had me fill," he told his wife. "It is the thing I am going to do."

Dinah slipped down from the bollard and tried to escape him. He almost had her in his grasp when the other man caught him by a shoulder and spun him around with a strength which surprised him.

"Keep your hands off her! She shall not go with you unless she goes of her own will."

The Irishman lowered his head. "I tell you I am her brother."

"You may be a brother to her, but to me you're a bullying black-guard. If you lay a hand on her against her will, I'll take you by the seat of your dirty britches and drop you in Cooper River."

Betsy screamed: "You mean her no good, with your fine clothes and your fine speech."

He gave her a little bow. Fury made him more polite. "Madame, the fine speech I just made to your husband goes for you, too, if you ill treat this girl."

He turned to Dinah. "Do you wish to go with them?"

She edged closer to him. "No! Oh, no!"

"Then you shall not. Only, for God's sake, don't weep again!"

Roddy was trying to bluster. "I will tell Mr. Bull."

"Do so," said Maurice. "He happens to be my kinsman, as well as my closest friend. I seem to have got myself involved in your very unpleasant affairs by coming out tonight to help him unload his horses."

It was soaking through Roddy's thick skull. His mouth fell open. Betsy pulled at his arm. "He will cause you to lose your job. Then what will we be doing?"

Roddy looked from her to Dinah to Maurice Bay. He, too, was alone in a new land and, in his way, lonely and fearful. Unlike his wife, he had no ugly suspicions of this arrogant stranger's motive for championing Dinah. He was a decent, honest lad, in spite of both roughness and weakness. His one overwhelming sensation was that of helplessness before a man who had the whip hand, and would not hesitate to crack the whip ruthlessly. He had instinctively feared Bay from the first moment he set eyes on him. But, at the same time, instinct told him that Dinah would be safe with Bay. She was of age now, he told himself, and stubborn enough to look after herself. He could not let her make him lose his new job by quarreling over her with his employer's relative.

Betsy jerked him harder. "Come on! She is not worth it."

Glowering but obedient, he picked up his bundles. Dinah watched them go off following a slave, who waited with a light-wood torch to show them to their night's lodgings.

Her eyes came back to find Maurice's fixed upon her. He said, a little uncertainly: "Are you sure that you have done right?"

She nodded and tried to speak, but her eyes overflowed again.

She wiped them with his handkerchief, which she was still holding.

"No," he exclaimed. "For heaven's sake, no!"

She misunderstood. "Ah, but I have spoiled your kerchief!"

She held it out with both hands and looked guiltily at it.

"I didn't mean that. I meant you mustn't cry any more." He stooped and picked up her bundle. "Come on now. I'll take you home to Mother before you have a chance for more tears."

She looked at him doubtfully. She knew that, upon Aran, every door was open to necessity. But this was a strange land and she did not know its customs. "Would your mother let me in her house?"

"She has never yet refused to take in anybody or anything I brought home." He put a hand under her elbow and smiled down at her, teasing. "I've brought her birds with broken wings and homeless dogs and cats, friends who were too drunk to dare go to their own homes, and once a starving poet from the court of the Prussian Regent."

Dinah sighed with relief. "'Tis the heart of honey she has."

"Bless your own heart," he exclaimed with surprise in his voice. "You've described her exactly without even seeing her."

He was guiding her over uneven ground toward the next wharf. Huge sheds loomed ahead of them where the cotton bales waited for shipment. Suddenly he stopped short in the darkness. "But I didn't bring the carriage! It went to Lowndes Grove for Hilt. I'm so accustomed to riding I forgot I was on horseback."

She tried to reassure him. "I never, in all me life, had a chance to ride in a carriage."

He was looking down at her anxiously, although he could not see her face. "But what will we do then? Can you ride pillion behind me? If not, we'll have to walk."

"If ye mean can I sit behind you and hold to your coattails," she answered, "'tis the only way I ever rode—on the donkey's rump on Aran."

8

TIMBUKTU, MORE INTIMATELY known as Buck, clattered over the cobblestones in the gait which is known as a running walk and which is appreciated by people who ride long distances. On his back Dinah clung with both arms to Maurice Bay's narrow, sinewy waist, and her right cheek was pressed close between his shoulder blades. He held her bundle upon his saddle bow, and he spoke to her occasionally and kindly. They had passed a dark building with double steps upon their left and a broad street running off to the right, and ridden a short way beyond when he swung the horse to the right.

"Lummy!" he shouted. "Lummy! Wake up and let us in!"

Peeping around his shoulder, Dinah saw a light blossom. It approached them through the darkness and silhouetted the wrought iron of the double carriage gates. The Negro Absolom, carrying a lantern, unbolted and swung them open. The horse stepped through, and its rider drew it to a halt.

"Take Buck's head, Lummy, while I get the lady down."

"Yassuh," said Lummy sleepily. He showed no more surprise than Buck had shown when she was lifted to his croup.

He swung her down and then swung down beside her. "No need for a rubdown, Lummy. The horse is cool. You can just water and stable him."

Then he turned and took her by the arm. "This way. The flagstone path leads through the garden."

She was speechless with fear and loneliness and she wished she had gone with Roddy. Tall shrubs brushed against her, and she smelled a dusty spice which she learned afterward to call *Opoponax*. The house rose before her, dark and enormous. Across the street she heard water breaking against a sea wall.

Maurice Bay opened a door and drew her into a big hall. Gas burned dimly in a chandelier of a dozen engraved crystal cups. A huge curved stairway seemed to soar unsupported into regions above. He propelled her upward, not seeming to notice that she was holding back and about to crumple up. On the second level he pushed a half-open door. "Mother," he announced casually, "here's a little girl named Corley. She had nowhere to go, so I brought her home to you."

Across the room a lady rose to her feet and laid a book on the table beside her. Her features were chiseled and her face almost stern in repose. A faint flash of surprise crossed it now, and then vanished. Like her son, she was of medium height but appeared taller, because she was as slim as a wand and as straight as a rapier. This slenderness was only enhanced by the pale yellow and bouffant skirts of the modified *robe à la Française* that she wore. Its square neck was modestly veiled by a small scarf of delicate lace, and the deep *V* of the bodice accentuated her small waist and divided the full, trailing overskirts. Her black hair was parted and drawn back on her head in a cluster of curls just touched, here and there, with silver.

But, when she saw Dinah lonely and woeful at the door, she took in the situation at a glance as her son had not. Surprise vanished and tenderness took its place. She came forward, seeming to glide under her yards of flowered silk, and she held out both hands in a gesture of gentle welcome. "You did right, Morry," she said.

Maurice slung the bundle on the nearest chair and pulled his guest into the room with him. He knew that he had done right and that his troubles were now at an end. For he knew now that his mother was taking over. He said: "She arrived tonight on the cattle boat with Rawlins' Irish horses."

Mrs. Bay had reached out and taken both of the chapped, rough, cold little hands in her own. "My dear child, how far you've come!"

Dinah broke under the kindness. She felt she was strangling. "'Tis—tis a wide way, ma'am, between me and Ireland."

Maurice spoke hastily. "Here now! None of that! If you begin to cry, mother'll cry with you. Then there'll be nothing for me to do but sit back on my hind legs and point my nose at the chandelier and howl like a hound dog."

Mrs. Bay had drawn the girl into her arms. "You shall cry if you choose. But you'll cry with my arms around you and have my shoulder to cry on."

Dinah clutched her desperately, cold and shaking from head to foot. She smelled the same dusty perfume that she had smelled in the garden, and she felt a hand touch her windblown hair.

"Such soft, pretty curls. What is your name, my dear?"

"'Tis no more than Dinah, ma'am. Me name is Dinah Corley."

"You are cold to the touch. Morry, what did you do with her cloak?"

Maurice, in masculine helplessness, looked from the bundle to Dinah. She raised her head. "I have no cloak at all, ma'am. I have me shawl, and I would be wearing it except that I have to carry me clothes tied in it."

Mrs. Bay's eyes went to the small bundle tossed on the gold brocade seat of a mahogany chair. She said with quiet courtesy: "It is an exquisite piece of weaving. It must be an heirloom in your family."

Diverted from her grief, Dinah drew out of the soft arms and tried to smile at them both. "It was me mother's shawl and she wore it for her wedding."

"I love all beautiful things. You shall tell me about it tomorrow. Now it is late and you are very tired. You must eat a little supper and then go to bed."

Maurice started toward the broad ribbon of stiffened brocade which was the bell pull beside the fireplace. "Shall I ring for Erasmus?"

His mother raised a restraining hand. "Of course not. Erasmus and all the other house servants have been in bed for hours. You may go yourself, and get the port and biscuits."

As he left she drew the girl down in a big chair alongside the wood fire. Its great chimney was set on a line with the door they had entered. Dinah now faced the eastern side of the room, which was also the side of the house but turned to the street. Its length of twenty feet was cut by four French windows, each hung with a panel of lace and overdraped with gold brocade. A chandelier, larger than the one she had seen in the lower hall, hung from the ceiling at center and lighted the large room. Dinah had never before seen gaslight. The lovely little wing-shaped flames quivered like yellow butterflies in the crystal cups that held them like flower chalices.

Mrs. Bay was saying: "You must drink a glass of wine and eat some biscuits, then go to bed and have a long, restful sleep."

The gas and the wood flames were dancing on wine-red mahogany. Dinah leaned back against softness of cushioned satin and silk. Numbness was taking over from fatigue and fear and cold. "Tis kind ye are, ma'am," she said wearily, "but have ye a bed to spare for me? I would not want to be turning out yourself or your grand young son."

"We have extra beds," Mrs. Bay reassured her. "You shall have a room to yourself and yet not turn anyone out. Sleep just as long as you can. When you wake your breakfast will be brought to you."

Horrified, Dinah grasped the arms of the chair and sat upright. "Oh, no, ma'am! I could never let you be cooking me breakfast."

"I have a cook. You will be giving me no trouble at all."

Maurice was coming in with a silver tray upon which were decanter, glasses and a silver dish. "Sleep as long as you choose, Dinah. My mother has sixteen cooks."

That brought her completely out of the chair. "Oh, me soul! Sixteen cooks?"

"Of course not," said Mrs. Bay. "Morry, stop teasing her at once and give her a glass of wine."

He poured it and brought it to her, and he set on the arm of her chair the dish of imported English biscuits. Then he turned his back to the fire and ran his hands down in his riding breeches' pockets. "I repeat that she has sixteen cooks. There's Erasmus first." He looked gravely at Dinah. "Erasmus would be outraged if I didn't put him first."

"Morry, stop!" said Mrs. Bay. "Drink your wine, Dinah, and don't listen to his folly."

He drew his hands from his pockets and began to count on his fingers. "There's Mauma and Aunt Jody and Aunt Jody's niece Elvira. There's Lulie and Ann and Clementine and old Venus and the stable men and—"

"Morry, you *must* stop! You're talking like a zany. Erasmus is a butler, not a cook. Clementine and the other two girls are housemaids. Venus and Jessie and Mary Jane do our washing. Mauma is too old to do anything. None of them cook except Jody and Elvira. The other six are gardeners and ostlers."

He grinned from ear to ear with delight at having made her

explain. "You'd better not let Mauma hear you say she can't do anything. She thinks she runs the whole ménage. And I'm inclined to agree with her."

Picking up the decanter he approached Dinah, who was looking uncertainly at him. "Sit down and let me fill your glass. Don't you like the biscuits?"

She dropped tiredly back in the chair and accepted a second glass of wine. He set the dish of biscuits in her lap, and she began to eat them hungrily. In order to leave her to herself, Mrs. Bay addressed her son.

"Did Rawlins' horses come up to your expectations?"

His slow voice became enthusiastic. "They are magnificent. I've never before seen such bone. If they perform according to conformation, I think I'll run over next summer and get a pair." He stopped to pour himself a glass of port. "Here's to Ireland, Dinah! When I go, would you like me to take you back for a visit?"

Her eyes filled and she choked suddenly on the biscuits. "I—I could not say for sure. It might be I would have no roof for me head."

"Leave her alone, Morry," commanded Mrs. Bay. "We have plenty of time to talk with her tomorrow. Don't ask the child annoying questions when she's tired and hungry."

He refilled both Dinah's glass and his own, and then turned on his mother. "Very well, then. I'll ask *you* annoying questions. Why do I find a respectable Charleston lady sitting up alone at 2 A.M., after the servants have gone to bed?"

Although accustomed to managing a mansion and servant quarters, two children and sixteen slaves, her son's teasing always put her on the defensive. She looked around her helplessly. "I was reading."

He stepped toward her, eyes dancing as he sipped his port. "Something improving, I hope. Or was it *Godey's Ladies' Fashions?*"

"No," she denied indignantly. "I was reading a book." She looked toward the table where she had laid it when they entered. "There it is. A most interesting book."

He crossed and picked it up. "Goethe's *Faustus* in the original. It is an interesting book—for anyone who reads German. But I seem to remember that you never liked the language. In fact you called it uncouth and disapproved highly of your only son's going to Heidelberg. I gathered that you considered Oxford or the Sorbonne the only choice for a Charleston gentleman."

"And I still think so," she told him spiritedly.

"I know you do. So my bet is that, instead of reading, you were standing at that window watching to see that your little boy got home safe."

"Stop teasing me, Morry," she ordered.

Dinah, drinking her third glass of port and eating biscuits as if starved, was watching them between bites and sips.

"Here's a fair exchange," he said. "I'll stop teasing you if you'll stop sitting up half the night to see me come in. I know how many duties you have to keep you busy all day long, and it spoils my pleasure to know that I am making you lose your rest. It isn't fair, Mother. I'm twenty-two, but you seem to think I'm not yet out of diapers."

Horror was in Mrs. Bay's voice. "Maurice! That awful word— before an innocent young girl!"

He had spoken before he thought, and he was embarrassed. But Dinah saved him. She finished the last biscuit and wiped her mouth on the handkerchief he had given her at the wharf. "Sure, but I've heard it often, ma'am. And helped put them on the babbies."

He burst into laughter then. "You're the innocent young girl, Mother. Dinah and I know more about life right now than you ever will."

He put down his glass and caught her in both arms and kissed her. But she drew herself away. "Come, Dinah. You must be ready for bed."

Dinah rose obediently. "I am; for I have not slept in a bed since I left the loft in me father's house."

Startled, Mrs. Bay looked inquiry from her to Maurice.

He shrugged. "Steerage. Eleven weeks on a sailing ship."

Mrs. Bay put an arm around the blue serge shoulders. "You'll sleep in a bed tonight, dear child. And you'll stay with us as long as you like."

Dinah lifted her bundle from the chair. She looked at Maurice and said shyly: "Good-night, Mr. . . . Morry."

"Good-night, Dinah," he said.

He looked after them, half sympathetic and half amused. Then crossed the room and picked up *Faust*. He opened it, glanced down a page, slapped it shut and threw it across the room. Then he filled his glass, swallowed the port, filled it again and took it across to the grand piano. Setting it upon the mahogany top, he parted his coattails carefully and seated himself on the bench. He began playing "Tannenbaum." Strange air for a Charleston drawing room, for "Maryland, My Maryland" had not yet been written to the tune. He played by ear, with little skill but with a natural sense of touch. When he finished the old song, he started slowly and uncertainly upon a piece of music of a very different type. But, even his lagging tempo could not spoil the swing of its chorus. He played it again and faster and sang its last lines aloud:

> "Look away! Look away!
> "Look away down South in Dixie!"

Mrs. Bay came back into the room and stood behind him, listening. As he stopped she asked curiously: "What is the new song, Morry, and who taught it to you?"

He swung her around and pulled her down on the bench, beside him but facing the other way as if they sat in a love seat. "I don't know what it's called, but that red-headed lieutenant over at Fort Moultrie has been trying to play it."

She said resignedly: "Red-headed lieutenant? I do wish you would learn to be more explicit. Among all the army officers whom we meet at balls and dinners, how can I identify a red-headed lieutenant?"

He laughed and ran a treble trill, speaking over his shoulder. "It's that fellow who tries to paint and who is so fond of music. We met him at Old Uncle Bond'Ion's house on Sullivan's Island, and he comes over to Charleston to the drawing-room musicales."

"I asked you his name," reminded Mrs. Bay.

"Oh, his name," said Maurice carelessly. He stopped to make a run in the treble. "His name is William——"

He paused for another run.

"Tecumseh——"

He gave a last and most spirited trill. "Sherman."

Then he spun on the bench to face his mother again. "You were sweet to the little Irish lass."

"Tell me about the poor child," she said. "I'm thankful that you found her."

"I don't know anything except that she's unhappy and alone and afraid of her brother. I knew you'd take her in and take care of her."

"Of course I will. I put her in the room next to Dorry's. Mauma always sleeps in the dressing room between, and I woke her up and turned Dinah over to her. I don't mind waking her," she added excusingly, "because she sleeps all day as well as all night."

His voice was anxious. "Did Mauma take to Dinah?"

"Thank heaven she did," said Mrs. Bay. She turned on her son. "I wish you had half as much wholesome fear of your mother as you still have of your Mauma."

He said sheepishly: "I'm scared to death of her. But I want her, and everyone else, to be kind to Dinah. I found her sitting weeping on a bollard, ready to jump in the river but pluckily refusing to go with her oaf of a brother and his virago wife." He paused and frowned. "Ireland is suffering from both famine and war. Here in South Carolina we are so happy and so safe from those two Horsemen of the Apocalypse that we ought to be glad to help others less fortunate."

"You are right, darling," she said. "We'll do all we can for little Dinah Corley. When she is rested and less afraid I'll talk with her about herself."

Then she rose and put a hand on the dark cloth of his shoulder. "But I'm sleepy, and you should be even if you're not."

He went across to the fireplace and picked up the small gilded pole which had a wick to light the gas, and a slot to turn off the valve. From the hall door she was watching him. "This wonderful invention is a laborsaver," she said. "When I think of the dozens of oil lamps . . . and the candles of my childhood . . ."

Her low voice seemed to go out with the gas. Under the chandelier which he had just extinguished, Maurice Bay began to whistle "Dixie" softly. He shouldered the pole like a musket and kept step to his whistling as he crossed to the hearth to replace it.

"See, Mother?" he demanded, as he put it down with a thump. She said reasonably: "I cannot see in the dark."

"I mean that tune you just asked me about has a catchy swing to it."

He set his feet down hard to its time as he went from the fire-place to the door. There he took her arm and spoke earnestly. "The Charleston Light Dragoons are always on the lookout for that kind of thing. If they haven't got it already, I'll play it for them next meeting. I'll play it in double-quick time. Because I have an idea that Lieutenant Sherman has introduced us to a mighty good marching song."

9

DINAH SLEPT DEEPLY . . . dreamlessly . . . and blissfully. . . .

As her tired body had sunk into the deliciously soft bed, between sheets scented faintly with citrena, her equally tired brain had sunk into oblivion. Like some shy, wary animal, it scented security. Here, in a land antipodal to the only land she knew, a strange and definitely overbearing young man had picked her up from a torch-lit wharf in the midst of night and confusion, and carried her to a house which seemed to her like a castle. She had pictured red Indians with tomahawk in hand. She had heard of covered wagons which rolled on endless prairies. But no Irish lad returning from America had described people who resembled the Bays, or houses which resembled their home.

Half-dazed and hugging her shawled possessions, she had fol-lowed Mrs. Bay up a second stair the night before. Only a candle under a tall hurricane shade lighted that third hallway. Mrs. Bay had opened a door and called *"Mauma! Mauma!"* There had been no reply except loud and steady snoring. Setting upon a table the candle she carried in a blue and white French china holder, she had moved toward a second door. As she disappeared through it Dinah looked around. The room was large, with two big win-dows curtained in ruffled blue taffeta. The same material covered its dainty dressing table and quilted the big low-poster bed set catercornered across from her. Underfoot the cypress floor was almost completely covered with straw summer matting in the fashion of the day. She had no time to see more, because Mrs.

Bay reappeared, followed by a blue-black woman almost six feet tall and made more immense by layer after layer of underwear and sleeping clothes.

"This is Mauma," said Mrs. Bay. She came to Dinah, took the bundle from her and held it out.

"Mauma," she begged, "this little girl is no bigger than our Dorry. She has come a long way and is all alone and homesick. Will you take her now and put her to bed, and take good care of her?"

The tall black woman came forward as lightly as a leopard. Her face was a network of age, but she walked like a jungle cat. She took the bundle from Mrs. Bay and stood looking down at the newcomer. Her eyes were dark stones rimmed with bloodshot yellow, and Africa inscrutable was just behind their gaze.

Mrs. Bay turned and kissed Dinah lightly on the forehead. But at the hall door she paused and spoke with emphasis. "Try to remember, Mauma, how you felt the day when you were first brought to Charleston."

Then she had gone and left them, closing the door, and Dinah had looked up into those sphinxlike, stony eyes and burst into tears of despair and loneliness.

Torn by grief and utterly beyond composure now, she had sobbed herself to rest with those black arms around her. For Mauma had gathered her, like a baby, to that powerful, flat breast and sat down and rocked her, crooning softly in Gullah. Although she could not understand a word of it, it finally pushed its meaning through Dinah's misery. She realized that the singer cared enough for her and her troubles to be trying to comfort her with a lullaby.

Twenty minutes later, when she was almost asleep, Mauma brought in the round hip bath with its high, slanting back. Dinah heard her pouring into it hot and cold water from kettle and china pitcher. Then, limp and drained of all effort, she sat while the Negress undressed her, lifted her into the warm bath and washed her like an infant. Some soft garment was slipped over her rumpled head and she felt a deep-stuffed mattress give under her. She turned her head on the pillow and sighed and fell asleep.

Through her awakening twelve hours later, lilted and leapt the

song of a bird. It fluted like the blackbirds in the Valley of the
Seven Churches. It ran a gamut of birdsong to her completely unknown. Then it quivered and heightened and soared like an Aran
lark.

She opened her eyes slowly and they fell on the dresser mirror.
In it she saw herself, very small between the four posts of a big,
high bed. The heat of the day had caused her in her sleep to push
down the covers. She saw she was dressed in a nightgown so fine
and sheer that the warm rose-tan of her arms glowed distinctly
through its long sleeves. They ended in frills of lace which half
covered her hands. At her throat the same lace foamed modestly
up to her chin. She wore no nightcap, and tangled brown curls
were spread on the pillow around her face.

She lay as still and as bright-eyed as a bird caught in the hands.
It all came back to her clearly, but she felt no sense of panic. These
people who belonged to the fairy tale of the night before had given
her what was, at least, a respite from panic. Lying in their luxuri-
ous bed, she knew without troubling about the why that she would
be closer to them than she could be to Roddy and Betsy.

However, she had no intention of imposing upon them. She
would thank them and find a place to support herself with her
needlework. She could make gowns like the one she wore, and
make them with finer stitches. The gentry who used them would
pay her well for them and for other garments. She could not go
back to her father, and she would not live with Betsy. The young
man whose voice took turns at teasing and commanding, and his
lady mother with the lovely, composed face, would tell her where
to get lodgings and how to get work. She would write to her John
and wait for him. He had said no matter when or where, he would
come for her.

She watched the blue taffeta curtains sway farther into the
room, as tide ran up the rivers and the breeze came with it. It
took her some time to realize that three of the floor-length panels
were blowing in and out, while the fourth stayed still. It was not
only still but bunched as if wrapped around a post. She raised her
head to observe it and, as she did, another head poked like a
turtle's from behind the forget-me-not silk. She looked into a small
face, pointed and elfin and eager—a face with long-lashed, big
brown eyes, and brown hair held by a yellow band.

For a few heartbeats their gaze stayed locked. And then Dinah smiled.

The blue curtain was pushed, and ballooned away. The elf skipped free of her hiding place. Catching her long, primrose-yellow skirts high with both hands, she crossed the room in a series of leaps and brought up standing beside the bed. Her mouth was cherry-red and curved, her eyes alight with excitement.

"You're Dinah," she whispered. "My Dinah Ducklegs. I knew that the story would come true someday!"

Dinah sat up and held out a hand. "Ah, but you're nowt but a child! With all you're as tall as I am and as lovely as a fairy, you are no more than a gossoon. What do they call you?"

"They call me Dorry. My name is Dorothea. I'm eleven years old and I can read. I read a story about 'Dinah Ducklegs,' and I prayed at night that she would come out of the story and be my friend."

Dinah leaned and lifted her to a seat on the side of the bed. In spite of her height she weighed hardly more than a willow wand wrapped in the organdy. Her little feet, in heelless black slippers strapped over white cotton socks, stuck straight out before her.

"I heard Mama tell Mauma that you came on a big boat. I didn't know how you were coming, but I knew you'd come some way."

"Me home is across the water. The bowt brought me in last night."

"This is your home now," said Dorothea gravely. "We'll walk out on High Battery. Mauma will never walk far. I'll show you the forts in the harbor, and we can watch the sailboats. Morry loves boats. He sails them, and he knows how to make them too."

Dinah put an arm around the little, velvet-belted waist. "'Twas Mr. Morry that found me, in the cold and the night, on the quay. He brought me here to your mother who gave me the food and the bed. Sure, but I cannot be putting them to further inconvenience. Just as soon as I have me clothes, I will give them me thanks and be off."

But the child cast herself with such violence upon her that she fell back flat upon the bed. Two thin young arms were around her neck and a petal-smooth cheek pressed close to hers.

"Dinah—Dinah Ducklegs—don't go away from me! I want

you for my sister. Morry and Mama are so old! Mauma won't let me climb the fig tree or dance to Uncle Samba's drum. She makes me eat melongona and practice my pianoforte scales—"

Mauma's arrival stopped her recital of injuries. Dinah, still flat on her back, looked up into an ebony mask. Her arms, before she knew it, closed protectingly on the child.

Mauma towered above them. Her face was expressionless, but there was complete disapproval in her tone. "Git outa that bed, Miss Dorry. Don't you know no better than to climb in anybody bed with your dirty shoes on your feets?"

Dorothea climbed out and stood, slender, forlorn and rumpled. When Mauma used "Miss" before her name it cut her to the quick. She knew the old nurse reserved it to emphasize disgrace. Dinah sat up to intercede, but the black woman ignored her.

"Way you been hidin' all this time wile I been lookin' for you? Your ma and Mr. Morry settin' down to dinner now. You know you sposed to eat your vittals at half-past one o'clock. You keep on runnin' off every time Rasmus bring your waiter and you goin' to shrivel up and blow way like a boo-hag."

Dorothea put her arms behind her back and locked her hands together. Pivoting on the balls of her feet, she swayed her body impertinently. "I don't like to eat all by myself, and I'd like to be a boo-hag. I didn't run away this time, I just came in Dinah's room. I hid behind the curtain and waited till she woke up."

Mauma began: "You got no right to wake up Miss Dinah. She tired."

But Dinah broke in. "She didn't, ma'am. Twas the birds that woke me. I am rested entirely and ready to get up now."

She swung her feet over the side of the bed and would have stood up had not a strong hand come down on her shoulder. "Is you talkin' to me, wite gal? What that name you call me?"

Dinah quailed in terror. "I didn't mean anything wrong. I—I was trying to tell you about the little girl, ma'am."

"Take shame on yourself," said Mauma. "What kinda place you come from? Aint nobody teach you better than to call black people *ma'am?*"

Dinah felt her eyes blurring with shame and her brain with confusion. What phantasy was this when a sword-straight woman, who held herself like a queen and appeared to command others, ordered her to omit one small word of courtesy? But the unrelenting voice went on. "You got to be mannersable. Your skin witer than anybody I ever seed. Hit witer than Dorry's or Mr. Morry's or Mr. Morry's pa. Don't you never let me hear you call no nigger *ma'am.*"

Dinah rubbed knuckles into her eyes, and the child went into action. She screamed aloud and jumped up and down, stamping her slippers upon the floor. "You've made her cry, you old devil," she shrieked. "I'll kill you! I'll kick you! I'll butt you!"

She bowed her head like a small goat and rushed upon her nurse, who picked her up by the shoulders and shook her violently. When set down she let her whole body go limp and collapsed and rolled on the floor, drumming her heels and beating her head with audible thumps on the matting.

Dinah jumped up and bent over her, crying: "Acushla, be still!" But Dorothea continued to yell and kick as if in a spasm.

Above the noise rose the black woman's voice. She said in completely commonplace tones: "Is you listenin', boo-hag?"

Dorothea continued to writhe, but she stopped screaming to listen.

"Listen good, boo-hag, because I got errand for you to do."

The little black slippers drummed more slowly, and the big eyes in the tear-streaked face looked up with wary glances.

"Listen, boo-hag," said Mauma. "This chile so bad I can't do nothin' with she. You fly to hell quick as you can and tell devil to send plat-eye. Tell him to send plat-eye tonight and take she out she bed."

The dying shrieks of temper rose and fused in a scream of pure terror. Dorothea lay on her back and looked up with a white, tormented face. "No, Mauma, no! I'll be good! Don't let the plat-eye get me! Tell the boo-hag to come back. Don't send for the plat-eye, Mauma!"

She had jerked her slender body into a sitting position and was staring out of the window as if at something she saw. Dinah's eyes followed hers. The sky was blue and cloudless. Not even a bird-wing crossed it. But Mauma was staring too. Her purple lips moved and she said: "Boo-hag, you aint got no need to go to hell yet. Jist wait round and see if this chile behave sheself."

Dorothea rose and stood, still limp but compliant now. She hiccoughed a small sob as she implored: "I'll behave, Mauma. Won't you please, please let Dinah eat dinner with me?"

"You got to wash your face first, and lemme comb your hair. I aint goin' let any chile of mine eat wile she looks indecent."

"I'll wash my face! I'll comb my hair! Just let Dinah eat with me. If you do, I'll always eat what you tell me to."

Mauma went across the room to a tall mahogany wardrobe, opened one of its double doors and revealed the blue dress hanging. "I made Lulie clean your dress with a sponge and hot water and iron it. But your underclothes aint dry yet, so Miss Clelia send you some of hern."

She held out a hand to Dorothea, who took it obediently. "You come with me now and let Miss Dinah dress. If you wash your face and behave yourself, I'll let her eat dinner with you."

Dorothea left, with her pixie face turned back over her shoulder, and as the door closed Dinah began to dress. The underwear was of sheer cotton, trimmed with narrow thread lace. She had not yet learned that, to the servants, Mrs. Bay was still the Miss Clelia who had married into the house.

By the time Mauma tapped on the door, Dinah was ready to follow her down the hall to a small bright room lined with books. In one corner was a hobby horse, lacking a tail and one leg; in the other a doll's house of exquisite detail. By a window stood a small table set with two places, in its center a covered tureen of chicken soup. Dinah ate two plates of it, along with some hot bread that Mauma and Dorry called "Sally Lunn." Then Mauma pulled the bell ribbon, stacked the dishes on a tray which she called a waiter, and Erasmus appeared with a second service. He helped Dinah first to a green vegetable which she had never seen before. As he went on to Dorothea, she closed her eyes tight and shook her head violently. The butler addressed her politely but in determined tones.

"If you don't eat your broc'li, I won't give you no dessert."

Dinah, starved for vegetables, was devouring hers. "Why would you not eat it, avourneen?" she asked in real surprise. "It has a fine taste in the lovely green leaves of it."

Dorothea at once opened her eyes, allowed her plate to be helped and began to chew. Both Mauma and Erasmus looked at Dinah with admiration in their eyes. Completely unconscious of it, she finished off her dinner with a tall glass of the syllabub which was its dessert. Dorothea, draining hers to the last sweet, wine-flavored drop, upset its goblet, shrieked *"Morry,"* and rushed to the door to meet him. He lifted her featherweight and tossed it to a shoulder.

"Good-day, Dinah," he said. "What fare amid the alien corn?"

She knew her Bible as well as he did, and she looked back at him gravely. "You and your mother have given me kindness with both hands. I am fit to earn me own living if ye will tell me where—"

Dorothea interrupted with a wail of anguish. She clenched both hands in her brother's hair and kicked with both her feet. "Don't let her go away, Morry! Make her stay with me forever!"

He managed to pull and shake her loose. "For heaven's sake stop kicking my stomach!"

But, as he set her on the floor, she caught him around the waist. "Why can't she stay with us, Morry? Why can't she be my sister?"

"I haven't the faintest objection," he told her crossly. "Both Mother and I wish her to stay as long as she will."

Dorothea let go of him and cast herself upon Dinah. "You heard what he said! He wants you to stay. Won't you stay with me, Dinah?"

Dinah pushed the damp hair away from the flushed, intense little face. "Avourneen," she said, "I cannot do that because of the inconvenience. You and your mother and brother have done too much for me. I must make me living with me own two hands."

She looked at Maurice, who was standing and watching her closely. "All I want is your kindness to find me a decent lodging. I have skill with the sewing to earn me own keep."

"You'd earn your keep," he told her, "if you'd stay with this sister of mine and teach her to be a lady instead of a young wolf cub."

Dorothea seized the opening with the canniness of childhood. "If you let Dinah go away, I'll be a wolf and I'll bite. I bit Mauma once," she bragged, "until the blood ran down her arm."

"Both Mother and Mauma spanked you then," he reminded her. "If you ever do it again, they'll spank you harder. And I'll spank you too."

He looked back at Dinah, with interest in his dark eyes. "But what about it? Will you stay with us?"

She shook her head slowly, still smoothing Dorothea's silky crown. "I must be earning me own keep. I am not afraid of the work."

He shrugged his thin shoulders and his voice dropped to a bored drawl. "As you wish, then. Your brother is waiting downstairs. He and that harridan of a wife have found out that you are here, and he seems as determined to take you away as Dorry is to keep you."

10

RODDY HAD LEARNED several things and had come to his senses in the interval since he had last seen his sister. It is not easy to frighten or awe an Aranman, but he had talked with Rawlins Bull and he realized he had made a mistake. His employer told him briefly and definitely that Dinah was safe with the Bay family, and advised him not to annoy either her or Maurice Bay. Then he dispatched him, on one of the Irish horses, down Charleston peninsula with a note to Maurice.

Cap in hand, he was standing in the drawing room when Maurice opened its door and made Dinah precede him. She stopped short, looking from one man to the other. Roddy did not speak, but Maurice said gently: "I'll go now and leave you with your brother."

She clutched his sleeve and cried aloud: "No! Oh, no, Mr. Morry!"

Roddy's face darkened. "Ye'll not yet come with me?"

"Never," she said quickly, then calmed herself and continued: "I never fooled you, Roddy. I told you on the bowt, when you and Betsy tricked me and took me away from Galway, that I would not stay with you. I meant the words I spoke."

Maurice broke in. "Now, look here! All this is deuced awkward for me. I have nothing to do with your personal affairs."

"That ye have not," Roddy Corley told him.

Maurice frowned. He liked the man better for his plain speaking, but Dinah's hand still clutched his coat sleeve. He looked down and saw that it was clenched in desperation—and a sudden picture came to him of Mel's hand on his sleeve. Mel was coquette enough to make the touch infrequent,—and it was a soft, provocative touch, not a clutch of necessity. He recalled her fingers, white and slim, with almond-shaped nails which she polished with chamois until they shone lustrous and smooth. Looking at them, no man would have guessed that they could gather a hunter of fifteen hands for a five-foot jump which she took without rising from her side-saddle.

The picture came like a flash of light and was gone, but the little rough hand was still before his eyes. It was gripping hard enough to be felt through broadcloth and linen. He heard himself saying, with what he knew was sententiousness and hated as such: "I've nothing to do with your family quarrels, but any man has something to do when a woman needs his protection."

"Are ye fool enough," asked Roddy, "to be thinking that you have to protect her against her own brother?"

"Yes, since you've taken her away from her home against her will."

"Tis a matter of which ye know nothing. My father wished it done. The lass was not yet eighteen years old and was in the toils of a redcoat. But nowt has happened to her," Roddy went on stolidly. He added: "And tis meself who will see that nothing does happen, in this wild, uncivilized new land."

Those three adjectives were obliged to hit a Charlestonian between the eyes. But, although he lived on the Battery in a house built by his direct ancestor a hundred and fifty years before, Maurice had spent enough time in Europe to get perspective on age. He knew that the duns of Ireland, although simpler in construction, were as old and older than the castles of Central Europe. The man seemed to have his sister's welfare at heart, and she was, after all, a peasant with broad hands hard from work.

"Not yet eighteen?" he questioned thoughtfully.

"Ah, but I'm that," she told him. "Twas the day before me birthday that they took me away from me John. They found out that I was going to marry him the next day."

"It sounds like a dirty trick to me," Maurice commented.

"Tis a saying of Aran," said Roddy, "that the man who is not smart enough to think of the trick is the one first to call it dirty."

They looked at each other, deadlocked. Roddy's expression was no more revealing than the face of an Aran boulder. Maurice, on the other hand, was trying to keep his temper. His was the curse of a cool mind harnessed to hot blood. The first said: *Listen to this man;* the second urged: *Why don't you kick him out?*

He felt Dinah release his sleeve and saw her lift her head. Although the tawny curls were caught and fastened back with pins, some always managed to free themselves at the back of her neck and ears. They shone like gold against the white skin. He had seen real blondes in Europe, but they were scarce in Charleston. Mel Manchester was dark, flashingly dark, and was admired for being so. One of the Jockey Club's usual toasts was: *To a dark-eyed one!* It bore witness to preponderance of brunettes in a southern country. Looking down at the Irish girl, he saw all at once she was lovely—lovely and strangely different from all the girls he had ever known.

She was speaking to her brother with simple dignity. "I am eighteen years old now, Roddy. You took me away from me John, and I do not know how I will find him again. I can do no more than wait for him here, for I know well that he will come for me. I cannot go back to Aran, for me father would not take me in. But I tell you again what I told you before: *I will not live with you and Betsy.*"

"And what do ye think to be doing then?" he demanded.

"I can keep meself with me sewing. Ye told me, yourself, I could do it."

"I know ye are good with your needle, but ye are a stranger here. How will ye find the place to work, or the place to lay your head?"

"She can lay her head in this house, under my mother's care, for just as long as she likes," Maurice interpolated.

But neither brother nor sister paid any attention to him. Dinah said earnestly: "Mr. Morry's mother will tell me where to get work. And I know that Mauma will help me too."

Maurice suppressed a smile. Even the stranger within their gates fell under Mauma's dominion and acknowledged her power.

But Roddy was demanding to know: "Who might be this creature named 'Mauma'?"

"She's the head woman servant of the house," Maurice explained; "the slave who stands next to my mother and in charge of the other slaves. We've found her capable of caring for my young sister, so I think she can look after your sister too."

"I've seen them at Lowndes Grove," said Roddy. "I saw them last night and today. They are black and they are savages, and I have no liking for them. But, although they are black and savage, I am thinking that no man has a right to hold any other in slavery."

"Think what you damned please," snapped Maurice; "but have the sense and the manners to keep from telling another man what to do in his house and his country."

"If it's manners that's in it," said Roddy, entirely unperturbed, "ye might find yourself off on the wrong foot did we talk in my country of Aran."

Maurice not only knew that, but he prided himself upon having a broader view than some of his friends had. By the more conservative, he was considered a little odd because he did not hesitate to condemn the institution of slavery. He was kind as well as courteous, and it did not please him now to argue on the other side against a rough-mannered but honest-tongued man. He said: "We're getting nowhere by talking this way, Corley. I told you last night I had no idea of letting you force the girl to go anywhere against her will. She's eighteen years old and has a right to choose for herself."

Roddy gazed steadfastly back at him. "She may choose for herself, so long as I know she is living safe and decent."

"Don't you believe your employer? He told me in this letter that he had assured you the girl was safe with my mother."

"Aye," said Roddy; "but I have not yet seen the sight of your mother."

"Lord help me keep my temper," Maurice begged aloud.

He turned and jerked the bell ribbon, while Roddy watched him. The butler came, soft-footed as a cat and dignified as a king. "Erasmus," said Maurice, "will you kindly go and ask Miss Clelia to come here."

As the slave went Roddy Corley said: "'Tis the *missus* I'm wanting to see, and no *miss*."

Maurice tried to hold back his rising irritation. At that moment he would have enjoyed throwing the man downstairs and shoving his sister after him. But he managed to keep his voice even, for he saw he had to justify himself. "All the servants call Mrs. Bay 'Miss Clelia.' They started it when my father married her and brought her into the house where there was an older Mrs. Bay."

He turned in relief to his mother and took her arm as she entered. "Mother, this is Roddy Corley, Dinah's brother. He has her good at heart and has a right to inquire, and he's come to assure himself that she is safe in our hands."

Mrs. Bay moved a little forward and held out her hand. She saw a man just a few years older than her own son, a man with hard hands but clear eyes, who looked defiant, but unsure and lonely too. She said: "Mr. Corley, this is a quiet and old-fashioned home. Your sister is quite safe in it and is welcome to stay if she will."

Roddy shifted his cap to his left hand, wiped his right hand on his breeches, and gripped her fingers hard enough to hurt. He saw a woman of forty, dressed for the morning in severe black without hoops. Her hair, drawn back and looped over her ears instead of being arranged in curls, showed more gray than it had the night before. She released her hand from his grasp and turned to his sister.

"I hope you rested well, my child, and that Dorry didn't disturb you."

Her voice mothered the girl. Dinah felt it and Roddy heard it. He was watching, calmly and carefully.

"She did not disturb me at all, ma'am."

"She has been begging me to ask you to stay with us. The child is extreme in her likes and dislikes, but I've never known her to be so set on anything."

"She's a spoiled brat," said Maurice. "She knows how to get her way."

"She wants her way very much this time. In fact, I'm afraid disappointment will have a bad effect."

Maurice listened, wondering as he always did whether his mother was an accomplished diplomat or a completely ingenuous woman. She was still speaking to Roddy.

"Disappointment really makes Dorothea ill. If you've ever had a delicate child, Mr. Corley, you know how hard it is to get her to eat enough."

"There were six of us," said Roddy. "The only trouble I can remember me mother having was to get enough for us to eat."

Mrs. Bay dealt with that easily. She smiled at him. "Then you must understand, for you had the same difficulty that I have, only in reverse. Mauma tells me that Dorothea ate twice as much today because Dinah ate with her."

"It was the green food," said Dinah. "She did not understand. When she saw what a fair treat it was to me, she ate it with enjoyment."

"Whatever it was," said Mrs. Bay, "I am very grateful to you. Due to the difference between her age and that of my son, Dorothea is too much alone. Mauma takes good care of her body, but I am sometimes horrified by the things she tells the child."

"You needn't be, Mother," said Maurice. "I was brought up on the same. Most southern children believe in hags and plat-eyes and boo-daddies."

"You have always been strong enough to think for yourself, my son. They did not do you any harm. It is different with Dorothea."

"Ah, but I know what you mean, ma'am," Dinah exclaimed. "I saw it this hour ago. I saw your little daughter turn and look through the window. I saw by her eyes *she was seeing* what the black woman told her about."

"That is exactly what I mean, Dinah. If you've noticed it already, I think you can help her. Perhaps you can help her more than I, her mother, can."

"I will help her, and gladly, with all me heart. From the first I set eyes on her, I thought I was seeing the kind of child that the fairies lend—and take back."

But she did not see the stricken look in Mrs. Bay's dark eyes. Maurice saw it and understood, and came to his mother's rescue.

"She looks to me like a leggy young colt. There's nothing the matter with her except that she's outgrowing her strength and her appetite. Here she comes now," he added.

Dorothea entered demurely, with Mauma right behind her. Just over the threshold she stopped and made them a quick little curtsy. Mauma had dressed her freshly in white muslin. It had a round, low neck and a belt of cherry velvet, and several inches of frilled pantalettes showed below its hem. Swinging by cherry ribbons from her arm was a hat like a small straw basket, with a cluster of red-ripe cherries on its brim. Her hair had been brushed smoothly and she was unrumpled, but Dinah saw that she had been weeping again.

Mrs. Bay explained to her son. "I gave her permission to come, provided she let Mauma dress her and she behaved like a lady. She knew that Dinah's brother was here, and she begged to be allowed to speak to him."

Dorothea had been well coached by Mauma. She came on with her little round-toed, soft shoes silent on the floor, until she stood directly in front of Roddy. Looking down at her, he too thought of a silk-soft tender foal. But her hands were twisting the velvet bonnet ribbons, and her eyes were bright on his face.

"Please, Mr. Corley, will you let Dinah live here with me? I want her to stay in the blue room close by my yellow room. I want her to eat with me and walk on the Battery with me. I want her to stay *forever*. Won't you let her stay?"

Roddy shifted his feet and coughed. He looked from the child to Mrs. Bay. The latter spoke. "I realize, Mr. Corley, that you cannot be expected to decide so important a matter at a moment's notice. I see that you have your sister's welfare at heart. But, are you willing to leave her with us for a few weeks, then come back and talk with her? You could, by that time, decide whether or not you approved of her staying with us permanently."

"Aye," said Roddy, glad of escape.

He started toward the door, walking around Dorry, who turned and stared with interest after him. Upon the sill he had the grace to pause and address his hostess. "Good-day to you and to all here, ma'am." He cleared his throat awkwardly. "And I might as well be saying now that I take back all I feared. I can see that me sister is safe in the keeping of yourself."

Maurice looked after him as he tramped, unescorted, down the stair. "Of all the impertinence!"

Mrs. Bay held up her hand. "On the contrary, I have never had a finer compliment."

Dorothea was hugging her around the waist. "Dinah can stay; can't she, Mama? Didn't he say that Dinah could stay?"

"He said, my dear, that Dinah could do as she chose. If you wish to make her choose to stay, I advise you to be ladylike and to do as she tells you."

"I will! I will! Can we go out on the Battery now? Can Dinah and I walk on the Battery by ourselves?"

"Certainly not. Dinah is still a young girl, herself. You and she may go, but Mauma will walk behind you."

Mauma grumbled: "And I aint got no tention of walkin' fur, neither. The way my corns is killin' me, I know rain must be comin'."

"Can we walk to the end of White Point?" The child had caught Dinah's hand and was pulling her toward the hall. "I want to show her the school ship *Lodebar*."

"You may walk where Mauma tells you to. But, wait a minute, Dorry! Have you allowed her to put on your long pantalettes?"

"She aint 'low me," said Mauma. "But I put em on anyway."

Standing in the doorway and still holding Dinah's hand, Dorothea gave her skirts a swing. Below them the baggy atrocities which were a fashion of the day revealed their ruffles and lace to the four onlookers. Mrs. Bay gazed upon them and spoke approvingly.

"That is the way I like to see you look, my darling. No nice little girl walks on the Battery without showing at least four inches of pantalettes."

II

DURING THOSE FIRST days in a strange country, Dinah clung as closely to Dorothea Bay as the child was clinging to her. Although unaffected and natural, Dinah had her reserves. She could not open her heart to Mrs. Bay or Maurice as she could open it to little Dorry. She had always longed for a younger sister to love and to care for, and in Dorry she found a strange mixture of childishness and precociousness.

Mauma showed no jealousy when Dorry begged that first night that Dinah be allowed to put her to bed. So far as the old woman was concerned, Dinah had passed her first tests with flying colors. This grandchild of the first baby to whom she had been nurse could be safely trusted in Dinah's hands. Mauma was over ninety and very tired. She was growing backward now, instead of forward. Sometimes she dreamed that she was again in the Africa of her childhood. Mrs. Bay was always begging her to rest. But Mauma would have died at her post rather than trust this last charge to any one of the other Negroes in the Quarters.

To Dinah in her loneliness, the thing that counted most was that the child needed her. Maurice and Mrs. Bay were giving, and she was taking their kindness. But she had been born a giver rather than a taker. The first small spark of comfort in her grief had been kindled by Dorry's need of her, rather than by what the others did for her.

That night Dorry said her prayers aloud, on her knees by her bedside. She interspersed them with explanations to Dinah.

"Thank you for sending her, God. (I begged him to send you, Dinah.) And, please God, make her stay. I'll be good and not fight Mauma if you do. And don't let the plat-eye get me. I'm not afraid of the boo-hags. (The plat-eye is the next worst thing to the devil, Dinah. It can change itself into anything. A dog or a mule or a buzzard. If it turns into a buzzard, it spits tobacco on you.)"

Dinah felt just there obliged to interrupt. "Acushla, I would not talk to God about things like that. He will never be letting anything hurt you."

"But Mauma said—"

"Finish your prayers and I will tell you what I mean."

She knew she was walking on dangerous ground. She had neither the right nor the desire to destroy Mauma's work. She was glad of the few moments to think while she was tucking Dorry in bed. The room was exactly the same as hers, but done in yellow instead of blue.

She said: "Dorry, what is the prettiest color in all the world?"

Dorry sat upright again and replied with enthusiasm. "Yellow. I like it best of all. That's why Mama put yellow curtains and a yellow quilt in my room. She likes lilac and Mel Manchester likes red. Mel is Morry's sweetheart. She wears red all the time, and Morry sends her red roses and red ribbons on candy boxes." She popped down on her pillow again and said in a tone of certainty: "But I know that yellow is nicer than red or lilac. I know it's best because it's the color of sunshine."

Dinah shook her head as she smoothed the golden taffeta bed quilt. "You cannot *know*. You can only *think* it is prettier. Meself, I think blue is prettier than red or yellow or lilac."

The child looked at her questioningly. She said: "I mean this, me darling: I mean that God is the only one who really knows about things. You think and I think and Mauma thinks. Each one of us has a right to think. We must not blame each other if each thinks differently."

Dorry reached out a hand. "I'd never blame you, Dinah."

She took the hand and held it tight. "You must not blame Mauma, either. When she was a little child, people told her about plat-eyes. You know that she came from a far-away country that is different from this?"

"From Africa," said Dorry. "Morry told me all about it. Uncle Samba says there are men over there that turn into leopards in the night. Uncle Samba can kill people by making dolls that look just like them and then making Voodoo."

"Oh, no, Dorry! He cannot do that. Of course, if they are afraid of him, they may die of fright."

"I don't know what they die of," Dorry said, "but they die."

Conversation was getting out of bounds. Dinah made an effort to bring it back. "What I mean is only that people think differently. They think differently about colors and many other things. If Mauma believes there are plat-eyes, you must not be rude to her. But, do you really believe in your heart, Dorry, that God would let such things hurt you?"

"I don't believe it when I'm talking to God, but I do believe it when Mauma is talking to me."

"That proves that they are just fairy tales. You only believe in them when you let Mauma frighten you."

Dorry thought silently for a while. "Then Mauma told a lie," she concluded.

It was Dinah's turn to be frightened. She had tried to avoid this. Her mind went back to the tantrum she had witnessed just before lunch. "Dorry, I heard you say to Mauma, 'I will kill you.' But I do not think you wanted or meant, in the heart of you, to kill her."

"No," said Dorry truthfully. "I was mad, but I wouldn't kill her." She asked anxiously: "Did I tell a lie?"

"No, darling, you did not. That is what I wish to tell you. You were angry and you thought, in that moment, you wished to kill her. When Mauma thinks of the dark land from which she came and remembers the tales that were told her, she thinks there are hags and plat-eyes. But there are not such things in the world."

The child's eyes were shining. "Are you sure, Dinah?"

"I am sure, avourneen. Next time you say your prayers, do not trouble to ask God to keep them away. Just tell Him you thank Him because there are no such things, and that you are not afraid, because you know He will keep you safe."

"I'll tell him now," said Dorry. She shut her eyes and lay still.

Dinah watched the small, pale face and hoped that her words had helped. For the first time in many weeks, she had completely forgotten herself. But Dorry opened her eyes and brought her back.

"Will you tell me a story? Not about Charleston or Africa, but about where you live."

"It is nowt but a rocky island." Her throat swelled with the hurt. A rocky island where fuchsia dripped its vivid petals on naked stone. Where the boreens were emerald-green from the fog. Where the cottages climbed while she walked with her love. . . .

The swishing sound of taffeta skirts brought her back from that dream. Mrs. Bay had come into the room. "Dorry, I think you ought to let Dinah go now. She has done a great deal for you, and you mustn't be selfish."

Dorry spoke drowsily. "All right. You can put out the light, Mama. I'm not afraid of the dark any more, because there aren't any plat-eyes."

Mrs. Bay beckoned to Dinah and reached up and turned off the gas. In the hall she said: "Come to my room. I wish to talk with you, dear."

Dinah followed her down the stair to a bedroom on the second floor. It was larger than hers or Dorry's, less beruffled, and done in the lilac of widowhood. Between two of its windows stood a small Chippendale desk and a chair with slender legs.

"Sit there. You may wish to write at my escritoire. Morry said last night that you were in some trouble. He asked me, before he went out tonight, to find out how we could help you."

"'Tis good of ye, ma'am. But I would not wish to trouble ye

with me sorrow. Tis only that they sent me away from the soldier I
was to marry."

"It troubles us to see you sad. Does this soldier know where
you are?"

"I cannot say that for sure." She shook her head as she thought.
"It may be he will have asked at the pier and been told where the
bowt was going."

"I think you should write him at once. The mail goes off in the
morning."

She drew paper and ink and a quill pen from different compart-
ments.

"Where is he? What is his address?"

Dinah looked back at her in dawning terror. What was his address? She did not even know where in Galway were the British
barracks. Were they in Galway town or somewhere in County
Galway? How would her letter reach him if her knowledge was so
vague? How could she expect him to find her when he must be as
vague about her?

Mrs. Bay saw and put a hand reassuringly on her shoulder. "If
he is a British soldier, the Post Office will see that his letter gets to
the nearest British barracks. Morry told me that the ship on which
you came sailed from Galway. Have you a friend there, a friend
whom you can trust?"

"There is Mary Donovan. She is John's friend, and me own
friend, too."

"Then write to her and to your sweetheart. Tell them both
where you are, and explain that you were taken away against your
will. Tell the man— What is his name?"

"Tis John Croft."

"Tell John Croft where you are. I will give you the full address.
Tell him you will stay here with us until he can come for you."

The quill began to scratch and Dinah's head bent over. Mrs.
Bay walked to the window and looked out in the night. Under the
stars the harbor had a sullen, steely sheen. Nearly three thousand
miles of it, she thought, between here and Galway.

Dinah was writing swiftly.

> My John, they took me away. I went to Galway to meet
> you, as you told me to be doing. But Betsy heard us talking
> when you came to my father's cottage, and she and Roddy

deceived me and held me on board the boat. My heart was close to breaking when I saw the wide water around me. I am the world's width away from you, and I do not know what to be doing. A kind gentleman named Mr. Bay took me home to his mother. Tis herself that tells me to write you now and tell you that I will stay with them until you can come for me. Will you write me soon, my John? I love you and I am sore lonely for you.

She signed it and put the address dictated by Mrs. Bay. Then she said shyly: "I would like to pay you the price of the postage, ma'am."

"Wait until Morry finds out tomorrow. Now write your friend Miss Donovan exactly what happened to you, and ask her to see John Croft and find out if he gets your letter."

Things were beginning to look brighter. Dinah smiled as she took up the pen. Even if John Croft's regiment had left Galway, Mary would find him. Mary and Tim would know just where in England he lived.

Mrs. Bay had her seal both letters with a stamp like a sheaf of grain. Dinah looked at the delicate tracery in the wax and thought it a head of oats. It was the rice in harvest, seal of the rice planters' families.

"Leave them on the top of my desk. I will see Morry before you do. He will stamp them and get them in the mail before he goes to his office."

She took Dinah's face between her hands and kissed it. "Now go to bed and rest, my child. We will do all we can to help you find the man you love. While you are waiting we wish you to feel that this house is your home."

12

In CHARLESTON curiosity ran high about Dinah Corley. Ladies too well bred to ask direct questions called on Mrs. Bay in hope of some revelation. Ladies less well bred called and asked the ques-

tions and received snubs. They mentioned having seen Dorothea
on High Battery with a stranger. They spoke of passing the carriage as it waited in front of the confectioner Roumillat, with
Hilton on the driver's seat and a young girl beside Mrs. Bay.

Before the end of the week Old Uncle arrived from the Island.
Dinah, reading to Dorothea in the pleasant bookroom on the third
floor, heard his booming laughter and heard the stair creaking
below.

Mauma came in. "You best lemme change your dress, chile.
Your Cunnel Ole Uncle just come in, and your ma is liable to call
you."

"I'd rather stay with Dinah," said Dorothea, who had hitherto
always run to meet her favorite relative.

Dinah closed the book. "Go and do as Mauma tells you. After
you have done so I will read you the rest of the story."

Mauma glanced at her approvingly as she led a docile child
away. She had the Negro's sense of caste, which is stricter than
that of the white man. But, for her decisions as to who was who,
she did not depend upon the white man's confused standards.
Maurice Bay's grandfather had bought her and her baby more
than fifty years before. That baby was now a middle-aged man in
charge of the stables. Both he and she considered themselves members of the Bay family, and both he and she took pride in the fact
that the family had high birth and wealth. She was old enough to
remember her tribe in West Africa. They had held wealth and
birth to be useful and valuable. Like all other Negroes, her scorn
was razor-edged for the "low white trash." But instinct had told
her, when she first saw Dinah Corley, that the little Irish girl was
what she described as "quality." Friendlessness and poverty and
ignorance of the customs of the land where she had arrived could
not hide integrity from the dark wisdom of Maum Phoebe's eyes.
When Mrs. Bay called her that night from the sleep of old age, she
had come suddenly awake and alert as an animal. She had gone
into the guest-room and seen the unexpected guest, and fixed her
with those obsidian eyes which had frightened her into tears.

But it was not tears that had softened Maum Phoebe. She had
passed judgment and made her decision in the few seconds before
Mrs. Bay closed the door. Had her decision been different—had
she judged the girl unworthy—not all Dinah's tears or Mrs. Bay's

orders and pleas, or the reminder of her own unhappy arrival and purchase, could have made her accept Dinah.

Dinah knew nothing about this. She co-operated with Mauma in Dorry's training because she loved the child and respected the old woman. Except for the phantasmagoria of hags and boo-daddies and plat-eyes, she saw that Mauma was rearing Dorothea to be a good woman and a high-bred lady.

It had been decided that, for the present, she should stay in the blue room as Dorry's companion. Since Dorry was driven in the carriage to school immediately after breakfast and not brought home again until one o'clock, Dinah had the mornings free for her sewing. Mrs. Bay had mentioned to several friends that her protégée was a skilful seamstress and would "take in sewing" from a small and select clientele. Mrs. Porcher had already arrived with dark green velvet and the pattern for a basque. She had so far held out against hoops; but she planned a long and voluminous skirt of snuff-brown merino to be worn with the basque.

Meanwhile, Mrs. Bay had taken Dinah shopping and bought for her what she would need: yards of cotton for undergarments, dark-green serge for an everyday dress, cream-colored cashmere for afternoon, a bonnet with stiff green moiré ribbons, a fashionable green cloak, and a pair of soft brown slippers that tied around her ankles.

Dinah had made the light cashmere first and was wearing it this afternoon. She knew it was finer than anything she had ever worn before, but she did not know how well it became her. She had touched it lovingly as she sewed, wishing John Croft could see it. She told herself that the old blue wool, which had been her best on Aran, would do for mornings until she could make the green. The soft brown slippers were light on her feet after her heavy Irish boots. ·

Mauma brought Dorry back, fresh as a flower in pink cambric, and they had started their reading again when Erasmus knocked. He said: "Miss Clelia send for Miss Dinah and Miss Dorry."

Dinah looked at him in surprise. "Did she really send for me too, Erasmus?"

Her dignity and courtesy had impressed him favorably. But even if they had not, like all the other servants he would have adopted Mauma's attitude toward her. Without being put into so many words, information had been passed by the grapevine that served the Quarters that the head servant of the house approved the guest in the house.

"Yes, ma'am, Miss Dinah. Miss Clelia ax you to come, and the Cunnel Ole Uncle say he wanta see what you look like."

Down in the drawing room Colonel Bond'Ion had obliterated with his bulk a sofa meant for three. Erasmus had set a small table with decanter at his right, and he was drinking madeira and questioning his niece.

"I hear she's pretty as a sea pink blooming on a sand dune. The story has reached Fort Moultrie. I understand that the younger officers go down on the wharves every night hoping to pick a girl like her off a bollard."

Mrs. Bay said fondly: "You always were a horrid man, Old Uncle. I told you she came on the cattle boat with her brother, who is a horse trainer."

"I know she came on the boat, Clelia. What I'm wondering is why she came."

"Her brother took her aboard and detained her until the ship sailed. He was trying to get her away from an Englishman."

"Was he trying to get her away from an Englishman, or was *she* trying to get to a South Carolinian?"

Honestly startled, she looked up. "What do you mean?"

He chuckled and drank his wine. "I mean nothing out of the way. I'm only trying to find out if she, by any chance, followed Maurice here."

"You really are a horrid old man! How can you say such things? You know that Maurice studied in Germany. When he made his Grand Tour last year, he never even went to Ireland."

"You don't know where Maurice went. When I was his age, I didn't tell my mother where I went, not by a long sight! Maurice is an attractive young devil and all the more so for his pretense of liking boats better than women."

"That's enough," said Mrs. Bay, in terror that the young girls might hear. "That's enough about Maurice. Here are Dorry and Dinah."

Colonel Bond'Ion was too heavy to rise unless he had to. He set down his wineglass and looked at the pair in the door. His great-niece rushed upon him and threw herself into his arms. He kissed her and stroked her hair and seated her on one knee. Then he held out a hand to the older girl.

"My dear, will you come to an old man who is too fat and gouty to go even to a young lady as pretty as you are?"

She smiled reply and went to him and put her hand in his. He drew her down in the narrow space between himself and the sofa arm. She felt herself wedged so tightly that she feared she would never get out.

"What did you bring me this time?" Dorothea demanded.

"Dorry!" cried her mother. "I have told you not to ask."

"Why shouldn't the child ask, Clelia? She knows that I always bring something. I approve of people speaking their thoughts, not keeping them pent up inside."

"If you approve of children speaking their thoughts," Mrs. Bay told him amusedly, "it is fortunate that you are an uncle instead of a parent."

Dorothea, encouraged, said: "I hope it's a sugar pig. Pigs are bigger than angels."

He set her on her feet on the floor. "Go in the hall and look on the table where you see my hat."

She went in a run and came back with two boxes and a bag. He gave her the last and watched her draw out a substantial sugar pig and a more ethereal angel made of the same clay. Then he handed one box to Mrs. Bay and the other to Dinah.

She went rose-red with surprise and delight. "Ah," she cried, looking up in his face, "'tis the first box of sweets I have had of me own!"

His kind old eyes twinkled at her. "But it will not be the last. I have had many sweets in my life, and I am grateful for them. I am not yet too old to seize one when I see it within my reach."

He took her chin between his thumb and forefinger and kissed her cheek.

Maurice spoke from the door. "You old reprobate, are you at it again?"

Colonel Bond'Ion laughed boomingly. "You're jealous, you young whippersnapper! Since the campaign in Mexico, our young men have gone soft. They can't kiss a girl or sit a horse or spit a rascal on a saber the way we used to do when we rode with General Scott."

"I can still drink your health, sir," said Maurice.

He filled his own glass and refilled that of the uncle whom they all adored. Then he looked down at Dinah. "You're squeezing the life out of her!"

Colonel Bond'Ion looked down at her. She was gasping with the pressure and, with every movement he made, being mashed a little flatter. "Are you at all uncomfortable, my dear?" he asked anxiously.

She said politely and breathlessly: "Not at all, sir."

But Maurice leaned and took her by the elbows and jerked. At the second pull he drew her out, as a dentist draws a tooth from the jaw. He pushed a chair under her knees and gave her a glass of madeira. "Sit there, or that naughty old man will have you in his lap like Dorry."

Dorry was climbing over him and he was well smeared with the sugar pig. Mrs. Bay intervened. "Dorothea, go and wash your hands."

She began to protest, but Dinah rose. "I will go with you and help you." She clasped the candy box with both hands and looked at the old man with shining eyes. "I thank you, sir, for the lovely gift. Good-by, and may God keep you!"

Maurice closed the door after them. The halls were unheated and drafty. He said: "What brought you, Old Uncle? You don't often give us this pleasure."

"No. I expect you to come to me. I'm too fat to get in and out of small boats."

"He came," said Mrs. Bay, "to find out about Dinah."

Maurice laughed. "Other people have the same idea. They even stop me on the street."

"You can't pick a girl as pretty as she off a wharf in the middle of the night without causing people to ask questions, my boy."

Maurice shrugged. "Perhaps not. But we needn't bother to answer."

Colonel Bond'Ion shook his head. "Then they'll make up their own answers, and you know what those will be. I came to tell you what should be done."

The head of the family spoke now, and they fell silent to listen. Mrs. Bay sat with her hands in her lap. Maurice leaned on the mantel. Respectfully and expectantly they looked at the colonel, while they waited for his advice.

"M'lanny gives a musicale on Saturday afternoon. She has asked a few officers from the fort. I shall make it a point to come with them."

Mrs. Bay nodded. "We have already received invitations."

"Oh, Mother, *must* I go?" Maurice exclaimed little-boyishly.

Colonel Bond'Ion decreed: "You must go—all three—and take the girl with you. She is pretty enough and refined enough to be introduced to your friends. In her position of lady companion to Dorothea, it is correct for you to take her into the home of a relative."

Mrs. Bay said gravely: "I think you are right."

Maurice asked rebelliously: "But why do *I* have to go? Hilton can drive you and Dorry and Dinah."

"Hilton will drive them, and you will ride alongside the carriage. You will enter your aunt's drawing room with your mother on your arm. Your sister and her companion will be following you."

"You seem to have it all planned. I had expected to go down to the Southern wharf at the foot of Water Street and do some work on a boat with Hals Sturm. Saturday is the only day he has half-holiday."

Colonel Bond'Ion began to heave himself up from the sofa. "I had it all planned before I came—in case the girl was presentable. The four of you make the pattern I want."

Maurice was disappointed and consequently cross. "You're talking the way Aunt M'lanny sings. We'll have to listen to "Weavers," I suppose. Hals and I are making an experiment. He's been telling me about that undersea boat which rowers operated in the Thames in 1620."

Colonel Bond'Ion's laughter boomed. "Are you and that German boy trying to make a submarine? That Dutchman's craft in the Thames was a joke and Bushnell's *Turtle* a failure."

Maurice flushed. "Of course we're not trying to make an undersea boat. We are building a sailboat shaped for minimum wind resistance. But, can't you stay for supper? We were counting on keeping you."

"We would love to have you, Old Uncle." Mrs. Bay laid a hand on his sleeve.

"I would like to stay; but the officers with whom I came have to be at Fort Moultrie by six o'clock. Ring for Erasmus to get my hat and cape, Nephew."

"I'll get them myself for you, sir. I'm going downstairs with you."

He offered his arm and the older man took it and leaned on him heavily. "Ha!" he said approvingly. "You hold up two-hundred-and-sixty pounds. You're strong enough, for all that you are no more than skin and bone. What you need is to drink more wine and do more racing and tilting, instead of working on boats like a laborer."

Mrs. Bay agreed. "It doesn't seem appropriate for a gentleman to use a hammer and saw with his hands."

"I'm not a contortionist, Mother. I can't use them with my toes."

"You're an impudent young dog," said Colonel Bond'Ion delightedly. "You must watch your ways with this girl. She's sweet as a moss rose and we must be good to her. But you must not let anyone think—"

He stopped and allowed to remain nameless what anyone might think. But Maurice asked rebelliously: "Think what, Old Uncle?"

"Ah-ha! So you're trying to catch me up? You know exactly what I mean. You must avoid gossip."

"Perhaps the day is coming when people won't be so hidebound and narrow," Maurice said.

"Oh, it is; is it?" demanded Old Uncle. His righteous indignation made him lean so heavily that Maurice's strong young body was braced to support him. "Let me tell you this. There is a pattern in life, and the one who plans it is bigger than you. When it changes it will change without your help and in spite of approval or objection from you and from other men. You are an insignificant thread in its tapestry, but you will be used in its design."

13

A FEW DAYS later Maurice made another vain attempt to get out of escorting them to the musicale. His mother chided: "My dear boy, you're the only man in Charleston who would refuse if lucky enough to be asked to M'lanny's soiree. M'lanny is the beauty of the family," she explained to Dinah. "She is so exquisite that half of the unmarried men in Charleston have courted her."

"Has she never fallen in love and married?" asked Dinah, whose mind ran to love affairs.

"She married my younger brother, Middleton Rowand, and he died five years ago. People think her a butterfly, but he was the love of her life. She has no intention of remarrying. Most of her beaux realize that now. Only the Frenchman does not."

Dorry said: "Aunt M'lanny gave me some of the Frenchman's plums."

Mrs. Bay laughed. "Poor Monsieur Serrurier! M'lanny leads him a dance. He is a horticulturist and raises the most marvelous fruit. He names prize specimens after her: *Pêche Mélanie* and *Poire à la Blonde*."

Dinah saw his garden next time they drove out. Peach and pear and plum trees were espaliered against the warm brick of dwelling and coachhouse. But Maurice told her that the grapes which he ripened under glass were the pride and joy of Monsieur Serrurier's heart.

"He sends Aunt M'lanny a basket of fruit every day. She doesn't like it. She stuffs herself on bonbons that his rivals send and gives his fruit to Middy and the house servants."

"Who is Middy?" asked Dinah. She already felt herself a part of the family and took an interest in it.

"He's a bad boy," said Dorry. "He took Coaxum's hatchet and scalped my doll named Goldilocks. Next year he's going on the schoolship *Lodebar*."

By this time Dinah knew the slaves out in the Quarters. Coaxum was not an old family servant. He had begged to be bought from a neighbor when he married Mary Jane, daughter of Venus and

Samba. He was a carpenter by trade, a mean-eyed, surly mulatto.

Maurice was enlarging upon his sister's description. "Middy is a bad boy, and both Mother and I have told you to keep away from him. Aunt M'lanny lets him do as he chooses and only laughs at his devilry."

Dinah was thinking about the beauteous Aunt M'lanny, the adoring suitor, and the naughty son as she came downstairs at quarter of five on Saturday afternoon. Maurice, having given up all hope of escape, helped her and his mother and sister into the carriage, mounted his own horse and cantered off beside them. As they turned west on Broad Street, Dinah saw on her right the gray building she had seen on the night of her arrival. A group of gentlemen and a young boy were standing on its steps. The gentlemen bowed to Mrs. Bay and she inclined her head. But Dorothea turned hers around and made a frightful face and stuck out her tongue.

Maurice, replacing his hat and keeping Buck alongside on the turn, got the full benefit of it. "Behave yourself, Dorry," he ordered.

She argued: "It was Middy on the Post Office steps. He made a face at me, so I had a right to make one back at him."

Hilton, without moving a muscle as he held his lines taut on the bright, broad backs and his whip diagonally across, joined in the family conversation. "That-there boy go long whenever Tom go for Miss M'lanny mail. Tom tell me he pure pizen. I wouldn't stand for him. I done tell Miss Dorry if she miss her lessons I'm goin' to stop drivin' her to school."

"I don't blame you in the least, Hilt," Maurice told him gravely. "Nobody wants to associate with little girls who miss their lessons."

Dorothea cast a wary glance from the coachman's straight back to her brother's face. But, just then, another rider created a diversion. He cannoned out of a Broad Street driveway on a rangy gray that reared, lashed out with both heels, and began to buck.

The young man's long coattails flapped like the wings of a huge bird; but he sat his flat Somerset saddle and, by the time they reached him, had his mount under control.

Dorothea stood up in the carriage and shrieked: "Cousin Sedgwick Lewis, make White Cockerel do it again!"

Hilton muttered: "Voodoo name ain't no fit name for a horse."

Neither Maurice nor his mother showed any emotion. They seemed to Dinah to accept the sudden eruption in their midst as Sedgwick Lewis' normal way of joining them.

He took his high hat from his thick brown hair and bowed low to the ladies. The gray horse seized its chance as he did and stood straight up on its hind feet again. He batted it hard over the ears with the stiff hat, which made it come down. Dinah saw that he had blue eyes, straight features and an engaging grin.

"Cousin Clelia," he said, "I was waiting for you. May I escort you, with Morry?"

"Of course, my dear. We are delighted to have you. Dinah, it is our cousin Sedgwick Lewis Simons. Sedgwick Lewis, this is Dorry's lady companion, Miss Corley."

Sedgwick Lewis bowed again and they all started off. They turned north on Rutledge Avenue with the Pond on their left. As they approached Aunt M'lanny's house they saw other carriages, and riders cantered by them, lifting their hats as they did. Dinah, assisted to alight by both Sedgwick Lewis and Maurice, was seized with sudden shyness. Hand in hand with Dorry she followed Mrs. Bay and Maurice. For Sedgwick Lewis had left them as suddenly as he had joined them, when he caught sight of a slim girl in huge hoops and a rose-trimmed bonnet.

The drawing room was as long as that of the Bays' home, but it was on the first floor and its drapes and upholstery were of turquoise blue. Aunt M'lanny, a golden-blonde in pale gray mousseline de soie, hurried to meet them and kissed Dinah as warmly as she kissed her niece and sister-in-law. Then she tilted her cheek toward her nephew, and as he did his duty, Dinah caught sight of the Frenchman watching the tableau. He could not be mistaken for anyone else, because he still wore the satin knee breeches which had gone out of style in Charleston long years before. He advanced and kissed the hands of the three lady guests, assuring them that he was enchanted to see Madame's family. His English was poor, and gave one the impression that he was still thinking in French and using some English words whose meaning he did not fully command.

"Good-afternoon, sir," said Maurice. "Are the new grapes doing well?"

"Ah," breathed Monsieur Serrurier, "zey are wat you call purple diamonds!"

Maurice suggested politely: "Amethysts?"

"I tell you I would not sell zem for diamond or ametiste! Zey hang like ze jewels, I tell you! I watch zem day and night."

Maurice left them hanging and steered his three ladies to seats by a long window that gave on the garden piazza. An old gentleman was already seated at the piano, and a younger one stood by him, tuning a violin. Dinah had a confused impression of bright bonnets and curls and flounces, interspersed with darker coats and trousers and with a half dozen blue uniforms.

Men were coming up to Mrs. Bay in a steady stream and she was repeating casually: "Miss Corley . . . from Ireland . . . my daughter's companion and friend. . . ."

Suddenly Dinah looked up and saw Old Uncle approaching, with an officer just behind him who carried a large chair. "Put it here by the girls," said the colonel, "and pull up one for yourself. You know my niece and grandniece. Miss Corley, Lieutenant Sherman."

The old gentleman at the piano struck a furious chord for silence. It fell, and Aunt M'lanny's musicale began.

At the end of an hour the violinist tucked his fiddle under an arm. The pianist rose and, side by side, they bowed to the applause. It did not abate and through it Dinah heard calls for "Miss Camellia." Aunt M'lanny rose and held out her hand to a girl in a dark red dress who was sitting in a corner between Maurice and an officer. She got up at once and came forward with the two men following her. She walked with an almost feline grace and with a rare lack of diffidence. Dinah, catching sight of her face, was startled by its beauty.

With perfect self-possession and excellent showmanship, Camellia Manchester paused and, before she sang, untied the strings of her red velvet bonnet. She half turned, hesitated, and handed it to Maurice. But she hesitated just long enough to make both men step forward, and the young officer flushed painfully. She lifted a hand to her soot-black hair, which needed no improvement. Then she moved to stand at the shoulder of the old gentleman who had resumed his seat at the piano. The whispers died to expectancy. Mel Manchester began her song.

It was "Drink to Me Only with Thine Eyes," and the girl had a true contralto. The voice seemed to Dinah as beautiful as the singer, but she felt it lacked sweetness. As soon as she finished Mel bowed and, although the room rocked with applause, went back to her tête-à-tête with two beaux instead of one. There were cries of "Bravo" and "Encore," but she shook her dark head, and the smile on her red mouth was, Dinah thought, almost scornful.

Carolus came in just then, followed by several Negro maids. Decanters were set upon tables, and glasses of punch were passed. Dinah, accepting one of the latter, saw Old Uncle's eyes on her as she sipped.

She smiled back at him. "'Tis sweet, yet sharp. Would it be wine and water, sir?"

"It's the Charleston Light Dragoons Punch. Liquid dynamite. You're likely to hear and see things if you drink it, child."

To her horror, she both heard and felt something as he spoke. Something was breathing hotly and heavily down her neck. She turned her head by inches and came face to face with the un-washed countenance of the boy she had seen on the Post Office steps. "I want Dorry to come and play with me," he whispered hoarsely. "Will you tell her to come out in the garden?"

Before Dinah could reply, Colonel Bond'Ion caught sight of him and aimed a blow at him with his cane. Young Middleton dodged it. Dorry jumped up. "I want to go outside and play with Middy!"

Mrs. Bay reminded: "The last time you went with Middleton, he pushed you into an ants' nest."

But Aunt M'lanny was coming, with half the men in her wake. She called, "My precious boy loves music so he creeps through the windows to listen!"

"He crept through the window last time," Old Uncle told her, "in order to jab a nail through the seat of Will Sherman's chair."

She smiled appeasement at the craggy-nosed, reddish bearded lieutenant, who had risen at her approach. But her blue eyes rested on her son. "Where have you been, my angel? I haven't seen you since dinner."

"I've been in my room, studying," he answered brazenly.

"He was at the Post Office," said Dorry. "He made a face at me."

Middleton said softly: "I'll put a bug down your neck for that, you tell-tale-tit!"

But Aunt M'lanny's formula for remaining unruffled and beautiful was simply to disregard discrepancies and discords. "He makes such funny faces. And he loves his little cousin. Go out to the summer house and play party with him. Eliza will bring you sherbet and Shrewsburys and almond cakes."

Mrs. Bay looked uncertain and Dinah started to rise. Maurice came up. "Oh, let her go. Don't send Dinah with her."

Dinah confided to him. "I must go, or the boy will destroy her entirely. I heard him say he would put a bug down her neck."

"He's done it before, and it won't hurt her if he does it again." He sat beside Dinah in the chair Dorothea had vacated.

Aunt M'lanny was being implored, as she moved among her guests, to sing. Two of the officers had already drawn forward her harp. Another was placing her chair. A fourth was leading her forward.

She clasped her hands, and Dinah thought of an angel garbed in mist-gray cloud. "But I had not expected this. I cannot even think of a song. . . ."

Maurice spoke into Dinah's ear. "What would that be if *I* told it?"

"So it will have to be an old song that I fear you have heard before. Have you heard it too often? Are you tired of 'Weavers'?"

No man dared be tired of any song that Aunt M'lanny sang. They clapped and called encouragement. She seated herself at the harp with the four officers assisting. The cloudy gray sleeves fell back as she lifted her arms to the strings. Dinah heard them ripple like water between cool stones.

> All men are weavers. Set within their reach
> Are varied spools which have been wound by fate
> With threads of love or sacrifice or hate.
> But choice of what he spins is left to each.

Her voice was a small and somewhat unsure drawing-room soprano. But it had a sweetness that Camellia's lacked.

> No man can work alone; for every line
> Has long ago been intertwined and crossed
> With other stands. . .

A silvery cascade of notes filled the small pause like a waterfall.
Across the room Mr. Pettigru and Mr. Rhett sat side by side. Lieutenant Sherman, between Dinah and Colonel Bond'Ion, folded his
arms.

> And better far a man should have been dead
> Than he should break or soil the running thread!

Maurice thought: It's nothing but words. Then he glanced
down and saw Dinah close at his shoulder. The thread of her life
had been warped, possibly broken, by others. He wondered if she
saw its connection with the song.

But Dinah's thoughts were quite literal. The word *weavers* had
brought before her a picture of her shawl from Inisheer. She
recognized some technical words by her knowledge of Irish weaving. It made her feel more at home and no longer out of place.
She liked the punch and the Shrewsbury cakes, and she was
watching the Frenchman. . . .

The only weaving he cared about was upon a loom of purple
and green, shot by tiny tendrils and patterned by swelling clusters.
He had counted every ripening grape upon every growing bunch.
His heart would break if, by any chance, that symmetry was
broken. Dinah watched him rise and cross to their hostess. He
kissed her hand, made his adieux and departed for his hothouse.
As he did so, he stumbled and stopped to apologize.

Mr. Rhett drew back the foot which had caused stumble and
apology. "My fault," he muttered. He wished the man would go,
with his funny pants and his funny talk. *The sovereign state,* he
was thinking, *is the only perfect pattern. The thread of her life is
states' rights. That thread must not be broken. . . .*

He frowned so hard as he thought of it that Lieutenant Sherman, across the room, wondered if he had in any way offended
Mr. Rhett. He hoped not, for he liked the South; Fort Moultrie
and Charleston even more than Florida. He admired the social
graces which had been denied him in youth. Thomas Ewing's pattern of life had had more strength than luxury. Its colors were red-
white-and-blue. He had bred the Union in young Cump's bones.
That thread can never be broken, thought William Tecumseh
Sherman.

The little Irish girl next to him cried: "She is wiping her hands on your lovely britches!"

He started violently and looked down at them. Colonel Bond'-Ions grandniece had come back through the French window and, while he sat wrapped in thought, managed to transfer a quantity of sticky stuff from her fingers to his uniform trousers. The Irish girl, who seemed sensible, had seized her and drawn her away. He examined the darker spots on the blue. "What can it be?"

"Grapejuice," said Dorry. "We ate all we could, then squeezed the bunches that were left. We got *handfuls* of juice."

He saw that her mouth and chin were smeared with purplish shadows. She put her hands on her stomach and began to whimper. "I've got a pain. It's Middy's fault. He dared me to eat the seeds and skins."

Across her head Dinah and Sherman looked at each other. Both had heard of the hothouse of Monsieur Serrurier next door. At no other place in Charleston could winter grapes be procured. What would the hot-headed Frenchman do? Had he discovered the outrage?

He had. Shrill cries were making themselves heard above the babel of talk. The crowd parted before the advance of the avenger. He rushed through the door from the hall, dragging Middleton along by the ear and shrieking the story of his wrongs for all assembled to hear. Aunt M'lanny still sat at the harp, but a space had been cleared all around her. Into its circle he jerked the boy and threw him with violence on the floor. "Species of an assassin," he yelled—then looked from him to his mother.

The tender sympathy of her eyes met and defeated his inflamed glare. She looked as grieved for his sorrow as if it had been her own. She showed no ugly resentment. She was the perfect hostess. Guests in her house might yell aloud or dash out her children's brains.

It was too much for the Frenchman. He took a step toward her and bent his knee. "Madame," he said, "I kees your hand." And he suited the action to the words. "Madame," he said, "you are great lady. But your son is *fou!*"

14

IN CONTRADICTION to the happy-go-lucky ways of Aunt M'lanny, Mrs. Bay and most other Charleston ladies led busy lives. Her house was large enough to be called a mansion. It and everything in it were kept immaculate. The housemaids swept and dusted, polished brass and scoured floors, but the mistress inspected personally its every room every day. She selected and "gave out" towels and bed linen from cedar-lined closets in the third-floor hall. She, with her own hands, gathered baskets of citrena leaves and, as the maids laid the laundry away, sprinkled them between its folds. She planned meals with cook and butler. She listed what was to be purchased and, several times a week, Erasmus marketed with these lists. She kept account, to the pound, of the grist and rice and flour and sugar in the storeroom barrels. She carried the house keys in a bunch on a silver chain worn round her waist. She cut and arranged flowers and directed the gardener.

She went about these duties after breakfast every day and, as soon as they were finished, went out in the yard to the Quarters. This was a two-story brick building with a one-story wooden addition built onto each end. In it lived all the slaves except Mauma.

The yard was a man's job, and Maurice had taken it over as soon as he finished his education. He inspected stables, oversaw building repairs and ordered wholesale the provisions for the Quarters. His mother's duties there were confined to religion and medicine. Old Samba was shriveled with age and nearly blind. But, in spite of his talents with the voodoo drum, he both professed and practiced Christianity. She read him a chapter from the Bible every day, and stayed long enough afterward to discuss it with him. His wife, old Venus, could not read but cooked for him and cared for him. She had been a skilful laundress when young enough for the work. Although unable to do it now she refused to retire. She drove Mary Jane and Jessie, her competent, middle-aged daughters, frantic with her fault-finding and contrary orders.

There were five children under twelve years old in the Quarters.

At twelve each one would begin training for his or her work in life. It was the custom to assign them, even younger than that, to young white masters or mistresses to learn to be "body servants." But Maurice, queerly ahead of his time, had always scorned a valet. Absolom was his personal groom and ready to serve him whenever allowed. Mauma's jealous possessiveness had so far prevented Dorothea's having a little Negro girl in the house to be taught as her maid. So the five children were looked after by old Venus while their parents were at work. She assembled them every morning after the Bible reading and made them show well-scrubbed faces and hands, and stick their tongues out as far as they could. Mrs. Bay then examined them for sore throat, sore eyes and vermin. From a practical as well as humanitarian standpoint, it was a necessary precaution. Diphtheria, which filled so many churchyards with little graves, often came to the Big House from the Quarters.

But with smaller afflictions the mistress of the house was expected to cope without doctors. She had a well-stocked medicine chest, and Erasmus brought it when needed. He stood by while she bathed running eyes with boric solutions, or made the owners of inflamed throats suck on lumps of potash. Calomel was administered like a rite at certain seasons. Soda was stirred into molasses which rose and foamed over its cup, while the waiting victim roared aloud, although the taste was pleasant. In addition to all this a quart bottle of raw turpentine was kept upon a shelf in the harness room. It was not used for the horses. Neither Maurice nor Titus would have permitted that outrage. It was said to burn animals far worse than it burned human beings. But any child, white or black, who cut a finger or stepped on a rusty nail was held by main force while turpentine was poured into the wound. They were then released and were believed to be safe from infection or lockjaw.

Such tasks kept the lady of the house busy until near noonday. From that time until dinner at three she wrote letters or sewed. She brought her embroidery, hemstitching or humbler hemming into the bookroom where Dinah did dressmaking. It was there that she talked with the girl while needles flashed and scissors snipped, and won Dinah's heart and learned all about her.

Dinah's letters to Croft and Mary Donovan had been mailed

promptly by Maurice. But the overseas mail was slow and unsure and both Dinah and Mrs. Bay knew that the wait might be long. The older woman, more sophisticated and less optimistic, did not speak her fears as to what could have happened. She had never seen this soldier in a scarlet tunic. It was possible Dinah's father and brother had judged him rightly. Perhaps he was only amusing himself with an inexperienced girl. Even if he had been in earnest and honorable, how was he ever to find her after what had occurred?

As if reading her thoughts, Dinah looked up from Mrs. Porcher's snuff-brown skirt. "Me John told me he would come for me." She smiled at the very memory. *"No matter when it is or where you are,* he told me, *I'll always come back for you."*

She stood up and shook out the garment. "Tis done."

Mrs. Bay took it and examined minutely its seams and hem. She spoke with an expert's approval. "And skilfully done."

The gray eyes on her face were glad. She knew the girl needed the money. "Dinah"—she hesitated—"Mrs. Porcher likes your work so much that—"

She stopped again. Dinah still smiled. "It is glad that I am to hear it. I owe her the satisfaction. She is kind and she pays me well."

"She likes your work so much she is willing to pay twice the usual price if you will make a complete layette. Perhaps I should not tell you, but—but her daughter expects a baby."

"I would like well to make its clothes. Not only to earn the money; I'll be thinking of the wee darling with every stitch I take."

Mrs. Bay thought: "Thinking of a baby that's not yet born? A young, unmarried girl like you?" She was thankful to see Erasmus entering with a tray. The time between breakfast and dinner was too long to go without food. Today she had directed him to bring shortcake and hot tea. He placed it on a table and she said: "Dinah, will you pour?"

The girl was pretty and ladylike, as well as instinctively nice and good. At M'lanny's musicale her conduct had been perfect. She was eating the sweetened shortbread and stirring cream in her tea. She stopped to admire the tiny sheaf engraved on the handle of the silver spoon. "Tis pretty, and I have seen it on the fruit knives and letter paper. Would it be the barley or the rye?"

"Neither," said Mrs. Bay, delighted to get away from the embarrassing layette. "It is a sheaf of rice in grain. More than one rice planter used it as mark."

She began to tell Dinah about the rice plantation on Winyah Bay where she had been born and had spent her childhood. It was named *Belle Isle* and was still the home of her older brother. Almost as soon as she could walk she had ridden with her father, along the dikes, across the trunks, in and out canals, beside reserves. When the bobolinks came by in May and August, going to or returning from South America, all the plantation pickaninnies turned out as "bird-minders." They beat tin pans, cracked long wips, shouted as loud as they could, and thumped with metal or wood upon other pieces of wood. These "ricebirds" came in such numbers that they could destroy a crop. They were delicious for eating and were also shot by the men of the family or the plantation huntsman. They were usually roasted whole and served upon a bank of rice or curry in an enormous platter. She had seen as many as five dozen ricebirds brought in by the butler to serve a dinner party. But such numbers, although large for the table, made hardly a break in the ranks of the migration. They still had to be kept away by the bird-minders' noisemaking.

Dinah loved these intimate morning hours. They made her feel at home in the house. She was no longer a stranger. Mrs. Bay was, this morning, still talking of her childhood when Mauma came in. She said belligerently: "I give Hilt Dorry cloak and tell him to make she put it on when he get she out of school."

"Thank you, Mauma," said Mrs. Bay. "Will you sit down and eat some shortbread?"

The tall old woman did not seem to hear. She was prowling, like a black leopardess, along the windows that overlooked the sea wall.

"Wind like that too cole for that chile to go without she warm cloak. Same kinda wind was blowin' day when I first come to this-here place. . . ."

Mrs. Bay knew the temperature of the bright early-winter morning. She had already been outside with a light shawl over her shoulders. But she knew the wind carried for Mauma a chill that it did not for her. She had been through this so often before, when it was blowing straight out of the East. She wondered if, given all the right conditions, it could bring across three thousand miles the scent of Africa.

"I 'member when Ole Maussa take me long with him," said Mauma. Her face had changed. Even through tears, Dinah could see that the agony was easing.

Mrs. Bay translated: "Old Maussa was Maurice's grandfather."

Mauma nodded. "He the one I mean. First time I see that wite man I know he good man. I been standin' on the block, at the market in Chalmers Street, holdin' my baby Titus in my arms. I see him and I say: 'Maussa, please buy us.' "

"My husband," explained Mrs. Bay, "had just been born. He was my father-in-law's first child, and a nurse was being bought for him."

"That right," said Mauma. "That what he say. He say: 'Woman, you a fieldhand. I come here to buy house servant. I want nuss for my baby.'

"I say: 'Maussa, they just sell tother chile way from me. I scared they gwine sep-rate me from my baby.' I say: 'Maussa, if you buy me and my chile, I take good care your chile till I die, even if I is fieldhand.' I say: *Maussa, for Lawd sake buy us!*"

15

DINAH HAD A visitor at an early hour next morning. Erasmus announced him while she and Dorry were at breakfast. "Is it me brother, Erasmus?" she asked. She could think of nobody else who would call.

"No, ma'am. This gen'l'man wide as he, but he aint tall as your brother. He call heself some kinda cannon."

She found Mr. Kincannon, in his going-ashore clothes, sitting stiffly in the drawing room. She had not forgotten his kindness and was truly glad to see him.

"But I thought that your bowt had gone away. I did not think to see you again."

"We needed repairs, and we had to wait for a cargo."

"But are you not taking the cattle, for cargo, to Ireland?"

He smiled. "Yes. But we don't load cattle at Charleston. We take what we can get here and work our way to Texas. The cargo we have under hatches now is consigned to Key West. When we unload in Florida, we'll pick up something for New Orleans or some other Gulf port—maybe direct for Galveston."

She looked at him with a sweet gravity that reminded him of Ellen, the young wife whom he had lost. She was thinking he seemed less at home here than he had on the deck of his ship. A drawing room could cramp a man who was used to the spaces of oceans. His shoulders were stretching the seams of his ugly blue civilian coat. She said: "Will ye not be seeing your home before you cross the sea again?"

He shook his head. "We're sailing south, so there's no chance of home this voyage. Once we carried tierces of rice from Georgetown to Boston. I don't know when I'll see Maine again." He paused and added, "Or Charleston."

"'Tis not your home," she said, surprised; for his voice had been regretful. "Would it give you sorrow if you did not see it again?"

He looked steadily at her. She could see the tiny wrinkles that sun and wind had formed like rays in the skin around his eyes. They had the look that comes to eyes accustomed to gaze into distances.

"Until this voyage it would not have troubled me never to see it any more. Now I would like to think we were going to touch at Charleston again."

She smiled so warmly at him that he almost spoke out right then. "I hope that ye will," she assured him, "and that before long. I wish to be asking a favor, if yourself will do it for me. And I shall be waiting in hopes to see you when you come back."

He leaned forward and spoke eagerly. "What can I do for you?"

"You can carry a letter to Galway. I have sent two by the post. But I mistrust that the twelve pennies that the clerk charged for each one of them is enough to pay their passage on a bowt."

So she was still thinking of the man in Ireland. . . . He swallowed his disappointment and told himself that he had not given her time to forget. But a sailor could not afford to wait.

Least of all a sailor on a cattle tramp that went to any port for which it got a cargo. He had no idea whether or not they would ever call at Charleston again. He could not afford to take a leave, for he hoped very soon to be master. Captain Swanson was old and ready to retire. He would certainly recommend his mate, for they had worked well together.

"I'll do anything I can for you," he said with sincerity.

"Then I will write it before ye go. But"—she remembered her manners—"what have ye done in the two weeks that have passed since the night we came in?"

"We went back to Quarantine that same night, and we stayed anchored there for several days. Some of the children in steerage had spots, and the doctors took them to the lazaretto for observance. They discovered the cause to be vermin, rather than pox. So they cleared the ship. She has been tied up at the Central wharf ever since."

"And you have been working hard, I think. I saw well enough, upon the voyage, that you were not afraid of work."

He was not afraid of work. In that he and she were akin. He sensed it as he thought of the seacoast town in Maine where his mother cared for his motherless little son. Ellen had been a Maine girl, accustomed to work, as he was. In all the four years since her death he had never wished to remarry. Not until he met this gray-eyed colleen in steerage.

"There was somewhat to be done," he said. "The ship is old. The last voyage was long." He hesitated. "I tried, at first, to find you through your brother."

"Roddy? He works for Mr. Bull, at a plantation three miles away. Ye knew that I would not stay with him and Betsy upon the voyage. Nor would I go with them upon land."

His keen eyes went around the room: mahogany and gold brocade. He had heard of these South Carolina planters. They were said to start drinking juleps and punches before breakfast; to work their slaves to death in the fields; to be a menace to all womanhood with their fancy manners. . . .

But he was a man who tried to keep the Second and great Commandment. Also, he was too intelligent to condemn on unproven rumor. He said abruptly: "But why did you come to this house? Who are the people in it? How do they treat you?"

The light that came into her gray eyes reassured him. "Mr. Morry brought me here because I had no place else to go. His mother, God keep her, treats me like her own daughter. As for the little girl—"

The little girl, just then, burst through the door. She was dressed for the drive to school in a bright green cloak with a hood. She was panting from outrunning Mauma, and she flew to Mr. Kincannon. "You shan't take her back on the boat with you! You shan't take Dinah away from me!"

He picked her up and set her in his lap. He was at home with children. "I did not come to take Dinah. Although I'd like to."

Dorry looked up into his steady eyes, and she suddenly clasped him around the neck. Just then the pursuit arrived at the door: Mauma, with Maurice behind her.

Mauma was scolding as she advanced. "Take shame on yourself for a no-mannered chile! Aint I tell you not to bust in on Miss Dinah comp'ny?"

Kincannon rose, holding her easily and tenderly. Although much older, she weighed hardly more than his own sturdy four-year-old. He saw her brother in the doorway, the arrogant fellow who had come on board with another of his kind and bowled over port regulations like ninepins. For a second they looked at each other—the two of them poles apart, and yet each typically and admirably American.

Then Maurice Bay stepped toward him. "I apologize, sir, for my little sister's unceremonious behavior. My mother and I are glad to have Miss Corley's friends call on her. We meant the drawing room to be entirely at your service."

Kincannon looked back at him over Dorothea's head. In spite of his bull neck, she was beginning to choke him. But he liked her, and he did not like her big brother. Words came less easily to him than they did to the southerner. Mauma saved him by laying hold on Dorothea and pulling. Dinah joined in the struggle and, when it was at its height, her hair became caught in the top brass button of his coat. Maurice did not attempt to assist. He merely leaned an elbow on the mantel and laughed. Mauma dragged her charge away. Kincannon finally freed the last curl.

Dinah was not embarrassed. She smoothed her hair with her hands. She smiled at him and informed him: "The reason that it happened is because the top of me head comes just to that very same button on you."

He had been intensely aware of that, with her head against his chest while she tried to intervene between the nurse and the child. Maurice saw the look in his eyes and stopped laughing.

"Won't you sit down again, Mr. Kincannon? I'm on my way to my office, so will ask you to excuse me. But I know that Miss Corley will enjoy your visit."

Kincannon said shortly: "I must go. We clear in two hours, with the tide."

"Ah!" cried Dinah. "Me letter! Can you not wait till I have wrote it?"

Kincannon drew an enormously thick watch from his pocket. He frowned at it. The tussle with the child had taken the rest of his short time.

Maurice saw and suggested: "If you haven't time to wait, the coachman can drive Dinah to the wharf. Dorry's school is on Hasel Street, so the carriage will return directly. Dinah can write her letter. I'm sure my mother will chaperone her."

But, in spite of the suggestion, and although Maurice himself saw the visitor out, Seth Kincannon walked up East Bay reflecting that he did not like the young Charlestonian.

Dinah flew upstairs to lay out her bonnet and cloak and then write:

> Mary darling:
> I wrote you before and I wrote to my John, but it was by the Post. I have only time for the one letter now because the boat sails with the tide. It is best that I write it to you not him, for his regiment goes on the New Year and the boat is slow and will not reach Galway for long months after that. It may be I will get a letter from him or from you Mary any day. Tis thirteen weeks since I left Ireland, but it could be he does not know where I am. The only way he could find out would be if he sent you his address and you wrote him Mary and told him what was mine. I am sure he will think to be doing just that.

She stopped and turned the long quill between her fingers. Surely John Croft would think of that. He would try to find her by every means. Her father would never tell him; not even if he dared to go to Aran and ask. Her father thought her with Roddy. Mary Donovan would naturally think the same, until she got one of Dinah's letters. If she or John Croft wrote Dinah a letter to Roddy's care, Roddy might never give it to her. Betsy would surely destroy it if she saw it. She had told Mrs. Bay of such fears when, upon Mrs. Bay's advice, she wrote both John and Mary the day after her arrival. She did not know that Mrs. Bay had asked Maurice to speak to Rawlins on the subject. Sweetwine, the man servant who fetched and carred the Lowndes Grove mail, had orders to watch Roddy's mail for a letter addressed to Dinah.

I told you in my first letter of this fine city and this great house. Tis almost as big as Lynch Castle and its windows are bigger and more and the sun comes into it every day. I will put between these pages the small sweet yellow flower that grows in the garden and is called Poponack. They are good to me but I want my John. I send my love, and may God keep you and your mother and father and Timmy. Please write Mary to

Your Friend Dinah Corley
In the Care of Mistress Bay on East Battery
Charleston in South Carolina
The United States of America.

When finished she tied on her bonnet, put on the new cloak, and went downstairs with the letter clutched tightly in a hand. Mrs. Bay had talked with Maurice and hurried through her morning work. The carriage, complete with Hilton and the fat horses, was waiting outside the garden gate. As they passed the Post Office at the foot of Broad Street, Dinah thought again of what she had written. Any day, perhaps today, that old gray building must yield up to her a letter from John Croft.

North of Broad Street, East Battery became East Bay. The wholesale district was crowded at this hour of the morning. Hilt guided Brandy and Soda between wagons and carts and drays. All along Cooper River sprang a forest of masts. Dinah had not yet learned the names of the wharves in their proper order, and the signs and Hilton's comments made a jumble in her mind. By little muddy ways that led them close to the river, they passed Vendue

Range and reached the foot of Cumberland Street. She and Mrs.
Bay got out and walked along the Central wharf.

There Dinah saw that the ship making ready to sail was the
cattle boat which had brought her from Ireland. Mr. Kincannon
ran down its gangplank to meet them.

They talked awkwardly together of all the irrelevant things of
which people talk when waiting to start a journey. Time was
closing in on them and space was yawning wider. Kincannon took
the letter and promised, with his own hands, to put it into Mary
Donovan's hands whenever he got to Galway. Although he disliked Bay he could not help liking his mother. He saw, through all
the unimportant differences of customs, manners and speech, that
she was proud with the same unbending pride of his stiff-backed
mother and other New England women. What meant more to
him, he saw that she loved and watched over Dinah.

Then came the minute to shake hands with them both and go
aboard. Mr. Kincannon was now on the bridge along with the
captain. Hawsers were released and thrown back from stanchions
on the deck. The dirty strip of dock water was growing wider as
the ship drifted out with the tide. Already her sails were blossoming like pale flowers on winter boughs, and on Central wharf Mrs.
Bay and Dinah had ceased to wave.

From the foot of Tradd Street, blocks farther south, Maurice
was watching the ship. He never watched a ship put out to sea
without wishing he was aboard. He hated his work with Coffin &
Pringle, Factors & Commission Merchants, at 7 Adgers wharf.
He hated loans and liens and the daily report which was chalked
on the blackboard as soon as it came in from New York. To him it
was merely figures; to the factors it could mean a fortune. But it
might cause some poor devil of a cotton planter to mortgage not
only his crop, but his slaves and his home as well.

He remembered how he had started to study for the law, but
dropped it and hurried home when his father died. In honesty he
could not believe that he would have liked law any better. But he
was glad that he knew enough of it to manage his father's estate
and look out for the interests of his mother and sister.

He envied that straight-eyed, bull-necked mate whose ship was
going out with the tide. The sea was clean of all the things that

troubled a man ashore. He loved the citron-green harbor and its broad tidal rivers. From childhood he had built his own boats, and he loved them better than horses. He could have steered that tramp as well as Tom Surtis was steering her. The man was taking her by Sullivan's Island Channel rather than by the Main Ship Channel. Maurice Bay knew them all: depth, direction, effects of varying wind and tide upon them. He knew Charleston Harbor as he knew the palm of his hand.

There were no jetties. The ocean lay out beyond Fort Sumter. He had liked the Yankee mate of the ship that was passing between the fort and the beach. The man was sweet on Dinah. It might be a good thing for her. . . .

It reminded him that on the way home he must stop and see the British Consul, Mr. Robert Bunch, at 58 Tradd Street. Mr. Bunch had promised to do what could be done. But he had shaken his head at the thought of finding one redcoat in all the British armies. Dinah did not even know the name of Croft's regiment.

The cattle boat was passing close in front of Fort Moultrie. On its parade ground the soldiers were drilling. Kincannon saw the sun flash back from their muskets. He had never taken this Beach Channel before. He looked from Moultrie to Sumter, wondering idly if, in the event of another war, any vessel could run between their guns. As he meditated, he was twisting around a calloused finger a few soft, bright-brown threads of hair, which he had found on the top button when he changed his civilian coat. He would go back and try again someday. He felt the ship rise and lunge for the bar.

Maurice, ashore, knew just where the ship was and felt her stress beneath his own feet. Out where she was going were clean wind and green sea. He knew she would be bearing south, around Charleston Light, which the uninitiated called Morris Island Lighthouse. He knew the uninhabited and jungle-grown island called Folly. She would stand clear along its beach. Kiawa . . . Seabrook's . . . and Edisto. . . .

He shrugged his shoulders and turned west toward East Battery. In thinking of Dinah's errand he had forgotten Camellia's. He had an engagement to call on her after supper that evening, and the only candy she liked was imported marzipan. Now just why couldn't she eat acorns and Black Chocolate Devils and other less exotic bon-bons? But, although exotic and expensive and hard to get, a dozen men kept her supplied with marzipan. Even though she fed it to her maid, to whom she was frequently unkind, she would expect him to arrive with a box that outdid all the others.

He took a deep breath of the salt wind, and it cleared both lungs and brain. At any rate, he smiled as he thought, Dinah's letter was on its way.

16

SEDGWICK LEWIS SIMONS had invited them to spend a plantation Christmas at Middleburg. Dinah helped with all the preparations for their departure a week ahead of the day, and with the wholesale buying of presents for family and Quarters as well as for the cousins on Cooper River.

Hilt drove the carriage northward on that winter morning. In it were Mrs. Bay, Dinah, Dorothea and Mauma, with as many personal belongings as could be crowded in. Lummy had started hours earlier with a wagon full of round-topped, brass-bound trunks.

Although Brandy and Soda stepped out handsomely, night fell before they crossed French Quarter Creek. Dinah saw lightwood flambeaux blazing in sockets to mark the gates of three plantations, The Blessing, Camp Vere and Halidon Hill. They made great fiery arches in the darkness, and the Spanish moss on their edges hung in lurid tatters. Then they were turning toward another gate, and its flambeaux were repeated to mark the road to the house. She saw Maurice and Sedgwick Lewis cantering ahead. Black men stood with other torches, along a low, long piazza. A gentleman was helping her out. The Bays' cousins were welcoming her.

She was glad to escape and go upstairs with Dorothea. The child was tired and cross and sleepy. A manservant brought a huge silver waiter with cold venison, hot biscuits and country butter, brandied peaches and feathery sponge cake. Then Dinah slipped into the big double bed alongside of her now-sleeping bedfellow. Mauma was sleeping on a pallet in the same room. She voiced her disapproval of the open window. Through it came the fragrance of tea olive in the garden, and the beat of a thousand thousand tiny silver drums from the frogs in the ricefield marshes.

In the next few days Dinah learned her way around the unpretentious house of black cypress. She walked with Dorothea on the lawns under oaks and magnolias, cedars and sycamores. They followed the pleached alley of camellia japonicas, with crimson blossoms above and around and fallen under their feet. Sedgwick Lewis took time to show them the rice mill and the slaves' burial ground. He told them with gusto the ghost story of the plantation: the tale of Old Fanny, long dead, who rose from her grave and wandered around all in white with a light in her hand.

The plantation was managed by Sedgwick Lewis' father and older brother Royall. The three young men spent most of their time riding to other plantations for dinners and dances and visits. The Cooper River clans were gathering for Christmas, and there were several large house parties. There was talk among the young men of getting up an informal lancing tournament. These tilts were usually held in spring or early autumn. But there were attractive guests across the river at Bossis: two handsome girls from Baltimore and their brother, who was a sportsman. All three had expressed a desire to see the Low Country lancing. Besides, Mel Manchester was coming to Quinby Barony to visit Jane and Polly Ashby. Camellia did not exactly fit into a quiet country life. Wherever she went she expected—and got—excitement.

Dinah and Dorothea watched the plantation carpenter fixing horizontal arms on the three uprights in a level field. It was an old lancing course, laid out merely for practice; but its distances were correct and its terrain safe and even. The rings looked tiny as they hung suspended just at the height of a horseman's shoulder.

Sedgwick Lewis yelled: *Look out,* and she and Dorry ran to one side. He came tearing along the course; but, as he approached each ring, the gray horse shied violently from its post and carried him in a series of scallops and out of reach.

Maurice selected a lance then, and took all three rings in a gallop. But, when they cheered him, he shook his head and said it was child's play. He said any man who could hold a lance could take them when riding so slowly, and he and Buck would have been disqualified by the judges. He said there would be enough entrants without him and he would not ride.

Royall Simons looked at him hard. "Not even to crown Mel Manchester? Those Baltimore girls at Bossis are a couple of beauties. Suppose the winner crowns one of them?"

Maurice seemed amused at the very idea. "I fancy Mel would survive it. In fact," he added reflectively, "it might be good for her."

Dorry demanded her mistletoe, and Sedgwick Lewis shed coat and boots. He clasped the trunk of the biggest oak and ascended, foot by foot. They stood beneath it and looked up while he swung from limb to limb, dropping branches with brittle stems and delicate, waxen fruit. Then he came down and they carried it into the house and, standing on chairs, hung its clusters from chandeliers and lintels. During the evening Sedgwick Lewis caught and kissed his mother and Mrs. Bay. But Dinah and Dorothea eluded him, slipping from room to room in challenge just as soon as he turned his back.

Maurice and Royall watched them, not taking any part. Since leaving Charleston, Maurice had been thrown constantly with Dinah. Here in the country he had no engagements with Mel and no office hours to keep. He found himself looking forward to morning walks along ricefield banks and to driving her and Dorry in a sulky through neighborhood roads. Looking on at this childish fun he envied Sedgwick Lewis. He had never realized before just how pretty Dinah was: white throat above the pale cashmere, curved lips, soft eyes and shining curls. Royall, eying him, smiled as they drank their after-dinner port.

"Shall we join in the game? We ate supper too late to allow us to go anywhere tonight. Even if we did, we couldn't find a prettier girl to kiss."

To his surprise, his casual cousin flushed an angry red. He said sharply: "I don't know what you are talking about. I wasn't thinking about kissing anybody."

Royall raised his eyebrows. "Weren't you?" he asked drily, as he lifted the decanter and refilled their glasses.

Just then, with a final Indian whoop, Sedgwick Lewis clutched at Dorry and missed. She and Dinah dodged through the hall door before he recovered, and ran up to their bedroom, laughing and breathless.

It was still mid-evening however, and Dinah was not sleepy. She had found on one of the bookshelves a little volume written not long before by Dr. Irving of Charleston. It was entitled *A Day on the Cooper River,* and it told about the plantation where she was staying, and other places. She sat reading by the light of a candle under a glass shade, while Dorothea tossed in her sleep and Mauma snored in a corner. At last she heard the others coming upstairs. Mrs. Bay's quick, light footsteps passed, went into her room next door, and then came out again.

Dinah hurried to the door. "Can I help you any way, ma'am?"

"I've left my reticule downstairs and in it are several things I need. Since you haven't undressed, Dinah, I'd be grateful to you."

"I'm all dressed, ma'am, and I'll be glad to get it."

She turned and picked up the candle, crossed the hall and started down the stair.

The house was quiet and pitch-dark. As she descended she could see the huge bunch of mistletoe that hung from the doorway leading to the dining room. She went first into the drawing room, but the reticule was not there. Perhaps, she thought, Mrs. Bay might have left it hanging on the back of her chair when she left the supper table.

She was in the dining-room doorway when two arms went around her. She started, and dropped the candle, and then recovered herself. She was not nervous and she recalled Sedgwick Lewis' nonsense.

"So ye've caught me?" she said, laughter in her voice. "But you must leave me go quick. I have come to seek the small satin bag of Mrs. Bay."

He was holding her gently but firmly. In the darkness she felt his mouth feeling for her lips. He kissed her hard but carefully. Then, as she tried to pull away, he clasped her with all his strength. The thrust of his head pushed her head far back and his mouth bruised her mouth. She cried out and pushed against his shoulders with both hands. He released her suddenly. She heard him cross to the mantel and fumble for candle and matches.

As he turned with the candlestick in hand, she saw his face and cried out again. The dark hair that he wore brushed back fell over his forehead. "Only it wasn't Sedgwick Lewis," he said, and his voice sounded strange.

She looked back at him, pale and afraid, her breast lifting and falling under the closely fitted bodice.

He took a step toward her. His voice was no longer slow and soft. "Well—what did you expect?"

He was holding the candle high and his shadow moved in its moving light. She stepped backward as he came toward her. She had known he could be sarcastic, but never bitter and sneering. "I must be a southern gentleman, mustn't I? Always chivalrous and—"

He stopped short as he caught sight of her face. "Oh, my God! What have I done? Dinah—little Dinah!"

She burst into tears as she snatched Mrs. Bay's reticule from the chairback where it hung. Then she wheeled and ran, leaving Maurice alone with the moving shadows.

17

DOROTHEA WOKE EARLY on that Christmas morning. Dinah, who had cried herself to sleep the night before, was still sleeping quietly beside her. It seemed to be a clear daybreak and the birds were singing loudly. Dorothea was glad of that, because she looked forward to seeing the tournament. She was eager to get up and unwrap her Christmas presents, and she tried to get out of bed as quietly as possible. But Dinah opened her eyes and smiled from a tangle of golden-brown curls. With a shriek of joy the child clutched her and kissed her. "Merry Christmas, Dinah! Christmas gift!"

That formula of the Negroes brought Mauma awake and upright. She caught them both before they could speak. "Christmas gift, chile! Christmas gift, Miss Dinah!"

They had their presents ready for her, and they trailed in long white nightgowns over to the wardrobe. Dorry produced a jeweler's box holding a small silver brooch which she had been allowed to select to celebrate Mauma's eleventh Christmas as her mentor. Dinah had made a pair of warm woolen bed socks for the old woman.

Then, before Dinah could give Dorry the little bright green gloves she had knitted to go with the winter cloak for school, Dorry was holding out another box to her. It was a longish, flat leather box, and she had to press a spring before its cover flew up. Upon parchment-yellow satin lay a thin circle of gold, with a round and empty depression alongside it.

"It's one of my bracelets," Dorry said. "Morry told me they came from France more than a hundred years ago. I want you to wear it, Dinah. I'll wear the other as soon as I grow up."

Dinah looked at it without touching it. "Oh, no! Your mother would not like this at all."

"Yes, she does like it. I asked her before we left Charleston. She asked Morry what he thought, and he said to let me give it to you."

Dinah lifted the small, rigid hoop made of three twisted strands of gold. She slipped it on her left wrist and something flashed. "Oh, me soul! Tis a diamond!"

She managed to tear her eyes from it, and dress and go down with Dorry. She had never known a Christmas like this. She compared it with the simple Christmas days that she had spent on Aran, before she had even heard of Charleston.

There was a gay breakfast downstairs and the presentation of other gifts. Dinah was overcome by her share: an ivory-handled parasol from Mrs. Bay, kid gloves from Maurice, bonbons from Sedgwick Lewis and Royall; a small painted fan and a lace handkerchief from Mr. and Mrs. Simons.

Dorothea, entranced, sat on the floor, winding and rewinding a little French music box. Childlike, she did not hesitate to show her preference for one present among many. It played "Malbrouck s'en va-t-en Guerre," and it had been given her by Sedgwick Lewis. But he had gone, with his brother and cousin, to see that all was ready for the tilt that afternoon.

The carpenter and his apprentices had built a small stand opposite the uprights where the rings were hanging. At four o'clock in the afternoon the guests began to arrive. There were carriages from Longwood, Quinby and Silk Hope. But Camellia

Manchester was not driving with the Ashbys. The young Baltimore sportsman who was a guest at Bossis had procured a tandem team and high-swung phaeton, and crossed the river at Huger's Bridge in order to escort her. The South Carolina horsemen who saw him swing his high-stepping blacks around the field and into position saw that O'Fallon Howard knew all that was to be known about coaching.

Camellia was dressed in her favorite color, dark red. But, instead of a bonnet, she wore a small, dashing hat with a long plume that curled off, then curled back to touch her cheek. She was at once surrounded by young men on horseback. But these attendants were not enough for her. When Royall rode up to welcome her, she sent him for Maurice.

Maurice was sitting Buck close by the stand where he could explain things to his sister. He wanted, more than anything else in the world, to try to explain other things to Dinah. He had been alternately seeking and dodging her all day. She acted just as if nothing had happened between them, but she had taken care not to let him get her alone. It cut him so deeply that it had spoiled Christmas and was spoiling the tournament. He cursed himself and wondered what to do. He would apologize and promise never to let it happen again. Yet he felt that no apology could reach the roots of the matter. He would like in some way to show her admiration publicly; to prove that he was not trying to take advantage of her position. Telling Dorothea about the tilting, he was really talking to Dinah.

He left her, however, when Mel summoned him. As he cantered across the field to the phaeton, he felt the old excitement that her summons always aroused. Her cavaliers made way for him. He held the enviable place of first among her beaux. Also, he already knew and liked Howard, the guest from Baltimore.

Mel said, "I sent for you to tell you that Rawlins Bull and Will Frost and Nat Pinckney and Lowndes Carew are coming."

"They rode from Charleston to Bossis yesterday," said Howard. "Waring White has a flatboat to bring them all over to Punkin Hill landing. But I don't think Bull expects to tilt. He said his mare was not trained for it."

Camellia tossed her head, and both men watched the bright feather brush her cheek like a kiss. "Don't let them fool you that it's so difficult, Mr. Howard. I've done it just for fun, and taken the rings."

Yes, Maurice thought, she had done it; but no one had timed her. He said: "I'm glad they are coming. We are going to have a full field. Of course Royall will wait for them. I suppose you told him, Mel?"

She bit her lip at the blunder. She had not told her host but had seized the pretext to send him for Maurice Bay. She had seen him lolling on that old horse and disregarding her while he talked to a child and an Irish servant. She said quickly: "I thought you were Master of the Lists. You've been on the inactive bench since Buck got so old and slow."

Howard was a gentleman. He spoke promptly. "That's a nice thoroughbred, Bay."

"Yes," said Maurice; "but he isn't young and I don't intend to stiffen him up."

He lifted his hat and trotted off to report the new entrants.

Dinah and Dorry just then saw the group from Bossls crossing the lawns. With Waring White and his four guests from Charleston were the riders from Kensington and Limerick plantations.

Royall Simons rode as the Knight of Middleburg. Being host, he would ride last. He knew that most of his guests had been unable to lay hands on their elaborate costumes. So he had compromised by wearing his blue-satin coat and flowered waistcoat over ordinary riding trousers and boots. Also, it had been agreed to ride bare of head, since only a few had brought the plumed hats that were customary.

Sedgwick Lewis, reckless as he was, realized that White Cockerel would make a spectacle of them both. He was acting as Master of Horse. He and Maurice were assembling the entrants a hundred yards away by the rice mill. The only Heralds available were little Tim Trescott and Harleston Du Pré, who had come in carriages with their parents. With a blue sash around the waist of one and a red around the other, they were mounted on two quiet saddle horses. Beaming with pride and trying not to drop their bugles as they rode, they led the procession in a walk toward the lancing ground. Riding twenty feet behind them, the Master of Horse and the Master of the Lists told them when halfway to blow the fanfare.

A burst of handclapping from the stand, the carriages, and the older men on horseback, answered the trumpets. The sight was a pretty one, although the tournament was not formal. The Knights of Longwood, Quinby, The Hagan and Silk Hope were riding two and two at its head, because they had happened to come in full dress. Two and two behind them came the other twelve, some in ordinary riding clothes, some distinguished by a bright waistcoat or a broad sash; but all sitting as straight as the wooden lances they were holding upright.

Around the field they went at a walk, with Tim and Harleston tooting joyfully and the gallery applauding and commenting.

Dinah's eyes were starry. She whispered to Dorothea: "Tis the grandest sight me eyes have seen, and your brother and your cousin are the grandest of them all!"

In the phaeton, O'Fallon Howard's heart beat faster as Mel leaned to look and her shoulder pressed his arm. Maurice was not in the running and Brailsford Cain had not come. If Lowndes Carew or Will Frost or Dick Ashby or Pierre Roche was declared to be champion, she knew that she would be crowned queen. If it had not been for the presence of Kitty and Janet Howard, she could have been sure, too, of Swin and Tavvy Ball, Broughton Keating and Warry White. But the Howard girls were blonde enough and handsome enough to make their host and his neighbors remember duty to guests. She was determined to impress her new beau by letting him see her crowned Queen of Love and Beauty.

Howard said: "This is splendid! I've heard of it all my life."

Mel lifted her long lashes and looked up into his face. "I've seen it so often," she said, "that there is only one thing which could make it splendid for me. It would be splendid if you were riding— as my knight—under my colors."

"But it's different from any riding, even point to point, that I've ever done."

The Heralds were announcing the Knight of Longwood. Jim Trescott flashed, in scarlet and black, on a black horse down the course. He took two of the three rings and finished well in the time limit.

One after another they followed. The man from Maryland was horseman enough to see the skill they showed. It involved holding with one hand a running horse to a narrow track, while the other hand balanced a heavy lance and took the small rings in their center. Divergence of the lance's point by a fraction of an inch merely knocked them from their hold. Delay of one second disqualified a man on speed by the timing.

Dinah was watching with breathless interest. After Royall, the fourteenth and last rider, had run the course, the little Heralds blew a long blast and Maurice rode forward. He announced that Will Frost and Royall were tied for first place. They would ride off the tie as soon as smaller rings could be put in position.

Mel Manchester's gaze was now fixed on the course as hard as that of her escort, but for a very different reason. She held her crimson lower lip cruelly hard between sharp white teeth. If Will won he would crown her. But she could not be sure.

Her slim fingers slid down O'Fallon Howard's sleeve. "There's no rule against postentries in a tournament like this. I believe you could outdo them all. I've been sitting here, seeing you carry my colors to victory."

He spoke to the groom who had ridden on a perch behind them. "Take the lead horse's head."

He was already down and helping her out. They crossed directly toward the stand. She was holding Howard's arm and, with the other hand, waving a red-velvet glove at Maurice. "A postentry," she called aloud.

Maurice looked at her, then swung down from his saddle as they drew near. "Are you really going to ride, Howard?"

The Marylander bowed. "If I can procure a horse."

Royall and Will had ridden up. Both dismounted, and they said in chorus: "Will you take mine?"

Howard's eyes went over them. He had seen them show speed and handle well. His excitement was mounting with the pressure of Mel's fingers. But she spoke first. "The fastest horse here is the three-year-old thoroughbred called *White Cockerel*."

Royall answered her plainly. "Use sense, Mel! Even that crazy young brother of mine had sense enough not to try to ride him in this."

She tilted her chin. Two spots as red as camellia petals stained her cheeks. She knew the exact words to use to silence both him and Maurice. Her voice was slow but distinct. "After all, Roy, the South Carolina Low Country is not the only place in the world where men can ride. Have you and Morry never heard of Maryland races and hunts?"

It made no difference that they knew she knew they had heard of them and seen them. They had both been guests at hunt balls in Baltimore. Royall spoke to Howard. "Do you wish my brother's horse?"

Sedgwick Lewis, close by and listening, practically fell from his saddle. He leaned to tighten the girth, and White Cockerel swung his neck around and would have nipped him in the seat of his pants if Maurice had not slapped him.

Sedgwick Lewis straightened up. "Are the stirrups right for you, sir?" He hesitated and his boyish voice was worried. "I tried him more than once on this course and he bolted the posts. But you've got more weight than I, and can probably ride him better."

Mel laughed. "I'm counting on that." Her fingers were squeezing Howard's arm, for she had no intention of letting him be dissuaded. "They put smaller rings for the ride-off and cut the time too." She gave him a look that would, she hoped, awaken jealousy in Maurice. "I wish my knight to have the fastest horse. I have no doubt of his horsemanship."

Royall said: "Will you ride first?"

Maurice said: "How shall we announce you?"

Sedgwick Lewis held White Cockerel's head and off stirrup while Howard mounted.

He settled himself in the English saddle with a horseman's ease. The leathers were right for him, although he was thirty pounds heavier than their owner. He looked down and met Mel's eyes. She unpinned from the front of her pelisse a huge crimson puffball japonica, and handed it up to him.

"Announce me as the Knight of the Red Camellia," he told Maurice.

The bugles blared as Tim and Harleston tried vainly to blow together. On the stand Mrs. Simons was thinking about the venison pastry. She said nervously: "I hope it isn't overdone. What is happening out there now, Clelia?"

Mrs. Bay was beckoning to Camellia to join them. The girl

should never have crossed the field, not even on her escort's arm. "It's a postentry, Placidia. He's up on that horrible horse of Sedgwick Lewis's."

Young Sedgwick Lewis had not troubled to escort Camellia to them. He was standing by Maurice's stirrup, and Rawlins Bull had joined them on the Irish mare. But Camellia turned and, with her head high under the red plume, walked the short distance to the stand. She passed Dorothea and Dinah without glancing at them, stopped to speak with her hostess and Maurice's mother, then settled red-velveteen skirts on the other side of them.

Howard was setting himself for the start. Maurice had told him to take his time. He was getting used to the feel of the lance as he rode in narrowing circles. The gray was moving under him with the long, free fling of a thoroughbred, and he told himself Miss Camellia knew more about horses than these men knew. He had ridden in many a point to point—and he wore a red camellia! He signaled to Bay he was ready. With lance couched, he took off in a run.

Dinah and Dorothea watched as intently as Mel was watching. They bore down on the first post with Howard riding perfectly and the gray horse doing better even than the speed required.

But, as the Knight of the Red Camellia thought he had lance point in the ring, his steed threw its head down viciously with all its weight behind the pull. It got one end of the bit between its powerful teeth and, with a twist of its rear end, whipped its body sideways and away from the structure on its right. Although it lashed out from under him as swiftly as a striking snake, he could have kept his seat except for the heavy lance. So delicate is balance in horsemanship that the unaccustomed weight dragged him around in the saddle and loosened his knee grip. He felt himself going, but he still clung to the lance and tried to keep his right stirrup and stay on the bucking horse. But his left foot had already slipped free, and his frantic pressure only served to turn and catch his boot in the right iron as he fell. Young and old, the men on the field were riders to a man. What they saw before them was every rider's nightmare: a runaway horse dragging a man whose foot was caught in a stirrup.

18

DINAH HAD BEEN frightened when she saw Howard mount. She and Dorry were too far away to hear what he was saying; but they had both seen Sedgwick Lewis try to hold his horse on the course, and seen it bolt. Dorry had remarked in a tone of pleased anticipation: "I think White Cockerel's going to throw him; don't you?"

Just then Mel had come by, lovelier than ever because of her easy triumph. She was standing now; no longer triumphant, but with her hands clenched and her teeth in her lower lip, staring out at the turmoil of men and horses.

For the men, afoot and on horseback, had rushed the field. White Cockerel was caught by Rawlins Bull before he had dragged Howard far. Dr. Gibbs was pushing through the crowd, calling: "Let him lie where he is! Don't pick him up until I get there."

The handsome Marylander lay sprawled in the dust churned up by hoofs. Blood was spreading in his hair and running from his mouth. Maurice and Royall had, in misguided sympathy, been just about to lift him.

"Get back," said the doctor gruffly. "You've done enough to him."

He kneeled by the unconscious man and began first to examine his head. His fingers were gentle, but his voice was rough. "You ought to be shot, you young fools, for putting him on that horse. It's a killer, and it tried to kill him."

Royall and Maurice, feeling guilty and wretched, did not answer, but Rawlins did. "Nobody put him on the horse. He chose to ride it. I heard him."

"The more fool he," said Dr. Gibbs. "It's broken his jaw and kicked him in the head."

Sedgwick Lewis came up and asked in hushed tones: "Is he dead?"

"Of course he's not dead. His head is nearly as hard as yours. No horseshoe yet forged could crack it."

He stood up. "Go get my carriage, Royall. We'll take him to the house. Maurice, tell your mother and cousin to keep the women from the house for the next hour. I won't have them having hysterics and getting in my way."

Maurice obeyed, thanking heaven that Howard had not been killed. He walked straight to the stand where Mrs. Simons and Mrs. Bay had risen and descended to meet him. He saw their distress through their quiet self-control.

"He's not too badly hurt, Mother. Cousin Placidia, Cousin Gibbs begs us to stay out here on the field. He wants us to keep the crowd away until he examines further and decides what to do."

The hostess put a hand to her distracted brow. "To think of it happening here! I feel as if it were our fault. O'Fallon is such a good-looking young man. And his grandmother was a Charlestonian."

Maurice put a comforting arm around her shoulders. O'Fallon was no longer good-looking and might never be so again. Those face wounds were deep, and they would probably scar. "If it's anybody's fault, it's mine. I'm Master of the Lists."

His mother said sensibly: "Nonsense, Morry! He and Camellia crossed the field to make the postentry. We saw it all. You could not have refused without insulting a guest."

Camellia was close enough to overhear. She stood, with her small head high and her cheeks ablaze, waiting to question Maurice when he left the older women. She was frightened and yet elated. O'Fallon Howard had been riding for her favor when he nearly lost his life. She was honestly glad that he had not been killed. That would have carried matters too far. She wondered why he had not had sense to drop the lance and recover his seat. She was thinking of it entirely from a selfish point of view, wondering in what way its consequences would affect her. Excitement of the thought increased her loveliness. She knew that the men were looking at her and the women talking about her. She stood, defiant and vivid, with her eyes fixed on Maurice. None of the others mattered, but she feared his disapproval. He still had his arm around that silly old lady. Mel heard her say: "But I feel that we should go to the house and help."

Mrs. Bay shook her head. "McMaster Gibbs told us to stay here. He doesn't want us, and he'll bite our heads off if we disobey."

She took the other woman's arm and spoke to her son. "Go on

now, Morry. The best thing to do is to run off the finals and keep the crowd together. We may have better news for them before they scatter. Besides, your cousins have arranged refreshments at the house."

He was grateful for her common sense. As he turned he saw Mel beckon to him. But he wished to avoid her, and escape came with a call from Dorry. "Morry," she said in her clear, childish voice, "Dinah's crying. She said not to bother you, but she's unhappy because Mr. Howard got hurt."

He stopped and looked up. The two girls sat on a tier just above him. Dinah dried her eyes hastily. Dorry was pressing into her hands the posy of mixed garden flowers that she had picked and carried for the festive occasion. "Take my tussy-mussy," she said. "And don't cry, Dinah darling. Won't you tell her, Morry, that he isn't really hurt?"

He looked up into Dinah's face and she managed to smile back at him. "I didn't wish Dorry to trouble you. I can see ye are fair distracted. But I thought that the poor young man was destroyed entirely."

The contrast was too marked for him to disregard it. This girl, who considered his own worry and who grieved for a man she had not even met, was in no way to blame for what had happened. All she was getting out of it was to sit and watch with a child, and to accept and hold tenderly a few flowers that the child gave her. But she never wasted time in thinking about herself. A stranger's hurt had moved her to tears. She was selfless, while Mel—

Behind him Mel called distinctly: "I wish to speak to you, Morry."

He gave Dinah the first smile he had managed since Howard's fall. "Don't worry. He's not very badly hurt. Now, take good care of her, Dorry."

Mel was at his shoulder. "Did you hear me call you, Morry?"

He turned and looked her in the eyes. "Yes. I was occupied. There seem to be people more distressed about Howard than you, although he was riding as your knight."

She drew herself up. He knew she lacked heart. But he could not help admiring her because she was utterly fearless. "I am not in the habit of showing my feelings in public." Her eyes grew blacker and bigger and her voice dropped to a whisper. "You are the only person, in all the world, Morry, who has ever seen me with my guard down."

She was disarming him. He knew it—but she was too lovely. Perhaps a man whom she really loved could guide her in the right way.

"Why do you think I called you," she pleaded, "if not to find out how badly Mr. Howard is hurt? I'm sorry now that I urged him to tilt; but I thought he rode well enough. The trouble about me, Morry, is that I measure all men by you." She hesitated, and the red in her cheeks grew even deeper. "When you are riding, Morry, I don't look at anyone else."

She saw that she was breaking him down and she pressed her advantage. "Would you, of all people, wish me to have rushed out to him and thrown myself upon him as if he were my fiancé? You, of all men, know that we are not engaged and that I do not love him."

"I know that, Mel," he said softly. "And I am glad that I know it."

But Will Frost interrupted. He approached, leading his horse. "I wish you Masters would call it all off, Morry. Roy isn't coming back to tilt, and I don't want to win by default. Besides, I think we should stop, out of respect for Howard."

Maurice thought so too, but Mel spoke before he could. "That's ridiculous, Will," she said. "Mr. Howard isn't dead. You've won the tournament." Her eyes called him hither. "You have a right now to crown your queen."

Maurice looked hard at her. She was no longer soft. She was just as beautiful, but she sparkled like hard, bright stone. She was holding Will with her eyes, as a magnet holds a piece of steel. Anyone could see that he loved her with all of his honest heart. Anyone could see that all she wished and all she was playing for was to make him crown her Queen of Love and Beauty before the field.

The rage that rose in Maurice's own heart frightened him. He tried to speak and found that he could not. The only thing plain to him was that he would like to kill Will Frost if he dared to crown Mel Manchester. His thoughts were too complex to understand, but he felt that he must prevent that. He felt that he could, and would, prevent it. When he got his voice back he was surprised to hear it low and even.

"If you don't want to win by default, I'll get you a runner-up, Will," he said.

He turned on one heel and walked directly back to Rawlins Bull. "Will you lend me the mare for a postentry? I've been wanting to try her. Besides, the doctor would like us to keep the crowd from the house for awhile."

Bull got down at once. "Of course. But, aren't you doing just what Howard did?"

Maurice was already shortening the leathers. "That gray is vicious. The mare is not. I rode her bareback the night she arrived."

Dorry and Dinah stood up to watch. Mel sat when Will left her, but she looked on with triumph in her smile. So, after all, he could not bear to see another man crown her! This was better than Howard. Her heart was pounding. She did not care for any man except Morry Bay. She had only been using Howard as a spur. The touch of Morry's hand on her arm thrilled her. . . .

The Irish mare moved under him with strength of steel and smoothness of silk. When Sedgwick Lewis handed him a lance, she cocked her ears forward and blew and trembled with fright. But he patted her and talked to her as he moved it around her head, and she realized that he was not going to strike her. He wheeled and cantered her slowly, thrusting the stick here and there, and she gained confidence and began to enjoy the game.

Meanwhile Sedgwick Lewis and Rawlins had cleared the field. The latter yelled to him: "Under what name are you riding?"

He galloped Kathleen Avourneen across and by the stand, taking a poke at Dorry with the lance as he went by. Dinah was clasping her bouquet to her breast and gazing, enraptured, at the mare in action. He shouted back to the Masters: "I'm Knight of the Aran Isles!"

Mrs. Izard from The Elms drew the carriage robe around her and said disapprovingly to Mrs. Middleton: "That must be one of those new places on Wando River. There's no plantation called Aran Isles around Goose Creek or the Ashley or the Cooper."

Will Frost was going down the course like a streak of green, leaning now for the first ring, his satin coattails flying. When he brought his horse to a stop all three rings were on his lance point. It had been agreed that, in case both riders took all three rings, the winner should be the one making best time. The winter sun was getting low.

Maurice brought the mare to the line of start and touched her with his spurs. One leap took her into full charge. He kept his left knee hard and steady against her side. She got the message. He wanted her to run close by those ugly posts. She feared them, but she already felt safe with this man's hands on her lines. He was talking to her through them, as all decent riders do. She would take him wherever he wished, would give him all of her strength and speed, because she knew with certainty now that he would always be kind to her. She heard three tiny metallic clicks as his lance point took the rings. She was running evenly but like the wind. Muldoon's lads had trained her well.

The timekeeper shouted something and, on the stand, Dorothea began screaming: "Morry has won! He's won!"

He led the mare back to Rawlins Bull, and lingered to run a hand in caress along her mane. Someone handed him a small wreath of crimson camellia blossoms from the pleached alley in the garden. He started with it toward the stand.

Everybody was clapping. Mrs. Bay and Mrs. Simons, in spite of anxiety about Mr. Howard, were trying to smile congratulations. Mel's dark head was proudly held and bare. She was holding the small red hat in her lap. She looked up into his face as he came abreast of her.

He did not even look at her. He walked directly past her, stepped up on the lowest bench of the stand and placed the crown on Dinah's head. Underneath it, her big gray eyes looked up at him in surprise and alarm. But he smiled down at her reassuringly and, putting his hands on either side of the soft little face, kissed her very gently on the forehead.

It was the kiss that the winner had a right to give his queen. But, from him to her, it wiped out that other kiss between them. It told her so as plainly as words, and the startlement in her eyes died out. She gazed back at him in joyful surprise and gasped: "But you are too good to me!"

He shook his head, still holding her face between his hands. The crowd was holding its breath. This was something more startling to see, even, than a horse trampling a man.

"I'm not being good to you, Dinah," he told her. "It's just that I want you to know—and want everybody else to know—that I'm proud to acknowledge you my friend and to crown you my queen in public."

As he turned the field broke again into applause—applause scattered and slowed by astonishment. Rawlins Bull's long face was gashed by its sardonic grin. Mel Manchester rose and took the arm that Will Frost was offering her. She knew Maurice's temper. She had pushed him too far. She smiled like a madonna into Will's eyes. But already she was planning to make the little Irish immigrant suffer for this slight to her vanity.

As they dismounted at the hitching rail and one of the waiting Negroes took their horses, old Mr. Heyward poked old Mr. Hayne in the ribs with an elbow. "That little lass from Ireland is pretty as a peach. Always thought young Bay was a gay dog, in spite of his quiet manners."

But, on the stand, Mrs. Bay leaned against her cousin and moaned: "Placidia, *what shall we do?*"

Mrs. Simons was stunned; and not only by Maurice's eccentric behavior. From childhood her cousin Clelia had always taken the lead and left her to follow, free of care. When she appealed for help, the end of all things must be at hand. With that support withdrawn, poor Mrs. Simons clutched with her mind for something else to stand through earthquake and flood and war. Instead of seizing upon her lawfully wedded husband or the Episcopal Church, her mind seized upon her several dozen pans of pastry. She rose and waved wildly at her younger son.

"The best thing to do, Clelia, is to have the Heralds announce that hot punch and cold supper are waiting for them all at the house." She clasped her hands devoutly and registered her thanks. "Praise heaven that we made ten gallons of punch—and made it strong!"

19

IN THAT New Year of 1859 time wove with driving shuttles. Hardly to be seen in its immense plan were the thin red threads converging on a small section of a great land that the old world still called new.

Dinah, returning from Middleburg Plantation, wept in secret when she found no letter from John Croft.

At a dock in the Thames a troopship lay, and a regiment was going aboard. It was one of many regiments ordered to India. Men shouldered each other to reach the rail and wave good-by to their families. But one young Englishman moved and gave his place to an older soldier. A man who had just been jilted had no one to whom to wave. His trade was soldiering and, in his disappointment and hurt, he had re-enlisted. He was indifferent as to whether he ever saw England again. That deep green valley with gray stones, which lay on an Irish island, was falling behind him as a dream falls when a man wakes. He knew now that it had not been true but false. He still woke in the night, thinking he heard a voice say *My John!* Then, listening to his comrades' snores and the beat of the crude propeller, he cursed himself for a fool. Had there been the slightest chance of mistake, she would by now have sent him a letter to explain. Besides, in spite of her big gray eyes, she had played the same game with that drunken ruffian in Galway who had told him.

But Dinah never doubted him. She wrote him another letter. "My John," she told him, "I know well enough that you have not got my letters. Tis the reason why you do not answer me at all. But I shall not stop writing you and, sooner or later, I know that one will find you wherever you are."

Mrs. Bay's first move upon returning to Charleston had been to announce that Dinah was in love with an Englishman and engaged to marry him. It seemed to her the best way to repair the damage that her son had done. She consulted Dinah about it, not mentioning her reason. Between the girl's innocence and Maurice's obstinacy, she felt that her way was indeed a hard one. He had laughed and then frowned when she broached the subject to him.

"Why should anybody talk about Dinah and me? A man has a right to crown any girl that he chooses queen. She's young and pretty, and she deserves some fun."

"Morry, I know that she is and she does. But people will think that you care for her."

"I do care for her. Nobody could live in the house with Dinah and not care for her. I love her—almost like Dorry."

His mother sighed. "Your friends will never realize that you can love her that way. They, being friends, will not start scandal. But others may."

His young face hardened. "If they do, I know how to stop them."

That, she knew, would make things worse. Dueling was barbaric and she had a horror of it. She thanked heaven that Dinah was always compliant. She seemed pleased at the idea of making her engagement known.

"I know that John will come for me as soon as he gets the letters. Tis kind you are to tell your friends, for they have been good to me."

So Mrs. Bay told, discreetly but emphatically. She explained that the reason she and Morry were tender with Dinah was because of the girl's love for an English soldier. "Her family managed to separate them, but she thinks of nothing else. Maurice is very anxious to find him for her."

She did not fool them in the least. They knew why she was, at just this time, producing an English soldier. Kindly disposed people believed in him and the story. Malicious ones said that it was all an invention. But, kindly or malicious, they continued to tell each other of that unlucky Christmas tournament. "My dear, I wish that you could have been there! You should have seen Mel Manchester's face!"

The last statement was libel. Mel could control her face. She had been gay and vivacious at the plantation supper. She had upon the young men exactly the same effect as the generous supply of whisky punch. Will Frost had almost had to fight for his hard-won place as her partner. She despised him for losing to Morry, but she struck at Morry through him. Dinah had sat, happy but serene, with Dorry sharing her hour. The young men came up to pay compliments and congratulate her, but she made no effort to hold them. They soon went back to crowd around Mel. Only the older ones lingered. And, at Dorry's bedtime, Dinah got up and excused herself to them with a smile.

But, back in Charleston, Camellia had Maurice again in her toils. She saw that something had to be done, something more than the lift and fall of long eyelashes and the hesitant touch of fingers. So she wrote him a note, telling him that she was anxious about Howard's recovery, but afraid of rebuff if she wrote to his sisters. She told him, truthfully, that many people had been unkind about it. She asked him, as her most trusted friend, to come and advise her what to do.

He went that evening—and walked into the web of her firelit drawing room. She had given her maid and the butler leave to go out, and warned her invalid aunt not to interrupt her.

With wistful dark eyes on his face she told him her troubles. She was clever enough not to overdo and to leave the most to suggestion: her orphaned childhood; her girlhood spent between cousins' homes and a New York school; her final haven in Charleston with a sick and complaining aunt. She asked his advice and he thought she was going to take it. When he stood up to go she was close to his shoulder. She looked younger and slimmer in the white muslin belted with black. It was simple with the simplicity of ultra-elegance. He did not know that, and he did not know what was the intriguing perfume he smelled. It was heady and different from the verbena or violet that most Charleston women used. When she lifted her face, her curved red mouth was not far from his chin. But her eyes were sad and appealing. She believed in a rôle while she played it.

"Morry, I'm all alone. Other girls have brothers to advise them. I want to do what's right." Red rose in her cheeks and her dark eyes fell. "Even more, I want to do what you want. Will you help me? Don't ever get angry with me! Don't stop being my friend!"

He took her in his arms and she made no resistance. She had never before allowed him to do it.

"Mel, I want you for more than a friend. Don't you know that, my beautiful?"

She did not dare to open her eyes for fear he would see their triumph. She had him, after all. But he had made her suffer. She would show him what it was to be tortured by jealousy; by jealousy of a girl as far beneath her as the dirt. But her voice was low as she drew herself out of his arms. He should have provocation. She knew she could arouse him. But he belonged to a school that put women on a pedestal.

"Morry, you must be quite, quite sure. And you must make *me* sure of your love."

He was quite sure, he told himself later, and he would make her as sure of him. He wooed her with ardor and tenderness. He was in no hurry for marriage, but he was a perfect lover.

He was so happy that he paid little attention to politics. But, as he went to and came from his work each day, he saw men gathered around the office of Mr. James Pettigru in Saint Michael's Alley. Far larger crowds went in and out of Mr. Barnwell Rhett's offices on Broad Street. They were older men than he and he knew them only casually.

But there was unrest everywhere. It was even reaching the slaves. On a January morning, when Mrs. Bay had gone to a meeting of her church guild. Dinah sat alone by the sunny east window and sewed. She was thinking of John Croft, as she always did when she found herself alone.

Her thoughts were interrupted by wild shrieks from the Quarters. The southeast room gave on the long third-story piazza which faced south and overlooked the yard. She dropped her work and started for it, hearing as she ran, yells, of *"Help"* and *"He killin' me!"*

As she got outside she saw Mary Jane, with clothes torn half off and blood streaming down her face, break from her door and rush into the open. After her came her husband, the mulatto carpenter, with a heavy piece of firewood in his hand. Before Dinah could cry out, he struck his wife on the head with it. She went down, rolling at his feet and screaming for mercy.

Dinah leaned over the banister and called aloud: "Coaxum, put that stick down at once! Do not touch Mary Jane. Mr. Morry will punish you."

He turned up to her the face of a fiend. She wondered if he was drunk. She knew that in Charleston the punishment of a white man who sold liquor to a slave was public whipping.

"Oh no, he won't. Mr. Morry gone and take Lummy with he," said Coaxum. "Hilt and Titus gone too. The horses gittin' shoed today."

She had forgotten hearing Maurice mention that all the horses were going to the blacksmith. Hilton had driven straight there after taking Dorry to school. Titus had followed with the wagon mule. Lummy had walked the few blocks after Maurice and ridden Buck on to the forge. When Mrs. Lucas stopped for Mrs. Bay in her carriage, and Erasmus sallied forth to market with his basket, it had left Dinah alone with women slaves, Jessie's young son Rex, and the carpenter Coaxum.

He grinned viciously up at her. Mary Jane groveled and howled. Old Venus appeared at the step of her room to do battle for her daughter. She was so crippled with rheumatism that she could hardly walk, and Dinah knew that Samba could not rise from his chair without help. From her point of vantage she could see the five terrified children, hiding behind the stable and peeping out. Of Jessie and Rex she saw no sign. Coaxum raised his weapon.

"I gwine kill this 'oman," he yelled. "She my 'oman and she won't do what I tell she. I gwine be free like witefolks and live in witefolks' house. I gwine come up there and kill you too. You aint no better than me."

He dealt his victim another blow that made her cry out in agony.

Dinah turned and ran for the stair. Maurice's room was on the second level and, in her capacity of assistant to Mrs. Bay, she knew it well. She flew to the tall wardrobe of gleaming mahogany, opened its left hand division, and pulled out the highest drawer. She snatched the silver-bound box that lay in it, raised its cover and picked up one of the pair of long dueling pistols. Without shutting box or door, she raced on down the stairs.

She passed the women house servants, huddled in terror, as she ran through the kitchen, which was the shortest way to the yard. She heard the thud of wood on flesh. Coaxum was beating his wife hard. He wanted to kill her and she, now unconscious, was no longer screaming. From behind, Old Venus threw herself upon him. He turned on her savagely, dashed her to the ground, and raised the log of wood to strike her.

"Coaxum," said Dinah clearly, "if you strike Venus I'll shoot you."

He spun around, and looked into Maurice's pistol barrel. Dinah was less than twelve feet away and still approaching. Venus' interference had prevented his seeing her come. He froze in his brutal attitude, wondering if he could reach her.

Dinah had never before touched a pistol. Maurice, like most other men, gave his womenfolk orders that neither they nor the servants were to lay finger on them. He, himself, kept them cleaned and dusted. But Dinah had seen them lying, shining, pearl-handled, wicked toys, when she opened drawers and boxes to inspect the maids' cleaning. She felt the long barrel bobbing unsteadily, so she put her left fingers around it to steady it. Her right hand seemed to fit the slender, ornamental stock, and her right fingers felt the small projection underneath it. All she knew about it was from which end the bullet came, and she pointed that end at the drunken carpenter. She had no idea of firing and had not stopped to think whether or not Maurice kept it loaded.

Coaxum eyed her cunningly. He had chosen his time with care. All the men except Rex were gone, and the boy was afraid of him. He had watched the neighbors drive out. Their women servants would not dare to interfere, even if they heard the noise across high walls and big gardens. He guessed that Dinah knew nothing about the pistol. Had she known, she would have stood off and not dared to come within reach. He crouched, threw the log straight at her, and leapt toward her, still crouching.

All that Dinah knew then was confusion and terror. She saw Coaxum leap and threw herself to one side. The movement made her muscles jerk and her fingers clenched on the trigger. The pistol went off with a roar and recoil that sat her down flat on the flagstones.

She sat, with the breath knocked out of her and her right index finger smarting. She saw Coaxum running toward the fig trees at the back of the yard and the other Negroes emerging from their hiding. Somebody was picking her up. She heard Maurice's voice. He spoke in gasps, as if out of breath from some effort.

"Dinah! How did you get out here? Why didn't you—lock yourself—in the house? Did that devil touch you? If he did—*Oh, God, Dinah!*"

20

THIS WAS A Maurice she had never seen before. His face was as pale as death and convulsed with fury. He had taken the pistol out of her hand and ordered her into the house.

"Take her along, Mauma. I'll attend to Coaxum."

As she turned, a squad of four policemen from the guardhouse came in the gate. Looking back, she saw Maurice speaking quickly with them. Then he and they fanned out and began to search yard, Quarters and other buildings.

In the kitchen Dinah was glad to drop on a chair and accept the ministrations of Mauma, Jody and Elvira. Not only were they devoted to the Bays and afraid of Coaxum, but the people of the Quarters were all related by marriage. He had beaten his twin daughters Lulie and Ann and nearly killed Mary Jane, daughter of Venus and Samba. The three in the kitchen loved Dinah and were alarmed, besides.

Jody turned to Mauma, her mother-in-law. "If my man Titus been in the yard, he'd a killed that yella nigger."

Elvira put in a word for her own husband. "Lummy done beat him up once. He say he goin' to cut Lummy throat."

The housemaid Clementine came in.

Dinah asked anxiously: "Clementine, did Coaxum hurt Lulie and Ann very badly?"

They were only seventeen years old and worked with their cousin Clementine. Dinah was fond of all three of them. She supervised their cleaning and, although she was particular, they found her always kind and just.

Clementine was in a state of wild excitement. "My ma say Coaxum been talkin' to a strange wite man last night. That-there buckra give him whisky and some little paper books. Coaxum been drinkin' that whisky and readin' them books all night. He tell my auntie Mary Jane he goin' to be free. He tell her he goin' to kill her and Ann and Lulie, all three, if they don't do like he say."

Mauma said violently: "You fool gal, why ain't you tell Mr.

Morry? Mr. Morry woulda shoot that buckra and save all this trouble."

"I ain't know nothin' 'bout it, last night, Maum Phibby. My auntie and her chillun scared so bad they 'fraid to talk. They think maybe Coaxum just shootin' off he mouth and he be all right when he sleep off that whisky. But he wait till the yard men go off and he bust loose worse than ever. He grab my ma too, but she git loose from him and run in the house and out through the front door, and run to where Mr. Morry is on the wharf. She say Mr. Morry holler to her to go tell the patteroll, and he start runnin' for here faster than a horse."

Dinah had ceased trembling. "Has the guard caught Coaxum?"

"No. They find the carpenter ladder up against the wall. He done climb over and git way through Mr. Alston garden."

Mauma spoke ominously. "Coaxum aint git way. The patteroll goin' to ketch him. And they goin' to hang him."

"I hopes they hang him," said Clementine. "I goin' to ax Miss Clelia to lemme go see when they does hang him."

Dinah listened in horror. Mauma and Jody shook their heads. They were old enough to remember the insurrection of 1822. They had no sympathy for the carpenter; only fear of him and fear of what he might involve them in. But they could not help feeling the call of race in a crisis. The warm blood in their veins ran cold at thought of hanging.

Jody asked worriedly: "Clementine, how come Coaxum git this way? Did Mary Jane tell you what make him ack so?"

"My auntie say them little books that wite trash give Coaxum say he must rise and kill the witefolks. He tell my auntie to rise with him, but she tell him no. He say she got to rise, 'cause she his wife and she b'long to him. He say he goin' to beat her brains out with a log of firewood if she don't."

Clementine paused and looked admiringly at Dinah. "My grumma tell my auntie Miss Dinah save she life."

Dinah tried to suck her finger. The trigger had caught and cut it to the bone. The taste of the blood nauseated her, and bright drops still oozed onto her dress. Jody saw and lumbered around behind the stove.

"I lets the spiders build they house back here where Miss Clelia can't see." She came forward with a filthy mess of cobwebs in which were caught dirt and dead insects. "I know this-here the only thing will stop the bleed."

She was just about to apply it to Dinah's open wound when Maurice banged through the door from the yard. He pushed the hair out of his eyes. "For heaven's sake, Jody, are you trying to give Miss Dinah blood poisoning?"

He took her hand and examined the wound. "How did you hurt it?"

"Twas only your pistol that pinched me. Tis of no matter," she assured him.

"It's a deep cut. Did you, by any chance, shoot yourself?"

He had his ideas about guns in the hands of women. He looked at it and felt it so anxiously that his own fingers were as bloody as hers. "I can see it's a cut, but it's deep." He took her arm, thereby staining the sleeve as well as the skirt of the new green dress. "Mauma, come on and help me wash it and tie it up."

"Boy," said Mauma, "what you know 'bout them kinda thing? You best let Jody stop the bleed with spiderweb like she goin' to."

He hesitated. He had run three blocks prepared to face and, if necessary, kill a crazed man. But he had never lost his sense of inferiority before Mauma. Besides, everybody he knew put cobwebs on bleeding wounds. It was no more than a personal fastidiousness that made him shrink from seeing them applied to Dinah's fingers. His Cousin Placidia often repeated the story of how a servant had ridden in a gallop from a nearby plantation to bring her a note. "I can find no cobwebs in my house, but I know that you always have them. Please send some quickly by Cedric, for the cat has clawed the baby." She liked to tell of it, taking pride in the fact that she furnished the cobwebs and appearing to see no slur on her housekeeping.

Fortunately for Dinah, Mrs. Bay walked in just then.

"What is the matter? I found the front door wide open and none of the maids around. Clementine, you should be attending to your business. Morry, why are you and Dinah here in the kitchen?"

Just then she caught sight of Dinah's hand. "Oh, my poor child! What has happened?"

Maurice said grimly, "Plenty has happened. Come upstairs and I'll tell you. Clementine, go and shut the front door and take charge of the house. Lulie and Ann are in no condition to come back to work today. I've sent Rex for Dr. Leger to attend to them and Mary Jane and Venus."

That afternoon and evening there were grim conferences in the Bay home. Upon hearing the story Mrs. Bay developed a migraine headache. Faint with pain, she could hardly sit up, but refused to retire until she had heard Old Uncle's advice.

"I feel that it's a disgrace, although I see nothing we did to deserve it."

"You needn't feel that way, Mother. It isn't our fault."

"I know. But I've always said—and thought—that bad owners made bad slaves. The poor creatures are dependent on us, body and brain and soul."

"Coaxum is not to be pitied. He's a fiend. He would have killed his wife if Dinah hadn't stopped him. Not that I approve of her doing it." He frowned so angrily at her that her eyes smarted and her heart raced. "If anything ever happens in the Quarters again, *stay in the house and lock all the doors.* I order you to. Do you hear me?"

She had to blink to get rid of the tears, but she answered him clearly. "Coaxum was killing Mary Jane. I could not leave him to do it. And—" it was hard to say the words, because he was being unfair to her—"and I would do—would do the same thing again. I will not lie to you."

He looked at her. And then he smiled for the first time since he had dashed through the gate, wild with fear for what he might find. "You shouldn't have done it. But, by Jove, you've got more courage than I thought! I would have expected it of Mel. Never of you."

Mrs. Bay went back to her theme. "It was all started by some low, vicious white man. The Abolitionists, in some way, are getting their pamphlets around."

"I know," said Maurice. "If we catch him, we'll hang him along with Coaxum."

But that comforted neither of them. They both knew that the white man who was evil enough to instigate the Negro to crime, always had planned his way of escape and left the Negro to bear the blame.

The wretched carpenter had been caught almost immediately.

He was not of the stuff of Denmark Vesey. He howled for mercy, said he had been drunk, and gave all information he could about the agent who had furnished him with drink and literature. A charge of insurrection from Maurcie, backed by evidence from Dinah and reliable Negroes, would, he knew, send him straight to the gallows.

Immediately after dinner Lieutenant McRae brought Colonel Bond'Ion over on the government boat.

"I just came in to ask what I could do, Morry. I know this is both family and Charleston; and I'm a Yankee."

Maurice said: "Please stay, Robin. I have a feeling that all trouble could be avoided if decent Northerners and decent Southerners would get together and thresh it out."

A number of Charleston men had come in, for the news had spread by now. They were not bloodthirsty, but Coaxum had a bad name. He had several times talked insurrection to their servants. Now he had committed the act.

Mrs. Bay said: "I want you all to know that my husband offered Coaxum his freedom when we came to live in Charleston. We had bought him, at his own request, when he married Mary Jane. Samba was then our carpenter and, in the city, we had no need of another."

Old Uncle said: "I remember perfectly, Clelia. Now, suppose you go and lie down and leave this matter to men."

She could hardly speak. "But—Old Uncle—I can't bear to have him hanged. Maurice senior offered to give both him and Mary Jane their freedom. We don't need sixteen servants. But she wouldn't leave her parents and Coaxum wouldn't leave her."

Mr. Colleton said: "Mrs. Bay, your husband did all that he could, and more than was necessary. A man like Coaxum endangers the whole community. I don't see how your son can do less than bring against him a charge of insurrection."

Mrs. Bay began to weep quietly. "Couldn't we force him now to take his freedom? I mean just turn him out and order him to leave Charleston."

Old Uncle boomed: "Clelia, go to bed! Set that devil free to stir up other Negroes to butcher us and, themselves, be hanged? I thought you had a grain of sense! Take her to bed at once, Dinah!"

Maurice and Lieutenant McRae helped them to the bedroom. When they left, Dinah took off Mrs. Bay's shoes, let down the dark hair and bathed the throbbing head. Except for the dozen low-voiced men in the drawing room, the house was ominously still. The house servants had gone out to the Quarters to commiserate with Mary Jane and Venus.

Out there, Samba said softly: "I gwine conjure he."

Venus wailed: "Oh, Lawd! Oh, Lawd! Miss Clelia tell you to be Christian."

Samba moved his clawlike hands deftly along the arms of his chair. His eyeballs rolled yellow and his blue lips moved. "This aint no time to be Christian."

Clementine told him practically and hopefully: "You aint got no need to conjure him, grumpa. You just waste your conjure if you do. The wite folks gwine hang him."

Samba's thick eyelids drooped. Years of blindness had taught him patience. He could wait.

In the big house Mrs. Bay sat up suddenly in her bed. "Dinah, I have an idea!"

"Yes, ma'am?" said Dinah.

She picked up the damp handkerchief which had fallen at the movement, poured more camphor on it, and touched the aching temples.

"We can send Coaxum to Belle Isle. My brother's slaves are devoted. He could never stir them up. My brother not only has a good overseer, but he rides his own ricefield banks and superintends it all. He is a widower. There are no women in the house."

Dinah could not help wondering whether the rice planter would be grateful for such a gift. But she only repeated "Yes, ma'am," softly, and went on applying the camphor.

Mrs. Bay swung her narrow, stockinged feet over the side of the bed and tried to stand. She turned pale green and fell back on the pillows.

"I—I'm too sick to walk. Dinah, you must go. Tell Old Uncle that I know Du Gué will take Coaxum. Tell Morry the whole thing has made me ill, and I'll be worse if the man has to be hanged. Tell him I know his Uncle Gay can manage Coaxum and make him behave."

Dinah knocked timidly at the door, and Maurice called sharply: "Who is it? Come in!"

All the men rose as she entered; all except Old Uncle. She went to stand in front of him, and he did not smile at her as she delivered Mrs. Bay's message. Then she turned and told Maurice exactly what his mother had said. He looked sternly at her, but in his heart he was glad of some alternative. When she finished he thanked her and took her arm and led her to the door.

"Tell Mother we'll consider it.

But, before he put her out, she turned on him with brimming eyes. "I beg you, Mr. Morry. I beg you, along with your mother, not to hang the poor creature. Tis a fearful death."

He gave her a pat, and then a push, and closed the door behind her. All the men were looking at him, but he spoke to the colonel. "Well, Old Uncle, what do you say about that?"

Colonel Bond'Ion frowned as he thought. "Du Gué could manage him. He treats his slaves well, but he stands for no nonsense. At Belle Isle Coaxum would work under Madison Monroe Jones. He's the head carpenter; a black giant who works hard and makes his assistants work."

He looked around the room. "What do you think, gentlemen?"

They were beginning to cool down. If they could get rid of the Negro without taking his life. . . .

Mr. Colleton was first to speak. "I think we should consider Mrs. Bay's wishes in the matter."

Maurice said: "There was practically nothing for him to do here in the yard. Idleness always makes for trouble. I know Uncle Gay's slaves. They work and they'll make a newcomer work. Busy Negroes don't stand for loafers among them."

There was more talk about it, for it was a matter that concerned the city as well as the Bay household. Agreement was finally reached and the colonel turned to Maurice.

"The decision lies in your hands. You are the man of the house."

"Coaxum goes to Belle Isle," Maurice answered quickly.

21

COAXUM'S DEPARTURE for the Winyah Bay plantation left the family and other servants in peace. Mary Jane was recovering, although seriously hurt. Venus and Ann and Lulie had been only bruised and frightened. Clementine thought wistfully of the hanging she had missed. The menservants who had been absent agreed that they would kill the carpenter if he ever came back in the yard. Samba kept his own council; but they heard more often his drum talking softly in the night.

Dinah tried to forget. It had been a bad experience. By common consent she and Mrs. Bay and Maurice never spoke of it. Mauma was charged to keep it from Dorothea. She was growing fast, and was busy with school and dancing school. Sometimes Maurice borrowed White Cockerel and took her riding on Buck. But the weeks between Christmas and Lent were gay and he was taken up with parties and balls, suppers of the Jockey Club and Light Dragoons, and with paying attentions of every kind to Mel.

It seemed to Dinah that Mrs. Bay had as many social engagements as her son. She often took the girl to informal gatherings and to pay visits at homes of cousins and especial friends. Beryl Porcher Winthrop's baby had arrived and, to Dinah's joy, she was asked to come and see it. She had the pleasure of holding it, dressed in one of the dainty gowns she had made, while Mrs. Winthrop and Mrs. Porcher thanked her and complimented her work.

It was upon this occasion that she first met Mr. Twigg. When she and Mrs. Bay came downstairs, Mr. Winthrop was talking with a gentleman in the hall. His dress was impeccable, but Dinah's observant eyes at once detected the subtle difference between his dandified elegance and the careless ease of his host. He bowed to the ladies far lower than young Campbell Winthrop bowed. Then, as he straightened, his narrow gaze crawled slowly from Dinah's skirt up to her face. His eyes were small and close-set, and he never opened them wide.

The man was speaking to Mrs. Bay. "This is a rare pleasure. I have not seen you for months. May I escort you home?"

"I thank you, Mr. Twigg, but there is no necessity for that. Miss Corley and I are together. Our coachman will care for us."

Winthrop had taken the older woman's arm. Twigg put his hand under Dinah's elbow. As she stood by the carriage while the other man drew the robe over Mrs. Bay's knees, Dinah felt Mr. Twigg's fingers moving along her arm. When he leaned to whisper she smelled brandy on his breath.

"Where has Bay been hiding you away from the rest of us?"

She was too sensible to tell anyone about it. But she was glad there had been several thicknesses of clothing between his hand and her arm. She had a feeling that his fingers would be slimy. He was, so far, the only person she had met in Charleston whom she really disliked. She had no idea that Mel Manchester hated her.

But on a winter afternoon that happened to be the child's birthday, she and Dorry were together in the drawing room. Dorry's gifts, stripped of their gay wrappings, were on a table, but Dorry had abandoned them for her beloved music box. The lilt of "Young Marlborough" was drifting on the air when the door opened and they saw Maurice with Mel on his arm. She wore a tight green velvet basque over a long green silk skirt with small hoops. Over each ear was a white camellia, making her black hair look more black.

Out of the small, green velvet muff that swung from her left wrist, she was now drawing a little box. She smiled at Dorothea. "Many happy returns of the day!"

Dorothea seized and opened it. "Oh, Miss Mel, thank you!"

It was a miniature silver button hook, meant to button skin-tight kid gloves upon tortured wrists. Mel said: "You'll need it before long, even if you don't just now. And, since you're twelve years old, why don't you call me 'Mel'?"

Dorothea smiled back at her, pleased. "I'd like to. I call Dinah 'Dinah.'"

For the first time, Mel looked at the Aran girl. She smiled slowly, amusedly, contemptuously.

"I wasn't exactly inviting comparison with Dinah." Her eyes flicked the other girl like the lash of a whip. "After all, there is a difference, Dorry."

Maurice saw Dinah shrink as if a whiplash had touched her. He saw the color flaming in Mel's cheeks. He knew her temper, her jealousy, her intolerance of rivalry. But he also knew she was in his blood. He could not keep away from her. She had humbled herself to him and apologized about Howard. Without telling him so in words, she had made him feel that the blame was his because she had flirted with Howard only to dare him. For the first time she had let him take her in his arms. Holding her, warm and slim and sweet while his heart pounded in his ears, he had persuaded himself that she was really repentant. Startled and shocked, he watched her now as she tried to recover herself. He was honestly ignorant of her dislike for Dinah. His own worst fault was arrogance; but he had no conceit. He could not but realize that the speech had been insulting; but he still tried to think its insult accidental and not malicious. Before his normally quick wits could find something helpful to say, Dorothea continued innocently, "I know it's different," she agreed; "because Dinah is so much younger than you."

Mel's flushed cheeks went pale with anger. Out of that velvety pallor her eyes looked undisguised hate at the other girl who had not yet spoken.

"Dinah is more like Lulie and Ann," said Dorothea, interested in the subject. "They are seventeen and a half and she is just eighteen. If they were six months older, they would all three be twins."

Mel laughed aloud, but it was not pretty laughter. Maurice put a hand on her arm, but she pulled away. Her voice was still low, but it seemed to cut like a knife.

"That is what I meant, Dorothea. Dinah is like Lulie and Ann. But I am not. And I do not care to be compared either to Lulie and Ann or to Dinah."

"Mel!" exclaimed Maurice.

He tried again to catch her arm. She evaded him. He saw, as he turned, that Dinah had moved away from Dorry and toward them. She faced Camellia, her face white and her gray eyes stricken. But, although her lips quivered, he saw her lift her chin. "'Tis small chance," she said, "that anyone would compare you to Ann or Lulie. Their faces are black but their hearts are not, while with you tis the opposite."

Her voice failed there; but she choked and went on, with more hurt than anger in it.

"They have given me kindness and courtesy since I came to this land as a stranger—which—which is different from what you gave, though I have done nowt to wrong you."

Then she brushed softly but quickly by them both, and the cream-colored dress that he knew so well disappeared through the door.

Amazement was struggling with anger upon Mel's face.

"Morry," she gasped. "Morry, did you hear what that girl said to me?"

"I heard," he told her between his teeth, "and I think you deserved every word of it."

"You think I deserve to be insulted by a servant in your house? By an Irish immigrant? Are you crazy, Morry?"

Her voice was rising now. He stepped close and gripped her arm hard. "Behave yourself, Mel! Dinah isn't a servant. You had no right to speak to her as you did."

"I know how to deal with underlings. I'm accustomed to being the mistress. She isn't a fit person to be in charge of Dorry."

The carriage was waiting for them. In silence he helped her in. "Drive slowly, Hilton," he said as he stepped in beside her.

But she had drawn herself away and into the farther corner. When he reached for her hand she jerked it from him. "Hold hands with your little Irish tart," she whispered viciously.

"Mel," he asked, "have you lost your mind? Dinah is no such thing. Besides, that isn't a word that ladies use."

"What do you know about ladies, with your backstairs flirtations? Anyone can see she's after you. She's trying to be compromised."

He caught her shoulder roughly. "Stop it! I won't listen."

"Oh, yes, you will!" she said.

He gestured toward Hilton's back. "Haven't you enough self respect to refrain before servants?"

She threw herself, again, to the other side of the carriage seat. The horses' hoofs clopped on the cobblestones and the metal tires rolled harshly. By the time they stopped at her door the winter darkness had fallen. The butler let them in. Hoping to escape further quarrel, Maurice spoke.

"No, Craven; I'm not staying. No need to take my hat."

Mel said curtly: "Craven, you may go."

The old man withdrew. Maurice looked at her, frowning.

"So you still want to have it out?"

She laughed softly. "Oh, you fool! You fool—I love you so! Can't you see that nothing matters to me except you? Can't you see that it drives me mad if another woman looks at you?"

She came so close to him that he felt the hard hoops in her skirt against his knees. Her face was tender and softly flushed and upraised to his. The flame in her black eyes was not anger.

But he tried once more. "You were abominable, Mel!"

She laughed again, and raised her arms. He felt them go around his neck. "I know—but I'm sorry now. So we'll forget it, Morry."

He tried to frown, but her face was too close. He could not even keep his jaw set when her lips were touching it softly. "How can I forget it?" he asked. But his arms were closing around her.

"You can forget it. You can forget everything in the world except me. You can tell me that nothing matters except me, Morry."

She felt his arms tighten and heard him give a quick breath, half-cry, half-groan. "Nothing matters, Mel, in all the world except you!"

22

RACE WEEK began on the first Wednesday in February. The city thought and spoke of nothing else: "Would anyone this year challenge Colonel Hampton for the Tattersall Whip?" "Who would win the Citizens Purse of a thousand dollars?" "How many states were represented by the horses which had already arrived at the stables adjoining the Washington Course?"

Dorothea begged Maurice to tell her about the dinner which always took place on the first day. He described it all to them. The Stewards, who were gourmets, would see that the table was laden with every delicacy. Then, when they had finished eating and the long board had been cleared, sudden stillness would fall upon the guests. Mr. James Rose, President of the South Carolina Jockey

Club (oldest in the United States of America) would rise and start the song of the club: "The High-Mettled Racer."

"I want to hear it," begged Dorry. "Please, Morry, sing it for me!"

"Not all of it. It's too thundering long. I'll sing you the first verse."

So, with Dorry on one side of him and Dinah close on the other, he sang in his pleasant, untrained tenor:

"See the Course thronged with gazers! the sports are begun:
The confusion but hear! 'I'll bet you, sir—' 'Done!—Done!'
Ten thousand strange clamors resound far and near;
Lords, hawkers and jockeys assail the tired ear.
While with neck like a rainbow, erecting his crest,
Pampered, prancing and pleased, his nose touching his breast,
Scarcely snuffing the air, he's so proud and elate,
The high-mettled racer starts first for the plate."

"But you should hear them shout it," he said. "Everybody joins in."

"Do they sing it at the ball, too, Morry?"

"Oh, no, not at the ball. The Jockey Club Ball on Friday evening of Race Week is the most important occasion of the year."

"Are you going to escort Mel? Did she tell you what color dress she was going to wear?"

"Stop bothering your brother now," her mother ordered her. "He has been very patient with your demands. He doesn't know what Mel will wear, because young ladies do not discuss their clothes with young gentlemen."

He not only knew what Mel would wear, he had seen and touched the dress. She had sent her maid Hester to bring it downstairs. Then, because Hester, holding it up as high as she could but being herself shorter than Mel, let its hem touch the floor, she had slapped the girl's face.

He had taken the flame-red, diaphanous thing, drop-shouldered and foaming with ruffles, from the little Negress. "Go back upstairs, Hester."

As she went and he turned on Camellia, he felt the vein in his temple throbbing with short, hard jumps. "No lady strikes a slave, Mel."

"Are you daring to tell me I'm not a lady?" she blazed.

"Now does any decent man or woman strike a slave, Mel."

She loved to quarrel with him, to see how far she could go. "You look as if you'd like to strike me now."

"Just at the moment there's nothing I would enjoy more. And let me tell you this." He turned and threw the gown from Paris violently on a chair. "Before you decide to marry me. If, as my wife, you ever do what you did just now, I'll take a riding whip to you!"

He told his mother and sister and Dinah nothing of that; nor of Mel's sudden surrender as she threw herself in his arms. He left them in the drawing room and rode up to the racecourse where members of the Farm Committee were assigning stalls to visiting owners.

By Wednesday all stalls at the farm were assigned and all hotels in the city filled. The Convention of the Episcopal Church in South Carolina chose that week of the year to meet in Charleston. Hundreds of other racing enthusiasts came from far and near. As Hilton drove them north on Rutledge Avenue that morning, the crowd moving with them increased, and the dust grew thicker. Buggies, tandems, curricles, gigs and dogcarts mingled with the carriages, or dashed ahead. Wagonettes from various hostelries drove slowly with their loads. Old men rode sedately, alone or in pairs. Young men galloped in groups, calling to each other. Besides the favorites of the day, which they were discussing, Dinah heard names of the great horses of the Carolina Turf: Young Brutus, Flag-a-Truce, Shadow, Sentinel, Noble, Babraham, Skim, and Borrock Billy.

By the time the Bay carriage reached the entrance to the Washington Racecourse, a procession of vehicles stretched for miles behind it. Hilton, holding north and right of the fence, drew up in front of an arcade. Two of the officers helped Mrs. Bay and Dinah from the carriage. They ascended a stair and found themselves in a large saloon with rooms for refreshment and for retiring at its either end. Looking south were large windows cut from floor to ceiling and giving entrance to a balcony of several hundred graduated seats. Gentlemen of the Jockey Club greeted them and escorted them to chairs overlooking the Starting Post.

The balcony was rapidly filling with women. Men moved

among them. Wade Hampton, Vice President of the Jockey Club, came up to pay his respects to Mrs. Bay and was introduced to Dinah. Maurice and Rawlins Bull appeared.

"Are you comfortable, Mother? Have you picked a winner, Dinah?"

Rawlins Bull said: "Miss Corley, will you honor me by a bet on the race for the Jockey Club Purse?"

She opened her mouth to tell him that she knew nothing of horses, and could not afford to pay her debt if she lost. But Mrs. Bay's hand on her arm checked the words.

"Of course she will, Rawlins. Which horse is going to win it?"

Bull grinned, but he said seriously: "I would advise her to pick Mr. Fenwick's black colt."

Mrs. Bay smiled at Dinah. "If Rawlins recommends it, it is sure to come first."

To Dinah's practical mind, the procedure seemed peculiar. She asked: "But which beast will you bet on then, if you give me the one you think best, Mr. Bull?"

"I'll take young Hampton's gray. Maurice shall be our referee. Now watch the track carefully, Miss Dinah. It may be my gray will nose you out."

They went downstairs to rejoin the men, and Dinah looked her question at Mrs. Bay.

"No lady pays any forfeit at this track, Dinah. If the horse you bet on comes in first, Rawlins will send you either a pair of gloves or a box of bonbons. It is sure to come first. I've heard Maurice speak of it. But if by any accident, Rawlins' choice should win, that would be the end of the matter. Young men neither expect nor wish to win from young ladies. They offer to bet to make the race more exciting, and because they wish to give a girl a small present." She added: "But no gentleman, needless to say, dares send a lady anything more personal than a pair of gloves."

The bugles were sounding for start of the first heat. Dinah gazed down on the track, a sandy, one-mile oval with its length east to west, and thought of the wild, crosscountry leaping on Aran. But she was more interested in the crowd milling below her than she was in the actual running. The Judges' Stand was just west of them. Its occupants stirred with importance and several individuals swept the track with opera glasses. In the fields beyond,

booths had been erected. Hawkers were crying sweetmeats, pro-
grams, fruit and souvenirs. Between track and paddock grooms led
horses wearing hoods and body-clothes. Along the fenced arena
across from the Ladies' Stand, carriages minus their horses were
drawn up three or four deep, and filled with men and women who
could not find seats in the stands. Numbers of young men watched
from their saddles. Others ran to and fro between Starting Post
and weighing shed, placing last-minute bets or giving a last look at
entries in which they had an interest. Blankets were being unbuckled, girths and surcingles checked; jockeys flung up into
saddle. The horses were coming to the Post.

Below Dinah, the brilliant colors seemed to weave and then un-
tangle: scarlet and green and purple and gold and pink and silver
and black. A second ago they had been bunched. Now they spread
far out along the track. Mr. Fenwick's black had taken the lead
from the start and was holding it.

When he came in well ahead, Dinah was as delighted as if she
had picked him herself upon her own judgment. She was smiling
with happiness as she looked up and saw Mr. Twigg bowing before her.

"I spied you from my saddle on the field," he told Mrs. Bay.
"So I dismounted and hurried to thank you for honoring us with
your presence."

Mrs. Bay inclined her head, wondering at the use of the pro-
noun *us*. She knew that Mr. Twigg was one of those rather
pathetic persons who go through life clinging to its fringes. He
rode well and spent his money freely; he had managed to join a
first-class Militia company; but neither the Saint Cecilia Society
nor the South Carolina Jockey Club had seen fit to admit him. He
had killed an elderly man in a duel in Savannah, and he was said
to be the best pistol shot in Charleston.

He said: "Let us bet, Miss Corley, on the Hutchinson Stakes.
You take the favorite, of course. I'll risk Mr. Singleton's bay
mare."

Dinah answered: "I have just now won a wager from Mr. Bull.
Tis enough, I think, for the one day."

Mrs. Bay's eyes were approving her.

Twigg laughed. "That sounds like a boast, and I cannot let it
pass. You may not win from me with the ease that you did from

Mr. Bull. I'm willing to risk my judgment for—let us see—" He was caressing his small moustache as he spoke. "Shall we say something to wear on a pretty little hand?"

She knew her hands were not pretty, and empty flattery did not please her. She tried to reply, but he talked her down. "The bet is made! I must go to my horse. The bugles make him restless."

Mrs. Bay told Maurice about it later, before he went to the Jockey Club Dinner. He said disgustedly: "Odds changed from the favorite to Singleton's mare a half hour before the start. Twigg must have heard that on the field. He knew it when he asked Dinah to bet."

"It doesn't matter," she said. "I am glad that he won, because that makes an end of the affair. Had Dinah won, he would have had an excuse to bring her gloves."

Dinah did not go on Thursday. When Dorry came home from school, she and the child dined together and then took a walk along White Point with Mauma in attendance. Off the wharf at the foot of King Street rocked the three-masted *Lodebar*. Dorry pointed a finger from the turn of High Battery, for Mauma refused to go any farther. "Middy is going to ask Captain Aimar to take you and me and Mother over his school ship someday."

But today Dorothea must go back to study her French and her history. Dinah, after setting her to work, took yellow sewing silk, thimble and needle and scissors down to the drawing room. She had observed a small rip in the brocade of one of the chairs, and she knew she could mend it as well as any upholsterer could. She had finished the self-appointed task and risen, sewing basket in hand, when the door to the hall opened and she heard the butler's voice. "If you will walk in and wait, sir, I will call Miss Dinah."

Mr. Twigg entered. As he saw her he smiled. She saw his white teeth, as he did so, gleam under his moustache; and she saw his eyes gleam between narrowed lids.

Erasmus, having seen her too, shut the door and departed. Mr. Twigg came forward with long steps. He took her hand, bowed over it, and did not let it go.

"My lucky star must be in the sky! To find you . . . and to find you alone. . . ."

She tried to pull her hand away, but he was too strong for her. He was taking something from a pocket with his left hand and pushing it on the tip of the middle finger of her right hand. "Something pretty to wear on a pretty hand," he was repeating.

She stared at the small gold thimble. The one she owned was of horn. But she did not wish anything from him. "Mr. Twigg, you won the wager. You have no need to be paying me."

"No need perhaps; but desire—yes! Since you mention my winning the wager, I will settle accounts for a kiss."

"No, you will not," said a voice from the door.

Dinah, still struggling to get away, looked and saw Rawlins Bull. Tall and cadaverous, he advanced purposefully.

"One can easily see, Mr. Twigg, why you do not belong to the Jockey Club. One of our unwritten rules is that no lady pays a debt."

Mr. Twigg had released Dinah. He stood as tall as Rawlins Bull and he stood straight, with his head high. But Rawlins Bull ignored him. He said: "Miss Dinah, I came to pay the wager I lost on the Jockey Club Purse. Will you accept this pair of gloves, with my congratulations upon picking the winner?"

She took the box from him. "But twas you who told me how to bet. I have never been able to tell one of the beasts from the other."

He smiled crookedly at Twigg. He had heard that story from Maurice. "It is not my habit to take advantage of the Ladies' Stand by trading on information which gets first to the field."

Twigg said furiously: "I could call you out for that!"

But Maurice had come in behind Bull. "One small correction, sir," he said. "If you call anyone out, it should be not my cousin but me. It is I who stand in the position of this lady's protector."

Rawlins Bull looked at him and checked the words on his tongue. He saw that Morry had something up his sleeve.

Twigg stared from one to the other, enraged, but slightly baffled. These damned fellows worked together like a pair of trained bird dogs. Bull had insulted him by insinuating that his bet with Dinah was not fair. But Bay had twisted the matter around until it now sounded as if he, Twigg, was insulting a woman and she had to be protected from him. It would do him no good in Charleston to fight on that side of the question. He knew that both Bay and Bull looked down on him. But he also knew that he could shoot either one of them through the heart or the head before he cocked finger on trigger. Why did they have to make a fuss about a little immigrant? She was fair prey for any man who wanted to buy a gold thimble.

She burst into tears and held it out to him. He took it. Bay said sternly: "Dinah, go up to your room!"

She went. Twigg put the thimble back in his pocket. It had been a good try. He was sorry he had failed. He would not have dared to give her jewelry. There were cases where a thimble of silver or gold could have been given and accepted. But he was not the kind to give it or she the kind to accept. It was a great impertinence, and he knew it.

Bay was saying: "Do you care to explain and apologize, sir?"

He smiled in amusement. They thought they could shoot; but his skill was professional. "And if I do not, sir?"

"You will, in that case I suppose, follow usual procedure."

Twigg smiled thinly. "Do I understand that you wish me to challenge you instead of Mr. Bull?"

"You understand correctly, Mr. Twigg."

He enjoyed his advantage and wished to prolong its pleasure. "I did not realize you attached such importance to a servant girl."

"She is my little sister's companion and the friend of my family. Anyone who calls her a servant is a liar."

As he spoke he recalled with horror that Mel had called her that. The memory made him angrier and he vented his fury on Twigg. He could punish Twigg, although he had not punished Mel.

Twigg was saying: "You seem determined to make me challenge you, Mr. Bay."

"It is a matter of complete indifference to me, Mr. Twigg. But I advise you to remember the advantage you give me by doing so."

Twigg's eyes went even narrower. "You mean—"

"I mean that the man challenged has choice of weapons and that I should choose swords."

Twigg remembered belatedly that Maurice Bay had served his apprenticeship in the *Mensuren* at Heidelberg, and he saw too late where he had been maneuvered. He had heard of the student duels and that they slashed for the face.

Maurice said: "While no *beau sabreur,* I am a *Bursch* of the *Verbindung.* Knowing your reputation as a duelist, I should stipulate no masks and sharpened swords. That would, at least, keep it from being too tame for you. One can easily lose an eye or take a swordpoint in the throat."

"This is unprecedented," said the other man furiously. "The Code of Honor says that no honorable man chooses a weapon which puts his opponent at disadvantage."

"I know the Code as well as you do," Maurice told him scornfully. "I am choosing this method to show my contempt for it; and for you."

Twigg's fingers fumbled with the thimble in his pocket. When you knew you could shoot before the other man cocked his pistol, it was easy to sustain a reputation as a duelist. He could be brave about pistols; but—a swordpoint in eye or throat. . . .

"You are overhasty," he said. "I have not yet challenged you. I ask you, Mr. Bay, to convey my apology to the lady."

23

As summer—known to Charlestonians as the "sickly season"— approached, the Bay family planned to spend it on Sullivan's Island. At Moultrieville, below the fort, was a comfortable hotel. It took the combined efforts of Morry, Hilton, Titus and Lummy to get the four women and Dorothea's pug puppy across the harbor ferry and into it.

Old Uncle's house was nearby and his carriage was at their disposal. Every afternoon they drove above the little village to the northeast end of the low, sandy barrier. Beyond the fort were low sand dunes with sea pinks, yellow buttercups, clumps of Spanish bayonet and lower-growing yucca. The myrtle, which grew there in scattered clumps, became a forest farther on. Carriage roads and bridle paths wound in and out among it, over its soft, brown, fallen leaves which silenced horses' hoofs. But it grew higher than carriage top or head of a mounted man. The sun distilled its spicy scent and the birds swayed on its slender twigs, and billions of small black mosquitoes rose from it at the smell of blood.

Sometimes the colonel went with them, but when he did there was room only for one grown person and Dorry. The grown person sat by the coachman, and Old Uncle, taking up all of the back seat, held Dorry on his knee. But he made these rides delightful by the stories he told. He told them how Captain Florence O' Sullivan, the Irishman for whom the island was named, had been authorized when the colony was young to keep a cannon at the mouth of Lord Ashley's river. Whenever he saw a sail about to enter harbor, he fired this cannon from the beach to warn the city. As he spoke Dinah could picture the excitement along the old sea wall, which followed Cooper River south from Craven's Bastion to Granville Bastion. Soldiers would have been kneeling behind its low curtain, training small cannon on the ship until sure that it was friendly.

He told them, too, of square-sailed craft which had slipped into Breach Inlet, captained by men with names like Richard Worley and Steed Bonnet. Across that same strip of treacherous water the British had tried to advance from Long Island and had been repulsed by Colonel Thompson's Battery. Dinah covered her eyes with a hand as she saw those scarlet tunics picked off by the Continental sharpshooters and struggling more and more weakly in the roiling current. Colonel Bond'Ion saw the gesture.

"What is the matter, child? Is the sun too hot for you?"

"Tis not, sir," she said. "Twas but that I thought of John Croft, to whom I am promised. He serves in the same British army and they wear the same red coat."

"You're a faithful little thing," he said. "We will not fight England again." His merry face sobered. "I fear, if war comes, it will come from nearer home. You are more apt to see Morry under fire in Charleston Harbor than to see your sweetheart's red jacket in that situation."

She twisted around from where she sat in front by the coachman, and faced him. "God between Morry and harm!" she cried; "for that would be even worse."

He looked back at her sharply as he balanced Dorothea on a knee. He had grown to love her like a niece and had told her to call him "Old Uncle." They were passing a ramshackle, ghostly-

looking house, and he changed the subject by pointing it out to
them.

"A young man named Edgar Poe wrote a story about it. It's a
very unpleasant story and he was a queer young man. I saw him
more than once while he was a soldier at Fort Moultrie."

Dinah had seen a book of his poems which was passed around
at the hotel. The ladies read it aloud as they rocked on the piazza,
and she listened, sensing its music but not understanding it. She
preferred stories and verse that dealt with young love or quiet
domestic bliss.

But, while her days were quiet, Maurice's were not. As soon as
he returned from work on an afternoon ferry, he was in demand
for horseback rides on the beach or through the myrtles; or for
maroons and picnics on other beaches. On dance afternoons he
escorted Mel back from the city with him, and she spent the night
at the Moultrie House under Mrs. Bay's chaperonage. It had long
been a custom of Charleston equestrians to take themselves and
their horses across on the ferry boats for an afternoon ride on
Sullivan's Island. But there was now no need for Mel to bring her
horse. Maurice was keeping both Buck and the Irish mare at the
hotel stables. He was trying to trade his cousin Rawlins out of her,
and had taken her for the summer while Rawlins was in England.

As he dismounted late one afternoon he saw Dinah and Dorry
coming up the path from the beach. He walked to meet them.

"Where have you been?"

"Hunting for shells," said Dorry. "Afternoons that we don't go
to ride in the carriage, Dinah and I walk on the beach and fill
our basket with shells."

His heart smote him. Dorry was a child, but Dinah was a young
lady. He looked at her with remorseful eyes. "Do you mean to tell
me that all you do for diversion here is to gather shells with
Dorry?"

"Ah, no," she said, and the surprise on her face was genuine. "I
talk with Dorry and read to her, and we play games with the
others. We have fine rides with Old Uncle and walks on the beach
as well."

It was as varied as any life that she had ever known; but to him
it sounded dreary, and he felt he had been selfish. With his usual
point-to-point tactics, he set about remedying it.

"It's midsummer, and you haven't yet been on a picnic!"

"I haven't either," said his sister pointedly.

"Well, I'm going to see that you both go in future. We're sailing to Morris Island on Saturday, and tomorrow I'm rowing around to Shem Creek."

He told his mother at supper. She asked: "Why are you going? There's nothing at Shem Creek except the old shipyard."

"That's why. I want to talk with Mr. Mullen about a boat. We'll row across the cove and around Mount Pleasant bluff."

"Oh, Morry! Take two girls in a rowboat out on the harbor? You'll frighten Dinah to death."

He smiled at Dinah across the table for four. It was not often he had meals alone with them. He was popular.

"I have an idea that Dinah isn't as timid as you think. I believe she has something as tough as her island stone underneath her pretty face and her gentle ways."

The compliment pleased and confused her so that she sat tongue-tied and flushed rose-red. He continued to tease her.

"Would you be afraid to trust yourself to me and a rowboat I built myself?"

She shook her head slowly. "I would not. I have seen the boat down at the cove. Tis well built; and broad enough of beam, without being broad to clumsiness."

He clapped a hand to his head in consternation. "Was there ever a bigger fool than I? To ask a daughter of Aran if she was afraid of a boat!"

She smiled. "Tis many a hide I have helped to cure for the currach frames. And I mind one night so wild that I feared we would not make shore with the currach. I have rowed them since I was a child. I can help you if you weary."

"Horrors, no!" said Mrs. Bay. "It would ruin a young girl's hands."

Maurice was laughing. "I won't weary between here and Shem Creek."

But as he settled her and Dorry in the rowboat next day, rolled his sleeves high on his thin, strong arms and pushed off from the wharf, he was thinking.

Dorry sat on the thwart amidship and Dinah astern. He ducked his head as he stroked, and grinned at her. "I shan't forget your offer, rowing or not. A girl who will help if you weary is a good one to have around."

She smiled at his nonsense and dabbled a hand in the water alongside. The live oaks leaned from the high shore which he hugged to avoid currents. It was pleasant to have them along, and they were giving no trouble. Dinah seemed as happy as Dorry was. The parasols upon which his mother had insisted were lying, still furled, across her lap. He could not help contrasting it with the progress of Mel and Suzette. Either one of those belles, if they had condescended to go in a rowboat, would have taken for granted a parasol and a beau in attendance to hold it.

They swung into Shem Creek with the tide and his rowboat leapt under every stroke. He drove it up on the soft mud bank close by the oyster shell path.

"Step lively now! I'm holding the boat, and I can't let go to help you ashore."

They needed no help. They jumped nimbly ashore. He stepped out and dragged the boat higher. Walking single file, they followed him up the narrow white walkway between feathery tamarisks.

The boat sheds looked down on the channel. Small wooden wharves jutted below them. Mr. Mullen was superintending the launching of a whale boat, but he ceased operations to hail Morry heartily. He was a short man, immensely broad, and his figure was highlighted by the three-quarter length, culotte-like trousers and the horizontally striped shirt in which he worked. His stocking cap took Dinah back across the world to the Cockle Strand. He was coming toward them on large, flat, bare feet.

"Tis yourself, Mr. Morry! I looked for you the week ago today."

They shook hands hard. They were old friends, and their love of boats drew them closer.

"I was detained," said Morry, "by important business."

Dorothea saw fit to explain. "Mel came that afternoon, Mr. Mullen. She is Morry's sweetheart, and she is very pretty."

Mr. Mullen took his pipe from his teeth and removed the stocking cap. "She is that, begorra," he agreed, and bowed politely to Dinah.

Dorothea laughed aloud at the joke. Dinah blushed, then joined in the laughter. But Maurice did not. He was embarrassed and was provoked with his sister.

"Dinah," he said formally, "this is my friend Mr. Mullen. Mr. Mullen, Miss Corley is a guest in our home. She came to Charleston last autumn from the Aran Isles."

Mr. Mullen was highly pleased. "A hundred thousand welcomes! Have I not been to the islands and taken the greeting meself? If twas of Galway that you were, I would say I had known your Da. A dour devil named Corley farmed there when I was but a boyeen."

"Twas me father, I think," said Dinah. She recognized the portrait but bore Mr. Mullen no rancor at all.

Dorothea, feeling that she had launched the conversation, decided to give it impetus and to take part in it.

"Dinah's sweetheart is a soldier. He's lost, but we're going to find him. He's an English soldier and wears a lovely red coat."

"Begorra," said Mr. Mullen, "if tis a red coat he wears, the best place in all the world for him to be is to be lost."

He turned back to Dinah gallantly. "As for yourself, me colleen, the sweetheart for ye to have is a lad like Mr. Morry. He has been building the boats with me since he was more small than his sister there. Many is the time I have offered to give him a shipwright's job."

Like Dorothea he laughed heartily at his own joke. But Maurice again refused to join in. He spoke abruptly.

"Where is the sailboat? Did you locate the trouble?"

"I did," said Mr. Mullen. "Twas nowt but a matter of balance. If ye will be building a boat like a fish with the bow heavier than the stern . . ."

Still talking, he turned toward the dock, and Maurice followed him.

"Let's pick gaillardias," suggested Dorothea. "Mama likes to have them in a low dish on the table, and Morry loves them. I heard him tell Mel last week that he loved them because they were the color of the dress she wore."

Dinah looked down at the orange-red, daisylike blossoms around their feet. She remembered Mel in the sultry silk of that dancing dress the last weekend. She began to gather the flowers. By the time the men came back, she and Dorry had enough to decorate the whole dining room. But Maurice had evidently forgotten his love for the color.

"Quit picking those weeds and come on," he said. "The sun is almost down."

He shooed them toward the path and turned back to Mr. Mullen.

"I'll get Robin McRae to run me across in the government launch, so I can sail her back to the Southern wharf."

Mr. Mullen helped them push off, and Morry leapt in at the last second. It was a hard pull to the creek's mouth, for tide was still running in. As they rounded the mainland and reached the cove, he shipped his oars and drifted. He stared west at the huge, smoky half-circle of the sunset.

"That haze could mean a storm on the way. Have you seen a hurricane, Dinah?"

She shook her head. "I have not, and I have no wish to be seeing one. I got me fill of black winds when I lived on Aranmore."

He blinked from the glare. "They're different winds, but they all make up at sea."

He threw back his head and began to sing. He always wanted to sing when at sea. He rowed slowly, for the current was taking them into the cove now. Dinah and Dorry joined in and their words blew on before them.

> Where the scattered waters rave,
> And the winds their revels keep.

Waiting impatiently at the wharf, McRae and Sedgwick Lewis heard. As they leaned down and caught the boat's bow, the latter addressed his cousin.

"I wish you were like the wind and kept your revels on schedule! Had you forgotten that I was to bring Mel and Suzette for the weekend?"

"Oh, Lord," said Maurice. "Is today Friday?"

"It's Friday," McRae told him.

"It's more like Doomsday for you," said Sedgwick Lewis.

"What did Mel do? Did you tell her I had an important appointment about a boat?"

"We told her that, but she's mad anyway," said his cousin candidly. "She's been locked up in her room ever since we got here and found you gone."

"What's worse," said McRae gloomily, "Suzette's with her and won't come out with me."

But Maurice was listening to nobody else's troubles. With one leap he was up on the wharf. As he ran along it he shouted back: "Tie the boat up and bring the girls! I haven't time to stop for that."

The four of them followed him slowly, discussing the misadventure. Dinah was troubled and Sedgwick Lewis amused. Dorothea's interest was keen, but she was more interested in the fact that her nose and cheekbones began to prickle. McRae was unhappy because events had involved his courtship of Suzette. He had lost a long summer afternoon while she stayed closeted with her sulky friend.

"Mel's a vixen," said Sedgwick Lewis. "If I were Morry I wouldn't give in to her." He took Dinah's arm and looked down in her eyes as he helped her up the steps. "There are too many pretty girls in this very pleasant world for a man to bother his head too much about any one."

"Get along with ye," said Dinah, glad for the relief of laughter. "If you were Mr. Morry, you would love her and do as he does."

Mrs. Bay, in genuine distress, met them in the lower hall. "Hurry and dress for supper, girls. You're late, and Mel's upset."

Dorothea clasped the newel post. "Mama, I don't want any supper. My face burns like fire. I want to go to bed!"

"Sunburn!" exclaimed Mrs. Bay, as if she were saying "leprosy." "I suppose you forgot the parasols. You'll both be a sight by morning. Go on to Mauma! I'll find a maid and get soda and lemon."

Dinah delivered Dorry, now weeping with pain, to Mauma. Then she took the gaillardias and ran down the back stairs. Her fair skin, accustomed to Irish mists, was smarting; but that was a small price to pay for escaping supper with Mel. She made the Bay table bright with the beach flowers, and then carried the sunburn cures upstairs. Dorry was safe in bed, under a mask of wet soda, and she was putting it on her own face when she heard a knock at the door.

She opened it and faced Sedgwick Lewis. "Swing low, sweet chariot!" he exclaimed. "Does it hurt as bad as it looks?"

"Ah, no," she said; "it but stings a bit." She smiled, and the plaster around her mouth cracked. Then she asked anxiously: "Is it well with Mr. Morry?"

"On the contrary. My poor cousin is regarded by all the old tabbies here as a cross between Bluebeard and Torquemado. News has spread that he abandoned the girl who has a claim on him, in order to take you and Dorry out in a boat and maliciously fry your tender hides in the summer sun."

"Oh, may God help him!" cried Dinah. "Twas not his fault in the least. Tis your place to be denying such lies, and you a man of his own blood. You must tell them he went entirely for the sake of seeing a bowt."

He grinned in delight. "I'll do it, me darlin'. But—did he?"

"He did," she said in all seriousness. "Twas that and that only which made him forget."

The supper bell began to ring. Room doors opened and guests came out. Sedgwick Lewis leaned closer to whisper.

"If it was a boat made him forget Mel, all I can tell you, Dinah, is that you're the sweetest and trimmest craft I ever saw in this harbor. And Morry's a blind blundering fool if he doesn't see it too!"

24

NONE OF THEM ever knew what Morry said to Mel. It must have been satisfactory, for she appeared next day with her beauty unimpaired by bad temper or late dancing. She let bygones be bygones and only laughed at Dorry and Dinah, who were red of nose but still undaunted in spirit.

"I'm glad it's stopped hurting," said Mrs. Bay. "But you really look utterly dreadful. Morry, I don't think they should go on the water this afternoon."

Dorry gave a wail of protest and her brother upheld her.

Mrs. Crawford, who chaperoned them, gathered Dorry and Dinah, Mel, Suzette and four other girls from the hotel into the wagonette. At the wharf Morry and Sedgwick Lewis, with four of the younger lieutenants from Fort Moultrie, awaited them. Dinah and Dorry had no escorts and were not at all disturbed by the lack. They sat in the stern with their chaperone and enjoyed every moment. The big sailboat moved out through the cove and around Sullivan's Island. On the hotel piazza handkerchiefs waved, and they waved back in delight. Lieutenant McRae had managed to get Suzette to one side. Except for Morry who skippered them, and Lieutenant Brook who acted as crew, the rest had clustered around Camellia. She sat on a cushion, looking more vivid for white dress and sunshade, and kept an eye on Morry while she laughed and talked. She knew nothing about the boat and saw no reason why he couldn't put down the rope he held and come and sit by her. It seemed to her he was staying in the stern to be near Dinah. She saw him pointing out the forts and other harbor marks to her and Dorry and Mrs. Crawford.

Upon Morris Island beach, in the long shadow of the lighthouse, they built a fire of driftwood in spite of summer heat. Dinah was in her element unpacking the picnic baskets. She and Mrs. Crawford spread and weighted a cloth. They heaped plates with cold chicken and spiced beef, with salad and pickles and muffins. Dorry was running up and down, hunting for starfish and sea biscuits. The others were strolling in couples on the beach or through the dunes.

After supper they sat around the driftwood fire and sang and talked. It flicked long, varicolored tongues from the minerals it devoured. At dusk a great shaft of light shot out from the lantern room far above their heads. Watching it, Dinah stood again on the deck of the cattle boat and heard Seth Kincannon's voice as he told her about it.

Because of the driftwood's heat, they had drawn back and widened their circle. She and Dorry were on one side, Maurice and Camellia directly across. Presently he got up and strolled down the beach. Dinah was too far away to hear him say he was going to make sure the incoming tide would not reach their rowboat. She could not know that Camellia was displeased because he had not asked her to stroll with him. She did not hear Lila Lou Blake whisper teasingly: "He's the best-looking thing I ever saw, Mel; but he's got a roving eye. Is he in love with you or with the pretty colleen from Ireland?"

The first thing she heard was Mel's voice. It called clearly across the circle. "Dinah, does this remind you of the night you arrived in the steerage? My aunt had an Irish cook who came on an immigrant ship."

Dorry, lying with her head in Dinah's lap, sat up. She saw no offense in the words, but she sensed their undercurrent. Nor was Dinah offended. She came back from her memories.

"I was thinking of it this moment," she answered easily. "'Twas sad and lonesome I was that night, without a friend. But, thanks to Mr. Morry, it is different with me now."

She was not trying to provoke the other girl. She had made up her mind to try not to quarrel, for Morry's sake. But she could have chosen no other words more calculated to inflame Mel. She heard Lila Lou chuckle softly. She saw Lieutenant Chapman smiling.

"Morry has always been soft-hearted," she said. "At times he can be soft-headed too."

Sedgwick Lewis raised his head, like a turtle's, from the sand where he lay.

"What do you mean by that, Mel? Didn't all Americans, except the more objectionable of the king's henchmen, arrive in America as immigrants?"

"Mine didn't come on a cattle boat, and they didn't travel steerage. I mean that Morry was risking some dirty disease when he went near anybody who had lived in such filth."

Mrs. Crawford was on her feet. She had no intention of letting matters go further. "It's time to repack the hampers and leave now. Sedgwick Lewis, will you throw sand on the fire?"

He rose to do as she asked, but he could not resist drawling: "Maybe you're jealous, Miss Camellia Belle Manchester."

There was a moment of silence. The four visiting girls watched avidly. Mrs. Crawford seemed to be stricken dumb. The four officers looked as miserable as men look when forced to witness women's quarrels.

Mel asked with deadly quietness: "Jealous of what, Sedgwick Lewis?"

"Oh," he answered carelessly, "jealous because you've never made an ocean voyage; not even in steerage."

Mrs. Crawford caught sight of Maurice in silhouette as he came up the beach. "Hurry!" she called. "We must sail, skipper! I promised your mother to see that you brought Dorry home by ten."

Dorry was puzzled and sleepy. She held tight to Dinah's hand as they followed the others down to the water's edge. She wondered why Dinah suggested sitting in the bow, because that put them the whole boat length from Morry.

It was the last of their picnics. The storm season was approaching. Maurice awoke one night to feel the island suspended in stillness. He could not go back to sleep, and before day he heard the wind rising on a far-off, whining key.

At breakfast he asked: "Mother, do you wish to go back to the city?"

"Oh, no," begged Dorry. "You promised that we would stay here until my school started."

Mrs. Bay looked from her daughter to her son. "It may be no more than a gale. Even if we have a real storm, this house is sturdily built. Why don't you take the horses back to Charleston this morning, and find out what Dr. Chalmers thinks about the weather?"

Maurice rose. "I'll do that. If he predicts a hurricane, I'll come back on the next boat and get you."

He took the horses with him on that early ferry. As it rode free of the cove he saw that the harbor's citron was tinged with deeper yellow and laced by whitecaps. The boat lurched with the ground swell and, when a wave broke over her deck, the Irish mare trembled and whinnied softly. He stayed beside her and kept a hand on her neck. Buck stood without holding, as steady as a rock. But his eyes were alert, and he raised his head and sniffed the air at intervals.

Back at the Moultrie House a spatter of rain had begun. Guests from inland were getting nervous. A boatload of them departed as soon as the ferry returned. In every pause of the wind, those who remained tried to reassure each other by saying that the squall was over. But coast dwellers knew the threat of those death-still, waiting pauses.

Colonel Bond'Ion came before noon. He got out of his carriage and thumped up the walk with his stick, while his coachman drove away.

Mrs. Bay hurried to meet him. "I'm so glad you've come, Old Uncle! I wish I had taken the girls to the city as Morry suggested."

"The island's as safe as the city. Where's Morry?"

"He went on the first ferry, and took the horses. I hoped for him on the last boat. I'm sure he'll come on the next."

He did not tell her that the ferry had made its last trip. He had information from the fort, brought in by the beach patrols. Also, he had talked with Lieutenant McRae, who had just come in on the government launch and who said that no boat could now cross the harbor. He knew that tropical storms struck with varying degrees of speed. This one seemed to have taken them unawares. His butler had told him at breakfast that the hurricane was close because the seabirds had been flying inland all night. The Negroes had ways of forecasting weather. Over in Charleston Dr. Lionel Chalmers had a private observatory and put his knowledge at the service of fellow citizens. The commanding officer of Fort Moultrie had sent Lieutenant McRae across to check with him.

The colonel tried to speak cheerfully. "Cash is taking my horses to the regimental stables. They are on higher ground than mine and more strongly constructed. The officer in command always extends that courtesy. Don't look so worried, Clelia! If the storm is severe, the soldiers will come and carry civilians to the fort."

"I'm worried about Morry crossing on that low, flat ferry!"

"Perhaps he'll have sense enough to stay in Charleston," the colonel suggested. But he knew as well as she did that Morry would cross.

Dorothea rushed into the room, followed more slowly by Dinah. "A sailboat is trying to get in the cove, but it's being blown out to sea!"

"'Tis small as a birdwing," said Dinah. "It tilts like a wing in the wind." Her voice was troubled. "We were watching it, but the rain squall has hidden it now."

"Who can it be?" said Mrs. Bay. "Who would put out in such weather?"

"It's some fisherman caught on his way in," lied Old Uncle.

Dinah shook her head. She had grown up with small boats, and she remembered the one she had seen in Shem Creek. "'Tis not the shape of a fishing bowt. Tis even smaller, but different."

Mrs. Bay put a hand to her throat. "Morry was experimenting!"

Old Uncle caught her shoulder. "Clelia, you can do nothing! Besides, you don't even know whether or not it is Morry."

"I know it's Morry! He would come back! If the ferry had stopped he'd sail his own boat!"

She outdistanced Dinah and Dorry as she ran up the stairway. Old Uncle came last, with his cane loud on the treads. The group at the south-hall window made room for them. The rain was blowing like smoke across toward Morris Island. It lifted a moment to let them see, halfway between Castle Pinckney and the entrance to the cove, a small sailboat lifting and falling with the tremendous swell. They saw it lean perilously and scud southeast. Then a towering wave hid it completely.

Dinah saw Lieutenant McRae pushing through the group. He said: "Mrs. Bay, Dr. Chalmers told me this morning that his observations show these cyclones blow counterclockwise. The wind is now driving Morry out to sea. But its next turn will put wind and tide at his favor."

Dinah's heart hammered in her throat, but nobody noticed her. McRae was trying to comfort Morry's mother. He was answering the question that her eyes asked him. "There's no way to get help to him. Brook and I wanted to take a surfboat out, but the commandant forbade it. Frankly, I do not think we could even have launched it."

The rain squall still hid the harbor. They could not tell whether or not the sailboat had capsized. Mrs. Bay was shaking as if in a chill.

Old Uncle said: "Clelia, the boy swims like a fish. Even if the boat turns over, it won't go down."

"Nobody could swim in that sea," she said between chattering teeth.

There came a diversion just then with a tearing and thundering noise. Lower ground around the hotel was several feet deep in tidewater. Under their eyes an immense wave lifted a small house from its piling. It swung sideways, as if trying to feel for its place on the butts. But it found no support and its floors gave way. Walls caved and the roof toppled. It collapsed like a building of cards. A second wave lifted the wreckage and, as if with intent, drove its timbers like battering rams through the front of the house just behind it.

Dinah put both arms around Mrs. Bay's slender waist. She could not voice her feelings but could hold Morry's mother close.

She had seen storms on Aran, but had thought this a gentler land. Nor had she realized before that anybody in it could cause the agony clawing at her heart.

Soldiers and civilians were now out in crews. Dorry—not realizing what the others did—watched them, roped together, wading from house to house and taking women and children to safety in the fort. But the four grown people had eyes only for the boiling harbor.

The squall of rain veered and blew to one side, like a gray mosquito net blowing. At first they saw nothing. Then the boat rose on the crest of a forty-foot wave. For a second it was there . . . then it disappeared in the trough. . . .

Dorry was saying something. At first they did not listen. "Look, Dinah! The oleanders have turned a different way."

They looked, and saw the big bushes still flattened by the wind. At the ends of stems and trunks, bunches of draggled, rose-pink blossoms lashed torn petals against the water.

Dorry said: "I mean they were lying down before, but their heads were pointing a different way."

Lieutenant McRae yelled: "You're right! The wind's gone round to the southeast!"

As he went plunging down the stairs he shouted: "I'll get a crew to the cove!"

The red-hot band around Dinah's chest snapped and released her at his words. She had had to watch in silence while Maurice fought for his life. She knew that he did not belong to her. He belonged to his mother and Mel. Only his danger had betrayed her secret; and only to her. She was cold with another terror as she realized that the pain of this hour had an even keener edge than her slow grief for John Croft.

She felt Mrs. Bay go limp in her arms and clasped her tighter. "Old Uncle, help me!"

Together they got her into her room and on her bed. Old Uncle and Dorry only got in the way, but under Dinah's treatment she soon opened her eyes. When Robin McRae brought Maurice in, they found Dinah kneeling beside her and bathing her face with eau de cologne. She sat up and held out her arms; and Dinah moved aside.

She watched the other woman holding him close. Salt water

was running down the blue army overcoat which McRae had put on him. He released himself and stood up.

"We were watching the boat." Mrs. Bay's voice broke, and Dinah envied her the luxury of open grief. She was going on. "Are you hurt, Morry?"

"Not in the least, thanks to Robin. But I'm wet as a wharf rat."

McRae joked to relieve tension. "He's a poor skipper, Mrs. Bay. He claims he isn't hurt, but the boom cracked him in the head."

Dinah started for the medicine chest. It traveled everywhere with them. Her heart was lifting. She could at least do this small service for him.

But he backed away like a nervous horse and demanded: "Will it burn?"

"It will," she said calmly. She had herself now in hand. "Put your head down so I can reach it and wash the cut."

He danced from foot to foot and said a few "ouches" as she dressed it. When she had finished she held out a hand. "Give me that wet coat now, and get yourself into dry clothes."

He backed even farther away.

McRae explained. "He took off his pants before he swam from the boat."

"I didn't dare bring her close to the wharf. Robin had some soldiers there and they threw me a rope from one side. He climbed on that slippery dolphin and threw me one from the other."

Mrs. Bay said: "Lieutenant McRae, I can never repay you!"

"Oh, yes you can," he corrected her. "You can tell Miss Suzette that, in your opinion, I'd make her a good husband. Tell her I'll hang around the house and be at her beck and call. I'll give up soldiering. It never suited me. *And* I'll never try to cross harbors in tropical hurricanes."

Morry grinned back at him sheepishly as he clasped the long coat around him. His wet hair looked lank and black above his strained face. He mumbled: "I thought I had time to cross and get back before the storm broke."

Colonel Bond'Ion chuckled.

"My private ambition has always been to compile an anthology of famous last words. If I ever do, I won't fail to include your contribution, Morry."

25

CHARLESTON'S autumn was a long Indian summer. Dinah remembered it from twelve months before. Even the oleanders had wearied of blooming, and the white and lilac spikenard was shedding its fingery leaves. Rex worked with late flowers in the garden on East Battery: pale physostegia and jewel-colored asters, and scarlet salvia whose seed was imported from Italy. Japanese chrysanthemums were beginning to bud. Tea olive and opoponax burst out after every rain. All over the city cassia swayed its clustered golden bells.

Dinah remembered it all from twelve months before. But this was a different autumn and she faced a different problem. The other one had been simple. She could then only wait and hope. Now she asked herself if she had the right to keep on living in Maurice Bay's home.

It was characteristic of her that she dared to face the thought and did not try to pretend it had been a midsummer madness. I love him, she told herself; but he does not love me. He loves a girl of his own kind, who has beauty and charm and high spirit. She lives the life he has always lived and she does the things he likes to do. All that he has done for me has been from the kindness of his heart. He must never know that I feel for him in any way save as he feels for me.

She reminded herself, as she picked the fall flowers for Mrs. Bay, that he had done nothing to make her think he cared. He was kind to his mother and Dorry in the way he was kind to her. He had kissed her under the mistletoe, as any other man would have done. Looking back, she told herself honestly that her reaction to it had been due to the fact that it was Morry's kiss. She and Dorry had been daring Sedgwick Lewis to kiss them. Had it been he, or any other man, she would have laughed instead of taking it seriously.

She had two alternatives: to break away completely, or to stay in the Bay house and hide her secret in her heart. The former would be difficult and Maurice would oppose it. The latter would force her both to see him pay court to Mel and to endure his brotherly attitude toward herself. But if she could not endure both those things, she told herself, she had no right to stay. He had said she was tough as Aran rock, and she remembered it now. She told herself that she would stay, waiting for the man who had her word, and losing herself in the varied interests of the household.

One of these matters at once came up in regard to Dorothea. Hilton had discovered, during the vacation months, that she had failed in the last term on arithmetic. Upon the first morning of school, when she went out the front door, she saw the humbler Absolom seated on the carriage box.

"But, Lummy, you don't drive the carriage! You drive the wagon or do errands on horseback. Hilton is the coachman. Where is he?"

"Hilt right back there in the Quarters," Lummy told her. "But he say he aint gwine drive you no mo'. He send me."

Reinforced by Mauma, she rushed out into the yard. But Hilton was adamant.

"I shame to ride with you. I tell you last year I aint gwine drive no chile that miss she lessons."

She wept and pleaded; but neither her tears nor Mauma's scolding could budge him. Dinah was powerless. Mrs. Bay and Maurice refused to interfere. For six weeks Absolom drove her to and from Mrs. Heriot and Mrs. Ramsey's School for Young Ladies. Although he was kind and she had always cared for him, he was a constant reminder of her disgrace. Besides, other little girls asked embarrassing questions about the change of coachmen. She studied the hated arithmetic as she had never studied before. After six weeks she showed Hilton a passing report on all of her studies. Next morning he was at the door, and good-natured Absolom was back in the tackroom soaping saddles between naps.

"It's the best thing that could have happened," Maurice told his mother and Dinah. "When I tried to help her with fractions I thought she was half-witted. Nothing but the disgrace of Hilton refusing to drive her made her study hard enough to pass."

He was in his office on Adger's wharf when Mr. Kincannon came in. He was more sunburned than ever, and he wore a master's uniform.

Maurice jumped up and held out his hand. "Congratulations, Captain! Dinah will be pleased."

Kincannon turned the cap in his hand. He was not usually at a loss. Maurice drew out a chair. "Sit down. Have you seen Dinah?"

Seth Kincannon sat. He shook his head. "Not yet. I carried her letter and I have news for her." He looked sharply at the other man. "I'm afraid she will not be happy to hear this news, Mr. Bay."

Oh, Lord, thought Maurice. Is he going to ask me to tell her? His dread of women's tears returned. He wished none of them weeping on his breast. He supposed the soldier had forgotten Dinah and married another girl. If he had done so, he was a fool. Any man would be lucky to get her.

But Kincannon had neither intention nor desire to dodge a duty. He said: "It's a mixed-up story. Would you mind, Mr. Bay, listening to it first, then advising me how much of it to tell Miss Corley?"

Maurice drew his own chair closer. "You've been to Galway?"

"I was in Galway in August. We have now an auxiliary steam engine. I talked with Miss Mary Donovan. She is now Mrs. Tim O'Leary. But I found her and gave her Miss Corley's letter."

"What did she say?" asked Maurice. "Could she tell you about the soldier?"

Kincannon shook his head. "That regiment left Galway not long after Miss Corley sailed for America. There was trouble in India and, so far as the O'Learys know, Croft re-enlisted for foreign duty and went to the East with it."

Maurice gave an exclamation of anger. "The man must be a rascal! Why didn't he follow Dinah? He swore to her he would come for her, no matter where she was."

Kincannon was more moderate. "He may think she jilted him. The O'Learys never saw him again to tell him the truth of the matter. A tough lad by name of Larry O'Dell, who worked with Roddy Corley, was the only person I could find who talked with Croft before he left."

"Did O'Dell tell him how it happened?"

"No. He only made matters worse and gave Croft a false impression. He was under the influence when I talked with him, but he remembered seeing Corley's sister at the boat. He said he helped carry their luggage aboard, and the girl tried to fool him that she was not going and would meet him at Donovan's. He said, if he had not taken drink, he would have known all along that she was only trying to make a monkey of him. Her sister-in-law had her clothes there, and her brother told him that the three of them had a cabin for the States."

"Did he tell Croft that?"

"As well as I could make out, he did. That and even more."

Maurice swore.

"Why didn't these O'Learys write? Dinah wrote Mary Donovan. It's pitiful to see the way she hopes for a letter, day after day."

"Mary Donovan O'Leary wrote, but she wrote to New York."

He disregarded Maurice's exclamation.

"She has a friend named Annie O'Rourke who married a man named Sullivan. This Sullivan has made several trips between Galway and New York and thinks he knows all about America. He told the O'Learys he'd never heard of a place in the States called Charleston. He said America's only ports were Boston and New York. When Mrs. O'Leary told him that Miss Corley's address was The Battery, he told her The Battery was in New York City. She listened to him and she wrote to The Battery, New York."

Maurice ran his fingers through his hair. Kincannon gripped his hat with both hands and looked him straight in the face. "I've done all I could. I went to the barracks and talked with officers there. Even if Croft can be located in the East—even if he still wants to marry her—he's back in the British army for a term of years."

"I know," said Maurice. "It sounds hopeless."

"What I came to ask you," Kincannon said, "was whether you think I'd be taking any advantage of her if I asked her to marry me."

The other man looked so startled that he added hastily: "After telling her, of course, exactly what I've just told you."

He had suspected a year ago that the man was sweet on Dinah. He remembered thinking then that it would be a good thing for her. It should be even better for her now, because John Croft was as good as lost. He saw all that clearly. But he saw, too, the East Battery house without Dinah. . . .

"I don't think so, Mr. Kincannon," he said truthfully. "You've done all you could to find this Englishman for her. It's not your fault that you failed to do so. You've a right to go in now and try your luck."

The sailor rose. "I'll do it. Thank you, Mr. Bay."

Maurice sat in a window and looked out over the harbor. He was too restless to settle back to the work he had been doing. The house was only three blocks away, so Kincannon must have reached it now. He happened to know Dinah was at home. She always sewed in the mornings so as to devote her afternoons to Dorry. Besides, she had mentioned that she was making a dress. She had all the orders she could fill, and had to refuse some clients. But she always had time to help him or his mother or Dorry. He looked down at the buttons on his coat cuff and smiled. She had said gravely the evening before: "If you'll leave me the coat you are wearing, I'll mend the split of its seam and tighten the buttons. They are near to falling off."

He had taken it off and laid it in her lap as he went to his room to put on his best for a small party given by Mel. As he passed the drawing-room door and called good-by, he had seen her sitting with bright head bent as she sewed and his mother read.

She would be mending Kincannon's coats in some bleak little village in Maine. The house would be different without her. His mother depended upon her. Dorry would start having nightmares again and dreaming that plat-eyes were after her. But, in spite of all that, Dinah had a right to her happiness.

He thought about it until time to go home to dinner at three o'clock. While he was helping the terrapin soup, his mother said: "Dinah has had bad news."

He put the silver ladle back in the tureen and motioned to Erasmus to take it away.

"Kincannon told me that he had failed to find Croft. I suppose that is what you mean."

"Yes. He came to see her and stayed nearly two hours. I went upstairs and found her crying afterward."

He was surprised at the way his heart thumped under the

buttons she had sewed tight. She would not have been crying if she had accepted Kincannon.

His mother was saying: "I have an idea that Mr. Kincannon addressed her. He came downstairs so fast that he did not even see me in the lower hall."

"He's a fine fellow," said Maurice. He could afford to be generous now, and he felt sympathy for the man from Maine. "Dinah deserves the very best when she decides to marry. But you and Dorry will miss her."

After dinner he went up to the bookroom where she sewed, and where she and Dorry had early dinner together. He found her pale and sad but still hard at work. "Dinah," he said, "I'm sorry. Kincannon told me about it."

"He did his best," she said. "My heart aches that I have hurt him. But—but I promised John Croft I would wait. And he said he would come for me."

He frowned; for he had not the slightest idea that John Croft even remembered her now. But, if he could be found, it would at least settle things one way or the other.

He said: "Dinah, Kincannon talked to the O'Learys and to military authorities in Galway. Can you think of anyone else who might know anything about Croft?"

She thought for a moment before she spoke. "There's only Father Sweeney. He's the Roman priest on Aranmore and John talked with him." She smiled wanly, trying to hold with both hands onto that past. "He told John that he would do well to marry me. I knew him as a good man and I know that he would help if he could."

"I'll write him myself," said Maurice. He looked down at her. "But, Dinah—"

She looked up at him with eyelids still red from weeping. She wondered if any other woman had sat so, while the man for whom her heart cried out planned with her to find the man to whom she was promised.

"Dinah," he was saying, "do you feel sure in your heart that, if he knows where to find you, John Croft will come to you?"

"I know he will come," she said quietly. "I will wait, no matter how long."

Maurice was thinking about it as he rode the mare to Lowndes

Grove. He was returning her, for Rawlins Bull had come home. Dinah had come down and patted her nose and told her good-by in the driveway. It had added to his reluctance to give her up. As he rode out he had called back: "Stop worrying now! I'll write the priest."

It seemed to him that she still grieved as keenly for the Englishman. At first he had sympathized and admired her for loyalty. Now a spark of resentment was mixed with those feelings. It was too faint to be analyzed. He directed it against Croft, and told himself that the man had forgotten and was not worthy.

Rawlins Bull greeted him with delight. "Thanks for keeping the mare in the pink." He walked around her, surveying her critically. "She's a nice bit of horseflesh; but after the riding I did in England this summer, I've decided she's too light for me. I'll keep her for guests, or sell her."

Maurice almost shouted: "Sell her to me. Right now! I'd give my eyeteeth for her, Rolly!"

Rawlins regarded his cousin with a horse trader's eye. "I'd have to have another hunter in her place. Roddy Corley is going home for a visit."

"If you tell him exactly what you want, I'll commission him to bring the horse back for you."

He remembered the tears in Dinah's eyes as she waved good-by through the gate. Perhaps the return of the mare would distract her mind from John Croft. He said: "I've promised Dorry a horse."

"Couldn't be better," said Rawlins. "Dorry's quite old enough now to ride and hunt. Besides, two always travel more quietly than one does."

"When is Roddy going? Can I take the mare back tonight?"

"Of course," said Rawlins. "I didn't know you liked her as much as all that. Let's go and talk with Corley now. There's a ship in harbor that he plans to take."

They walked down to the small cottage that looked out on the Ashley's marshes. Betsy let them in, and proceeded to dust with an apron two already spotless chairs.

The commission delighted Roddy's heart. He had found and talked with Kincannon. He looked forward to seeing Muldoon's horse farm more eagerly than he looked forward to seeing his father on Aran. Already he was planning to get a cut from Muldoon on the business. He followed them out and down the steps.

"I was wondering, Mr. Bay—" He paused and coughed. "The matter is that me wife is sick on the sea. She does not wish to be making the voyage, and I would make it better without her. But she is afraid to stay here by herself. It is I was thinking that Dinah—"

Maurice cut him short. "I'm quite sure that Dinah would not stay with her. You'll have to make other arrangements, or else take her along."

He forgot it as he galloped happily home on the mare. "She belongs to us now, Lummy," he said as he dismounted.

His mother and Dinah were up and he told them all about it. Dinah smiled until he saw the dimple he liked in her right cheek. "I will take her a bit of loaf sugar the first thing in the morning."

"And ruin her teeth," he said laughingly. He was pleased with all the world. He stood with his back to the fire screen and with both hands in his pockets. "What do you think Roddy asked me, of all things in the world? He wanted you to come and stay with Betsy while he was gone."

Dinah rose swiftly to her feet, with a kind of eager relief on her face. "It is the thing I should do," she said. "I will gladly go stay with Betsy."

It had given him the surprise of his life. "Stay with Betsy?" he had exclaimed. "The woman is a virago. You have been avoiding her. Have you forgotten what she did to you?"

"I have not forgotten," she said slowly. "But a whole year has gone by. It is that I feel differently now." She caught herself quickly. "I mean—I mean that time changes the look of things."

"*You* haven't changed," he said stubbornly. "You love Croft as much as ever. I can't see anything in the world to make you go stay with that woman."

There is everything in the world, she thought, to make me get away from you. Do not try to keep me here, watching your love for another girl!

But she only told him gently: "I think that I should do it."

He gave an exclamation of impatience. But, before he could speak again, his mother intervened.

"Dinah must do as she thinks right. It would be a change for her." She turned to the girl. "We'll miss you, my dear, more than I can tell you. Dorry and I will call and take you with us when we go out to drive."

Morry said crossly: "You women always stick together. But—" he brightened. "I'll see you too. I spend a lot of time at Lowndes Grove with Rolly."

Perhaps she could avoid those times. Perhaps seeing him there would not be as hard as the enforced intimacy of his home. But whether or not it was, she was determined to fight it out. Escape from his presence, and life such as Betsy lived it, would be the best two allies she could have asked. They would help her find her way back to the life which belonged to her and the man to whom she belonged.

26

RODDY SAILED ON Kincannon's ship only three days later. Since Dorry was bewailing Dinah's departure and begging to be with her until the last minute, mother and daughter planned to drive with her to Lowndes Grove that afternoon. Mrs. Bay had on hat and gloves when Lulie brought the message.

"Hilt say when he go to hitch up he fine Brandy done cas' a shoe."

"Oh, dear me! What is to be done? I heard Roddy tell Dinah that his wife would have a fit if she had to spend the night alone."

"Hilton say he kin drive Miss Dinah in the buggy with one horse."

"If the buggy holds together! Nobody has used it for years. Morry prefers either to walk or to ride horseback."

Soda, almost too broad for the shafts, was harnessed to the buggy, and Dinah's more immediate luggage was put in. She was coming downstairs in her new blue tippet and little blue hat when Morry walked in the door.

"I thought you were going earlier. You should always wear blue, Dinah."

The reason for delay was explained. He said: "I'll drive her there in the buggy, myself."

"Hilton is ready to carry me. Do not trouble yourself," she pleaded.

"No," he said. "Hilton should lead Brandy at once to the blacksmith. I'll enjoy driving the old buggy. I haven't been in it for years."

Mrs. Bay saw that Dinah was anxious, but thought it fear of Betsy's temper in case she were late.

"You have an engagement this evening, Morry. How can you take that long drive and get back in time to dress?"

"I'm having supper with Mel at eight. Then we go on to the Parkers' for music. I tell you what—"

He was running up the stairs and calling over his shoulders. "I'll put on my festive raiment now; then I'll go straight to Mel after I leave Dinah."

He will always go back to Mel, her brain was telling her heart. He will always be kind to me, for kindness is in his nature. But, when he does what he thinks he should, he will always go straight to Mel.

She sat in the hall, talking with Dorry and Mrs. Bay, until he ran down the stairs in his best coat and his flowered vest. The two women kissed her good-by, but he hurried the parting.

"Put that luggage box in front, Hilt. It's too big to get under the seat."

"Mr. Morry," said Titus.

But Morry was going on. "Hilt, get Brandy to the smith before the forge closes."

"Mr. Morry," said Titus severely, "you better watch out for this weel. This buggy been laid up long enough for dry rot to git in the spokes."

Maurice, standing by the right front wheel, seized and shook it with all his strength. "It'll hold up if it stands that. Neither Dinah nor I are big."

He vaulted over it and into the buggy beside her, tossed her half of the buggy robe and tightened his lines.

Soda looked around reproachfully before starting. He was not accustomed to going alone or to having his fat sides wedged between shafts. Also, it came to him as he took his first step that he was pulling an unsafe vehicle. But Morry trailed the whiplash over his back in signal, and although indignant he trotted smartly.

"I hope twill not cause you to be late for supper with Miss Mel," said Dinah.

He drew out his watch and frowned at it. "I hope not; but I can explain to her."

She did not agree with him about that, but she did not offer advice.

"And don't get it into your head that I'm driving you as a favor. I'm enjoying every minute of it."

He leaned to tuck the robe closer. Her heart leapt, in spite of her head. She whispered happily: "Are ye that?"

"I am, by Jove! I've not driven the old buggy for years. I'm enjoying it so much that I intend to have it repaired and painted. Then I can take Mel for drives in this beautiful weather."

She sat silent. They were turning west, above the Washington Racecourse. Bushes were high on either side of the narrow, sandy road. Their shadow made the dusk darker. The clean, winy smell of wild fox grapes was strong on the autumn air. Morry sniffed it.

"That smell takes me back to my boyhood, Dinah. It makes me hungry. And, by the way, you look good enough to eat. I like that funny little blue cape and those blue ribbons tied under your chin. You're like the smell of the fox grapes, kind of sweet and natural. You make a man think of things like autumn and fruit and home. You make me feel younger, too; as if I could do things I've always wanted to do but kept from doing because of silly ideas."

To illustrate he put his feet in his best boots up on the dashboard, sprawled back against the cushions and began to whistle "Dixie" as loud as he could.

It startled Soda who was plodding between ruts in a slow walk. Hilton had better manners than to whistle while he drove. Besides, the left shaft was rubbing his side sore. He lurched to right, jerking the cracked wheel out of its rut and against an old stump. There was a sharp sound of snapping wood. Simultaneously the metal tire sprang off, the spokes splintered with the weight and the right front axle dropped. Maurice, with both feet on the dash, had no way to brace himself. As the axle struck the ground, he was thrown violently from the toppling buggy. Rolling on the grassy edge of the road he felt a double impact, as Dinah and the luggage case pitched out on top of him.

He tried to get up and found his arms and head entangled in grapevines. Dinah was lying across his legs and, although small, she was plump. He achieved a sitting position and boosted her to her feet. The whole left side of his face throbbed from the metal-bound corner of the luggage box which had hit him under the eye. He saw his tall hat smashed under the buggy.

Soda, stopped short and waiting, turned his head and gave them a glance of disgust. To show his contempt, he reached out and took a mouthful of grape leaves. Both he and Maurice knew he would never have dared eat in harness while driven by Hilton or anyone else he respected.

The blue ribbons were still underneath Dinah's chin, but her hat had slipped back off her head and was hanging by them. She smoothed her rumpled, grass-stained dress and looked down at him. "Are you hurt then, Mr. Morry? The left side of your face is red and that eye is almost shut."

He was blinking it from pain and from the water that ran out of it. "That blamed box hit me! But I ought to be taking care of you." He rose with one quick movement. "That was a terrible fall and all due to my carelessness."

"I am no more than shook up, for I fell fairly upon you. Ah, the pity!" She had spied his hat. "It is spoiled forever, I fear."

"I'm sure it is," he said; "but it's the least of my troubles." He was busy unhooking traces and unbuckling straps. "We have a half mile to walk. I'll be late. And I look like the devil!"

He dropped the shafts, and Soda stepped forward as accustomed to do. Maurice tucked driving reins and traces through the saddle rings. He stooped and lifted the luggage box back into the buggy. Then he took Dinah's arm.

"Come on! The horse will follow us. I'll ask Rolly to send somebody to get your things. Let's hurry now; so I can clean up and get back to Mel."

He walked so fast that she stumbled more than once in the sand. But he kept a strong grip on her arm and both upheld her and pulled her along. She heard the horse's feet, soft but heavy, behind them. A belated cicada in a pine tree was making the air vibrate with his harsh song. It was completely dark except for a red streak over the river.

The carriage lanterns which always stood on the Bull gateposts were lighted. Between them Dinah saw Betsy's shawled head and frightened face.

"God be good to me! Is it yourself? Why would ye wait until nightfall? And I all alone with dogs screeching and savages creeping around me!"

Over in the kennels one of Rawlins' foxhounds was baying mournfully.

Maurice said: "Go with her, Dinah. I'll have your luggage sent for."

He left them and went walking fast toward the lights of the big house.

Betsy asked inquisitively: "What might be his hurry? And why did you come afoot?"

Before Dinah could answer her, Soda loomed huge in the dusk and strolled unconcernedly and slowly through the still open gate. Betsy darted to one side.

"Saint Patrick save us now! How did the beast get loose?"

"Don't be silly," said Dinah. "He was following us, and he knows his way to the stables."

She told of the accident. "My case struck Mor—Mr. Morry—in the eye, and I fell on top of him."

"God help him!" said Betsy. "And fat as ye are! Tis a wonder that he was not murdered."

Dinah, following her on the path by the light of the lantern she carried, made up her mind to endure frankness and more if necessary. But Betsy had learned from loneliness and was anxious to be friendly. She took a key from her pocket and opened the cottage door.

"I take no chance of finding a thief hid under me bed. See!" She waved a bony hand, proud of her house and housekeeping. "I owe ye thanks for coming. Ye have a room to yourself. But the door of it opens into me own, and we can keep it open."

Dinah went into the clean, small room and began to untie her bonnet strings. Betsy was being pleasanter than she had expected. Already environment was taking her back to reality, away from a man whom she must not love and who did not love her. She sighed and hoped that, in spite of his absent-mindedness and his zeal to get to Mel, he would remember to have her clothes brought to her.

Meanwhile Rawlins had taken his cousin upstairs and was administering aid in spite of his amusement. "What you need is a raw beefsteak. I'll send down to the springhouse and get you a chunk. We butchered a steer for the hounds today, and most of it's hanging there."

"Oh, no!" said Maurice, frantic, as he sloshed his face with cold water. "My shirt and waistcoat are dripping now, and I'll be late as it is. All I need is raw meat on my eye and bloodstains on my clothes to send Mel into hysterics."

"You couldn't send Mel into hysterics if you tried; that is, unless she wanted to have them for a reason. But, if you ask me—" he threw his long frame into an easy chair and grinned—"you're going to have a difficult time explaining how you got that way."

Maurice wheeled, with water from the wet towel running down his neck. "What do you mean? And what are you laughing about?"

Rawlins was choking now. He rolled from side to side of the chair. "It may be all circumstantial, but the evidence is against you. You start out driving a pretty girl but get here with—with vine leaves still in your hair and a cock-and-bull story about falling out of a buggy."

"Now just what do you mean by that? I was bringing Dinah to Betsy."

"I know you were. What I want to know is what you did to make her get out of the buggy and walk the rest of the way rather than ride with you."

Maurice dashed the wet towel away. His right eye glared, but his left was by now completely closed.

"I did nothing, you darned fool! I told you the wheel gave way. Dinah fell on me, but it wasn't her fault. The box—"

Rawlins, enjoying himself, broke in. "I wasn't blaming Dinah. I think all the more of a girl who defends herself and who can hit hard enough to give a man an eye like that!"

Then he sat up and stopped laughing, for Maurice was pale with anger. "What's the matter? Can't you take a joke?"

"Not that kind of a joke. And not about Dinah."

He was struggling into his coat. His cousin stood up. "Then I apologize. You know I didn't mean it. But, Morry, take my advice and don't go to Mel looking as you do. Spend the night here, and let me send Sinny to tell her your ankle is sprained so badly you can't put it to the floor." He waved a hand toward his desk. "You can write her that—and write Cousin Clelia the truth."

It was so arranged, and Dinah, unseen, saw him ride off the next morning. She went out later and talked with Hilton and Lummy, who had come in the wagon to bring her small trunk and to collect Soda and the remains of the buggy. By them she sent messages to Mrs. Bay and Dorry. But, for the two months of her stay, whenever Maurice rode in the gate she vanished into the cottage and stayed there until he left. Twice he came up on the piazza and called her name eagerly. It happened that both times Betsy was not there; so Dinah simply stayed in her room and kept quiet until she heard him go away.

Absence helped. In the cottage she felt herself back in Ireland. Betsy had made no friends, and her thoughts and her talk were of the past. They spoke of Roddy and of people they both knew whom he would be seeing. Neither of them mentioned John Croft's name, but Dinah deliberately tried to think of him. She tried to conjure him up by her side as she walked the path above the marsh, where big live oaks leaned down toward the water. She reminded herself of his gentleness, of his kindness and his common sense. She trusted him still and could give herself no loophole by doubt of his loyalty. She thought she had him beside her again when she heard footsteps behind her.

"Dinah! I've caught you at last. I've been several times to the cottage but never found you at home."

She was wearing the shawl from Inisheer and she turned, holding it around her.

"We'll sit on this oak-tree root," he said. He took her for granted, as usual, and was spreading his handkerchief for her. "You've been as elusive as a will-o'-the-wisp. I used to chase them when I was a child. At Middleburg, once, one led me out in the marsh and I nearly got drowned."

You chase them still, she told herself, and probably will as long as you live. But she said: "They are nowt but fox-fire, and they will lead you astray. They have been the death of many people in Ireland."

He laughed delightedly. "This is a good lesson for me. I, who have followed them all my life, still know nothing about them. You, who do not approve of them, can give me advice about them."

She looked out over the slow river. Flood tide held it in pause. I could give you advice, she thought; but I have not the right to give it. Between them stood a sturdy man in a red coat, waiting; and a woman who used her beauty to lure like a will-o'-the-wisp.

Maurice was teasing. "Well, tell me why I chase them? And tell me what I'll have to hold if I ever catch one?"

She did not smile. "You chase them because tis your nature. But, as long as you chase them, you will not see the things right under your nose. No man can catch them. But, if a man did, he would find their fire cold flame."

He saw her shiver under the shawl, and he stood up and pulled her to her feet. He did not speak again until they reached Betsy's cottage. Then he said: "Dinah, I think you've taught me something without meaning to. Thanks! And good-night. I'm glad you're coming home to us soon."

She watched him disappear into gray dusk and gray moss hanging. Man dear, how can I teach you? she asked herself honestly. So long as I let my heart follow you, I follow something that can never be mine.

Shivering from head to foot, she turned back into the house to warm herself with the real fire that burned on Betsy's hearth.

27

DINAH CAME BACK to the Bay house in a more peaceful frame of mind. Nine weeks with Betsy had given her time at least to calm her heart. She did not try to fool herself that she did not care for Maurice, but she told herself that common sense and pride could hold that feeling in check. John Croft had been her first love. It had been a quiet and tender love, and she had thought it the love of her life. But it had never shaken her like the wind of terror that shook her when she saw a boat battling a storm. She tried to tell herself that terror and friendship and sympathy were in part responsible for that intensity. She wondered if jealousy had hold on her. She had no right to be jealous. Mel had had a claim on him before she came on the scene. She had known from the first, and she still knew, that he loved the dark-haired, willful girl in spite of her dangerous faults.

Even if the miracle occurred and he turned to her instead, she had given her promise to another man. "No matter when or where," she had said, "I will be waiting for you, my John." She believed in her heart that he was faithful and might come any day. She knew in her heart that he relied as securely upon her word.

Maurice was restless, but he did not realize what was causing that restlessness and taking all the zest out of life. Nor did he realize that Mel was now doing in her subtle way all she could to lead him on and make secure his conquest. He was her chosen escort wherever she went, and he saw that other men envied him for it. On a wine-sweet winter morning he was riding home with her after an early fox hunt and a hunt breakfast at Lowndes Grove. Their horses' hoofs were soft on unpaved Coming Street, and along with them were Will Frost, Suzette Manigault and Lieutenant McRae, Brook and Chapman.

Lieutenant Brook said: "I saw such a piece of trick riding when I was in England! A girl took her hunter up the steps of a public building and down again. I counted the steps—there were eight. I've seen that kind of thing in a circus; but never another girl who could do it."

Mel turned her head and smiled her secret you-and-me smile at Maurice. She wanted to do something to fix his attention exclusively on her. She knew she could ride. She was willing to take any risk to draw him closer.

"Shall I show him he's wrong?" she asked. Her voice excluded the others.

His eyes followed her glance. They were just in front of Saint Paul's Church and its iron gates were open. Facing them and to right and left, eight stone steps led up to the portico.

His face lit and he said: "A box of segars, Brook, that a girl I know does it here and now!"

The riders reined up. Brook looked at the steps—then at Mel. She laughed back at him, young and lovely and daring. He thought Bay was a lucky chap. He said eagerly: "Taken!"

Will Frost cried out sharply: "No, Morry! Don't try it, Mel!"

"Don't be silly, Will," she said, and swung her horse toward the gate.

Frost looked Maurice Bay in the eyes. He said: "I can't stop her, but you can. I tell you to do it now!"

The officers had begun to applaud. Suzette cried: "Mel *can* do it!"

The black thoroughbred was at the south flight of steps. Mel touched him with her heel. He raised his head and pricked his ears as he saw what she asked of him. He lifted his right front hoof and in the sudden silence it clashed on the stone.

They held their breath. They saw, too late, that the thing was wrong and dangerous. Frost, keeping quiet for the girl's sake, bit his lip and nursed the urge to kill. He loved her, but he knew that he would never get her. This man—this man who was his friend—could have her if he whistled to her. She was risking her life to please this man, and he sat by and let her risk it.

It was now too late for Maurice to do anything but sit by and not startle Mel's horse. The black thoroughbred struck the stone of each step as he set his hoofs. He was afraid of his rider. Sometimes he wished to kill her. But he was strong and proud and swift, and anxious to finish a strange new task. His body was strained at the wrong angle and it threw the weight on his kidneys. The surcingle of the heavy side-saddle cut into his ribs. Finally he got both front feet on the portico and drew his hindquarters up after them.

Mel was thinking: the worst is to come. When he starts down, will he plunge, or fall? But I don't care! I'll show Morry! I'll show him that I can ride and dance and love as that Irish girl cannot. She is the reason why he is in no hurry to marry me. I'm enjoying life too much to be in any hurry myself. But I want him to suffer and urge and plead. I want to hold back and torment him.

Maurice heard Frost say between his teeth: "If that horse falls, I'll shoot you, Morry."

The officers from Fort Moultrie sat their mounts like statues.

They knew they were watching something remarkable, something they would not see again.

As the black horse crossed the portico, his shoes struck sparks from the level stone. He paused, bunched his feet under him, and descended the north flight.

Suzette shrieked: "He's done it! He's down! Oh, Mel, you were wonderful!"

The officers kept clapping and crying out compliments. In the confusion, Will Frost bowed to Mel and cantered off. Only Maurice saw that. When the others looked for him he was gone. They rode on down to Broad Street laughing and talking about it.

Maurice's misgivings were gone. He was so proud of Mel that he could not take his eyes off her. She saw it. That look would have made her try to ride up Saint Michael's steeple. Of all the gay cavalcade proceeding down Coming Street only Will Frost had the sense to foresee consequences. In a rage, he had ridden directly home and, of course, held his tongue about it. Nevertheless, the news reached the house on East Battery before Maurice did.

At Broad and Church Streets he and Mel turned east. To McRae's disgust his two brother officers continued on down Church Street with him and Suzette. As they neared the Manigault house Evelyn Albemarle saw them and ran out into her garden, which was just next door. She was picking jonquils close by the fence when her neighbor drew up with more beaux than she needed.

Evelyn was a hopelessly dumpy girl with a poor complexion and a plain face. But, beneath acne and extra flesh, she longed for what all other girls had. Had she had it she would not, perhaps, have been obliged to get it through gossip vicariously. Suzette had always been kind to her; Mel had been definitely unkind. But she disliked them both. As the riders stopped she waved her yellow jonquils coyly.

"Was it a ripping run?" she called, in what she hoped was hunt parlance.

The officers stood there in polite silence. But Suzette was Mel's best friend and admired Mel from her heart.

"Oh, Evelyn, you should have been with us! Mel looked perfectly stunning. And she did the most marvelous thing, didn't she, Lieutenant Brook?"

Brook agreed with her perfectly. "Miss Manchester rides like a Cossack."

Suzette told the story. To Evelyn, starved for thrills, it was strong drink. She had seen Cossacks only when she saw a circus in England. She thought of them as part of the act, like the clowns or the women in tights. She saw Mel in pink tights and spangles. She said: "It sounds like a circus."

Suzette agreed delightedly: "It was better than a circus."

McRae saw where the conversation was leading and suggested that it was time for them to get back to the fort. One of the Manigault stablemen took Suzette's horse. She went upstairs to take a nap and forget it all. Evelyn rushed back into her house, dropping her flowers, and hurried to tell her mother and younger sister the story.

Mrs. Albemarle, having no daughter attractive enough to be a magnet for trouble, was naturally outraged. She was just setting out for a meeting of a charity board. She told about Mel's feat there, without charity, and Mrs. Bay was present.

As soon as her mother left Evelyn dispatched fourteen-year-old Marjorie, who was a schoolmate and friend of Dorothea Bay. A common wall at the back divided the two properties. Both Dorothea and Marjorie had often crossed it before. Marjorie, arriving by way of fig trees and servants' Quarters, found Dorry and Dinah alone at home and demanded details. It was the first they had heard of it. Neither thought any harm had been done, since Mel and the horse had come through unhurt.

When Maurice came in his sister rushed to meet him. "Oh, Morry, we heard about Mel! I *wish* I had seen her do it. Marjorie says that Evelyn says she was just like the circus ladies in tights."

He silently consigned Evelyn to a place he never mentioned before Dinah or Dorry. He had heard of her mischief-making before but never experienced it. Now worry began to gnaw at his mind. Neither he nor Mrs. Bay did much talking at supper. Since Dorothea was thirteen she and Dinah had the meal downstairs with them. In the drawing room afterward conversation was sustained by the two girls, who still saw nothing wrong. As soon as they went to bed Maurice turned a troubled face to his mother. Her eyes met his.

He said: "You've heard about it?"

"I heard, at the meeting, from Mrs. Albemarle. But I wish to hear it from you. I was hoping. . . ."

Her voice trailed off. He knew she meant that she hoped he could brand it a lie. But he could not. He said rebelliously: "Mel can ride better than any other girl in Charleston. She's better looking too. That's the whole trouble."

Mrs. Bay said very gently: "Perhaps it is. But . . ."

That was the dangerous thing about his mother. She had a habit of letting her words trail off that way. It put you on the defensive and forced you to say something.

He said it. "I wasn't drunk—in case that's what you are asking."

She shook her head. "No. But—but Saint Paul's has been our family church for generations."

He had not even thought of that; for he, too, loved Saint Paul's. He said: "It was only the portico. It wasn't sacrilege."

"Every stone of it is sacred, Morry. What you did was sacrilegious, although you did not mean it to be. What is even worse, it made a young lady conspicuous."

Now he realized why Will had left them. He knew that Will cared for Mel. But Will must know, as everybody knew, that she belonged to him, to Morry Bay. He had thought Will was afraid for her, afraid for the physical danger. There had been a moment when he, too, had been alarmed. But he had not thought. . . .

"Mel has no father or brothers," his mother went on. "She is beautiful and reckless; just the right target for gossip."

Fear made him rude. "Nobody will gossip except that spiteful old woman and her ugly daughter."

"Be honest with yourself, Morry. It was a foolish thing to do. Has any other young woman in Charleston's history ridden a horse up the steps of a church and across its portico?"

He could only shake his head.

"To do a thing like that is to invite gossip. How would you feel if your sister had done it?"

"I would not stop to think how I felt. I'd paddle her well," he said wrathfully.

"I do not know whether or not you and Mel are engaged. But you have given everyone the impression that you love her."

"I do love her," he said. But he had hesitated an instant. He was assuring himself that he loved her, for she was as beautiful and provocative as ever. It was his fault if dirty gossip touched her. He had caused it and he must protect her. Her very impulsiveness made her need protection. He saw her leaning her slender weight to balance the tilt of the big black horse. He knew she had done it entirely to please him and to draw him on. He had been a fool to allow it. No wonder Will said what he did!

His mother was still looking at him expectantly, waiting.

"Mel asked that we keep it a secret. There seemed no hurry. Do you—do you think we should announce it at once?"

"Tomorrow," said Mrs. Bay. "Tomorrow morning you and I will call on Mrs. Manchester."

It was a great load off her heart. It almost wiped out the sacrilege. Her son was doing exactly what a gentleman should do. Fortunately he loved the girl and she loved him. A husband would check her wildness and develop her better traits. And perhaps— Mrs. Bay sighed as she thought it—perhaps a wife would bring Morry back to earth and make him settle down. Dreams were for poets, like that young man who drank, who wrote "The Raven." She liked to read poetry, but she wished no poets in her family. Practical people like Dinah were easier to deal with.

Her thoughts moved on to Dinah, for she loved the girl very dearly. She hoped that this happy ending of Maurice's love affair was an omen of good luck for Dinah and her soldier. With Maurice's engagement announced and his marriage soon to be, people would forget he had crowned Dinah at a tourney. She said: "We must send Lummy across with a note to Old Uncle tomorrow. He would never forgive us if he heard it from anyone else."

Maurice agreed. "But the old rascal knows all about it, of course. So does everybody else. Nobody will be surprised."

For some reason it troubled her to hear him speak that way. He seemed a little too calm to her, and calmness was not his strong point. She thought he should show some emotion.

She said: "My dear, your father would have been so happy tonight."

He took her in his arms and held her close and long. "Even if I marry as many wives as old Solomon, you'll always be first with me, Mother."

"No, my darling. I would not wish it so."

She paused at the door and looked back at him, still hoping for some signs of romance. But he was lighting a segar. He frowned as he inhaled the smoke, and began walking restlessly the length of the long room.

Why should I feel this uncertainty? he was asking himself. I've always been jealous when Mel flirted with another man. It's not as if our affair had been sudden and transient. I've known her all my life, realized her faults and quarreled with her, yet desired her still.

But, he reminded himself, there's always been something elusive —something that excited but did not satisfy. I've never been able to grasp it. But it is a feeling as if I held my hands to a flame that gave light but no warmth.

Suddenly then he seemed to hear Dinah saying: "And as long as you chase them, you will not see the things right under your nose."

He stood stock-still with the thin segar dying between his fingers. A cold wind from the salt marshes seemed to blow all around him. The marshes were neither land nor sea, but an unreal country of fox-fires, in which he had wandered, dreaming, too long and had lost his way. Dinah had told him the answer. He might even then have turned back. When a man caught a will-o'-the-wisp did he not find its fire cold flame?

28

WHEN DAY CAME through the east windows Maurice came back to himself enough to go to his room and try to make himself look less haggard. He had been fighting it out all night, going over and over it. This tenderness which Dinah had from the first evoked was deeper and more enduring, he knew, than his feeling for Mel. He had been fooling himself that it was brotherly. In his subconscious mind he had probably known the truth from the first, and consequently fought to keep it from reaching his consciousness. There were reasons enough, he admitted, for it to be suppressed. Dinah's social status was the least of them. To get her he would be willing to tell all critics to go hang. A wife like Dinah would more than make up for the loss of a hundred so-called friends.

But that was truly the least of it. He could not now break with Mel. He had for years courted her with fervor, trying as hard as he could to drive away her other suitors. If his ardor had slacked now and then, he had always returned to her. He knew that he was not steady. He owned his faults: high temper, arrogance and carelessness. He had been too careless and too much of a dreamer to see sweet reality right under his nose. Mel knew how to beckon and still keep just out of reach. She was very tempting and he had thought he loved her. Except for the softer and deeper emotions that Dinah had stirred, he might never have learned that love was more than passion.

Dinah, sweet and fine and true, and sturdily brave in her own way! The two men closest to him, Rawlins and Sedgwick Lewis, had seen her worth as he had not done.

But why torture himself with thoughts which were not even might-have-beens? It could never have been. Dinah did not love him. She had arrived in his home in the depths of grief for another man. Her one thought in life was to find him. When he—Maurice —had lost his head as he kissed her under the mistletoe, he had only frightened her so that she had pushed him away. The only decent thing to do was to keep on trying to find for her the fiancé whom she wished for her husband. The only decent thing to do was to announce his engagement to Mel. He had dallied long enough to make everybody expect it. That was a sin of omission. But a fault of direct commission had been his urging her to ride up the steps of the Planters' Church. He could not dodge the fact that it had flung her name to gossip. He told himself that, in spite of her faults, she was getting a poor bargain in him. But no decent man could do otherwise than ask her to announce the engagement.

He came down to breakfast hollow-eyed, and his mother noticed it. He does love Mel, she thought tenderly. He belongs to a generation less frank about sentiment than my generation was. But he has been lying awake and thinking about her.

At Camellia's home they were met by a girl subdued to gentleness. Mrs. Albemarle had called on Mrs. Manchester the night before, in zeal to do her duty and snatch a brand from the burning. After she left, aunt and niece had fought a fight lacking quarter. The former had reminded the latter of all the things she liked to forget. She had no means of her own and owed her education, her visits to distant friends, the very clothes in which she stood, to a relative related only in law. That benefactor had always expected, and now demanded in no uncertain words, a return for her money.

"A girl with your looks could have married as soon as she made her debut. You've been out for three seasons now, with new and younger girls coming on the carpet each year. Twenty-one is really passé for an unmarried woman in Charleston. You have the most eligible young man of your set within your grasp. He can offer you everything: personal attraction, family background, and fortune. But, instead of snapping him up, you play with him and get yourself talked about by doing what you did today. In my day young men did not marry girls who made themselves conspicuous. You'll be lucky if you can hold him after this."

After which diatribe the belligerent old lady had gone into one of her attacks and had to be revived with ammonia and brandy. Then she had taken a sleeping draft and passed a comfortable night, while Mel tossed sleeplessly in her big bed.

However, sleeplessness softened her face while it sharpened Morry's features. As she dropped on a low stool at Mrs. Bay's feet, the older woman put a hand on the parted black hair. "My dear, you look like a madonna. Pallor becomes you. You know, my dear, I have hoped for several years now to have you for a daughter-in-law."

In her relief Mel reached up and clasped Mrs. Bay's white-gloved hand. The same impulse made her look up at Maurice with soft eyes and parted lips. She could have whistled Will back, of course; or Brook, with a little trying. But she had shown her preference for Morry so plainly that acceptance of anyone else would be branded a second choice.

Her eyes, wide and soft, still rested on Morry's face as she thought this. She loved him as much as her self-love would let her love any man.

He took both her hands, drew her to her feet, and kissed her on the cheek. She had small use for kisses on the cheek; but she reminded herself he must hold back before his mother.

"We've really been engaged since the first of the year, haven't we? What I came to ask you, Mel, is to announce it right away."

Mrs. Bay added: "I think it advisable, Camellia. I'm sure your aunt will agree with me."

Mel was quite certain of that too. She turned, all smiles, from Morry. "I'm sure you know best, Mrs. Bay. Shall I take you up to Auntie's room?"

From behind Mrs. Bay's back she gave her aunt a look of amused triumph. She meant to convey: It's easy as this! You could have left off that scene last night. He's mine for keeps now —unless I see a better chance.

But she was still gentle and soft-eyed when she went down to Maurice later. He had been pacing the room, calling himself a cad and a cur as he realized how hard it was to play his part. She found no trouble in playing hers. She went close to him, putting her hands on his shoulders and letting them move caressingly as she spoke.

"We'll be happy, Morry. We've always liked the same things. Maybe—" he felt her fingers touching his hair very softly— "maybe I'll turn into a staid Charleston matron to please you."

Maybe you will, he thought. The idea would once have pleased me. My ideal of a wife would have been: beautiful, dignified, self-possessed. But all I can see now is a gray-eyed girl in a blue dress. . . .

But he took both Mel's hands and held them tightly in his. "I promise to be good to you and—and to try to make you happy."

In the weeks and months that followed he turned more to Robin McRae. Robin had troubles too, although of a different nature. Suzette had at last raised him to the heights by saying yes. But he had at once been dashed to the depths by orders to leave Fort Moultrie for another post. Maurice, himself needing comfort, tried to comfort him.

"You don't belong in the Army. You've told me that often enough. Why not resign while you're still young enough to take up another vocation? You are the kind to be teaching ideas in some college, not to be enforcing them in battle with a bayonet."

"I know it, Morry. I'd give my head to pick Sue up and take her back to New England. She'd be happy there with me . . . in some college town with elm trees. But this is no time to resign my commission. You know that I'm a Unionist."

Maurice knew that and knew what he meant. Neither of them cared for politics, but only a fool could fail to see that trouble was gathering. Although he and Robin held opposite views they had always been able to discuss the question dispassionately. Until McRae left in midwinter Maurice got along fairly well. Both engagements had been announced and parties were being given in honor of both girls. The warm friendship which had always existed between Charleston and the Fort Moultrie garrison was, on both sides, cooling perceptibly. But Lieutenant McRae was still welcomed, on his own account and on Suzette's. The two and Maurice and Mel still went everywhere together. The quartette precluded intimacy and, while it disappointed McRae, made things easier for the other man. Mel was too busy with the season's gaieties, in addition to letters, gifts and plans for a trousseau, to demand more than he could give. She was happy, and kinder in consequence. Maurice saw less of Dinah, not guessing that she was avoiding him. He had no way of knowing that his engagement had made her even surer that he loved Mel Manchester and even more determined to hide her secret from him.

She turned more to her brother now and went several times to see Betsy. Rawlins Bull had put Roddy in full charge of kennels and stables. For Roddy was learning fast and improving. Pride in his new responsibilities and real pleasure in his work had developed his character to such an extent that he even dared to stand up to Betsy and keep her in her place. He joined the Irish Volunteers in the rush of that winter's enlistments. Rawlins was immensely pleased when he heard about it. He, like Maurice and Sedgwick Lewis, belonged to the Charleston Light Dragoons. All the militia companies were recruiting and drilling more often, and upon those occasions when they met about that common business, Maurice thought that Dinah's brother had become a more likable man.

Dinah wrote even more often to Mary O'Leary. In her last letter Mary had sent a message from Father Sweeney. "God knows," she wrote, "what this Mr. Bay in whose house you live said to Roddy. But Roddy told Father Sweeney he had done you a wicked wrong and begged him to write to any priests he might be knowing in India. Father Sweeney got a letter, too, from Mr. Bay. He said Mr. Bay was rampageous to find John Croft for you."

Then one January night old Venus died in her sleep. Maurice

was awakened at daybreak by long-drawn, shrill screams from the Quarters. Her daughters had discovered the death and begun to mourn. One by one the other women servants joined in.

Although he dressed fast, by the time he reached the hall he saw Dinah descending from the third floor. He stopped and looked up at her, frowning. Only unusual looseness of the brown curls betrayed haste. Even while frowning he thought she was prettier with them loose.

"Didn't I tell you last year to stay in the house if anything went wrong in the yard?"

"Tis nothing wrong," she told him. "Tis death. I have heard keening before."

As they went out together he was thinking it would be Samba. Samba lived in a half-world. He was nearer the other side. But Samba was sitting erect, with dark lids hooding his sightless eyes, while his daughters wailed for their mother. Maurice lifted the parchment-like hand from its grip on the chair arm and held it tight in his. "I'm sorry, Uncle Samba. She was good. We all loved her."

Samba spoke low and courteously. "Venus good woman. She gone to the Promise Land. But he bad. I gwine send he to hell."

Maurice, startled, inquired: "Who?"

"Coaxum. He hurt she when he knock she down. I gwine fix him. But I gotta git him closer."

Mary Jane, overhearing, gave an even louder yell. She grieved for her brute of a husband, although she still begged Maurice to keep him away.

He was watching Dinah as she helped the women. She was perfectly calm and was calming them. But her every word and movement were tender and sympathetic, full of understanding.

They carried old Venus back to Belle Isle to the slaves' burial ground. Her daughter Jessie and the four grandchildren, and Hilton and Titus went with her. So did Maurice. She had earned that mark of respect. Not even the urge to attend her mother's funeral could make Mary Jane go anywhere near Coaxum. Samba, of course, had to remain. He sat silent, with dark hands still, while anyone was with him. But when alone he whittled on a soft, small piece of pinewood. He had sent one of the children to get it from a half-made bench that Coaxum had left when he went away. Every now and then Samba stopped and fingered it carefully, as the blind feel with their fingers to recognize a face. His ears were still keen as those of a fox. When he heard anyone coming he hid it somewhere in his clothes and spread his strong hands on his knees. Mrs. Bay and Dinah and Dorry usually paid him a daily visit, and Jody and Elvira carried him tidbits from the kitchen. His daughter Mary Jane tended him faithfully. He endured their attentions politely, waiting. As soon as they left him he listened and, knowing himself alone, drew out the wood that Coaxum had touched and went back to his work.

At Belle Isle Du Gué Rowand stopped work for a half day so that several hundred slaves could attend Venus' funeral. He attended it, along with his nephew. Jessie and Clementine and Ann and Lulie wailed piercingly, and the plantation Negresses wailed with them. But the voices rose like angels' voices in the hymns and spirituals.

Coaxum was there but he stood apart. He was liked no better here than he had been in the city. As they turned away from the grave, upon which had been placed the small things that Venus loved best and that she had used last, Maurice saw the carpenter coming toward him. It struck him that the man looked healthier and more upright. He touched his forelock respectfully.

"Mr. Morry, I come to tell you I shame for what I do. I wish I been back with my wife and chillun."

Maurice shook his head. "You tried to kill all three of them. Besides, the Charleston police only released you on the agreement that I keep you out of the city. Mary Jane doesn't want you back. It was fear of you that kept her from coming here today."

The mulatto shuffled his feet in the dust. "I know I done wrong, Mr. Morry."

"Well, you'll have to make the best of it now. You look stronger and healthier than you did in Charleston."

Coaxum's thick lips twitched nervously. "I been feelin' all right; till before dayclean yesterday."

Old Venus had died before sunrise, but he could not have known it. Maurice looked at him, wondering if the man really felt remorse.

"Dayclean yesterday, Mr. Morry, I wake up with pain in my back."

"Maybe you sprained it at your work. The overseer has liniment. If that doesn't cure it, he will send the doctor to you."

He turned away. He could do nothing. He knew that his uncle took care of his slaves. But Coaxum's voice rose with his fear and followed after him.

"This aint no pain no doctor can cure, Mr. Morry. Seem like it sharp and stickin' in me. Seem like it tryin' to get under my shoulder and stick in my heart!"

29

MRS. BAY and Mrs. Manchester had hoped for a June wedding. Maurice had told Mel to choose the time, and then put it from his mind. He did not dread it. He still believed Dinah entirely out of his reach. Since she loved and longed for another man, he would do his best to console himself with a girl who told him she loved him and who was doing all she could to flatter and interest him as well as arouse his passion. Yet he felt a relief which startled him when she nestled close on the sofa and asked: "Morry, would you mind if we waited until a year from this April?"

He hesitated, feeling that it was his duty to object. "I wish to do whatever you wish. What is your reason for waiting?"

"Suzette and I have been talking about a double wedding. Robin goes tomorrow. He's sure he could get leave a year from April."

"Having to leave her has knocked him galley-west. He's such a quiet fellow that I wouldn't have believed it. I wish she'd marry him tomorrow morning and go north with him."

Mel sat up straight. Her tone was amused. "The little donkey would do just that, but her mother and father won't let her. I told her she was crazy to miss a military wedding. Big as Saint Paul's is, it would be crowded to standing room with our friends. I would go up last on Colonel Bond'Ion's arm, and you and I would come down first. Of course we'd have the Dragoons with crossed sabers outside the door."

He could not help seeing that he and she were to have the most prominent place, with his fashionable cavalry troop instead of McRae's brother officers.

"It sounds like a kind of a spectacle. I'd rather have a quiet wedding, and I'm sure Robin would too."

She laughed and threw herself back, with her head against his shoulder, drawing his arm around her and holding his hand in both of hers. "All of you men do. I believe you're scared in your hearts. Robin begged Suzette to elope."

"I wish she would. I'd hate to see anything come between those two. There's no telling what will happen by April after next."

But she opened his fingers and raised his hand and pressed it hard against the soft flesh between the hollow of her throat and the line of her low bodice. "You're not going to talk politics! Robin has been boring me and frightening Suzette."

"Didn't it frighten you, too?" he asked. But he smelled the gardenia scent on her hair and she was warm and sweet and satin-soft under his fingers.

"It takes a lot to frighten me! Haven't you found that out yet, Morry?" He felt her twist in his arms like a sleek, soft, sinuous cat. It brought her face closer to his, and even so close, it was perfect: dark lashes on magnolia-pale cheeks and red lips parted and taunting.

"But you don't want to talk about politics or anything else in the world! All you want is . . . to kiss me . . . Morry. . . ."

There were brief times like that when he thought she was right. He thought that he could forget everything else: yearning for Dinah's tenderness and lightning on the north horizon. But the National Democratic Convention met in Charleston that spring.

It made not the least impression on Mel. She still refused to listen. But she was cross at the prospect of a long, hot summer at home. She went to Flat Rock with the Manigaults in August. But she could not make him promise to follow her there.

"Things are in too uncertain a state. I can't leave the office at this time."

You could if you wanted to, she thought. She looked down at the cluster of ten small diamonds on her left third finger. That will hold you for me, she thought; hold you tighter than handcuffs! I won't wear it in Flat Rock, and I'll make Suzette hold her tongue.

She never takes off that sapphire that Robin McRae gave her. She told me she fell asleep at night with her cheek lying on that hand. But I'll take mine off! It's my last chance for a fling before I'm a married woman. The nicest men from Columbia and Greenville go up to Flat Rock.

She had been gone for a week before he dared go up on the third floor and to the door of his sister's sitting room. Looking in, he saw a large geography book on the table and two heads bent together over its maps. It was a rainy afternoon and the scent of jessamine came through the windows from small white stars of blossoms on the vines outside.

"What are you and Dinah doing? May I come in?"

He wondered whether he fooled himself that he saw a look of gladness in Dinah's eyes as she looked up, then looked quickly down again.

Dorry was saying: "We're trying to find the shortest way to India."

He looked over their heads at the map. "You sound like Columbus."

"Cousin Ramsey told us at school that a man named De Lesseps was cutting a way from the Mediterranean to the Red Sea. I told her I wished he'd got it done, so Dinah's letters could go faster."

She was still devoted to Dinah and still dreaded losing her. But she was now old enough to know Dinah's story and was anxious that Dinah's soldier should be found. Instead of shrinking from speaking about it, as she had at first, Dinah now tried to remind and reassure herself by talking to Dorry about John Croft.

Maurice's eyes were following on the map the long sea road to the East. Somewhere out there, he thought, was the man who inspired this faith and affection. Was he worthy of it? Was he still waiting for her? Could another man, if he tried, make her forget?

They were thoughts as shadowy as ghosts, which had haunted him since she came to the house. But they had taken substance enough to tear him with a beast's claws on the night he faced the fact that he must marry Mel. He had been fighting them ever since; he hoped at times they were laid. But he had been mistaken; they rose and walked in the rain. It was blowing through the east windows with the scent of the jessamine. Dinah jumped up to go and close them, but he put his hands on her shoulders and pushed her back in her chair.

"I'll do it. Don't you know that when you have a man around you shouldn't lift your little finger—except to beckon him?"

But you'll never beckon me, said his heart as he watched the gray squall coming in from the sea. You haven't a thought for me, because your thoughts are forever with Croft. If you beckoned with your little finger, if you did but a tenth of what Mel does, you could make me forget everything else in the world.

He tried to smile as he turned back to her, for his spoken words had been light. But it was so plainly a forced smile that she thought: He is longing for Mel. Tis because he is lonely that he has come upstairs to Dorry and me. I must not be selfish. He needs comfort. I must think of him, not of myself.

So she said, with her wide-eyed seriousness that was such a contrast to Mel's changing moods: "After a man has come home from his task, a woman should care for him. Tis she who should do the small things in the house while he rests from his work of the day."

He could not help being amused. "I really don't work hard enough to deserve to rest."

But he could not help wondering how it would feel to come home bone-tired from labor to a room shut in by the rain and a wife who would tell him to rest. He had always enjoyed working with his hands, but that had been playing at work, building boats. The thought that Dinah was waiting, in a pale blue dress in the lamplight, would make it worthwhile to work like one of Mullen's apprentices.

Dorry was saying: "Morry, I've asked you three times what it's called!"

"Suez." He leaned over the bent head and bright curls and put his finger on the map.

They talked about it through the long, rainy summer afternoon: about where Dinah's lover might be and how he could be brought back to her. But it was strangely different from times spent with Mel. With her would have been excitement. Here was calm and sweetness: a contentment that flowed over him like cool water. The room was almost dark when Dinah got up and lighted the gas. Instead of doing it for her, as he had said a man should do, he gave himself the pleasure of sitting and watching her. She moved with an easy deftness that he liked more than feline grace.

The next afternoon he let himself go to the bookroom. But it was empty save for Mauma drowsing in a chair. She woke with a jerk and asked querulously: "W'at for you hangin' roun', boy?"

"I thought Dorry might want me to help her with her geography," he explained.

"Hilton drivin' Dorry an' Miss Dinah up to the Grove. Miss Dinah say she wanta talk to she brother."

It never occurred to him she had gone in order to escape the dangerously sweet pain of being with him. He did not flatter himself that he made the slightest difference to her. He took it for granted her errand with Roddy was about Croft. Before Roddy left for Ireland he had given Roddy a talking-to and made him promise to see Father Sweeney on Aran.

As soon as Mel came back Mrs. Bay invited her to supper. Maurice had brought Sedgwick Lewis home with him from mounted drill. Mel was not fond of him, because she guessed rightly that he saw through her and only put up with her on Morry's account. But, until Mrs. Bay left them after the meal, she was carefully sweet both to him and to Dinah.

"How I wish you had all been in the mountains with me!" Her words included them all, but her eyes told Morry: *I mean only you.* "I met such delightful people, and they haven't forgotten me. Today's mail brought me a half dozen letters from them."

Dorry, not to be outdone, boasted: "Dinah got a letter from Mr. Kincannon today."

Sedgwick Lewis asked teasingly: "Is he one of her beaux?"

Dorry nodded. "Yes, but she doesn't care much about him."

Dinah was blushing and distressed. Maurice came to her rescue. "He's a nice fellow. Any girl would be proud to have him for a beau. But you shouldn't tell Dinah's private affairs, Dorry."

"Tis no matter," said Dinah. "He only wrote to say he was joining the navy."

Mel was not pleased that attention had been distracted from her many letters and centered on Dinah's one. She asked disdainfully: "Who on earth is this Mr. Kincannon?"

"He's a Maine man," said Maurice, "and a good ship master. Roddy Corley went to Ireland on the ship he captained."

"But he's leaving the Merchant Marine to join the Yankee navy?"

Maurice looked at her in surprise. She had taken no interest in politics. He could not know she had met in Flat Rock a young lawyer who was delegate to the Democratic Convention and, in order to impress him, had drunk in every word he said.

But Sedgwick Lewis asked her: "What else would a Maine man join? Hardly the Charleston Light Dragoons."

She gave him a look that confirmed his suspicion that he was not her favorite cousin-to-be.

Dorry persisted. "I like Mr. Kincannon. He held me in his arms, and Dinah's hair got caught in his coat buttons."

"Are you sure," asked Mel spitefully, "that it was *you* he was holding in his arms?"

Maurice demanded: "Mel, what do you mean?"

She meant: I'm trying to tell you what a fool you are if you think you're the only man this little minx runs after.

But she said: "If you insist, I mean I see no other way for a woman's hair to get caught on a man's coat buttons."

"Well, I do see," he told her indignantly. "And I saw the whole thing that day, from its beginning to its end. Mauma was trying to take Dorry from Kincannon, and Dinah was helping her."

"I'm so glad you told me, Morry," said Mel in honey-sweet tones. "You are quite right to explain it, because it needs explanation."

Dorry yawned, and Dinah seized the excuse. "Come, let us both be going upstairs. Will you say good-night to them, Dorry dear?"

In her room she tried to forget by rereading her letter. Kincannon had said more than that he was joining the navy. The first page ended: *"I still love you and want to marry you, Dinah."*

She could not marry him, because she was pledged to wait for John Croft. But, if John Croft never came. . . .

She sat thinking about it.

She could not stay on with the Bays. Maurice would bring his wife to the house. Then the situation would be unbearable. Nor could she live with Betsy. Seth Kincannon was kind. He had a sturdy goodness that appealed to her. Since she could not have love, the next best thing was home with a husband and little children.

However, she could not ask him to wait while she still waited for John Croft.

The first page had slipped from her fingers. She picked up the second:

> I don't know when I shall see you again, for I am no longer my own master. But the Navy needs men who have knowledge of harbors along the Atlantic coast, and I've called most of them from Maine to Florida. Is there no chance that you've changed your mind and can send me the word I want?

She gathered the pages, folded them and laid them away in a bureau drawer. Then, instead of going to bed, she sat by the open window. The night was warm and the wind whispered in the palmetto palms. Samba's drum was throbbing as softly as a pulse. Voices and Mel's laughter came from the drawing room up the stair and through her door. Both of the men had urged her to come back, but she knew that Mel did not want her there. She tried to fix her mind on John, but it kept going back to Morry. He always took up arms for her, even against Mel. . . .

Here Mel stood on her own ground, armed with her own weapons. She was a part of everything that Maurice had known from his birth. But if things were different. . . . She was daring to let herself dream. If she, Dinah, could make a home for him to rest when weary. There would be times in the years to come when life would try him sore! If she could work and wait for him and light the lamp in the evening . . . and stand at the door with her arms held wide when he came home from his task. . . .

30

SOME WEEKS LATER Maurice received a letter from Father Sweeney. He had heard from a priest serving in India that a British soldier named Croft had been invalided home. The disease called malarial fever was playing havoc with men not accustomed to the

climate. Doctors did not know what caused it, but they used a
bitter drug called "quinine" to treat it. The man in question had
been desperately ill, so ill that he had asked for a priest. A Father
Ferec saw him. A transport laden with malaria patients had left
next day, and Father Ferec knew nothing beyond that.

Maurice felt obliged to show the letter to Dinah. He had grave
doubts as to whether Croft could have survived the long voyage
home.

She read it and spoke calmly. "The letter from India was
written months ago. It is likely that John may be well again and at
his own home in England now."

"Father Ferec remembers only the last name, Croft. And you,
Dinah, do not even know where in England is his home."

She nodded sadly. "But I think tis he; and I think Father
Sweeney will find him."

It was a troubled autumn, for her and for everyone else. As
summer went the brittle fans of the Pride of India fell, and clusters
of berries hung palely-gold against a pale blue sky. The oaks
turned deeper yellow. But the palmettoes did not change. The old
fronds drooped and raveled and wove themselves in a weblike
fabric that resembled sacking around the trunks. New fronds took
up their low, harsh song, which is Charleston's lullaby.

She heard talk, too, of the convention which had been called to
meet in Columbia in mid-December. The columns of the *Mercury*
were full of it. Secession from the Union was the question coming
before it. Dinah knew nothing about it, but she heard Mrs. Bay
ask: "Do you really think South Carolina should secede, Morry?"

"Absolutely, Mother. I think it's the only thing to do."

Sedgwick Lewis brought them startling news. He pulled White
Cockerel to a stop, threw the bridle to Lummy and ran up the
steps.

"Morry, had you heard? Yellow fever's so bad in Columbia that
the convention is coming here!"

In Saint Andrew's Hall on Broad Street, at a quarter past one
o'clock on the afternoon of December 20th, its delegates adopted
the Ordinance of Secession without a single dissenting vote. Men
cheered and clasped each other's hands and the city bells pealed
out. James L. Pettigru had a small following, but Charleston stood
with Barnwell Rhett by an immense majority.

Dinah and Dorry, excited, had at last fallen asleep with the distant tumult still in their ears. They knew that something important was happening, but Dinah was not prepared for Maurice's abrupt words when she met him next morning.

"I've been looking up sailings, Dinah. I think you should go back to Ireland at once."

It took her too suddenly for her to call pride to her help. Her eyes filled and she cried out: "Ah, but what have I done? Why would you be banishing me?"

He took a step toward her. His face was tormented. "Dinah, how could you think—"

Mrs. Bay broke in. "My dear, it is because he fears for you. We have been talking it over. There may be war. You are not a South Carolinian. There is no reason for you to be involved in our danger and suffering."

Morry saw her eyes, bright with tears, fixed on his mother's face. "There is a reason, ma'am. I owe you everything. Did you not take me in your arms when my very heart was breaking? Did you not give me a roof for my head and bread to put in my mouth?"

"We gave you no more than you gave us—love and loyalty, Dinah."

Love and loyalty? Yes, she thought; but how great the love is you can never know.

"Think it out, Dinah," he said again. "It is your opportunity. If you delay, it may be too late."

It is my opportunity to cut myself off from you, she thought. It is what I have been fooling myself I would do if I had the chance. But it is already too late, although you do not know it. If you are to be in danger I must be near, at all costs. Even if I stay to see you marry Mel and bring her here, I cannot leave you now. I must be close to you.

Mrs. Bay added: "It would be a poor return for us to make if, after all you have done for us, we let you share our trouble."

"Have I not shared your happiness for more than two long years? Whatever is coming upon you now, I wish to share it with you."

He wanted to take her in his arms. Loyalty such as hers would make life worth living. But feeling she was making a sacrifice, and that he must try to dissuade her, he said: "You told me you thought John Croft was in England. The port is still open and ships sail every day. I can get you aboard one if you will go now."

He walked to the window and stared out at the harbor whose ways he knew as he knew the city streets. Castle Pinckney was not garrisoned. That was fortunate, he reflected; for it was near enough to mount guns in range of the city. Moultrie was occupied by Anderson's artillery. But Sumter, the key position, was in the hands of workmen for improvements and repairs. In the event of attack by sea, the side that held Fort Sumter. . . .

He must not let himself think of that. There must not yet be talk of attack. Governor Pickens was sending Mr. Barnwell, Mr. Orr and Mr. Adams to Washington to confer with President Buchanan and to ask the return of South Carolina forts and all other South Carolina property. The port was still open, as he had told Dinah. Intelligence and coolness might still keep it open. But a warlike act from either side could close it and send its ships down to the sea on strange and perilous errands. His mind saw this angle at once, while the minds of other men saw militia, artillery and cavalry. He thought of Middleton Rowand and other young naval cadets training on the *Lodebar*. South Carolina had once had a navy of her own. It had fought and had also protected the commerce of its sovereign state. Now there was no such navy and he knew that, without the escort of fighting ships, her merchantmen could not carry her trade or bring back supplies to her.

Dinah had been watching him. He turned back to her now. "If it's a question of expense, won't you let me take care of that?"

"Tis not at all the expense," she told him softly. "I have been saving the money for more than two years now. Your mother lets me pay nothing but gets me the work from her friends. Tis only that, unless John comes for me, I have no place else in the world to call home. I will be happy, whatever comes, if you and herself will let me stay."

Mrs. Bay said: "It shall be as you wish. I dreaded losing you!"

Maurice told himself it was fortunate that neither of them guessed how much he had dreaded losing her. He must lose her sooner or later. But the thought that he would still see her every day in his home was a ray of sunlight that shone through gathering storm. They dropped the subject of sending her away when Rawlins Bull arrived with the most recent bit of family news.

On the night before many men had celebrated in many ways. But Roddy Corley, Aranman, had toasted Secession so heartily that he had come back to Lowndes Grove roaring drunk, beaten Betsy and thrown the whole plantation into an uproar at 3 A.M.

"Oh, glory be!" said his sister. "Will you sack him, Mr. Bull?"

Rawlins grinned and shook his head. "Your brother got drunk in a good cause. Besides, ever since Morry told me your story, I've been wishing that Roddy could give that sister-in-law of yours what she deserves."

That Christmas was gay with a hectic gaiety. No word had come from Washington. The harbor glittered with citron waves and white foam in the winter sunlight. Charlestonians on the Battery looked out toward the forts. Charleston drawing rooms were bright with holly and mistletoe. From midday until midnight families were at home to their friends with egg-nogg and black fruitcake. The latter, Dinah had discovered, began its recipe with "take one hundred eggs and six pounds of butter."

Since Coaxum's going the Quarters had remained quiet. Samba kept his thoughts to himself and his daughters did not know what they were. Only the young gardener Rex kept in touch with current affairs. He did not tell his parents where he went when given leave, for he knew that Hilton and Jessie would not approve. But, unknown to them, he attended secret meetings and his discontent was growing day by day. Lummy warned him: "Boy, you aint doin' nothin' but lookin' for trouble. Lessen you changes your ways, you needn't come hanging roun' my chile Linda."

At parties and on the streets pretty girls wore emblems of secession. Mel Manchester led the fashion. But in her heart she cared less about the issue than did either Dinah or Suzette. Dinah's one thought was of Maurice. She knew the Light Dragoons would be in the thick of whatever occurred. In the carriage with Mrs. Bay and Dorry as they watched mounted drill, she sat silent with her eyes on him and his colors pinned on her cloak. Mel and Suzette were always the center of a group of men. The former, pleased with excitement, was more vivacious than ever. It gave her pleasure to torment her friend about McRae.

Early on the morning of December 27th the family was aroused by loud strokes of the big brass knocker on the front door. Erasmus admitted a messenger and he asked for the man of the house. Dorry and Dinah, peeping from the top of the stair, saw Maurice run down the lower flight in his black-silk dressing gown.

By the time they dressed and went down the messenger was gone. Maurice and his mother were alone in the drawing room. He turned from the east windows, worry on his face and a small naval telescope in his hand.

Dorry, unable to wait, rushed upon him. "Morry, who was it knocking so loud? What did he come to tell you?"

"He was from the *Mercury* and sent by Mr. Rhett. He and others are going around to inform the citizens that Major Anderson moved his artillery from Moultrie to Sumter last night."

Neither girl had the least idea of the importance of that move. Dinah knew from his face and his voice what he thought of it. But Dorry was interested only in the telescope.

"Can I see Fort Sumter all the way from here through it?"

Without words he gave it to her and she ran to the window.

In exasperation, he pushed his hair back from his forehead. "What were our picket boats doing? Do they think this is a picnic?"

Nobody answered him. He began to walk up and down, hands in the pockets of his robe.

"We hoped, and thought, that Anderson would wait. I mean wait to hear what the President told our envoys. But thinking that is no excuse. The guard boats should have been on the alert."

"I see them," screamed Dorry. "Dinah, come see the soldiers on Fort Sumter!"

Dinah went to the window. She was frightened because she saw that Maurice was deeply disturbed. He had never talked with her on the subject. But she was heart and soul in accord with whatever he thought. She took the telescope and adjusted it to her sight. Far in midchannel, above the dark brick walls, small figures were moving stiffly along the parapet.

"They moved during the night," Maurice was repeating. "How could the guard boats have let them slip by? Nothing was known of it until early this morning; the *Niña* was patroling and saw them there."

To Dinah's distress he hurried away without breakfast. The long morning went by and he did not return. Jody grumbled because nobody ate dinner. The ladies were still at table when Sedgwick Lewis dashed in.

"No, Cousin Clelia, for once in my life I don't want anything to eat. Morry asked me to tell you that he was so busy you'd have to look for him when you saw him."

"Tell me what is happening! I'm worried to death."

"Well, don't tell Morry I told you but these poker games down at the Drags' headquarters sometimes last several days."

"Sedgwick Lewis, tell me the truth!"

He threw an arm around her and kissed her cheek. "Forgive me for teasing you, but everything's really all right. The companies are meeting together to make their plans. You'll be able to see all that happens if you sit in an east window with the telescope handy."

Then he was off. Dorry and Dinah flew upstairs to the drawing room. When they saw one of the guard boats putting out from a Cooper wharf they shrieked for Mrs. Bay.

"Mother, look! It's the *Niña,* crowded with militiamen. Where can they be going?"

"To Castle Pinckney," guessed Mrs. Bay. Her son had discussed things with her as he had not done with the girls.

They watched as the boat drew nearer to the small island called Shute's Folly. The men in uniform went ashore in orderly file. It seemed to Mrs. Bay, who had seen them only on parade or as individuals at entertainments, that they had already assumed a more businesslike and soldierly appearance. She was trying to tell by the uniform which company she was watching.

"Is Morry with them?" asked Dorry excitedly.

"I think not. The Dragoons are cavalry. It looks like the Washington Light Infantry."

It was Dinah's turn with the telescope. She said: "They have stopped at the gates. I think the gates are locked."

"Are they going to fight now?" Dorry questioned eagerly.

"Of course not! Castle Pinckney has only one or two soldiers, and the family of one lives there with him. They have done their duty by shutting the gates, but that is all they can do. Our men will break the locks or else climb over."

"That's what they're doing, Mother! They are putting up ladders! The first ones are beginning to climb over now."

The three women watched that little force go up and over without haste. For a few moments all movements ceased. There seemed no life on the tiny isle. The boat stood off. She was the same that had brought the news of Fort Sumter to the city in the dawn of that same long day. They saw the strip of green water widening between her and the landing.

Then, out of that brief hiatus, the bare flagpole came to life. A flicker of blue ran up it and caught the wind and held taut. Through the telescope Dinah saw the pale fronds stir on the azure. Across that stormy meeting of tides called Rebellion Roads, the Palmetto Flag faced the Stars and Stripes.

31

FROM THEN ON events seemed to rush upon each others' heels. On New Year's day Morry told them that the Citadel cadets, along with the German Riflemen and the Zouave Cadets, had been ordered to occupy Morris Island.

Dinah saw Mrs. Bay turn pale. "What are they to do there?"

"Construct a sand battery. The Citadel cadets, although youngest of the lot, know more about artillery and will probably handle the guns."

"Have you heard anything else?"

He nodded. "A steamer is being sent to reinforce Major Anderson with men, arms and provisions. The guard boat is on the watch by the bar, to warn them at Cummings Point as soon as that steamer is sighted. I don't think it will fail us this time."

Nine days later in the quiet of early morning they heard the guns. Dinah and Dorothea ran out on the south piazza, holding their warm dressing gowns around them against the cold. Lights appeared in the Quarters and soft voices called to each other. From a window below they heard Maurice shout: "Saddle the mare, Lummy! I'll be out in ten minutes."

They could see him in the gray light as he ran out in the yard.

As he did Sedgwick Lewis galloped up to the gate. "Where are Rawlins and Roddy Corley?"

"They are to meet us at the wharf. Open the gate, Lummy!"

The mare went through in a gallop and the gray horse wheeled beside her.

Mrs. Bay knew all about it, although the girls did not. "They are too impatient to wait for news. They arranged beforehand with a man who owns a flatboat to get them towed from the Southern Wharf across to James Island. From there they can ride to a place back of Cummings Point and cross to Morris Island in a rowboat. Your brother is with them, Dinah. Rawlins is pleased with his interest in our affairs."

They came back after nightfall with the news, which had long since reached Charleston by the guard boats. But they had got it earlier and they had details. They had been on Cummings Point and seen the small battery with four cannon which had driven back the *Star of the West,* carrying supplies to Fort Sumter. They were hungry and tired and demanded hot supper.

Dinah and Dorry, still asking questions, tried to help serve them. The housemaids had gone to the Quarters, but Erasmus was still in command and he had a proper sense of fitness.

"Miss Dorry, you and Miss Dinah best sit down to this table or else go back in the drawin' room. You aint doin' nothin' but purely gittin' in my way."

Sedgwick Lewis jumped up and pulled a chair on either side of him. "Move over, fellows! I want the girls by me. I'll wait on *you,* sweethearts!"

"No, you won't neither," Erasmus warned him. "I still 'members when you and Mr. Morry got in my pantry and et two quarts of brandied peaches I was fixin' to serve for Miss Clelia company."

In spite of his share of guilt in regard to the brandied peaches Maurice felt a surge of sympathy for Erasmus. From his place at the head of the table it looked to him as if Sedgwick Lewis' head was touching Dinah's hair while he whispered to her.

So he turned the talk to the day's ride, and Dinah as she listened could picture the four men galloping at full speed on the sea island road. She had once driven it with Mrs. Bay to visit the Seabrooks at Secessionville. It twisted to left and right, with jungle on either

side of it and tree branches and gray moss making a canopy overhead. Mrs. Bay had told her that it had been laid out in curves to
protect the Continental cavalry from the sweep that British guns
could make on a long straight stretch. She wondered why men
kept on fighting wars.

Her glance fell upon her brother, and she too saw the improvement that Maurice had noticed. He no longer stood in the drawing
room, surly and twisting his cap. He held up his head and talked
with the other militiamen. An Irish Volunteer was brother-in-arms
to a Charleston Light Dragoon. Besides, these men respected him
for his skill with horses.

It was not very long after this that the Dragoons were ordered
to Sullivan's Island for guard duty. Maurice, although not an
officer, was acting as aide and courier. It brought him to Charleston often and allowed him hours and, sometimes, whole days at
home. Whatever his errand, he tried to be cheerful and to reassure his mother and the girls. But he knew of the mortar batteries
being constructed at old Fort Johnson on Windmill Point. Brig-
adier General Beauregard had resigned his commission in the
United States Army and was now in charge of the coast defenses
of the section. Other states had joined South Carolina and, instead
of standing alone, she was now one of the Confederate States of
America. More than three months had passed since Major Anderson had moved to Fort Sumter. He had not yet been starved out
and he refused to evacuate. A troopship and three gunboats, sent
to his aid, were being held off by the harbor batteries. General
Beauregard knew they were only part of a fleet that had been
despatched, and he had no intention of waiting for its arrival.

It was at just this unhappy time that happy-hearted Suzette
Manigault came in tears to Mrs. Bay. She only wept harder when
she tried to explain her errand.

"No, Dinah, don't go! Please stay. I've always liked you and I
know that you've had just—just the same kind of trouble I have."

"Suzette, dear," implored Mrs. Bay, "try to stop crying and tell
me what it is."

"It's Robin, Miss Clelia! Mel said—she said if Morry— Oh,
I'm just so miserable that I wish I was dead!"

"What did Mel say? What about Morry? I cannot help you unless I know."

"It's really only Morry who can help me. Because he—he is Robin's friend. I heard from Mel that he was at home on leave today. I hope you don't think me *dreadful* to come to see a man!"

"Dinah," said Mrs. Bay, "please go and call Morry. The less the servants hear of this the better."

Dinah tapped on his door, but he did not even open it. He called rudely: "What's the matter? Why is Suzette bawling?"

"She has reason enough to bawl," said Dinah sturdily. "'Tis myself who knows that, and I pity her."

"I pity her too, but I'm not coming out until she stops."

"'Tis a matter concerning your friend, Leftenant McRae. 'Tis only you that can help her," said Dinah with serpent's guile.

He opened the door and stood, frowning as he tied his cravat. "Is it straight, Dinah? You know well enough that this kind of thing upsets me."

She reached up and straightened it and drew his coat lapels a little closer together. She was very businesslike.

"I will go now and ask her to be quiet if you will come."

When he got there Suzette faced him, flanked by his mother and Dinah. She was flushed, and her wet lashes made her blue eyes sparkle. But, except for a small hiccough every now and then, she controlled herself.

"Shall we leave you with him now, darling?" asked Mrs. Bay.

"For the Lord's sake, don't!" implored Maurice. "She might begin to cry again."

Suzette clutched out on either side for a hand of either woman. "Don't go! You both will understand. But Mel—hic! Mel said if Morry—"

Dinah leaned and dabbed her eyes and squeezed the soft hand tighter.

"Mel said, Morry, that if you did what Robin was doing she would break her engagement and hate you instead of love you!"

"For mercy's sake, Suzette," he asked, "what is Robin doing?"

"He's fighting—or going to fight against us if there is a war."

"Why shouldn't he? He is a New Englander born and bred."

"But Mel said that if you—"

"If I fought against South Carolina I would be a renegade. Robin's state is standing with the Union. Mel is giving you very bad advice."

"It isn't only Mel," she wailed. "Both Father and Mother keep asking each other before me why I couldn't have chosen a Charleston man."

"I have no doubt that you could have chosen one. You've always had plenty of beaux. But I've always held you above the type of girl who is satisfied with any man she can get for a husband. I thought it was real love between you and Robin. I'm darned sure —excuse me! that it is on his side. And let me tell you one thing, Suzette." Dinah saw he was getting earnest to the point of anger as he pleaded the case for his absent friend. "If you break with Robin McRae you'll never, north or south, find another man as good and true and fine."

It was exactly the advice that she wished to hear. Her lips began to curve in their piquant smile. "Oh, Morry, I *couldn't* break with him! I could never love anyone else."

"Then stand to your guns, Suzette. And respect Robin for standing to his. He must follow his pattern, as we are following ours."

But it was at that time a confused and tangled pattern. There was no scheme of secrecy, and everybody knew what everybody else thought and did. This was realized later on when the invading forces were found to have maps and detailed information about every navigable creek and passable road for miles above and below Charleston peninsula.

Now, on April the eleventh, everyone in Charleston knew that General Beauregard had sent to Major Anderson his final demand for surrender of Fort Sumter. Morry appeared unexpectedly.

"No, I'm not on leave. All leaves are canceled. The Dragoons, with other companies, are holding the eastern end of Sullivan's Island. Captain Rutledge sent me across with messages to officers at the Arsenal. As soon as I get the information he wants, I'll go back."

They were glad to have him on his own terms. He brought Mel to the East Battery house, in order to spend the short time both with her and with his family. She was present when he inquired: "By the way, Dinah, have you ever answered Kincannon's letter?"

Taken aback, she looked at him. "No; for I have no idea at all where I would be writing a letter to find him now."

"If he's an officer in the United States Navy, I think you can safely send it to Washington. If you write it and give it to me, I'll get it out for you. I have an idea that there'll be a chance, in the next few days, to send it aboard a Union ship by a Union officer."

She wrote it and gave it to him and he put it in a coat pocket. Mrs. Bay shook her head. "Maybe he'll mail it. Maybe he'll forget."

To Dinah it did not seem very important. She had congratulated Seth Kincannon upon what she called "being gazetted." Then she had wished him luck and told him, very gently, that she would not marry him.

That same evening Morry took her and Mel and Dorry out on the high promenade of East Battery. The news of something to come had spread and the citizens were gathering. Men clattered by on horseback and carriages drew up. Dorry had insisted upon bringing her pug. Now full grown and of fearsome appearance, it was entirely harmless—except that it still nipped anyone who annoyed it. It wore a large yellow ribbon bow and a harness with bells and a leash.

Mel demanded: "Do you have to take that frightful thing with us, Dorry?"

"Let you and I and the creature walk behind them," suggested Dinah.

"No, you won't," said Maurice. "I want you right under my eye. The whole city seems to be coming down here."

"Whole city or not," said Mel, "I won't go around in a harem!"

Middleton Rowand saved the situation by appearing at just that moment. His eyes lit at sight of Dorothea.

"I've just been to your house. I wanted to ask you to promenade with me along the Battery. Aunt Clelia said you were out here."

Maurice looked from Mel's lovely, angry face to the concourse of people, swelling with every arrival.

"She can walk with you, Middy, if you keep us in sight. You take her and that blasted dog, and I'll take Mel and Dinah."

Dinah, on Morry's other side, could not see Mel's expression, but she felt a disapproval that chilled the warm spring night. Around them voices rose and fell, and there were occasional bursts of nervous laughter. But the harbor was still and dark, except for the lanterns on the parapets. It waited in watchful silence, like the hush in a cyclone's center.

Dinah, placid as she was, felt it like a weight upon her. She did not know what Maurice knew. She thought she was feeling only Mel's displeasure. So she said presently: "I will go back. Your mother is alone in the house, and it may be she wishes me with her."

He knew that it might come at any moment now; and he knew it was more important than Mel's tantrums or Dinah's duties.

"I don't want to leave the sea wall—not even to take you across the street. Where has that young devil Middy gone with Dorry? I told him to stay close by us!"

A little breeze from southeast sprang up suddenly then. Its coolness made Dinah draw her shawl around her shoulders.

But Mel's voice was cooler than the breeze that made wraps necessary. "In seeking solitude, he is more complimentary to your sister than you are to me, Morry."

He did not answer her. His thoughts were on that wind-blown point from which ran out a hidden shoal to terminate in what had been the foundation of Fort Sumter. He knew exactly where and when a small boat could cross its submerged bank. But, high tide or low, it was always there—a link secret and invisible—but a link between Fort Johnson and Fort Sumter. In midchannel Anderson had, months ago, raised the Stars and Stripes. Beauregard's shore batteries were under the Stars and Bars. The range of the guns that there looked out followed that submerged sand-bar. . . .

Maurice had seen them so many times when sent across as courier. Now, in the darkness, he could have found his way around and between them. He had hunted the woods behind them and sailed the irregular jut of their small semipeninsula. Clumps of "raccoon oysters" had built in the evil-smelling stuff that Charlestonians called "pluff mud" that lay between the point and Morris Island. The cat-faced, ring-tailed creatures came walking softly at night from the trees down to the water to feed on them at low tide. Up around the sand dunes the yellow buttercups were already thick around the stubby mortars. . . .

He saw the flash of gunpowder that preceded all sound. It flared for seconds against the black backdrop of the sea island.

Along the sea wall voices ceased. Men and women held their breath. And into that stillness roared the long, shuddering crash of the first cannon.

32

DINAH HAD NOT expected it. She stood, helpless with terror, one hand holding her shawl at her throat and the other gripping Maurice's sleeve. He released it, and put his arm around her waist and drew her close. She knew him well enough to sense that he did not know what he was doing. All of him that was real was out on Windmill Point with the guns.

They seemed to her to be ripping long seams in the black velvet of the April night. She felt the flagstones under her feet vibrate with the burst of every shell. The crowd was no longer holding its breath. Most people were cheering wildly. Men were throwing their hats in the air and several sailed over the sea wall. Dinah looked down at a tall crown bobbing away on the dark waves.

"Ah!" she cried. "'Twas expensive and 'tis a pity to lose it!"

Mel's exultation was so great that she laughed aloud with amusement. "You must be crazy to think of hats at such a time! But I can't blame you. I feel mad, myself! I'm mad with joy that, at last, we've struck back at their tyranny!"

He answered her so low that Dinah could scarcely hear him. "We waited as long as we could. I approve every shot; but I am not joyful."

She turned on him like a wildcat. "Why must you be this way? Why must you always hold back when other men wish to fight? They are not thinking of what is to come. Listen to them! They are cheering."

He did not even defend himself from her accusations. He said quietly: "All of them are not cheering. It is a law of life, Mel, that when some cheer and some hold silent, other men hear the cheering but do not hear the silence."

"Well, I'm cheering with them!"

She took the silk scarf from her head and waved it high, as other women were doing.

"Bravo!" she cried. *"Vive* Beauregard! Hurrah for Mr. Rhett! See him standing over there! All of the older people are here. I've seen the Porchers and the Trumbos and lots of your mother's friends. Even the Albemarles are out. Oh, here come the Manigaults!"

Suzette was holding her bright head high. The city lamps were dim. But Dinah's eyes were sharp enough to see that the small face was white and set beneath its halo of red-gold hair. Mr. Manigault swept off his hat in greeting to Mel and Dinah. Maurice came back to himself long enough to bow to the Manigault ladies.

"It had to come, Maurice. Thank God we have Pierre Beauregard in command!"

"I agree with you perfectly, sir. Do you know the general personally?"

"I knew him when he was a little boy and I a young man in New Orleans. Had you heard that at West Point Major Anderson was his artillery instructor? I know Robert Anderson, too. He told me once that, of all the cadets he ever taught, Beauregard showed most talent as an artillerist."

Mel laughed softly and delightedly. Dinah, still watching Suzette's pale face, saw it twitch with pain at the sound.

Mr. Manigault bowed again. "But, before we say good-night, my daughter has something to tell you—and all her other friends."

Dinah heard Maurice say hoarsely: "No! Oh, no, Suzette!"

But Dinah saw that it was too late. Mrs. Manigault was speaking, with real regret in her voice. "We respect the young man, Maurice, and we know that he was your friend."

Was? thought Maurice. *Can war change even the tense of friendship and love?*

Mel put her arm through his possessively. She smiled exultant encouragement on the blonde girl's agony.

Dinah stood with both hands at her throat, holding together the Inisheer shawl. It seemed to her that the harbor breeze was as cold as the wind on the Glassin Rocks. She could detect the acrid smell of gunpowder in it now.

Mrs. Manigault's voice was low, exquisite, inexorable. "Nevertheless, a mother must think of what is best for her child. I will not have her life spoiled by waiting for a man who is now our enemy, employed in fighting against us, and who may never return to her. Neither Mr. Manigault nor I take a betrothal lightly. But, under the circumstances, we can only be grateful that she had not yet married him."

She turned to the rigid, white-faced girl. "You may tell them yourself, Suzette."

Only Suzette's lips moved. There was no expression in her voice. She spoke like a child, or a talking bird that repeats just what it is told.

"My engagement to marry Lieutenant McRae no longer exists," she said.

Then her father took her arm and she moved away, stiffly, between her parents.

"Dinah! Morry!" screamed Dorry. "Did you see? Did you hear? Oh, Morry, what is happening?"

"Enough," said Maurice between his teeth, "without you two acting the way you did. What do you mean, you young scoundrel, by taking my sister off in this crowd?"

Dinah saw he was venting his grief for Robin McRae on the two young people. She left him and stood beside them, but before she could speak Maurice went on. "Don't you know better than to take your young cousin off in a mob like this with God-knows-who shoving and pushing her? Dorry, come home with me at once! You look as if you'd been in a fight. Get back to your ship, Middy! Come, Mel and Dinah!"

Mel gave a little amused laugh as she went. But Dinah stopped and held out her hand to the crestfallen boy. She knew he was only sixteen. He was fond of his younger cousin, but had been carried away by the excitement.

"'Tis no harm done, Middy," she said. "'Tis that he is troubled and angry."

He was improving with discipline but was still spoiled and impudent. "Old Morry thinks too much of himself and tries to order us all around. But he's due a surprise before long. The cadets on the *Lodebar* are in line for commission. I can't wait to see his face when I'm a naval officer and he's nothing but a trooper in state militia!"

She laughed at him. "Get along with you, lad, or else you'll be in the brig!"

But Maurice was not laughing. She heard him calling in a tone of barely controlled fury: "Dinah, I told you to come home with me!"

When she joined him he was too angry to speak. As he herded them across the street, between rolling carriages and riders now galloping home, she saw that the tall house on the other side was in darkness except for its second floor and its Quarters. The servants were clustered inside the gate. Lummy called: "What for the w'ite-folks doin' all that shootin', Mr. Morry?"

"It's our people on James Island," he told the man wearily. "We're trying to take Fort Sumter back from the Yankees. Go back to bed now, Lummy. And make the others go too."

In the drawing room he went straight to his mother. Just now he was angry with all women except her. Suzette, he thought, was a weak little fool and had let others sway her. Mel was willful and violent in her views, and he could not in his heart think patriotism her motive. Dorry had disobeyed him and gone off unchaperoned. Dinah, in spite of her gentleness and customary common sense, had betrayed him by giving aid and comfort to Middy. He said abruptly: "Well, Mother, it's come at last! You'd better send Dorry right to bed. It's past her usual hour."

Dinah went over and took her hand and led her from the room. Maurice, now ashamed of his temper, watched them in silence. But, as they reached the top of the stair he appeared at the door below. "Forgive me, Dorry," he called. "Please come down again, Dinah!"

She did not answer him, for she thought he had been unfair. She helped Dorry undress, bathing her face and brushing her hair. The accustomed ritual soothed the excited child. She began to yawn. "Will there be war, Dinah?"

"Acushla, I do not know. Go you to sleep now."

When Dorry's grip on her hand relaxed she rose and picked up her shawl. Dawn was not far away, and the wind through the windows was cool. Without stopping to look in the mirror, she went back to the drawing room.

Maurice was drinking whisky. She knew he was fonder of sherry. He was refilling his small, straight glass from a silver-collared decanter. Mrs. Bay and Mel sat in two chairs which he had placed for them in two of the east windows.

He wheeled as he heard Dinah enter. She saw that his hair was tousled and his soft cravat had slipped a little to one side. His eyes implored her: *"Forgive me—and understand that I'm hurt!"*

This new Maurice was far more appealing than his usual arrogant self. She knew that he never drank too much and that forgetfulness of personal appearance was only a symptom of deep mental distress. Her heart melted and she smiled back at him.

His answering smile was eager and full of gratitude. "I was afraid you wouldn't come. I want all three of you to drink a toast with me. I brought whisky instead of wine, and Mother and Mel don't like it. Do ladies in Ireland drink whisky, Dinah?"

"They do," she told him; "at wakes for the dead."

He had been coming toward her. It rocked him back on his heels. She saw the pale brown liquor splash over the rim of his glass. But he recovered himself at once.

"I have already poured three half-glasses there on the waiter." He turned to ask the other two: "Shall I get you Madeira?"

Mrs. Bay nodded her head and rose from her chair. "I will drink with you, my son, although I do not feel like it tonight. Perhaps it will make me sleep."

He gave her a grateful look with the glass, and he handed the other to Mel. She held out a hand, without rising.

"The bombardment of Sumter deserves a toast."

As she spoke jestingly another battery opened at Fort Johnson. He stood at the window behind her and Dinah stood behind Mrs. Bay. The James Island shore, still lying in night, was lighted by successive flashes. The smoke hung over the channel in fiery clouds like red moonrise.

Mrs. Bay murmured, as if to herself: "Felicia Vanderhorst was engaged to one of Major Anderson's young aides. She was so happy when he wrote he was ordered to Sullivan's Island." They heard her sigh. "Yesterday Mrs. Vanderhorst told me she was glad it hadn't yet been announced."

Before their eyes a shell struck squarely on Fort Sumter. Its burst lit up the three-tiered walls and the dark sea all around it.

Mrs. Bay put a hand up to her eyes. "Grief like that for so many young people . . . death in battle . . . all the horrors of war. . . ."

"It's war," said Maurice. His voice was hard. "I'm not sure we'll win. But that doesn't matter, in the long run, as much as it matters to fight for what we believe in."

Dinah's eyes were on his face. It was thin and strained and tired. She would have given all she had to take it between her hands and kiss away those lines of unhappiness. I believe in whatever you believe, my heart's treasure, she told herself. But I wish I could tell you that I would love you more, beaten and lonely, than as you are. I learned to love you here in your home, where you have so much more than I ever had. But I could love you even more if you had nothing in all the world.

Mel had turned from the window. There was real surprise in her voice. "Morry, that's the silliest thing I ever heard you say! Why would anyone fight unless they were sure of winning?"

"If you don't see that," he said, "I could not explain it."

He turned to his mother. "You said you would drink to whatever I drank. But I'm asking you to drink *against* something. It's something more cruel even than war and it will last long after war ends. It has already taken possession of most people on both sides. But I want you to keep free of it, you three whom I love! Will you try to keep from hating? Will you drink with me *against hatred?*"

Mrs. Bay raised her glass to her lips and swallowed, but that swallow choked her. She had to set the wine glass down and cough into her handkerchief.

Dinah did not hesitate. She crossed the room to Maurice and, raising herself on tiptoe, touched his glass with hers. Over the thin crystal their eyes held each other as they drained the toast to the last drop.

It infuriated Mel to the point of dashing her glass to the floor. In reality her rage was all against Dinah. But, seeing what she had done, she was quick enough to pretend outraged patriotism.

"I will not drink such a toast! It sounds disloyal, Morry. Of course nobody expects anything more of Dinah. She cares nothing for our affairs and can love our enemies. I know of one she loves, and writes letters to. You'd be a traitor as well as a fool to talk before her!"

He said: "You should apologize both to me and to Dinah."

"Well, I won't apologize. Let her hate me if she will, but I'm telling the truth."

Mrs. Bay's low cry of distress made Dinah look toward her. On her face was horror at the vulgar scene, verging on a brawl, between her guest, her son, and his fiancée. Memory of her kindness and motherly love swept over Dinah, washing away her anger. She could afford to be generous. The clink of Morry's glass against hers was still singing a song in her ears. I alone drank it with him, she thought. Mel cannot take that away from me. She cannot hurt me, and I will not let her hurt Morry's mother.

She walked to the door and, from it, looked back at them. "Tis no matter," she said. "I have need of no apology. I shall keep the pledge I drank with you. I shall keep it all my life. And, whatever she says or does, I shall not even hate her."

33

ON HIS NEXT visit to Charleston Maurice said: "By the way, Dinah, I put your letter to Kincannon in the hands of a Union officer a few hours before he went aboard a United States ship."

She looked at him inquiringly.

"I gave it to one of Major Anderson's lieutenants. He's a nice fellow and I'm sure he'll see that it goes where it should."

He turned to his mother. "He's the man who's in love with Felicia. I offered, in turn, to bring her a message from him. But he was pretty gloomy. He said his goose was cooked. He'd just been handed a letter from her, enclosing his ring."

"Cooked or not," said Dinah, "a woman is nowt but a goose if she forsakes the man she loves for war or anything else."

He was sent less frequently to the city now. The women in the big house missed him more and more. Mrs. Bay turned over the housekeeping almost completely to Dinah. The house servants liked her and she was capable. All that Maurice had been accustomed to do in overseeing yard and Quarters had devolved upon his mother. Titus was her lieutenant, in the literal sense of the word. He and Hilton were faithful, but Rex was troublesome. He neglected his work and more than once slipped off without leave

to meetings. She would not have known had Mauma not reported
it to her.

"Rex say he gwine cut Titus throat if Titus tell you. Coaxum
teach Rex he meanness before you send him away."

Above all things, Mrs. Bay wished to keep it from Maurice. She
knew that, for a man obliged to be absent from his home, no worry
on earth could equal the fear of turbulent slaves. So she sent for
Rex and told him that one more report of misconduct would send
him to the plantation and to a fieldhand's work. He was frightened and promised to behave. He was courting Melinda, oldest of
the yard children and now almost fifteen. She responded and
wished to marry him; but her parents Elvira and Absolom were
not satisfied.

"Then, if you don't want to leave Melinda, behave yourself,
Rex. All of the other people are helping me while Mr. Morry is
away."

He stuck out his lower lip. "I gwine behave. But me and Linda
wants to git married."

"Didn't you speak to Mr. Morry about that some months ago?
The truth is that Linda's parents are afraid to trust her to you."

He dodged the question. "Linda wanta marry me."

"I know that; but she's too young. We have always made it a
rule not to allow our girls to marry early. Besides, you and Linda
will have to persuade Lummy and Elvira."

Rex only pouted more sulkily and shuffled his feet.

"Speak up and be respectful. You and Linda will do whatever
Mr. Morry told you to do. Now go back to your work; and be
sure to sow the marigold seed."

He touched his forelock and went, but she heard him muttering
under his breath.

Poor Rex, young and confused, was not the only one who felt
the gathering speed of that onrushing urgency. Summer passed
and the Light Dragoons were ordered to Pocotaligo to help repel
Commodore Dupont's attack on Port Royal. Some of them took
body servants, and the news spread among the slaves. Absolom
came upstairs and into Maurice's room, where Maurice was fling-
ing belongings into haversack and satchel while his mother and
sister and Dinah hovered around him and got in his way.

Lummy addressed himself to Dorothea, with the customary in-
direct approach of his race.

"You best lemme take Red, Miss Dorry. Ole Buck can't keep up with that Kathleen mare."

Her bright bay had been registered as "Red Branch Knight." Muldoon knew his Irish history.

"Of course, Lummy! I'm so glad you're going to take care of Morry."

Lummy grinned from ear to ear. He had learned long ago that the women of the family were invaluable as allies.

Maurice wheeled from his packing, displaying in one hand an undergarment that he had been trying to stuff surreptitiously in with razor and full-dress gloves and boot polish and rolled-up shirts.

"Who said you were going with me, Lummy?"

Lummy stuck out his mouth even farther than Rex had done. But Mrs. Bay applauded its every inch.

"Was you thinkin' bout leavin' me?" he demanded with indignation. "Mr. Roy done send Little David all way from Middleburg to be Mr. Sedgwick Lewis' body servant."

Maurice dashed the undergarment violently on the bed. Dinah promptly picked it up and folded and packed it properly. He did not see her, for he was shouting at Lummy.

"I don't care if Mr. Roy sent Goliath along with him! We're marching fast and traveling light. Besides, I like to be alone, without people tagging after me."

"Who gwine shine your boots?" Lummy asked him. "Who gwine brush your clothes?" His voice grew sterner. "Who gwine clean your horse and your saddle and bridle?"

"I learned to do all that for myself over on Sullivan's Island. I can pack my own things, too."

He turned and caught Dinah in the act of doing it for him.

"Will you leave my haversack alone? I'll never be able to find anything if you women put them in all kinds of funny places."

But he faced them alone and he knew it. All three of them stood with Lummy. Lummy, emboldened by that knowledge, stated: "I gwine with you."

"No, you're not! Because I'm not going to take any body servant."

"Then," said Lummy, "I gwine run off and follow you on Miss Dorry horse. If the patteroll ketch me, you'll have to git me off."

"Mother," asked Maurice furiously, "does Lummy belong to me or do I belong to him?"

"I would say that you belonged to each other, dear. Lummy has been devoted to you ever since you were a baby and he was a little boy. In this case I think Lummy is right and you are wrong."

Absolom waited to hear no more. He turned and went down to the Quarters and called Elvira to pack his satchel while he groomed and saddled Red.

The autumn was lonelier than the spring had been; for Maurice and Rawlins and Sedgwick Lewis were too far away to get home on short leaves as they had done from the island. Mel came frequently to see Mrs. Bay and always brought news. Upon her last visit she had brought a thin man with too-large features and a small, sandy moustache. She introduced him as "Captain Gaunt."

"He's from northern Alabama. I've always wanted to see those big, old plantations in the Gulf states, and the cotton fields and magnolias by moonlight."

Although wearing Morry's ring, she could not resist giving the Alabamian a moonlight-and-magnolias glance between her lashes.

It appeared to make no impression on him. He said: "My home was little more than a cabin in the piny woods. I'm what you'd probably call 'poor white trash,' Miss Manchester."

Mel was not pleased. He was the newest captive of her bow and spear, and his importance might have redounded to her credit. She tilted her chin. "Don't try to be so modest. Everybody knows that General Beauregard asked that you be sent here. Even if you won't tell what you're doing, everybody is saying that it's something important."

"Everybody is saying too much. That's just the trouble," he told her.

"I'm sure it's some mysterious weapon," persisted Mel. "Hasn't a Confederate soldier submitted plans for a submarine gunboat?"

Mrs. Bay saw that he did not intend to answer that. She said: "I wish my son could meet you, Captain Gaunt. He loves the water and has built boats and sailed them since he was a child."

Gaunt looked at her attentively. "He would probably be of more use here in harbor defense than he is in the cavalry."

"How I wish he was here! I'd feel he was safe, tinkering with boats in the harbor he knows so well."

"Would you?" he asked her in his strangely expressionless voice.

Aunt M'lanny heard rumors of torpedoes and bombardment and arrived at the house one day in a state of terror. She was leaving. "I've sent Carolus and Tom on ahead to open the Flat Rock house. But I'll be horribly lonely. Why don't you come with me, Clelia?"

Mrs. Bay shook her head. Leave Morry? Leave Charleston? Not until she had to.

"Well—if you won't." She brightened. "The Kings and the Howes are still there, I believe. I'll count on you to look after Middy. He can come here when off duty, just as he would have come to his home."

So it happened that young Middleton, donning for the first time a naval lieutenant's uniform, displayed it to his aunt instead of his mother. He stood in the middle of the room while Dorry and Dinah walked around him, making admiring comments.

"I'm on a boat that patrols Stono Inlet. That's just as important as the bar, because it's the back door to Charleston. Wait till old Morry sees me in these do-dads! I'll make him salute me three times for every time he's thumped my head."

He came often, and sometimes Mel was with them when he did. She had no patience with him. "If Morry were here he'd tell you not to talk that way, Middy. You have no business telling your patrol route or where gun placements are being built on James Island and John's Island."

"I'm only talking in the family. There's no need to make such a fuss."

"Not entirely the family." Her eyes flickered across Dinah's face. "Somebody is sending the Yankees information about harbor defenses. I heard several officers discussing it this afternoon."

Dinah wondered how she could overlook the fact that the officers alluded to had discussed it before her and that she was in turn telling about it. But she went on.

"Suzette and I had driven up to the Citadel Green to watch the cadets drill. Captain Gaunt and Lieutenant Twigg came up to our carriage."

How on earth, thought Dinah, did Twigg get a commission?

She knew nothing of his reputation with pistols or that he was instructing recruits in marksmanship. She held to the age-old fallacy that officer meant gentleman.

"I've found out," said Mel importantly, "that Captain Gaunt has been sent here to investigate. I introduced him to Lieutenant Twigg and he seemed to think Lieutenant Twigg could help him. Oh, I know that Morry and Will used to dislike Mr. Twigg. But it's different since he has won his commission in the Salt Water Rifles. He seems to admire Suzette. I hope she'll forget that Yankee. He's probably forgotten her."

They made no comment on her information, for they knew nothing about it. Middleton was relieved to find, next time he came, that she was not there. He dropped in whenever off duty, and he was with them the night they heard the yard gates clang and the women in the Quarters yell: "*Mr. Morry and Lummy come home! Sweet Jesus! Looka them big as life!*"

They ran downstairs and into the yard. Hilton and Titus held lightwood flares. Morry and Lummy had dismounted and were surrounded by Negroes. They looked tired but happy and were shaking hands all round.

Maurice caught sight of Middleton's uniform. "Great day! The Navy must be hard up."

Mrs. Bay took up for her young nephew. "Don't say that, Morry. We're all proud of him."

He laughed. "Well, I'll have to add that the cavalry is hard up, too. They've given me a commission and transferred me to Virginia."

"Oh, Morry, why?"

"Because I speak German fluently. There are lots of Germans in the Union Army. When one is taken prisoner, you can get more out of him if you can chat with him in his mother tongue."

But his time with them was short and hurried. During its two nights and one day he never saw Dinah alone, and he thought rather bitterly that it was best so. The next morning he called on Mel, and was, to his own surprise, relieved when he found a half dozen officers already in her drawing room. Captain Gaunt was one of them. Although they talked together, Maurice told him neither where he was going nor why. He would have been startled to know how much Gaunt had learned in that talk. The summary was: Nice fellow, but soft from easy living. Sent to the front as interpreter; not sharp enough for Intelligence. Either in love with another girl or darned careless about this one.

It was raining when he said good-by. He took his mother in his arms, with Dorry and Dinah and Mauma standing near. He looked over her head at Dinah and wondered how it would feel to have the right to take her in his arms with all the world looking on.

She met his eyes, then looked away because she could not bear it. She knew that he might never come back, yet he would not even kiss her good-by. The day before, when he went to Mel's house, he must have held her in his arms—held her in his arms and kissed her until he made up for absence!

She looked out at the harbor he loved, where the sullen swells were leaden. Tide foamed up to the sea wall in slow waves that did not break.

Maurice unloosed his mother's arms. "Stop fretting about me! You forced me to take Lummy along. He looks after me as if I were a child. He'd fight the whole Union Army by himself to protect me."

He was laughing at her, but he kissed her gently. "Take care of each other, and write to me, all of you."

Dinah, eyes on the gray waves, did not see his eyes on her.

34

THEY WROTE HIM and he wrote to them: as often to Dinah as to Dorry. His to her were gay little notes and quite impersonal, telling her of what he thought would interest her. "I understand that the Irish Volunteers will soon be in Virginia. Congratulate Roddy for me. The rank of corporal takes some earning."

They went almost every afternoon to see the company drill. Everybody was there, from Betsy Corley to Mel Manchester. They cheered the emerald-green flag with its golden fringe, and Dinah's eyes were proud as they followed her brother's squad.

Mel was looking neither at him nor at his banner. Her eyes were

all for the officers who surrounded her. Captain Gaunt was always
one of them. He watched every maneuver of the militiamen who
had not yet been sent out. He was with Camellia upon every occasion; yet she could not flatter herself that he danced attendance
upon her. In fact, neither she nor anyone else could picture Captain Gaunt dancing. He drove instead of riding and when she
asked the reason replied: "All my life I've had to ride a mule or
follow one in the plow. It's only you people who don't have to
ride who consider it pleasure."

It angered and disgusted her, and yet he attracted her strongly.
She would not have been at all averse to a clandestine flirtation;
but he showed no desire for it and he repeatedly asked her about
Maurice. Whether or not she liked a man, she tried to make every
man like her. It had become an obsession with her to break down
this sandy-haired captain who had no social graces and whom she
hated at times.

But she had no idea of letting go of Maurice Bay. One afternoon when she and Suzette appeared at the drill ground on horseback, she left her group and rode over to his mother's carriage.

"Oh, Mrs. Bay, I had a long letter from Maurice today. May I
come and tell you about it? It was a treat, for I don't hear from
him often, although I write more than he does. Until now I didn't
even know exactly where in Virginia he was."

"Come to tea tomorrow at five, and bring Suzette with you. I'm
so sorry for the child. She grows paler and thinner every day."

Mel laughed unkindly. "It's nobody's fault but her own. A
woman's a fool to worry about any man enough to ruin her looks."

They came next day, and Suzette sat quiet while Mel talked
gaily.

"You know, of course, how amusingly Morry can talk and
write. He says that so far he's a failure at getting information, and
he hopes to be attached to a cavalry company for raids. He's right
on the border and in the thick of it."

Dinah's heart jumped and she saw Mrs. Bay wince, but Mel
went on as vivaciously as before.

"He says the only prisoner with whom he has spoken is a boy
from Bavaria. When this boy heard that Morry had been at
Heidelberg and had spent a summer walking in the Bavarian Alps,
he called him 'brother' and broke down and cried for homesick-

ness. Morry said he could have had all the secrets of Washington from him except for two things: the prisoner knew nothing at all and appeared weak-minded besides. I told Captain Gaunt and Lieutenant Twigg yesterday. How they laughed!"

Suzette did not even smile. Mrs. Bay seized the opening. "Mel, you and Suzette used to laugh at Mr. Twigg and refuse even to dance with him. Why do you now accept him? He is not one of us."

Suzette spoke for the first time. "I know that, and I loathe him. Robin always disliked him."

Mel turned on her. "You're a little idiot! Everyone says he's making sharpshooters of the men he trains."

Alight with enthusiasm she explained to Mrs. Bay: "He found that the old strawberry farm above the racecourse was too near the city and too many people watched them. He's very careful to keep secret what they're doing, for fear of spies. So they ride out now to a lonely place on James Island, near where the Stono River goes to sea. He keeps them shooting at the targets long after nightfall, by the light of fires they build. He says that when they go into action, they'll have to shoot in the dark as well as in the day."

"That sounds reasonable," said Mrs. Bay politely.

But Dinah's common sense told her that Twigg had been talking to make an impression on Mel. What secrecy was there about recruits learning marksmanship? Recruits, north and south, were doing exactly the same thing. She thought of the onlookers at parade, now mostly women and old men. It was not pleasant to think that one of them might be cheering South Carolina militia and sending out to the Federals information about it. She could not imagine anyone of the people she knew doing such a thing. It must be an outsider. Captain Gaunt was said to be an officer picked by Beauregard. But, after all, what did they know of him?

Mel's gay voice was going on. "How I wish I could watch them! I know a young man in the Rifles. He says that some nights they shoot by the light of three or four or even five bonfires. Sometimes they only have one, or none at all. Lieutenant Twigg says such conditions may exist on a battlefield."

Chaperoned by Mauma and Hilton, Dorry and Dinah went down to see the Irish Volunteers off not long afterward. When

Dinah kissed her brother good-by she said: "Roddy, if you see Morry—"

He waited with one arm still around her waist. From the train windows his appreciative comrades called:

"And you a married man, Corp'ril! But I cannot blame ye, begod!"

"Tis the luck of the Irish. But tis his luck and not mine."

She blushed and assured them naïvely: "He is my own brother!"

That occasioned a volley of redoubled whistles and comments:

"Ye look as much like him, me darlin', as Beauty looked like the Baste!"

"Whist, ye idjit! If tis true that the corp'ril is her brother, is it not true before God's gold throne that we are her brothers-in-arms?"

She kissed him again, embarrassed. "Tell Morry his mother is well."

Only Twigg's Salt Water Rifles were left now to watch on parade. They were a newer company and not yet in shape for action. The Citadel cadets were called on for missions and were restless to point of revolt when ordered back into barracks. Their ordnance officers were experimenting with rifles guns. So far, no cannon could reach Charleston from beyond Fort Sumter. The side winning the race for that discovery first would have an incalculable advantage.

Defense of the coast and the harbor was being pushed as steadily as the Confederacy's limited resources allowed. Walking on High Battery, Dinah and Dorry saw a huge raft being towed toward the shoal called the Middle Ground. They rushed back to the house for Morry's telescope and, with its aid, saw rock from following barges loaded onto this grillage until it sank. Day after day the barges took ballast stone from Charleston's wharves out to the spot and dumped it. Before their eyes it rose above high tide mark. Then they watched gun emplacements being set and guns mounted upon them. Mel reported that one of her numerous officers said the small fort on the Middle Ground was to be named Ripley for the commandant of James Island and Saint Andrew's Parish.

It was at just this time that Mrs. Bay got a puzzling letter from Maurice. It enclosed another letter and all it told her was:

> Lummy and the horses and I are well. I don't know how on earth Robin knows where I am. But he's right about Twigg. The man is unendurable. See if you can warn Mel and Suzette to avoid him, without bringing Robin into the matter. But do not, *at any cost,* show Robin's letter to anyone. I'm glad that Roddy's a sergeant. Dinah hadn't told me.

Mrs. Bay handed it to Dinah after Dorry had gone to bed. The two women were now accustomed to spend the long, lonely evenings together. Dinah read the brief note and then the unsigned scrawl from McRae:

> Morry, I'm risking more than my skin to send you this, but it's worth it. Will you, for the dear God's sake, keep Suzette from getting entangled with that devil Twigg. If she should—well, I can't tell you what might come of it! Let it go that I'm jealous. That's true. She's the only woman I love. If you can stop Mel, stop her too. We always thought him a swine. Now I have proof that he's one, although I can't tell you why. You can tell Miss Dinah that Sergeant Corley is well.

Mrs. Bay puzzled over it. "Perhaps Robin McRae has been captured."

Nor did Dinah understand, but she sensed a hidden danger. "If he were taken prisoner, ma'am, Morry would be seeing him. There would then be no reason for him to write the letter."

"That is true. But how can I warn Mel and Suzette without showing them the letters?"

Dinah cried out: "I beg you not! Morry said show it to no one."

"Yes, he did," said Mrs. Bay. She read the letter over again. She read it aloud and slowly and Dinah, listening, took heed upon second thought of what in it concerned herself.

"Roddy is nowt but a corporal."

"He was when he left Charleston, but he may have been promoted."

"He may that," said Dinah. She was pleased at the thought. Then her eyes went wider. "But how would Leftenant McRae be knowing?"

Mrs. Bay remembered wild tales of espionage where agents delivered lists of enemy officers' names and rank. But she had no idea of frightening Dinah. She said: "I hate to reprove Mel. I don't want her to think me an interfering mother-in-law."

For another reason she was troubled about Mel. Mel had always been a beauty and popular. She had always sought attention and been the center of interest to men. But it seemed now to Mrs. Bay that her behavior was not dignified for an engaged girl whose fiancé was in the front line of battle. Her name seemed to be linked with that of every new man who came to Charleston. Many came now, for harbor defense and on the blockade runners. Houses were thrown open to them and women made them welcome. But Mel's attitude toward them had nothing in common with hospitality. She flirted with them and openly exhibited them as her latest conquests. Mrs. Bay's friends mentioned it, as friends are prone to do. M'lanny wrote from Flat Rock as ingenuously as she talked:

> Are Mel and Morry still engaged? I hear she accepts attentions from some captain who either catches spies or is himself a spy. Will you ask Dinah to pick and send me a box of opoponax? As you know, I like to keep them in my bureau drawers. I know that my angel looks handsome in his naval uniform. It seems hard that his own mother cannot see him; but I have to make that sacrifice, with others, for this dreadful war.

Mrs. Bay did not show that letter even to Dinah. Thought of Morry's being hurt either by Mel's neglect or by gossip was unendurable to her. She tried to be fair and remember that Mel was young and pretty. She still wore his ring and, in Mrs. Bay's presence, spoke of him possessively and proudly. Perhaps any other girl, if sought after as she was, would do as she was doing. War times were not normal times. Perhaps patriotism caused Mel to be kind to all southern soldiers. Yet, she remembered, Mel had not volunteered for work at the Trapman Street Hospital where workers were needed badly. Dinah gave several hours each day, and returned with her eyes red from sympathy and her hands red from work in carbolic fluids. Mrs. Bay herself visited there and read to and wrote letters for patients. They both gave as much time as they could spare; but Dorry needed them too. It was hard to make her eat enough of the unappetizing fare they now lived on. She suffered from headaches and complained of pain in her legs and chills down her back.

"What would I do without Dinah?" Mrs. Bay kept asking herself. She recalled the night when Morry, happy and carefree then, had brought her home as casually as he brought any homeless thing. Her only thought that night had been to help the forlorn little stranger. She saw again the sad gray eyes and the clothes bundled in the Irish shawl. But gently and unobtrusively the stranger had twined herself around their heartstrings and into their very lives.

As she entered the house now, sad from hours with wounded men, Dinah met her and gently relieved her of hat and cloak. "I have a cup of hot tea made for you. Come drink it before you go upstairs, ma'am."

It was a treat they seldom got. Middy had brought a few pounds a week before. "The *Lodebar* brought it in from Bermuda," he said proudly. "She's a blockade runner now, Aunt Clelia."

She sat at the table, facing the front windows as she sipped it. She was grateful for its heat and strength, but felt selfish because Dinah refused to share it. Out in the street it was dusk but not yet dark. She heard heavy wheels on the cobblestones. "It sounds like a wagon, Dinah."

Dinah went to the window and looked out. Into their range of vision came two mules drawing a covered vehicle. They both saw such vehicles unloading day after day at the entrance to the Trapman Street Hospital. They saw it stop at the gate. They could not mistake an army ambulance.

35

Servants and family rushed together into the garden. Mrs. Bay cried: "Thank God I hear him swearing!"

Dinah was thankful too for every angry word she heard issuing from the ambulance. "I can walk, blast you! I won't go on that stretcher! You'll scare my family to death. Give me an arm and help me along."

They lifted him out and he walked after a fashion, shuffling between two orderlies. But he was alive and they could see that he still had two legs and two arms.

Elvira cried: "Where's Lummy?" She began to howl.

"He's all right. And so is Dorry's horse. Lummy's riding it home. All trains are now needed for the wounded."

He stopped—and Dinah saw his mouth twist with a pain that was not physical. "But he isn't bringing the mare. She—she was killed under me."

He told them all about it during the long days of nursing. "A shell burst close by us. It killed her at once, thank God! Before I lost consciousness I crawled close to her with my pistol. But I saw there wasn't any need for that."

Dinah, sitting by his bed, leaned and took his hand in hers.

"She was magnificent, Dinah. She never once refused me. Sometimes I felt her shiver. But she did what I asked her to do."

Dinah was seeing her shiver in the crude stall on the cattle boat. She felt again the velvet-soft nose nudge her for reassurance.

"You were good to her and she loved you. I'm thinking real love is like that. It is not to do the thing you want but the thing that is best for the one you love."

He felt his eyes blurring. "Remember the tilting at Middleburg? She had never done it before. She was puzzled at first and afraid. But as soon as she knew what I asked of her she gave me all she had."

He turned his face away from her and lay, still and exhausted. What thread in life's pattern had brought the mare from Ireland to joust by a brackish river and die in Virginia hills?

Dinah was thinking of it too. During the hours she spent with him her thoughts went back repeatedly to their too-brief times together. He was often strangely silent. She laid it to suffering and to his grief for the animal he had loved. She could not know that he, like her, was counting every hour past. He felt her face between his two hands when he had crowned her his queen at the tilt. That was, he told himself, the only sensible thing he had done.

In all else he had blundered. He had been a blind fool. If from the beginning he had been gentle yet shown that he loved her honorably, he might have made her love him.

But he had not known that he loved her, he reminded himself. He had been thinking only of his pursuit of Mel. Her beauty had drawn him on into a morass from which he could not escape.

He groaned. Dinah rose quickly and put down her sewing. She came to him. "Is it the pain? I will call Ann to bring more hot water for the jug."

"It's hot enough—and it isn't the pain. It's just that when I think . . ."

She leaned and put a cool, firm hand on his forehead. He caught it and held it in both of his. "Talk to me! Tell me what you do at the hospital when you leave me every day?"

"Scrubbing is my work. I am good at it." She smiled at him but drew her hand away. "I had choice of that or the operating room. I am strong, but I would rather scrub floors and wash garments than to see the surgeons work."

"I don't blame you. What do Mel and Suzette do?"

She turned to draw the chair with her work nearer his bed, and she answered carefully. "Suzette writes letters for soldiers, as your mother does. I do not know what Mel does. We are not there at the same hours."

He looked at her sharply, but she held up between them the shapeless garment upon which she was sewing. He recognized it.

"A hospital shirt! They had me in one like that in the ward in Richmond."

"God be thanked," she said softly, "that we got you home again!"

The words gave him heart. "I feel better," he said. "Will you put more pillows under my head?"

"Ah, but should you be sitting up? The doctor has not yet said that you could."

"He hasn't said I couldn't. Please help me, Dinah!"

She put her arms around his shoulders and helped him pull higher in the bed. He could have done it himself, but he pretended he could not. She packed the pillows carefully, then stood off and gazed at him.

"Now you look like yourself again!" She knew that he needed

cheering. "We will soon have you strong and raging around. I hear your mother coming upstairs. She will be proud to see you so."

But it was Mel. She exclaimed with surprise to see him sitting up. "How nice, Morry!" She gave Dinah the coolest of nods. "You'll soon be well enough to go driving, or even riding, with me."

He laughed. "Perhaps I will, thanks to Nurse Dinah. She's got me up this far, and she says she'll soon have me 'raging around.' "

Dinah saw Mel's face change suddenly. "Do you mean Dinah undertook to let you sit up without the doctor's permission?"

"She helped me because I asked her to. It can't hurt me."

Dinah was already moving toward the door. As she went through it she heard Mel say: "If you have a turn for the worse, I'll know who to blame!"

She always left the room when Mel came. And at this time Mel came every day. She was proud of Maurice. It was easy to be devoted to a fiancé who had been wounded in one of the notable cavalry charges of the war. He redounded to her credit but, being confined to bed, did not interfere with her engagements with other men. She was at once kind and gay, affectionate and amusing. She told him all about Captain Gaunt. He began to piece things together. . . .

"Captain Gaunt likes you. He's anxious to see you again."

"Don't bring anybody yet, Mel. This leg still gives me fits at times."

He would not have had to tell Dinah that. She sensed it when he suffered and was quietly tender, although she humored him by letting him try to sit up. He had no broken bones; but a fragment of the same shell which had killed his horse had gone deep into his thigh. In Richmond it had been removed and the wound stitched. Then he had been sent home for ligaments and muscles to heal. Hospital beds were needed for more urgent cases.

Mel said impatiently: "I don't see why you suffer. A blockade runner came in today, and it brought a little morphine. I know a medical officer in the Trapman Street Hospital, and"—she smiled —"I know he'll give me anything I ask."

He was terribly angry. "Flirt with the swine if you choose! But never suggest such a thing to me again. Until that morphine came in men were being held down by force for operations. There's little enough of it and it will go soon enough. Do you think I'd accept a grain merely to ease me and make me sleep?"

"I think you're silly," she said. She leaned and kissed him good-by.

He felt the usual relief at her departure. It troubled him, but he had to face it. It was Dinah he wanted beside him. To have her there soothed him and made the pain seem less. For the first time in his healthy life he had leisure to think now. He went over it all. She had never heard from the English soldier. There was now no chance of his getting through the blockade. Dinah had waited long enough, and he would tell her so. His illness and the sweet intimacy of her attendance on him made him feel that he might have a chance and that he must try for happiness. His narrow escape from death had given him a new and clearer perspective on life. Why let convention keep him from the woman he loved, holding him to one he no longer loved and who did not love him?

He saw that Mel's visits were only to feed her own conceit by showing him as her property. Although he had told her he suffered too much to see company, she had brought Suzette one afternoon. He happened to be in pain, but the girl's pathetic face made him forget himself and think of her and his friend McRae. He said: "Cheer up, Sue! I had news of Robin while I was on the border and he loves you just as much as ever."

She had cast herself against the footboard of his bed. "Oh, Morry! Where is he?"

"Ouch!" he exclaimed. "Don't jar my leg. I don't know where Robin is. He apparently knew just where I was. I'm still wondering how."

"Did you see him? What did he say? Tell me, Morry!"

"No, I didn't see him." He tried to speak lightly. Robin had said: *Let it go that I'm jealous.* So he took that tack. "He said he loved you. But he told me to warn you that if you look at another man, or even glance sideways at one named Twigg, he has a pretty Yankee girl picked out in your place for Mrs. McRae."

Mel had scoffed unkindly. "There are other fish in the sea!"

But Suzette said stoutly through her tears: "Not for me! He's the only one."

Mel had at first, in interest and excitement, come too often and inconsiderably brought others. Now of a sudden, when he was better and really needed companionship her visits became less frequent. He did not actually miss her; but it piqued him, because he knew the reason. Two of the more noted blockade runners were in port and their officers were being entertained.

He thought it all out and told himself that he was a fool. What did he owe to a woman who treated him that way? Why let her spoil his life and deprive him of the woman he loved?

But at that point he gave up, as he had done so often before. The woman he loved did not love him, he told himself with finality. She was waiting for another man. He saw less of her now; because, since he was better, she had gone back to full time of hospital duty. She sat with him in the evenings, and he waited all day for that. Sometimes they talked. Sometimes he lay silent, watching her as she sewed. Was he a fool not to take a chance and try his luck? Or, if he did, would he be taking advantage of her and even risking making her leave his house?

More and more he was certain that he wanted her. He wanted her to sit with him, to put his pillows behind his head, to feed him soups and eggnoggs, even after he could feed himself. He made up his mind that he could not go on in this state of suspense. He had to tell Dinah he loved her. As well have all hope dashed as to endure this misery of doubt and fear and hope. As soon as he saw a time without danger of interruption he would tell her he loved her. He was waiting for the chance. It came when his mother said: "Darling, Cousin Ramsey is not well. She wants Dorry and me to have supper with her tonight. Dinah says she will be glad to stay with you."

Between exaltation and nervousness he ate nothing of that evening's meal. When Erasmus took the waiter away, he was seized with misgivings. Why should she love him? She had lived in the house with him and seen how selfish and careless and high-tempered he was. If he dared tell her it might frighten her away. Once he had frightened her with a kiss.

Standing by him Dinah looked down at his bent head and disconsolate pose. She cried: "You are suffering more, and your mother is not here!" She sat on the edge of the bed, putting her hands against his chest and trying to see his face. "Morry!" Her voice was anguished. "Do you want the doctor?"

The words and the tone gave him hope. There was nothing wrong with his arms. He reached out and pulled Dinah to him. He held her so tight that it hurt, and she loved the hurting.

"I don't want the doctor. It's you I want! I've wanted you so long, Dinah. I've always loved you and I can't wait longer to tell you. It was different before the war. But now I've seen death too close to risk any waiting. I have a right to life, and to love. You mean both to me."

She lay still against him. He did not know what she was thinking.

"Dinah, are you angry with me because I told you? I tried to hide it, but I couldn't any longer."

She turned so gently in his arms that he was not reminded of his wound. Her eyes looked up into his: tender and wide and gray. "How should I be angry with you, my heart, when I have done the thing myself? Had you not told me, I would have had to hide it forever!"

Joy flooded his heart so completely that it washed away all scruples. He had come back from danger and death, and held his own love in his arms. That was all he remembered while he held her close and kissed her.

But behind Dinah stood a long line of North Irish and Scottish ancestors. Duty, which they had made a harsh word, was bred more gently but just as firmly in her. Although younger than Maurice in years she was older in common sense. Until now he had always had his way. From childhood she had been obliged to submit to the will of others. She saw all the obstacles that he refused to see. Drawing herself out of his arms even in that moment she saw the quilt dragged sideways until it touched the floor and the pillows fallen aside from his back rest.

She smoothed the bed covering neatly, dodging his arms and disregarding his almost-incoherent appeals. She shook the pillows and put them in place, drew his gown together across his chest, let him draw her down for one more long kiss—then disengaged herself again.

Such coolness and efficiency began to make him nervous. He commanded, "Let all that stuff go and come back here!"

She pulled a chair just out of his reach and sat, with her hands in her lap. If she even let him hold her hand she could not think connectedly, for she was not as cool as she appeared. She had learned self-control in a hard school. This was by far the happiest and kindest home she had ever known, but it was not her home. She had been accepted into it by Morry's mother, who had given her trust and love. She knew Mrs. Bay's horror of anything like scandal. For her son to jilt a girl like Camellia Manchester: beautiful, high-born, popular, important in the city, having enough influence to carry opinion on her side and brand him in the speech of the day a cur and a cad . . .

He knew what she was thinking. "Mother loves you, Dinah. She loves you more truly than she could ever love Mel."

She nodded. "Your mother loves me, and she has proved her love. Tis the reason that I cannot break her heart."

"Dinah, nobody would know. Mel's as proud as Lucifer. The minute I gave her to understand I loved another girl, she would throw me over. I would be the one jilted."

Dinah's heart leapt. She could believe that. Mel would never humble herself to beg any man to stay if he did not wish to. About Mel's feelings she cared no more than Mel had cared about hers, but the endurance of Aran stone was in her blood and in her voice. She said: "I have given my word to John Croft."

He exclaimed in impatience: "You've waited long enough! If he even remembered that promise, he would have come by now."

Her eyes lit again. Then the light died out and she spoke slowly and sadly. "Had I not kept on writing to him, I might hold by that. But I know that he could not come so long as he was in the army. It is only since you and I have asked Father Sweeney to find him that there has been a chance of any word reaching him."

He cursed himself as he recalled how he himself had written to the priest and had ordered Roddy to go to see him and explain. He groaned and dropped his face in his hands. The gesture was more effective than words. She jumped up quickly, went close to him and drew his head against her breast.

"Dinah, I swear to you, I don't believe he's coming. He could never get through the blockade now, even if he tried," he said.

She held him close and smoothed his hair back from his hot forehead. "Do you mind the night you found me sitting alone on the wharf? Had you not come, my heart was so hurt that I might have jumped in the sea."

"I remember! I've loved you ever since I brought you home, sitting behind me with your arms around my waist."

"Aye," she said. "And I loved you, too, although I did not know it. But the grief of that night is still on me, whenever I think of it. How can I let him cross the long sea, alone and lonely as I was, to find that I have not waited though my letters told him I would?"

"You can write and tell him not to come. Your letter will reach England in three weeks. We'll wait that time, and then tell everybody."

Her voice was a lilt. "I will write now as I sit here beside you."

36

HE RECOVERED more quickly after that. In a week he was hobbling around, although still unable to go downstairs. The drawing room was on the same level as his bedroom, so he shared young Middleton's visits.

"You talk too much, Middy! Don't tell these things elsewhere."

"Of course not. I know when to be cautious. But Mel bit my head off. She's crazy about this spy business, and from the questions she asks I think she's got some idea of who it is."

Sedgwick Lewis dashed in one day on his way to Middleburg. He kissed the three women, demanded all details of Maurice's experience, then gave them news of the Light Dragoons.

"We're still on picket duty. But they've issued us Enfields."

"Enfields for light cavalry are an innovation," said Maurice.

"They caused a near-riot. When they were handed out, the fellows took them by the wrong end and asked if they were hockey sticks. I heard Lieutenant O'Hear say: 'They must think us Artillery.' Somebody hollered: 'Let's have a race on our hobby horses!' We got astride of them and galloped around. They're ugly, clumsy weapons, but Captain Rutledge reminded us that they kill at longer range than pistols and sabers do."

He had as yet seen no killing. He amused them with tales of recruits from the hills who had never seen the sea and rubbed their eyes and took the pledge when they woke to see a tidal creek running the opposite way it had run before. Then he was off with a clatter of hoofs, calling back to write to him often. As she watched him go Dinah was thinking of the first time she had seen him. His comings and goings were always like that: happy and hurried and laughing. In this house they all loved him as much as if he had been a younger son. He loved them too. But he was off now on the long road to the plantation, to spend his few days of precious leave with his mother and father. His older brother Royall had long since enlisted and gone.

Mel had brought Captain Gaunt in once. Then he had called again and alone to talk with Maurice.

"If transferred, would you be willing to take duty here on coast defense?"

"Not only willing but glad!" To help defend the harbor he loved and to be near Dinah, Maurice thought.

"I've found out all about you since I've been in Charleston. It's a costly waste to put men in the wrong jobs. As soon as you are able to make the trip to Fort Johnson, I'll arrange an interview with General Beauregard."

Now it was nearly three weeks since the night he had talked with Dinah, and he was on his way to James Island. To his disappointment Gaunt was not going with him. A young sergeant had arrived to drive him in a buggy. Maurice had not been in a buggy since the time he drove Dinah to Lowndes Grove. He thought of it to take his mind from the pain the jolting caused. Then he forgot the leg as he thought that next day the time would be up. Next day he could tell them all about Dinah. Next day he could hold her in his arms with all the world looking on, instead of waiting around hungry for a stolen kiss.

The thought of Mel no longer troubled him. That was not going to be hard. She had outdone herself in flirtations recently. Kind friends had not failed to tell him; but they had no idea that he thanked God devoutly to hear about it. She seldom came to see him now, neglecting him for days at a time. He felt he could say honestly: "Mel, we no longer love each other. Marry whichever of these men you prefer. Everyone knows you prefer them to me— and I'm going to marry Dinah."

He wondered what Dinah was doing. She would be alone in

the house. He knew that his mother and Dorry were going to see Cousin Ramsey.

Dinah was alone in the house when Captain Gaunt was announced. She felt sure he wished to see Mrs. Bay. She went to meet him with hand outstretched. "Morry has gone to Fort Johnson, as you probably know, sir. But his mother will soon be home. Will you sit down and wait for her?"

He stood looking at her in silence, trim in his gray uniform. Then he spoke with eyes still on her face.

"It is you I have come to see, Miss Corley. I took care to come when the others were out, so as to talk to you alone."

If it concerned her alone, she thought, it must be her family. He saw her go very white. For just a second he wondered. . . .

But he had run into mare's nests before. Facts and intelligence pointed one way. He believed in facts and intelligence. He heard this girl whispering: "Is it—is it bad news of Roddy?"

He took her arm then and guided her to a chair. She did not know that from him it was a rare gesture of gentleness. But she called forth gentleness from a man, which the other girl did not, although he could not put the other exquisite face from his mind's eye. But he let nothing interfere with his work. He drew up another chair for himself.

"It's nothing like that, Miss Corley. So far as I know your brother is unhurt."

She wondered suddenly how he knew enough about her affairs to know that Roddy was her brother. Perhaps Mel or Suzette had told him when they went together to see the Irish Volunteers drill. He read the thought.

"I've had to find out all about you, because it has been reported to me that you are sending information out to the enemy."

Keeping his eyes on her face as he spoke, he saw that she was not frightened. The shock of his words had merely dazed her. It confirmed what he already thought. She looked back at him with gray eyes wide and utter amazement on her face.

"What would I know of secrets to send? And how would I send them?"

"Of course I don't have to answer that, but I don't mind telling you. An officer from a patrol boat visits this house frequently. He, like too many others, tells what he is doing and why. According

to my informant you have a friend with a commission in the Union
Navy. When Fort Sumter surrendered you persuaded a southern
soldier to get a letter out to this man by one of the outgoing
garrison."

She knew she had to be careful then. It did not matter about
herself, but it mattered about Morry. He had made her write it;
he had offered to take it; he had given it to Felicia's sweetheart.
He had trusted her utterly; and had involved himself.

She said very slowly: "I did that."

Gaunt asked her: "Who is the man?"

"His name is Seth Kincannon and his home is the state of
Maine. Twas he who befriended me when I came from Galway
to Charleston. It is true that he is a leftenant in the navy of the
North."

He let her finish. "I know all that. I am asking you who is the
man who got your letter out to him?"

She looked him straight in the eyes. "That I will not tell you."

He laughed shortly. "Luckily for us both, it doesn't matter. I
know who he is. Have you kept letters from Kincannon? If so, I
wish to see them."

"I have kept only the last," she said. "I am quite willing to show
you that."

He could not hurt Seth Kincannon, she thought as she went to
her room. If she showed him that letter it might turn his questions
from Morry. She drew the two small separate sheets from their
envelope and glanced over them as she started downstairs. Upon
the first he had opened his heart. She could not show that to anyone. Surely Captain Gaunt's interest would extend only to Kincannon's link with the navy.

She handed him the second page and he read it slowly. When
he looked up his face was stern and his eyes were dangerous. "So
I guessed wrong and she was right," he said between his teeth.
"No wonder you destroyed the first page, Miss Corley! It must be
incriminating if it is more so than this."

Involuntarily she put a hand to her breast. She felt the stiff
paper crackle where she had folded and tucked it.

He saw and held out a hand. "Give it to me at once."

She drew it out of the neck of her dress. He read it as slowly as
he had the first—then looked up at her and began to laugh sound-
lessly.

"You women complicate the whole war! First a woman sends me after you, on what I'm sure is a wild goose chase but which I cannot disregard because of your connection with a Federal officer. Then you go to the trouble to hide proof of innocence and give me a half-letter which could easily convict you."

He held the pages one in each hand and looked at her over them. "Let me read you this second one.

"I don't know when I shall see you again, for I am no longer my own master. But the Navy needs men who have knowledge of harbors along the Atlantic coast, and I've called at most of them, from Maine to Florida. Is there a chance that you've changed your mind and can send me the word I want?

"Don't you see, Miss Corley, that without the preceding page that question has to refer to harbors? By his own confession he knows them. He sounds like the man to make use of any information about sea patrols, shore batteries, sunken mines. You live in the same house with a man whose hobby is the harbor. So much so that I've called him to General Beauregard's notice for service in its defense. I've been told all about the Rowland boy. He's going to get a reprimand. So is another person who has been talking too much."

He paused, but she did not question him. She stood looking at him silently. He thought to himself: It's lucky for me I haven't got to make her talk!

Dinah was having upon him a strange effect, making him talk more than usual. He seldom bothered to explain, but he wished to explain to her.

"Almost ever since I got here I've been sure I knew who was guilty. In fact I'm expecting news of the arrest any moment now. But people have interfered and confused the case. Can you not see why I had to ask you? You had every opportunity and you are, after all, not one of us. The last page of that letter, alone, could have sent you to prison. As soon as I read the first page I knew he meant 'will you tell me you'll marry me?' "

She managed a small smile. "It did not seem fair to him to show you that."

"My branch of the Service, Miss Corley, is not a pleasant one. I do not stop to consider what is fair and what is not. The enemy I fight is unfair, underhanded and treacherous. Information is my weapon, and I get it by what means I can. Now I wish to see a letter written by Lieutenant Bay when he was in Virginia. I am not sure to which one of you it was written, but it refers to Major McRae."

Dinah thought: It has come! I did all I could to prevent it. I gave him my friend Seth Kincannon to make him forget about Morry. There is danger in that letter, for Robin McRae or for Morry. But how did he know of it? Could Suzette have told?

He said: "Are you going to get it? If you tell me it is destroyed, I can keep you here until the house is searched."

"I know where it is," she said. She was cold to her fingertips, but she turned quietly and went out into the hall.

Mrs. Bay's room was in twilight. Dinah stopped to light the gas. Then she went to the Chippendale desk and drew out a bundle of letters. As she removed the one on top and replaced the others, she thought of that autumn night she had sat at that desk and written John Croft. So long ago, and she had never heard from him. He must surely by now have got her letter about Maurice. Tomorrow the time would be up and she and Morry would no longer have to hide their love.

She was already holding his letter over the gas jet. It blazed and scorched her fingers. She dropped it, then picked up the fragment. She burned the last corner of it and then burned the one from McRae.

As she went out, empty-handed, a man in the uniform of the Salt Water Rifles was running up the stairs. He pushed by her as if he did not see her, stepped into the drawing room, stopped short and saluted Gaunt.

"Sir," he said. "Sir!" His voice seemed to fail him.

"Deliver your message, Sergeant," snapped Captain Gaunt.

Standing behind the man, Dinah saw his disorder. Sweat stains on his riding pants and muddy boots showed he had ridden hard. She also saw that Maurice Bay and Mel Manchester were now in the drawing room. Mel looked angry and reckless. Her cheeks were ablaze with excitement. She held a letter in either hand, but her eyes were fixed on Gaunt. Maurice was looking at him, too, but glaring rather than looking. He braced both hands on the back of a chair, his face so drawn that her heart ached. The long drive must have jolted and inflamed his leg, she thought.

But Gaunt appeared to see nobody but the man in the door. He repeated: "Sergeant, I told you to give me your message."

"Sir," said the sergeant, still gasping, "he—he escaped us."

There was no mercy in Gaunt's voice. "How did he escape you? You are an agent of Confederate Secret Service, and you were planted in the company to apprehend him. You had your instructions. Why did you let him escape?"

"Sir," said the man in the uniform of the Salt Water Rifles, "we did all that you told us to do. But Lieutenant Twigg must, in some way, have been warned of danger. He must have known and planned his escape and got word out to the blockaders. Before our eyes he was taken aboard a Union gunboat."

37

MEL'S VOICE ROSE almost to a scream. "Lieutenant Twigg?"

Gaunt paid not the slightest attention to her.

"Didn't I order you and Winters to stay with him? He has been signaling to the gunboat with the fires he built on the Stono bank. I made sure he got plenty of false information out to it while I was making sure about him. Thanks to Miss Manchester, I finally trapped him with Lieutenant Bay."

"With Morry?" asked Mel. She was whispering now, so low they could hardly hear her.

Gaunt looked at her. "Yes. You told him all about Bay's letters: where he was, what he was doing and why."

"But I was telling *you,* not him. He happened to be along with you. You and he were together so often that I thought he was helping you."

"I kept him with me all I could, to keep him out of mischief and to keep my eye on him. Immediately after you told us where Bay was, an officer of United States Intelligence betrayed the fact that he knew it by sending or writing a message to Bay. You gave

Twigg his warning by telling him that, too. I should have taken no chances and arrested him then. But I had no complete proof yet and I still do not know what that message was."

He turned his back on her and turned again on the sergeant, who was still standing miserably at attention. But he showed the man no more mercy than he was showing Mel.

"How did you blundering fools let him get away?"

"Sir, your instructions were not to take him in custody until he had already built the fires. You wished a report of the number and exactly how they were spaced."

"I did. I've been trying to make out the cipher they spell. Go on!"

"You know the location of that rifle range. It's on the bank of a creek that runs into the Stono. A hundred yards downstream, where it turns, is an old channel marker. Lieutenant Twigg has remarked several times that the navy patrol should remove it. This afternoon he said: 'If they won't do their duty and get it out, I will. Navigation marks like that are guideposts for invasion.'

"Those were his words, sir. I listened because I thought its removal a signal, and I wished to be able to report it to you. We had not built the fires yet, so I did not interfere. He ordered Winters and Ansell to row him down to the marker. Ansell, of course, left his rifle ashore, but I knew Winters had his pistols. I thought all was well, but I loaded my rifle and stood on the bank and watched them.

"The next thing I saw Ansell and Winters overboard, and Twigg rowing like the devil. I shot then, and I know I hit the boat. But I must have hit it above waterline. It disappeared around the bend of the creek. The tide was running out, and he was less than a mile from the ocean."

"Why didn't Winters stop him?" demanded Gaunt.

"Winters is badly hurt, sir. He was still unconscious when I left. Twigg evidently knew he was one of us and was armed. Ansell says Twigg suddenly hit Winters over the head with the butt of his revolver. Then he ordered Ansell to jump, and he threw Winters overboard. Ansell had a hard time getting Winters ashore against the tide."

"What did you do then? Did you even try to catch him, after letting him get away?"

"I rode to the nearest farm to get another rowboat, and I picked a couple of fellows who can really row. But it had taken minutes to fetch the boat and get started. As soon as we got within sight of open sea, we saw the gunboat standing off and Twigg already approaching it."

"That creek plays out in the marshes. You should have realized that the channel marker could give no information. You should have realized that Twigg was up to something." Gaunt's face was stern.

"I did, sir. I thought that by letting him get the marker we might find out something more."

"You thought wrong," barked Gaunt. "You failed in your duty. You may go!"

The unhappy sergeant saluted and went. Mel was looking at Gaunt with stricken eyes.

"Do you mean that Lieutenant Twigg took fright when he heard me tell you that Morry had heard from Robin?"

"I mean that. I know more about you people than you realize. I've learned that, while McRae was at Fort Moultrie, he and Bay here were thick as two thieves and both despised Twigg. I still can't think McRae would have dared to warn Bay that Twigg was a traitor. But Twigg, knowing how both men hated him, decided to clear out when he knew Bay had heard from McRae."

Dinah was thinking: Then Suzette didn't tell after all. . . .

But Gaunt was looking hard at her. He reached out and took her right hand and examined the blister now risen on the tip of a finger. "That wasn't there fifteen minutes ago. I suppose it means you burned Bay's letter?"

She shrank away from him. Did nothing escape him?

"It doesn't matter now," he said. "But if I'd caught Twigg it would have helped to hang him."

Mel cried out: "It does matter! Why do you try to excuse her? She has destroyed evidence. I told you she was against us. I was trying to help you, to work for my country. That's why I told you all I knew."

He laughed at her then. "Madam, your motives were utterly selfish. You were not trying to help your country or Bay or me. And, by the way, one thing you knew and failed to tell: Bay was the man who sent Miss Corley's letter through the lines."

Mel wheeled on Dinah then. But when she spoke there was no concern for Maurice in her voice. There was instead vindictive pleasure and triumph. "So you told him that? You treacherous little fool! You're trying to work on both sides. Do you hear that, Morry? She told on you!"

"No," said Gaunt. "She refused to tell. But you have just told me."

He picked up his hat and turned for the door, but Mel was following him. She said in a strange tone: "Are you really going?"

"Why not?" he asked her curtly. "I told you so in my letter. The only change in my plans is that, due to you, I'm leaving Charleston with a failure behind me. I had expected to leave Twigg in the guardhouse and another case completed successfully."

But Maurice had let go his grip on the chair and thrown back his head. Dinah saw now that the strain on his face was repressed fury rather than pain. "You are not going," he said, "until I tell you what I think of you for sending me out of the house so you could come here and bully a girl. When I think of Dinah, alone and at your mercy, I could kill you—you—!"

Gaunt's sandy eyebrows went up. His voice was amused.

"Before the ladies, Bay? Really, I am surprised at you. But where I come from that's an expression of comradeship. I wasn't raised, as you were, to think it called for a fight. So don't bother to challenge me. I have no time for such idiocy. I've never fought a duel. I save my bullets for the real enemy. You know more about your fancy code than I do, and might possibly put an end to my work for the Confederacy."

Mel spoke before Maurice could. She lashed out venomously. "You have no time for being a gentleman. I should have known it. But you tried to fool me. I've met planters from the Gulf States, but they were not like you. Only patriotism made me kind to you. Now I wouldn't wipe my shoes on you!"

Dinah saw the hurt of it darken Gaunt's eyes swiftly. Then they were again unreadable.

"This is untrue. I told you from the first that my people were piny woods crackers. I'm not ashamed. I'm proud of it. I've had to fight a harder fight and come a longer way than men born to the things I want. I told you what my life had been, and that you could take me as I was."

"Take you?" she said. She used each word to lash him across the face. "I wouldn't take you if you were the only man on earth. I'm glad you failed in your mission; and glad that I caused you to fail. How dare you write *me* a letter of formal reprimand!" She clenched her fingers into a fist around the letter in her hand and crushed it. "You dare to write me this—you low white trash?"

"Maybe you'll eat those words someday," he said. "I'll make you, if I can."

As he reached the door and turned he did not seem to know that Maurice and Dinah were there. He was looking at Mel.

"Maybe, someday, you'll take me on my own terms. Remember that. Because, although I know just what kind of a woman you are, I'll take you, any time, on any terms."

Dinah was watching the play of emotions on Maurice's thin, tired face. Rage had convulsed it. Then it had relaxed in complete surprise. A look as if of relief followed.

Mel was still watching the empty door. Her hands were clenched on the two letters. She was listening to Gaunt's footsteps grow farther away on the stair. She held her breath as she heard the front door open. It closed, and she gave a small gasp.

"He's gone," she said very low. She repeated: "He's gone!"

She looked from Maurice to Dinah. Dinah, being a woman, saw in her eyes what Maurice was only beginning to suspect.

He came back to himself with a jerk. "What do you mean, Mel? Of course he's gone. We're well rid of him. But I should have broken his neck for what he did to Dinah."

"That's what I mean!" she cried. Her voice was rising again. "Why didn't you kill him? Not on account of Dinah, but on account of me. You heard what he said to me, and you stood by like a coward. Why didn't you kill him? I'd enjoy seeing you do it!"

He said wearily: "I couldn't have killed him, even if I'd wanted to. I think he's a better man than I."

"He is," she screamed. "He's a better man than you ever were or ever will be. He's ruthless. He'd do anything to get what he wants. He's cruel. I'd read and I'd heard of men like that. But I'd never met one. Now he's gone."

Dinah stared at her in pity, Maurice in a kind of horror. She stamped her foot. "But he's a beast! Why didn't you kill him for what he said to me?"

"Because, Mel, I haven't the slightest idea of killing anybody for you. I know now you care nothing for me. You and I have come to the parting of our roads."

She began to laugh very softly. "Oh, have we?" she asked him.

She held a letter out to him. "Not after you read that and know what it has caused. You've let this little cheat turn you against me. But I'm still wearing your ring, and you're still bound to me. You ran after me and took me away from the other men I could have married. Now that I'm helpless and everyone is against me, you can't go back on me!"

He took the letter but did not look at it. He felt that the sky was falling. He watched her as she handed the other letter to Dinah. "This should interest you," she said, "you paragon of loyalty!"

It was unsealed and Dinah was drawing the page free. As she did so, Mel went on speaking. "The messenger from the ship arrived as I was coming in the door. He asked me if I was one of the family. I told him I was." She smiled maliciously at Maurice. "I meant that I would soon be your loving wife."

Maurice felt numb. He looked back at Dinah. She glanced from the page she held to Mel, with startled eyes.

"But this isn't for me. It's for you, and it's from——"

Mel snatched it from her. "I meant to give it to Morry and the other to you. Yes, it's for me and it's from him: a formal reprimand from an officer of Intelligence for the damage I've done and a threat if I do any more. But you're more particular, Dinah, than my aunt is about my letters. She got hold of it first and read it—— and has turned me out of her house."

Maurice did not appear to take it in. He was looking at the envelope he held. He said hoarsely: "This is for you, and it's from England, Dinah."

"I thought so," said Mel. "Isn't that nice? Happy endings for all three of us."

"Stop it!" said Maurice. "You've gone mad, but you aren't going to ruin my life. I know what you are now, and if you think——"

His voice failed him as he saw his mother coming in the door. She said: "Morry, light the gas! Why are you three here in the half-darkness?"

Her voice was unsteady. All three of them saw her hands shake as she stripped off her gloves. She dropped them on a table and sank into a chair. The yellow flames blossomed one by one at the touch of the lighter. Dinah watched them flutter and thought of the first night that she had come into the room. She saw Morry's mother, under that same chandelier, opening her arms without reservation to a stranger.

"What are these dreadful reports going all over Charleston? I hear that there is a spy ring and Mr. Twigg is arrested." Her voice trembled so that she could hardly go on. "But I hear that others are involved—some of them close to us. Mel's name has been mentioned." Her voice broke then. "I—I could stand anything except scandal."

Her face was so white that Dinah, frightened, started toward her. But Mel moved more quickly.

Mel threw herself on her knees at Mrs. Bay's feet, put her dark head in Mrs. Bay's lap and burst into a storm of tears.

"I'm a victim, Mrs. Bay, of this cruel slander! I was trying to help Captain Gaunt and help the Confederacy! He made me tell him all I knew, then he turned on me. It was because—it was because—I hate to say it but I must! It was because he tried to make love to me and I put him in his place. I told him I loved only Morry and was going to marry him soon. So he hated me and to punish me wrote me a letter full of lies. Aunt Julia saw it and believed it and told me to leave her house."

She was weeping uncontrollably now, and Mrs. Bay's arms were around her.

"Oh, Mrs. Bay, what would I do except for you and Morry? I have nobody else to whom to turn in all the world. Thank God for your arms around me. Thank God that in my trouble I can still count on your love and his chivalry!"

Maurice took a step toward them. "Mother, listen to me!"

But Dinah reached out and caught his sleeve, and he turned to her. For long seconds they stood, looking into each others' eyes.

"Tis no need to trouble your mother more by explaining now," she said quietly. "My letter is from John Croft, and he left England long weeks ago. He is on his way to marry me and take me back with him."

38

MAURICE HAD GONE to his room and slammed its door behind him. He could have fought back against Mel and told his mother what he knew; but what Dinah said had knocked the solid earth from beneath his feet. He felt that nothing mattered now. He sat on the edge of his bed with his head in his hands. As he came back to himself his leg began to punish him for the long rough drive on country roads and for hours of standing.

Still, he was ready for duty. Fortunately he had received notice of his transfer to harbor defense and his orders to report next day. He had assured General Beauregard he was able to start work at once. He knew the Confederacy's need of men. But he had forgotten, in all that ensued, his pleasure at being told that everything was already arranged and that Gaunt had recommended him for a captain's commission. What mattered most to him now was that work would get him out of the house and away from both Mel and Dinah.

Erasmus came in. He said anxiously: "You best come down and lemme give you supper, Mr. Morry."

Maurice shook his head. The butler looked at him. "Taint no need to worry too much bout Miss Dorry. The doctor come and gone, and he say her fever aint too high."

"Oh, my God! Is Dorry sick too?"

Erasmus looked at him even harder. He knew there was trouble but had thought it due to the fact that Mrs. Bay had handed a feverish child over to Mauma as soon as she came in the house. Before she went in the drawing room she had sent Rex for the doctor.

"Miss Dinah takin' care of Miss Dorry. Miss Clelia done put Miss Mel to bed in the comp'ny room, and Lulie carryin' a tray up to her now."

Then he could safely go downstairs. He went directly to the sideboard and poured himself enough brandy to make him feel there might yet be some hope. He was eating supper alone when his mother came in and sat next to him.

"Serve me here, Erasmus, instead of at the head of the table."
He saw that she looked both unhappy and ill.

"Oh, Morry. I am afraid that Dorry has in some way caught malarial fever! Cousin Ramsey has it, and I've been taking her there."

He put his hand over hers. "Why should you imagine, just because Dorry has one attack of fever, that she has contracted that disease?"

"It is not the first attack. We kept it from you while you were ill. This afternoon she had a chill in the carriage coming home." She began to weep softly. "I can eat no supper. If anything happened to Dorry . . ."

He got up and leaned over her, putting his arms around her. "Nothing is going to happen. Cheer up! I've got duty right here in the city."

"Thank heaven for that! And thank heaven I have you, Morry. I've leaned on you ever since I lost your father. If you ever failed me I'd die. But I know that you never will."

He ached all over: his head and his heart and the leg that throbbed from knee to hip. He said: "Can I see Dorry now?"

The room was dim, with one shaded candle burning on the bureau. Dinah sat in a low chair on the other side of the bed. She did not look up at him; but Dorry, drowsy with fever, raised her arms.

"I'm glad you came to tell me good-night. I'm so tired, Morry."

"You'll soon feel better, dear. Just take your medicine and rest."

Outside in the hall Mrs. Bay told him: "That's just the trouble."

"What do you mean?"

"I mean the quinine has given out. Dr. Leger hopes to get some by tomorrow. But there is none for her to take tonight."

He was aghast, although he knew what the blockade was doing to them.

"Dinah and I will take turns sitting with her and sponging her when her temperature goes up. That's all we can do. But, Morry, Mel can help us! She told me to let her know if Dr. Leger failed to get it and she'd get it from an Army doctor she knows. I'm so thankful to her. It may mean saving Dorry's life."

He managed to stumble into his room and throw himself across the bed. What an actress Mel would make! She had fooled him for years, kept him crazy about her. Now she was playing a perfect scene for his mother. She cared nothing for Dorry; he had often seen her snub the child. But there was no denying that quinine might save Dorry's life.

The brandy made him sleep, and next day he lost himself in the work. His knowledge of channels and currents and tides made a place for him at once. Torpedoes were to be laid, in addition to the mines. In late afternoon he got out of the carriage in the yard and limped slowly along the flagstones that led through the garden to the front door. The opoponax scent was so heavy that he stopped short. He was bringing Dinah home again on an autumn night along that same path. . . .

From a stone bench under the blossoming tree Mel rose and stepped in front of him. "I know you're avoiding me, but we've got to talk."

"There's nothing to talk about. I'm letting you break the engagement."

"Are you?" She smiled. "And suppose I don't break it?"

"Then I'll break it and tell why I'm doing so. I know what people will call me, but you won't escape their tongues either."

"Why won't I? Your mother has taken my side by taking me into the house."

"If you stay here, I shall move into barracks."

She looked at him speculatively. "There is little use for us to quarrel. I don't want to marry you any more than you want to marry me. But, if I break the engagement at once, people will think of gossip about Captain Gaunt and of the mean things my aunt said."

"I can't help what they think. Break it; or I will."

"If you do you'll cause a scandal that will kill your mother. She looks like a ghost today, because Dorry is worse. Besides, do you imagine I'll let you throw me to the gossips without telling all about you and Dinah?"

"What are you talking about?"

"All Charleston will be talking about you if you give them cause to say a word about me. Do you imagine they haven't asked questions and wondered since she came into this house? It would have been better for her if you'd treated her as a servant, instead of crowning her at lancing tournaments!"

His voice was dangerous. "Have you been spreading these lies?"

"On the contrary. It suited me better to be shocked and hurt. I gave the impression that I knew nothing of such things and was sure my fiancé was true to me, as I to him. But I could easily explain that my trust and innocence had been betrayed. I might say you had turned on me because, when your own mother took me in, I came face to face with conclusive proof that you and Dinah—"

"Oh, my God! What do you want? Why did you wait here to talk?"

"All I want is a little time to let talk die down and to make up my mind. I'm willing to make a bargain. If you keep quiet, I'll ask your mother to take me back to Aunt Julia and explain that it wasn't my fault. She'll believe your mother. That will suit you, because you'll be rid of me, and it will suit me. The scandal-mongers will hear that the prodigal niece has been received and forgiven. That will shut them up."

He had agreed; for there had seemed nothing else to do.

That night Lummy rode in on a thin, long-haired, footsore horse. He was himself weary and emaciated from five weeks of difficult riding. But he forgot it in relief and joy at finding Maurice alive. They had last seen each other in the hospital ward where Maurice had given him what money he had and instructions to start for home. But even with money to buy, there had been nights when neither he nor Dorry's horse had anything to eat after day-long travel. Maurice held the sick girl up in his arms at the window next day to see Absolom and Red Branch Knight safe back again.

Mel's plan had worked. Mrs. Manchester was so impressed by Mrs. Bay's sincere distress at her niece's misfortune and wrongs that she welcomed her niece back with tears and apologies. Even Mrs. Albemarle could make little of the affair, since Mel's mother-in-law-to-be had championed her, and her aunt confessed that it had all been a mistake.

Dorry's illness kept Maurice from seeing Dinah alone, and his work was of a nature to keep his thoughts away from everything else. He threw himself into it completely. He and the men on his detail were submerging explosives at key points in Charleston Harbor.

Rex and Melinda came to remind him of his promise. They had at last persuaded Lummy and Elvira to give their consent. After the wedding, the dry wartime cake and a little punch were served in the yard by moonlight. Then the younger Negroes danced to Samba's drum, while the older ones looked on with Dinah and Mrs. Bay and Maurice.

Dinah moved her chair close to the old blind carpenter. "Sometimes, when I lie awake in the night, I hear your drum, Uncle."

He did not cease stroking it. "Does you lies awake too, missy?"

He could not see her, but his keen ears heard her sigh. "I never used to; not even when I first came here. But I lie awake now, and I like to listen to it. I've heard you make it laugh or shout, or dance as it is dancing now. But when I hear it in the night it seems to be always calling."

"It kin call," he said softly. His fingers flexed and stiffened with every beat of the rhythm. "It kin call; and whoever it call he got to come, soon or late."

On a day in late October Maurice was off duty and in the tack-room overlooking leather with Lummy. He had attempted more than once to ride but found it too painful. Dorry was better but still in bed.

Maurice never saw Dinah alone. More than once he made up his mind to talk with her again. But he decided his arguments would have more force if he waited until Mel had set him free publicly.

He heard the yard gate open then and slow hoofs come up the drive. From the small window he could see only the gray's heaving sides and the legs of a Dragoon uniform.

"Sedgwick Lewis!" he shouted in delight.

As he stumbled through the door Rawlins Bull swung down from White Cockerel.

They looked at each other in dead silence. The horse's legs and flanks were black with sweat. His head hung down on his long neck and he breathed in quick, harsh gasps.

Maurice's lips felt stiff, but he said: "Take him at once, Lummy. Rub him down, and keep him walking. Wash out his mouth, but don't let him drink."

He turned to Rawlins and, by that time, was able to utter the one word: "When?"

"Yesterday. They landed a force of more than three thousand men."

Rawlins lurched slightly and put a hand on the nearest post. "By the Broad River. There were two brigades of infantry under General Brannan—small detachments of cavalry and sailors, a battery, sections of Regular Artillery. We were camped at Mc-Phersonville. Walker dismounted us to fight. Counting the sixty Drags, he had four hundred and five men."

He paused. Maurice said sharply: "Yes? Go on!"

"The only reason we held them was because we knew the woods. We shot from behind trees, Morry! We scuttled through the grass and bushes like Bob White running! Every man of us thanked God for those Enfield rifles we'd laughed at."

Maurice nodded somberly. "Sedgwick Lewis told us about it."

Rawlins closed his eyes and moved his head from side to side. "Well, those same rifles saved a good many Drags yesterday, but they didn't save him."

He swayed and clutched the post with both arms. "I've been fighting—and riding so long. Give me a drink! We've got to go on, at once, to Middleburg."

Maurice got him into the house and left him at the table, a decanter beside him, and Jody bringing food. Then he went out into the hall and began to climb the stairs painfully. From Dorry's room he could hear voices and the sound of the music box.

They listened in utter silence. Mrs. Bay caught her breath and covered her face with both hands. Slow tears were running down Dinah's cheeks. But Dorry only stared at him, as still as stone, except for her fingers which wound the painted toy tighter and tighter.

"Put it down, for heaven's sake!" he cried. "You're going to break the spring!"

She did not take her wide eyes from his face. But she reached out blindly and set it on the table and it began to play.

He bolted then for the door, but he paused on the threshold. "I'm going with Rolly, Mother. We've got to catch Little David. Rolly sent him on to change horses at Lowndes Grove and go on and call the ferryman and have him waiting at Dover."

She whispered: "Yes. You and Rawlins must tell Placidia."

"Littie David is so crazy with grief there's no telling what he'll do. He may not wait for us, but push on and tell her in the worst way. We're leaving now on Buck and Red, but we'll get Rolly's horses at the Grove."

He looked from one face to the other. No one of them answered. The music box played on the table. He went out and shut the door.

Going downstairs was harder than going up. He thought, with savage pleasure, of the physical pain of the ride.

The little music box still played, but it was running down. On his slow descent he heard it, faintly . . . and more faintly. . . .

> To war has gone young Marlborough
> And he—has not—come home. . . .

39

WHEN THEY GOT BACK, Rawlins rode south again and Maurice was almost immediately sent across to Fort Johnson. From there he continued to take part in the torpedo trials. While in Virginia he had learned all he could about experiments made with them against the Union fleet in the Potomac. His work threw him with both Captain Lee and Lieutenant Glassell. In the late winter of 1863 Captain Bay was detailed to place fixed torpedoes at various places in Charleston Harbor. Used that way they were new in war, and they were uncertain and treacherous. By March Captain Lee's "spar torpedo-boat" was completed: a semi-submarine carrying a submerged spar with a thirty-pound torpedo on its nose. Maurice, on trial trip in the canoe that propelled it with oars, realized that it was a step nearer his dream.

His work took him from point to point of harbor defense, and he was in Fort Sumter on that Sunday, April 5th, when the Union Fleet came in sight. In Charleston Mrs. Bay and Dinah climbed with the crowd to the top of Saint Michael's steeple to see it. As beautiful and terrible as the battleships of today, the armada advanced upon fortifications inadequate in proportion. Maurice, upon the parapet, counted the ships as they came: *Weehawken,*

Passaic, Montauk, Patapsco, New Ironsides, Catskill, Nantucket, Nahant, Keokuk.

In Sumter the band was playing. The flags had been raised and saluted. The artillerymen were lifting their scarlet caps and cheering. Young Darrell Drayton was serving the gun just below. Maurice could hear him repeating: "Aim at the *Passaic!* Don't bother with the others!"

From Charleston steeples and rooftops the citizens of Charleston watched. On the parapet Captain Bay stood up, forgetting to take shelter. Below him young Darrell shouted to outshout the noise: "Leave the others alone, boys! Give the *Passaic* hell!"

The ironclads were all firing now and the shore batteries had opened. Lee and Moultrie and Beauregard and Gregg and Sumter were answering. It was early afternoon. The attack had been delayed to wait for clear weather. The arc of each shell could be seen plainly as it curved from its gun to its target. Fire and water rose like waterspouts everywhere. The outer harbor appeared to be in the grip of a cyclone. Along the inner harbor, within the torpedo defense, moved the Confederate ironclads *Chicora* and *Palmetto State*. Outside the bar were waiting the Union transports and gunboats.

When it was over and the attackers had withdrawn, officers of of the harbor defense argued its significance. Except for the *Keokuk,* which was sinking, the armored ships seemed to have taken small damage from the guns. They were slow and clumsy at offense, but cannon balls were seen to bounce off their sides.

"Besides, they seemed to know and avoid our mines," said Captain Bay. "The Union has more ships and more men. They'll come back in far greater numbers. Our only chance is to learn how to drive torpedoes against them."

On his now-infrequent visits home, he did not discuss torpedoes with his mother and Dinah and Dorry. Instead he told them of young gunner Drayton.

Dorry asked: "But why did he want to sink the *Passaic* especially? Is she the flagship, Morry?"

He began to laugh at the memory. "No; the *New Ironsides* is their flagship. But Darrell had found out that Captain Percival Drayton was in command of the *Passaic*. In an interval between salvos I leaned over and yelled at him, 'Why are you trying to sink the *Passaic* first?' He waved his red artillery cap and yelled back, 'I've got nothing against the ship! I just want to sink Cousin Percy from Philadelphia!' "

Mrs. Bay's smile died on her lips. She could guess how many others were fighting against kinsmen in a war between the states.

But although the harbor attack was abandoned for an interval, a Union force had been landed at the mouth of the Stono and upon the southern end of Folly Beach. Along its highest ridge of dunes and directly through its jungle, their engineers were constructing a military road. In spite of fire from Morris Island batteries, their gun carriages rolled northeast upon it. There came a day when Maurice, now weary and desperate, saw their cannon unmasked to command the inlet crossing and their boats with howitzers put out from Folly's north beach. In a rifle pit on Morris Island's southern tip, he fought with the defense until Colonel Graham ordered retreat. Walking backward for three miles in deep sand under the July sun, they tried to cover exhausted and wounded comrades and to reach the shelter of Fort Wagner. He was among those who reached it; but they had been obliged to leave behind nearly three hundred men, captured, wounded and dead.

He knew in his heart that it was the beginning of the end, unless the torpedo rams could be made practical. A new and improved one was being built at top speed at Stoney's Landing.

But he knew that the Union sappers were now digging their way with steady and perfect efficiency where no woods gave them cover. From Morris Island, now in their hands, their heavy guns began to bombard Fort Sumter. Maurice, in charge of small boat patrols, brought back to Fort Johnson the warning that sheet piling was being driven into the marsh, less than five miles from Charleston.

There were officers who scoffed. "That marsh won't hold up a big gun."

"We thought their sappers couldn't tunnel a barrier island's sand," Maurice reminded them. "What can they expect to use it for if not for a gun? From there the city is within range of rifled cannon."

In order to watch, he and Lieutenant Glassell went dangerously near one night in a canoe. They saw that a grillage of logs heaped with sandbags surrounded a deck upheld by piling. In the starlight they watched the gun platform surmount this deck.

At Fort Johnson they discussed means of reaching it with explosives. But not even a suicide boat could get through the marsh to ram it. Guns from shore batteries failed to destroy it. Hidden in the marsh they watched the great Parrott rifle skidded out and bolted to its foundation. Before dawn, in the sultry August night, its first shell howled over the harbor and burst in the center of Charleston. While Maurice cursed as he watched, the Swamp Angel dropped fifteen other shells on the city.

When he reached his family that morning and found them unhurt he implored his mother to leave the city. "Take Dinah and Dorry and go to Columbia!"

"I don't want to leave you, Morry! I don't want to leave your father's home. Besides, I'm not sure your sister could stand the journey."

"I think she would be better off in Columbia. Take the carriage and drive there by easy stages. Spend the first night at Tranquil Hill with the Warings."

"The servants must be considered, too. I have a letter from your Uncle Gay that we must discuss."

"What did he say? Is the old boy still trying to get into Service?"

"They have accepted him, although he's fifty." She smiled as she thought of her brother. "That shows how young and strong he's kept."

Maurice knew that it showed how desperately the South needed men. He said: "Commissary, of course?"

"Yes. In Georgetown. But this is what I want you to hear."

Ever since the war measure of January 1st proclaimed freedom for slaves in those states in rebellion against the Union—*but only in those states*—there has been, of course, some of the trouble it was meant to cause. Up to the time I left Belle Isle my people seemed contented. But Flanders sent me word yesterday that Coaxum and two fieldhands had disappeared. I warn you because he may try to see his wife.

Maurice took the letter from her and read it slowly. "Flanders is a good overseer. Sometimes runaway slaves run home again. If they do he'll have sense enough to take them back with some mild punishment. But I'll warn Titus and Hilton and Lummy, and I'll tell Erasmus to be sure that the house is securely locked at night."

His nerves were now tight as violin strings; his work laid before him the whole panorama of coast defense and he knew that the blockade was closing in. Only now and then could a blockade runner glide through like a ghost on some black night. The last one he had recognized as the former schoolship *Lodebar,* but no layman could have recognized her. Seeing her drop anchor, he was seized with a sudden terror that she might be bringing John Croft.

The new ram had been rushed to completion in two months and was an improvement on Lee's torpedo-canoes. He and Lieutenant Glassell took her on her trial trip. She was fifty feet long and incredibly narrow of beam. Maurice, acting as commander, sat on deck only ten inches above water line and steered while she was propelled by three men in the hull below. Since they planned an attack upon the *New Ironsides,* a giant, they began to call the ram the *David.*

But when plans were completed for the attack it was Glassell who was given command. His crew consisted of but three men: Cannon for pilot, Toombs for engineer, and Sullivan for fireman.

Maurice, in bitter disappointment, went to General Beauregard. "I think you owe me a chance, sir. I'd be glad to go as Glassell's pilot."

"I can't afford to lose you both, Captain Bay."

"We've taken care of evrything, sir. We anticipate success."

"Arrange it then with Commander Glassell. But remember that it won't help coast defense to get yourselves killed or captured."

Mrs. Bay was accustomed to wake early these mornings. When the wind was from the south she could hear, very faintly, the bugles blowing reveille at Fort Johnson. It made her feel nearer to Maurice. She knew more of his affairs than he guessed. Camellia, with no good-by to them, had suddenly gone to Columbia, leaving Mrs. Manchester alone and hysterical. For years now Mrs. Bay had hoped for the marriage. She sensed that something was wrong, but the engagement had not yet been formally broken. Her son's happiness was as close to her heart as his safety was. As she heard the faint notes dying she recalled happily that he had said he expected to see them that afternoon.

Arrangements with Glassell and the crew took almost all day. When he ran into the house and upstairs it was late afternoon. He saw nobody until, as he reached the third floor, Dinah came out of the bookroom with something gray in her arms. He went to her. "Where are the others."

"Your mother was called to the Trapman Street Hospital. She told me to tell you she would not be long. Dorry fell asleep, so I left Mauma with her."

He put an arm around her and steered her back into the room. "Thank heaven for a minute with you. Put that thing down— whatever it is."

She laid it on the back of a chair and stroked it very gently. "Tis the cavalry cape that you brought back from Virginia. Had I known that it was torn I would have mended it before."

He caught her hands away from it. "Forget it! I've so little time. And my heart needs more mending, Dinah, than the cape."

She let him draw her to him. "Ah, if I could, I would!"

"Mel has gone. That sets me free. I came intending to tell Mother the whole thing, with you present."

"I have heard no different from John," she said. The name made her try to pull away. "Tis the same with him. He is coming, thinking as he comes that I kept my word."

But he held her. "Dinah, the only thing to do is to make up your mind what matters most. We love each other. Will you break your promise to him or break faith with your own heart and mine?"

She clutched him wordlessly. He pressed his advantage.

"I honestly think that Mother would tell you what I'm telling you. If you loved Croft I would not try to take you away from him. I'm sorry for him; but it's two against one to suffer. Do you not love me? Don't you want to marry me?"

"So much," she whispered, "so very much that I beg you not to persuade me!"

"I will persuade you. I'm fighting for what I want more than life. If you turn me away now I won't care what happens tonight."

She clasped him with all her strength then, and lifted a frightened face to his. "Morry, what is going to happen tonight?"

He groaned. "I'm as bad as Middy! I let a secret slip. But it's nothing important, Dinah."

"Tis something," she said. He felt her trembling in his arms. "You are going into danger in one of those boats like a fish."

"Dinah, for God's sake say nothing to Mother or anybody else!"

"I shall not tell. For I know that it could help no one to do so. All I'm wanting is to do what you wish."

"All I'm wanting is to kiss you," he said.

The minutes passed and dusk crept into the room.

He raised his head at last, and turned hers to look him in the eyes. "Dinah, after that can you tell me I have no chance? At least let me tell Croft the truth when he comes. Or—" he saw she was breaking down—"will you send me away tonight for good?"

She cried out again at that. "Morry, where are you going?"

"Only on a mission which I'll try to make a success. If I succeed and come back, shall I come back to you?"

"Come back to me!" she implored him. "Come back in spite of all! You and I can only tell John Croft the truth and then let him decide. But come back to me, Morry! For, until you come, I'll be on my knees to God to keep his arms about you."

40

A FEW BLOCKS AWAY he met Glassell on the wharf where they had agreed to meet. A little breeze blew from the north, and the stars came out through a faint haze. The long, narrow craft, painted a murky blue for invisibility, lay deep with ballast in the dock below them. James Stuart, who called himself Sullivan, was getting up his fires in her segar-shaped hull.

They waited for complete darkness, then cast off moorings. The ebb tide took them silently out toward the bar.

They knew that the Union flagship was now stationed within it, where she could support the forces on Morris Island and from which point she could fire upon Fort Sumter.

They drifted by Fort Sumter and the line of picket boats. Toombs and Sullivan had her steaming now, without noise. They were below. Glassell, Maurice and Cannon crowded the tiny deck, only a few inches above waterline. They seemed to be cruising in an undersized rowboat just within Charleston bar. Suddenly they could see the entire Union fleet silhouetted against the Union campfires on Morris Island.

They steamed in silent circles then, waiting for the tide and the moment. They heard the fifes and drums give their martial commands and fall silent. On the admiral's ship the nine o'clock gun boomed its order for "lights out." The three men on the *David's* deck crouched with their eyes upon that ship. Her starboard side was turned toward them.

Cannon whispered: "Let's have the guns ready, Commander! The last prisoner we got from the fleet said every ship had men posted on deck watching for these torpedo boats with loaded rifles."

Glassell's voice was just as low. "I'm ready. Captain Bay, will you tell Toombs we want full steam ahead?"

Maurice stuck his head through the manhole and gave the order. Steering with his feet, Glassell was turning the *David* slowly. Through the darkness they drove directly down upon the *New Ironsides* which lay exactly in the middle of the fleet.

Forty yards from their objective a deck watch began to hail: "Boat ahoy!" The cry was taken up on other decks. Maurice knew that, fourteen feet ahead of their bow, the copper torpedo containing one hundred pounds of rifle powder was being driven along on the end of its hollow iron shaft. Six feet below the surface it was gliding silently at the *David's* maximum speed of seven knots.

They were now close enough to see figures on the ironclad's deck. Glassell's gun went off by his ear, almost deafening him and causing the confusion it was meant to cause in the defense. Then the greater explosion of the torpedo threw him half overboard. He clung with his legs in the water, while the small boat lunged and rolled and the waterspout she had thrown up crashed down through her hatch and her smokestack.

He heard Glassell shouting to reverse and back off. He heard their engineer reply that the fires were flooded and the machinery jammed. Rifles and pistols were pouring fire down upon them. Drums on the flagship were beating "to quarters," and ship after ship took up the alarm. Glassell cried back to Toombs: *Cut her pipes and sink her! Each man for himself!*

Maurice, still half-submerged and keeping the hull between himself and the rain of bullets, had been thinking only of how much damage they had done the enemy. She was not sinking, but if she sank she would take them down with her. Glassell had given orders to abandon ship. He remembered suddenly that only four small cork mats were aboard. Life preservers had been provided for a crew of four. He, at the last minute, had made the fifth. He let go his hold and, throwing himself on his back, kicked off with both legs from the disabled torpedo ram.

They had counted on tide to take them out and turn of tide to bring them back. It had turned. Maurice rolled on his face and dived and swam under water in what he thought to be the direction of Fort Sumter. When he came up to breathe he was almost but not quite beyond the firing zone. A rifle bullet twanged inconveniently near his head. He breathed deep and went under again, then came up and floated on his back. From farther away than they had been before, he saw the ships ablaze with lights and heard shouts and drum calls. Except for a nervous watch here and there, they had stopped shooting in the water around them. That could mean either that his comrades were captured or that they had got away.

He tried to orient himself by the lights; but something had gone wrong. The tide should be taking him toward Fort Sumter; but Fort Sumter was now more distant instead of nearer. He trod water and risked holding up a hand. The wind had betrayed them. It had risen and was blowing hard from the north, driving the surface currents and a swimmer upon them out across the bar to open sea.

He was not yet tired and knew that he could swim. But, for a long pull of swimming under water, he would have to rest his lungs by spells of floating. Every time he came to the surface gasping for air, the rising wind and choppy harbor mouth lost for him more distance than he had gained.

Time after time he tried it. But he was losing the fight. He was now well out in the ocean with the lights of the fleet behind him. He turned on his back, fighting for breath and trying to think what was best to do. Wind from the south would have brought him ashore on some island north of Sullivan's and given him some chance to escape capture. Islands south of Charleston were in the hands of the enemy. General Beauregard had said he wouldn't help coast defense by going. . . .

He guessed that he had been in the water at least two hours. He had managed to get off coat and boots, but his other clothes were dragging him down. He trod water, discarding what he could. But the north wind chilled his exhausted shoulders and chest. His injured leg was giving out. Worst of all, he could now see no lights at all to guide him.

But he saw, as plainly as if on a map, the sharp southwest slant of the coastline. A wind that drove him south would drive him farther out to sea with every yard. He must by now be past Folly Island. There was no longer any need to fear capture by the Federals there. He must be somewhere off Seabrook's Island or Botany Bay; miles out to sea!

These were no longer harbor swells, or breakers reaching for the coast. They were the mountainous, tumbling rollers of the Atlantic. They were too rough to let him rest by floating any more. Several times they smashed him down under their tons of water. As he fought his way to the surface he realized that he had not enough strength left to spend that way. He must keep above them by swimming . . . although his lungs were bursting . . . although the wind was taking him hopelessly farther out with every stroke.

He was no longer thinking of what General Beauregard had said. He was thinking of Dinah. She had said: *Morry, come back to me!*

Thinking of that, he forgot he was cold and too weary to swim any more. . . .

Morry, come back to me! she was praying at that very moment.

It was midnight in the East Battery house. Mrs. Bay and Mauma and Dorry slept. Dinah, lying awake, was praying. Nothing mattered now except their love for each other. She and he would tell John Croft and beg his forgiveness. It was the only honest way. She had made up her mind. Nothing should come between them.

Ah! But if something beyond her control should come between them? He was out somewhere in the night on the sea and in danger.

"God," she begged, "will you keep your arms about him and the fish boat!"

As she got up, unable to stay in bed, she fancied that she heard the faint throbbing of Samba's drum. It was so low that it could have been the throb of pulse or brain. It was less a sound than an impulse to go to an imagined call.

She walked on bare feet through the hall and into the book-room. It was here that Morry had told her tales of the sea road east. It was here that he had held her in his arms and kissed her.

For long hours she stood there at the east windows, looking out. The tumult occasioned by the attack had long died down. Glassell and Sullivan, swimming, had been picked up and made prisoners of war. Cannon and Toombs had managed, by some miracle, to back the crippled *David* off and get her through the fire of rifles and howitzers.

The girl at the east window did not even know what had happened. Morry had not told her the details of his mission. The night was deceptively still. Distance and the southwest curve of Morris Island hid the outer harbor and the fleet's anchorage. Even in her terror she could not envision the dark, immense planes of ocean, rising and falling twenty miles off Edisto and thirty miles south of Charleston.

Her eyes, seeking him, looked too far to see the street below her. Later she was to wonder why she had neither seen nor heard.

For she was still standing there at dawn when Elvira began to shriek. Running out into the hall, Dinah located the screaming and knocking at the kitchen door. Maurice had given orders that only Erasmus should have its key. She let in the frantic kitchen maid, dressed like herself in a nightgown. Through the open door she had a glimpse of the other Negroes huddled together in the yard and staring at the gate.

"Coaxum dead!" screamed Elvira. "Lummy find him just now! He dead, holdin' onto the gate, and a knife stickin' clean through him!"

Titus had judgment enough to go at once through the front gate to summon the police. Mrs. Bay and Dinah dressed hastily and met them at the carriage gates. These were still chained and locked and, according to all three stablemen, had not been opened since sundown of the day before. Through their iron grill the two women saw the carpenter slumped on his knees against them and grasping them with both hands. They heard one of the guards say: "This man's been dead for hours. He's grown rigid with his fingers curved around these bars."

Mrs. Bay felt faint, but she had to protect her own servants. She asked: "Where did that knife come from?"

The guard examined. "It looks like a carpenter's knife filed sharp on both sides of the blade. It has B—Belle—*Belle Isle* burned into the handle."

She remembered that, in her childhood, she had often watched Madison Monroe Jones mark his tools so with a red-hot iron. Either Coaxum or one of his comrades must have brought the knife from the plantation. But the plantation was fifty miles away; there was no sign of the men who had been with Coaxum; her slaves, according to their own testimony, had not been outside the gates during the night.

To Dinah, those rigid hands locked in death's grip on the gate bars looked as if Coaxum had been trying with all his might *to get inside*. She heard again Samba's drum calling, softly but urgently.

As the horse-drawn vehicle called "Black Maria" took the police and the body away, Mrs. Bay thought too of the helpless old man.

"His room door is still shut. But he must have heard all this noise and be frightened. It's terrible to be blind and unable to move. We must go and tell him about it, Dinah."

Jessie joined them. She had just succeeded in calming her sister Mary Jane. "Pa been beatin' he drum all night," she informed them. "He wouldn't let me and Mary Jane put him to bed. He say this one night he gwine sit up in he chair. I hear he drum callin', callin' soft but callin' all night."

He was still sitting in his chair, but the drum had fallen from his quiet hands. His face was turned toward the door, as if he expected someone to come. His fingers, instead of being spread on his knees or on the chair arms, were clenched around a small object as tightly as Coaxum's fingers had been clenched on the gate. When Hilton loosened that grip they saw that it was a small wooden doll, low of brow and thick of lip, crudely like Coaxum. Its pine was smooth from handling through years of patient waiting. Driven under its left shoulder blade was a thin nail, the point of which came out in the ·chest on a line through what should have been its heart.

After breakfast, which nobody could eat, a subdued and frightened Middleton Rowand arrived.

"I say, Dinah, where's Aunt Clelia? No, don't call her! I'd rather talk to you. Has Morry, by any chance, been here this morning?"

She drew him with cold hands back through the door and to the bench under the opoponax.

"He hasn't been here since last afternoon. Middy, tell me what has happened!"

"For the Lord's sake, don't look that way, Dinah!"

He was barely seventeen; but for lack of Maurice and Sedgwick Lewis and Rawlins, he had to take up his burden as man of the family.

"Maybe nothing has happened. But he went on a mission last night, and—and all the others have been accounted for."

"I knew he was going somewhere." She could barely whisper. "You say—the others—are accounted for. Can they not tell of him?"

"I've been down at the wharf and talked with Cannon. He and Toombs stayed with the boat and got back to the inner harbor. He says Morry was on deck with him and Glassell when they torpedoed the flagship. Cannon never saw him after that. Dinah, for God's sake hold up! You've got to help me. We all count on you."

He put an arm around her shoulder. She leaned against it; for she had swayed on the backless bench. She held onto him gratefully while things came into focus again. She had to help him, she told herself. Whatever had happened, she had to help Morry's mother.

She managed to say: "You talked with the two who came back. What of the other who was on deck with Morry?"

"He was Glassell, the commander. He and the fireman tried to escape by swimming. They were in the midst of the fleet and were captured."

She breathed her relief. "'Tis likely that Morry was captured too."

He shook his head. She noticed then how young and unhappy he looked. His uniform was untidy and his face dark with fine, boyish stubble of beard. He had probably been up all night, either on his own duty or waiting with anxiety for news of the torpedo boat.

He said: "Morry wasn't taken by the United States Navy. We've had a report from the fleet. They've got Glassell and Sullivan. Morry's a captain, highest rank of anybody on board the ram. They would have reported him if they had him."

She was grasping at what she could for help, as if she herself had been drowning. "Old Uncle said he could swim like a fish. It may well be that he swam safe to Fort Moultrie or Fort Sumter."

"We've heard from every Confederate post. This happened around nine o'clock last night. A detail has been sent across Breach Inlet to search Long Island for him. But even a swimmer like Morry couldn't have made shore northeast with wind and tide against him as they were."

He felt her sag against his arm. He said quickly: "There's one other hope. If he took a chance of letting himself be carried out of the harbor rather than be captured, he may have got ashore on one of the islands south of us. If he did, the Yankees will probably catch him. But that would be better . . ."

He let his words trail off, but Dinah echoed them. "Twould be better by far," she whispered bravely.

She sat very still, holding the thought. Perhaps the thought would help him. There was no other way to help, or even to reach him with her love.

Presently she stood up. Middleton looked at her helplessly. Her eyes were huge in her pale, strained face, but she spoke evenly.

"Come into the house and get yourself shaved and tidied in Morry's room. Tis no way for a leftenant to look, and you will frighten your aunt even more."

He shot up from the bench like a jack from its box. "Do you mean *I've* got to tell her?"

"No," she said softly, "not until I have first told her myself." Her voice went even softer. "He would wish me to be the one to go first to his mother."

41

DAYS WENT INTO weeks and Mrs. Bay still refused to give up hope. If Morry had managed to get ashore, she told herself and told Dinah, it would have been to the south in enemy territory. He was a woodsman and had hunted sea islands and barrier beaches. He could have lived in their jungles on wild grapes and raccoon oysters. He would have done so indefinitely, trying to avoid capture and make his way home. But Dinah saw that her face grew thinner every day and that the white in her dark hair was spreading fast.

Weeks went into months, and Captain Maurice Bay was listed by the War Office, C.S.A., as having lost his life in discharge of his duty. Had he been taken prisoner they would have heard by now. In spite of their zeal for killing each other with efficiency, Union and Confederate forces maintained an exchange of courtesies.

Charleston was hard pressed by land and sea. Dorry was not recovering. Some people said that malaria was caused by a damp climate. Mrs. Bay consulted Dinah about going to Columbia. "But we would have to leave Mauma," she said worriedly. "The doctor told me her heart could not stand the journey."

Dinah looked out at the harbor. "Twas Morry's wish we should go."

There was no longer any need, she felt, to stay in Charleston. Middleton had told her things that she did not repeat to Mrs. Bay. He had said that, while the Federals would have reported capture of a live Confederate captain, they would not have reported one of the many unidentified bodies that washed up on beaches. It was like turning a knife in a wound to stay looking out at Fort Johnson and hear of the new submarine boat destroying crew after crew.

She looked out at the harbor, thinking how he had loved it. Before he went to Virginia he had said he would come back to it. He had come back to it at last . . . although he had not come back to her. . . .

The months had gone into a year when they started for Columbia. Hilton drove them by easy stages, so that Dorothea might not become overtired. The Warings kept them for a long stay at the plantation near Fort Dorchester. They rested at other places. It was January when they crossed the Congaree and drove up to the big white house on Blanding Street which Mrs. Bay had arranged to share with Mrs. Hyrne and Mrs. Cochet. Food was scarce, and Dorry's fever continued, but for a time they could rest.

Mrs. Hyrne and Mrs. Cochet were also Charleston refugees. The former had under her care two boys, her stepson and a nephew, as well as her own four-year-old son, a little daughter of two and a baby only a few months old. Her husband, fighting with the South Carolina Cavalry, had thought (as Maurice Bay thought) that Columbia meant safety.

But it was already too late for any safety. For the southern Confederacy twilight was closing fast. These women, cut off from their men, could not fully know the hopelessness of the situation. Major-General W. T. Sherman, at the head of seventy thousand veteran troops, was even then on the march from Savannah, with Columbia as his next objective and with total war as his plan.

News of his close approach came in mid-February. It was too late to flee. The day of the seventeenth was gray and gusty and threatening. Bands of Negroes, excited by the news that the Union Army was approaching, had been breaking into stores all day and were howling in drunken groups through the streets. Hilton posted himself by the front gate and defied Mrs. Bay when she called him back into the house. "I gwine kill the first one of 'em try to put he foot in this yard!"

"Hilton," she told him, "it's hopeless. We are not trying to defend the city. The mayor hopes for better treatment if we submit."

He said determinedly: "I gwine 'fend you and Miss Dorry and Miss Dinah. Last thing Mr. Morry tell me was to keep care of you."

She took his hard hand in both of hers and squeezed it tight. The tears looked gray rolling down his dark face. But her agony was dry-eyed. The only emotion she felt now was a great and terrible hatred.

The children's voices brought her back. Around the side of the house came a duck, running and falling grotesquely. Behind it was the youngest Hyrne boy. He threw himself upon it.

"Miss Clelia," he panted as he rose, clasping its pillowlike body, "a whole lot of ducks is coming through that hole in our fence. Something must have scared them."

She knew that the wholesale houses were destroying their stores. Orders had been issued, in particular about whisky. The owner of some poultry house had evidently opened its door, saying in duck language: *"Sauve qui peut!"*

The little boy said: "Sinkler and William Hume went over the fence to try to see where they are coming from. I'm keeping the ones we have penned up in that old shed."

"Darling," she expostulated, "I heard your mother tell you that not one of you must go out of the yard into the street."

"They aren't in the street," he told her with childhood's easy evasion. "They've just gone over the fence into the Crawfords' yard."

He turned to go back to his ducks, then turned again. "I'm having such fun!"

She and Hilton looked at each other in silence. She was thinking of the contagion of mass excitement. The hostile Negroes had been looting for days. Now the children were looting somebody's ducks. The thought was too dangerous for her to follow farther. All her life she had had some beloved man to lean upon. She had never been idle from girlhood, but always she had worked at woman's work. Father, brother, husband, son had in turn taken charge in emergency. Even Old Uncle was gone now. He lay in the plantation burial ground in Christ's Church Parish. What would she not have given for his arm around her and his advice?

She went back to Dorry's room where Dinah was sitting. The sick girl felt suspense in the air.

"What is the matter, Mother?"

"Nothing, darling; except that the Yankee Army may march into the city tonight. So do not worry if you hear a little noise." She knew she was understating the situation but had no idea by how great a margin.

Not long after that they heard the first, far, triumphant shouts and the drums. The children hung on the gate and watched the bright uniforms go by. The bands played "Yankee Doodle" and "Marching Through Georgia."

From the white-pillared piazza the women saw company after company of well-fed, well-drilled men in blue swinging past. Mrs.

Bay thought of the food she could not get for Dorry. Dinah thought of a ragged gray cavalry cape. . . .

Mrs. Cochet said hopefully: "At any rate, white men will protect us from rioting Negroes."

Young, stately Mrs. Hyrne sighed. "Yes, but surrender is a high price to pay for protection."

Her father and mother, who lived in a house nearby, came in. Both were over seventy and the old gentleman was choleric. As the strains of "Yankee Doodle" broke out he said a word he should not have said.

"Mr. Harris," his wife reproved him, "I am surprised at you." She looked severely at him under her white muslin cap. "I ask you to remember that there are young ladies present."

When the last line had passed they got the children indoors and to bed. Dorry's bedroom was upstairs and looked out on the garden. Dinah, keeping watch there with Mrs. Bay, first saw the red glow in the sky to the north. She called Mrs. Bay's attention to it very quietly, then left her with Dorry and went downstairs.

Groups of women were gathering in the now deserted street. From all four points of the compass red columns of smoke arose. Faintly at first, and then louder, came a hum of voices. It swelled to a tumult of yells and cheers.

Old Mr. Harris whirled his cane like a singlestick around his head. "The dam yankees are burning the city!"

"Mr. Harris," demanded his wife, "have you no respect for womanhood?"

He bowed to the frightened ladies. "I apologize to you. But I repeat that there is no other name for them."

His daughter tried to soothe him. "Perhaps the Yankee officers will make the soldiers extinguish the fires. Perhaps they have been set only by the ones who are drunk. Mrs. Simms told me one whisky warehouse had refused to destroy its stores."

Rumors were flying thick and fast. General Sherman had ordered Columbia burned . . . General Sherman had already had the looters causing the fires shot by a firing squad.

The fires were still far away but were getting larger and nearer. So was the noise of rioting. A group of soldiers came yelling around the corner. "Look at the damned Rebels," they cried. "Let's teach 'em a lesson!"

Old Mr. Harris, the only man in sight, raised his walking stick in menace. "Get back into your homes," he commanded the women. He stood, glaring at the men in blue. "I will deal with these ruffians!"

Dinah and his daughter dragged him by main force within the gate. The soldiers offered them no harm but went by jeering and singing.

Dinah went upstairs to Mrs. Bay and they whispered together outside Dorry's door. "I have just taken her temperature and it is a hundred and four. She must not be moved. Is the fire getting closer?"

"No," said Dinah comfortingly; "the wind is blowing the other way."

But she had already seen that the fires encircled them. Any wind that blew must blow one of them nearer.

Together they bathed Dorry's thin, hot young body and forced between her dry lips the last dose of the bitter powder. She murmured a while. Then her fever began to drop and she finally fell asleep. Mrs. Hyrne, who was staying upstairs with the five sleeping children, came into the room and offered to sit there.

"You and Dinah go downstairs. When you come back you can tell me whether things look better or worse."

They joined Mrs. Cochet on the piazza. Mr. and Mrs. Harris had gone to their own home. Outside the light was lurid now. Bare trees were outlined against it. It stained the old white houses and made bloody patches in the glass of their windowpanes.

Another band of drunken soldiers came in sight. As they did the three women stepped back in the house and closed and locked the doors. Through a window they saw the looters go in the next-door gate and into the house, from which came screams and a sound of smashing furniture.

Just then a group of officers rode halfway along the block. They stopped their horses across the street and sat, gesticulating as they conferred. The piazza columns, dark on a crimson sky, framed the man in the middle as he turned his face toward them.

Dinah cried out: "'Tis the red-headed leftenant from Fort Moultrie! You must go out to him, ma'am, and ask protection for Dorry. He will surely give it, for he was Morry's friend."

Mrs. Bay shrank back and Dinah saw the hatred on her face. "I cannot! I would rather die. And let my daughter die! I will not ask protection from the Yankee fiend who is putting Columbia to the torch!"

"I drank a toast with Morry," said Dinah very softly. "He asked me, whatever came, not to hate. I will go myself."

They saw her, in the increasing glare, go down the steps and the garden path. She looked a very small figure, holding her Irish shawl close. As she reached the gate, a figure lunged toward her from the shadows.

Dinah shrieked at the top of her voice: *"Leftenant Sherman, will you help?"*

The officers wheeled their horses. They looked at Dinah for a long moment, then Mrs. Bay heard Sherman's shout: "Major, break up that looting and put the looters under arrest!"

He came back into the house with Dinah. He looked the same, though he was heavier and his rust-colored hair was gray. He was as ill at ease as he had been when a lieutenant, but he was kind to them.

"Give me pen and ink and I'll write you an order of protection."

Dinah brought it. The General laid his hat on the table, drew up a chair and sat and wrote while his aides stood by. He handed the paper to Mrs. Bay.

"I was sorry to hear of Colonel Bond'Ion's death."

She shook her head. "I am glad he did not live to see this."

"It's war," he said. "War has to be merciless, madame. I'll place a guard here at once."

He saluted and left, and they read the brief order that meant so much to them.

> Officers and soldiers must not molest the property of Mrs. Bay, niece of Colonel Bond'Ion of the Old Army.

It was signed with the one word—*Sherman.*

The guard came within an hour, and it was Mrs. Bay who met him. On nights when Dorry was as ill as this, Dinah was accustomed to stay with her until midnight and her mother took over then. In the light of the fires still raging, Mrs. Bay, looking anxiously out, saw a stockily built man in uniform coming along the sidewalk and stopping to look at the house numbers. He opened their gate and came up the walk. As soon as he spoke she recognized an English voice. "I was detailed to guard this number, madame, but I was not given the owner's name."

"The name is Mrs. Hyrne," she said. "We are thankful that you have come."

He was not talkative but seemed polite and capable. He stationed himself on the piazza. "From here I can see and halt anybody at the gate. The night is no colder than a night of spring in England."

She asked impulsively: "Are you English? How does an Englishman happen to be in Sherman's ranks?"

"I served my time in the British army. But I was anxious to get to America."

"To join the Union army?" she questioned coldly.

"I have no quarrel with South or North. Soldiering happens to be my trade and I have to live."

She went upstairs then, thinking that he was little older than Morry. She had intended to reassure the others, but Dinah met her in the hall. "Dorry's fever is rising again, and we must have quinine! Mrs. Cochet knows the chemist has hidden his store of drugs. It is only to Lady Street, and I will go with her."

"I'll go myself. A young girl would not be safe on the streets."

Dinah wrapped her in the Aran shawl, for the gusty wind was still blowing. From the window she watched the two women go out of the gate. She could not see the guard on the roofed piazza below. She turned quickly as Dorry called out: "Morry! Where are you, Morry?"

She soothed the child and sponged her again, until she seemed about to doze. But every time she quieted, drunken whoops from the street awoke her. In her delirium she kept calling for her brother.

Dinah, tears running down her face, tried to take the girl's temperature. But Dorry threw herself from side to side so violently that it was impossible to do so, or to keep the wet cloth on her scorching forehead. Dinah was frantic with anxiety. Mrs. Cochet and Mrs. Bay should long ago have returned. It was only a few blocks to Lady Street.

Through the deeper shouts and the singing she heard sudden

screams of women's voices. She knew Mrs. Bay's, even in extremity. She left Dorry and dashed downstairs. As she reached the front door a voice spoke in the darkness outside. She recognized it even as it ordered: "Let go the women or I'll shoot!"

She saw figures moving in the dark by the gate. Several shots rang out. A man yelled in real pain. Then there was only the sound of running feet going farther away.

Mrs. Bay and Mrs. Cochet, blanched and disheveled, stumbled in. Behind them came a man in a soldier's tunic, blue now instead of red. In one hand he still held his smoking pistol. In the other he carried her torn Aran shawl.

He stopped at the door and looked at her. His face seemed to grow younger. "Dinah," he asked incredulously. "Dinah, my lass, is it you?"

She turned then to Mrs. Bay. "It is John Croft," she said.

42

WITH THE OTHERS looking on he kissed her quietly, firmly. His wooing had been like that, and it had suited her. She had not then known there could be wooing like Morry's.

Mrs. Bay was weeping with mingled nervousness and relief. "Dinah, my dear, is it really John Croft? Thank God that something good has come to you out of all this horror!"

Dinah was dazed. She looked at Croft. "I knew you would come someday. But"—she turned back to Mrs. Bay—"have you got the quinine?"

"I have," said Mrs. Bay gratefully.

She opened her hand to show the twist of paper she held—then cried aloud. It had been torn in the struggle at the gate. Only a dust of white powder clung to its ragged edges.

Dinah had forgotten Croft. She was thinking of Morry's sister. "By the touch, I know that her fever is up to a hundred and five!"

Mrs. Cochet grieved: "It was the last that the chemist had."

But their guard unstrapped his knapsack and laid it on the

table. "If you need the cinchona powder, I have here all you can use. Ever since I nearly died of malaria in India, I have taken care to carry a supply."

He handed a small box to Mrs. Bay. She took and cradled it in both hands. His calm, even voice was as comforting as his words.

"I have more than that. It is issued to soldiers entraining for the South. I kept all I got. I've always been a careful man."

Mrs. Bay's eyes were telling him he was not a man but an angel. He did not notice that; but, beneath his unmoved self-possession, his heart had leapt at Dinah's look of gratitude.

The other lady said: "God bless you! All I can do in return just now is to leave you with Dinah."

The night grew colder while they sat and talked in the library. For the moment the fires seemed to be dying down. Several times the approach of noise made him go out to the gate. She heard him order the looters away with quiet authority. They obeyed him. She was trying to remember all of his good traits. He was kind and calm and courageous, and he loved her still. But a little shiver made her draw her shawl more closely around her. He saw the gesture and remembered and smiled.

"Saint Kevin's spell must have brought me, lass! I shall not laugh at it again."

Ah, but Saint Kevin's spell was meant to bring the lover a woman still loved! It had not brought Morry back from the night and the greedy sea.

"The blockade runner on which I tried to cross was sunk by the Union fleet. I was captured and taken to New York and clapped into Fort Lafayette."

Something was constricting her throat, but she managed to ask: "What is it?"

"A military prison used mainly for blackade runners and Confederate officers. There I was, without a shilling and with no idea what to do. But in a few days I was told a gentleman had called to see me. He was a wealthy man who had just been drafted, and he offered me a large bonus to take his place."

"So they let you out?"

"At once—in charge of a recruiting sergeant."

She took the shawl from her shoulders and laid it across her knees. Saint Kevin's spell was a cruel joke, she was telling herself.

Lives were patterned from the start, like a weaver's warp and weft. The thread of her life had been patterned to leave Morry's and meet John Croft's again. Aunt M'lanny's song had said that a man was better dead than interfering with that line of destiny. How could a mortal man change it, even if he tried? In spite of what had been done to her—in spite of her love for Maurice Bay —it had brought her back to John Croft. What could she do except submit?

"Something brought me to you," Croft was saying, "almost from the world's end, lass. Could chance have brought me all that way?"

She looked up in his eyes. "It could not that," she said.

She was back in Dorry's sitting room and the rain blew over the sea wall. . . . Watching her, John Croft knew she was not with him but with someone else.

She roused with an effort and made herself hear what this other man was saying: this man whom she once had called "me John." He was trying to call her back to him by talking of Ireland and the past.

"At first I couldn't believe it. I went straight to the Donovans. I had arranged with the chaplain for us to be married at noon next day. At the Donovans' gate I met a big fellow coming out. He was half drunk and he asked me: 'Are ye lookin' for her too?' Before I could answer he went on: 'So she's made a monkey of you as well! She told you, I wager, as she told me, that she'd see you here?'

"Mary ran out just then. She was crying aloud and taking on. 'There's some mistake, John Croft! Dinah would not have done it!'

" 'She has done it, begob,' said the big chap. 'She has sailed for America—and after telling the two of us she would be meeting us at this house!'

"Tim O'Leary came up in a run. 'I have been to the wharf meself. I have talked with the boys who load cargo and who saw the cattle bowt clear.' I kept insisting there must be some explanation. I even suggested that your brother might have forced you aboard. Mary kept saying the same thing. 'There is a mistake, John Croft! There is.'

"But Tim told her: 'There cannot be that, Mary. I tell you I talked with boys who loaded the ship. They all saw her go aboard. They all say she went of her own will, laughing and talking with Betsy.'

" 'I saw her meself,' said the chap called O'Dell. 'Didn't I carry their luggage and see the three beds in their room? And wasn't I with Corley when he asked the mate if he had the cabin for himself and his wife and his sister? But she tried to make a monkey of me by saying she was not going! I was fool enough, the same as yourself, to think she would meet me here.'

"I went away then, Dinah. I didn't listen to Mary. My regiment left in a few days. I didn't even see her again."

Dinah thought to herself: So it was all as simple as that? She reminded herself that, all along, she had thought it could be explained. He had told her now, honestly and not sparing himself. She could not honestly blame him or think it was his fault. She had never, in her heart, ceased to trust him. Even her love for Morry, brief and beautiful, had not interfered with her trust in this man. But the two emotions were as far apart as the flame of a shark-oil lamp and lightning out beyond the harbor—lightning beyond that stormy bar where she had come in and Morry had gone out.

Croft shook his head unhappily. "I went through a bad time, Dinah."

She did not answer or look up. She was staring at the shawl on her lap. The weaver must have planned each thread, but to her it was tangled.

He came and sat on the arm of her chair and drew her head to his shoulder. "But it's all behind us now. We've found each other again."

She was trying to think of a red tunic though her face was against a blue one. For so long she had recalled the texture of that scarlet coat! Now it was gone beyond recall. She was seeing instead a worn gray cavalry cape. . . .

"Remember," pleaded John Croft, "the Valley of the Churches . . . and the wind on Straw Island's beach . . . and the green lanes of Aranmore. This war is almost over now. Summer will come in England. The lavender and the wallflowers will bloom in our own garden."

She had never smelled the wallflowers, although he had told her about them before Morry Bay had come into her life. Now, through the acrid scent of burned wood pervading Columbia, she smelled the star jessamine, achingly sweet in the rain. . . .

Suddenly she was weeping hot tears against Croft's blue shoulder.

He took her tenderly in his arms and smoothed the hair from her forehead. "My own good girl, I understand. It was not easy for me during the long years, either."

"It is just that my brain and my heart are tangled in all that has happened. Will you always understand—and help me to understand, too?"

"I'll always understand," he said, "and always hold you safe."

He bent his head and kissed her on the cheek, then sat holding her as if she were a child.

She closed her eyes, trying to hush her sobs. She was thankful for his restraint. She had been calm too—until she met Morry Bay. Had their meeting been no more than an episode in her life? Had it been brief as a perfume blown on a wind through a window? Had it been isolated as the oasis of beauty in her shawl?

She felt his lips on her brow and hair and was glad they did not seek her mouth. Would it be always this way? Would she always seek to elude him: to be again under the Druid mistletoe with Morry's strong arms around her and Morry's mouth on her mouth?

Although she had repulsed him then, she had known his embrace was different. It was different as the rose and gold in her shawl's design differed from neutral tints. But the shawl was woven of neutral tints, and the thread of her life might now have passed the only place in its pattern that blazed with beauty and brilliance. Must she go on to the end with only pale remembrance?

What else was there for her to do? she asked herself in return. She was still pledged to John Croft. He had come a long way to find her. He loved her still, and he said that he understood. His love was a quiet love that would never torture her by trying to challenge Morry's vivid memory. Would it not be better to go back to England with him and make the best she could of life in the cottage with the wallflowers? Could she endure Charleston again, with the harbor always before her and the scent of the jessamine bittersweet as love and death in the rain?

Croft said, as all other lovers have said: "We were meant for each other. Our lifelines touched, then were torn apart. They have come together again, Dinah."

That was what overpowered her. There was a thread of destiny. She had neither strength nor intent to turn it or break it. She said: "There is a thing that you must know."

"You need tell me nothing unless you wish to, Dinah."

"I wish to. I loved another man. Had he lived I would have married him. But he is dead. He died in the war."

He smoothed the hair back from her forehead. "Poor little lass. The time was so long. If you loved him, I know he was fine and good. Will you let me try to make it up to you? If you will, I'll do my best."

Outside the night was hell. The fires could still be seen, like hungry beasts in the distance. Screams of fear and drunken song and yells of triumph mingled into the awful, animal note that is the voice of a mob.

He held her close. He was kind and true. He was protecting them even now. There was nothing else for her to do. Besides, she owed it to him.

She said slowly: "I give my word—and I will be true to it."

He kissed her again then, gently. "You will never regret that promise if I can help it, Dinah."

Mrs. Bay came into the room. He rose, embarrassed, and set Dinah on her feet.

She smiled at them sadly but tenderly. "I came to tell you that my daughter is sleeping. Without your gift of quinine, I think she would have died, Mr. Croft."

That embarrassed him even more. He coughed. "It's nothing. I still have a surplus if you need it, Mrs. Hyrne."

Dinah said quickly: "Tis Mrs. Bay. Tis she who has given me a home since I came to America."

He looked puzzled. He was thorough but not quick. "I thought you told me the name was Hyrne."

She explained: "I meant that Mrs. Hyrne owned the house. I am Mrs. Bay. Both Mrs. Cochet and my family stay here."

"Then," he said, "I have to thank you, Mrs. Bay, for all you have done for my lass through six long years. And"—he paused, perhaps recalling the grim walls of the prison—"I have a message for you from your son, Captain Bay. I saw him when we were both prisoners in Fort Lafayette."

43

THE REAL NECESSITY of helping Mrs. Bay was Dinah's excuse for escape and for her own emotions. Realizing as Croft did not the shock of his message, she had caught Morry's mother in her arms and got her into a chair. During that first, frantic questioning the girl did not even think of herself. Morry was alive and unhurt. John Croft was telling them that. He had seen and talked with him while they thought him dead.

Mrs. Bay was begging faintly: "But why—why didn't I hear?"

"From what he told me," said the Englishman, "he had only got back to America and been put in prison a short time before I got there. He was picked up at sea off Charleston by an outgoing blockade runner."

"Still," said his mother, "that was more than a year ago!"

"You cannot realize, unless you try to run it as I did, just how tight the blockade is now, Mrs. Bay. I was allowed to talk with your son only for a few minutes. He said he had tried, time and again, to get back into the South. He nearly got in at Wilmington, but the ship was disabled and almost captured. He transferred to another, and they made several vain attempts to enter different harbors. Then, for several trips, they ran between Bermuda and England. They were caught not far from Norfolk and brought into New York."

"Is he well? What did he say? When will he get out of prison?"

He answered her last question first and frankly. "He will not get out of Fort Lafayette until the war ends. He sent you his love. He was very thin. But may I not carry you upstairs, madame? You look ill, and I think you should be in bed."

"I can walk," she insisted. "You have done enough for me."

But she could not even get to her feet. He picked her up easily. "Since I got home from India I've put on twenty pounds or so.

Dinah will have to keep me from getting overweight when I take her home with me."

Speechless, she followed them up the stairs. As he laid Mrs. Bay on her bed she implored: "Didn't my son say anything else?"

He shook his head, trying to recall, for he knew every word was precious to her. "I cannot truthfully say he did. We had only that short meeting. As I was called away he said there was something he wished to tell me about."

He stopped to smile at Dinah. "From Captain Bay's tone, I thought it was for me personally and was about my lass. But I was called away then and I did not see him again."

The happiness and confidence of his smile made her heart go cold. But she intended to tell him. Nothing else was thinkable.

"You can both sleep now," he said. "I will keep watch on the piazza tonight. I am sure that I can arrange to be sent back tomorrow night."

She slept, in spite of all, and she dreamed about Morry. She was in a boat with him again, and they knew just where they were going. Her waking thoughts had been confused as a tangle of threads. But in her dream all was clear. She was again with Morry. He had his objective in view and he was taking her to it.

Next day the city was calmer, but the fire still burned. Dinah managed to persuade Mrs. Bay to stay in bed. Dorry was better and there was a supply of medicine for her. Downstairs she told Mrs. Hyrne and Mrs. Cochet the news. Mrs. Hyrne was young enough to see romance, even through the smoke.

"To think, Dinah, that your sweetheart was bringer of all these good things! He is a fine young man, and you must love him very much." She broke off suddenly, glancing out of the window. "Oh, great heavens!"

"What is it, ma'am?" cried Dinah, joining her at the window.

"Here comes that Camellia Manchester walking along Blanding Street with a Yankee officer! She has made herself conspicuous ever since she came up here. People say she was chasing a Major Gaunt. That's bad enough, but he's at least a Confederate. She has outdone herself this time, the brazen hussy!"

Mel was not only walking with the enemy, she was walking straight up to their front door. Dinah couldn't face it. "I don't want to see her, and Mrs. Bay isn't able."

"I'll deal with her," said Mrs. Hyrne. "I'll send her about her business!"

She must have done so with vigor, for the call was brief. She reported: "Camellia said she wished to see Mrs. Bay and would come back again. I told her Morry was alive. I wish you could have seen her face! I hope he'll have sense enough not to marry her. I couldn't repeat to you, an unmarried girl, the things that have been whispered about her."

The day went by, and a shift of wind brought the fire nearer to them. By late afternoon it was only a block away. Mrs. Hyrne was frantic about the five children. Mrs. Bay and Dinah felt they must move Dorry. Word had spread that the Insane Asylum was not to be burned. Mr. Harris arrived and insisted that they take shelter in its grounds. They could not wait for Croft to return and help them.

The horses had been commandeered that morning. Hilton and Mrs. Hyrne's manservant offered to pull the carriage. They put Dorry, wrapped in blankets, and the smaller children into it. The two faithful Negroes drew it slowly along the street. All the others walked behind it.

Around them walls crashed and flames leapt and roared. Hot ashes and burning pieces of wood and paper filled the air. The streets were crowded with Negroes and with soldiers rioting. A man in blue reached out and snatched from Mrs. Hyrne's arms the bundle of pale pink flannel she was clasping to her breast. She opened her mouth and screamed wildly and the infant shrieked in his grasp. He thrust it back on her so roughly that it nearly fell to the ground.

"You can keep it, sister! I don't want it."

They camped in the walled park which surrounded the asylum. It was crowded with hundreds of other homeless ones. Cries from the terrified inmates made the night more hideous. Dorothea shook with chill after chill. The children wailed with fright. Mrs. Hyrne feared for her frail and aged parents. In and out among the crowd went the nuns, who had been burned out of their convent and who tried to tend the suffering.

At dawn an army ambulance rattled along the drive. An orderly descended from his seat beside the driver and walked from group to group, searching. At last he halted before them. "General Sherman wishes Mrs. Bay and her party brought to his headquarters," he said.

Mr. Harris, hardly able to stand, was forced by the women to get in. He demanded to be set down at his home. The driver consented. But as they turned the corner they saw that only its chimneys stood. A little farther, isolated by ruins, Mrs. Hyrne's house was still there, scorched but intact.

With the exception of Mrs. Bay and Dinah the rest got out there. At headquarters the two women were met by an aide of General Sherman and escorted into the building. It was the beautiful but still unfinished Talley mansion on Gervais Street. Orderlies were running in and out and officers kept riding up. Their commander-in-chief broke away from them.

"I sent for you last night, Mrs. Bay, when the fire reached your neighborhood. Your guard was there and traced you by questioning neighbors. I would prefer that you and your family stay here with me."

"I prefer not, General Sherman," she said. "But I thank you just the same. My house is still standing, although your men have burned those of my friends all around it."

Dinah saw him flush so darkly that she was frightened. "The South is conquered territory. What else do you expect?"

"I expect nothing, but repeat I am grateful for what you are doing. Our guard night before last was Private John Croft. He is courteous and is besides an old friend of Miss Corley. I would like to ask that, if possible, he be sent back to us tonight."

He turned to an aide. "Take the man's name and the house address and give the necessary orders."

The ambulance took them back to Blanding Street, where they found house and inmates in confusion. Poor Mrs. Hyrne was wringing her hands. "My children will starve! See what the wretches have done!"

Upon the pantry floor had been dumped the last of their scanty provisions: rice, field peas, grist, sugar, salt, butter and lard. Upon them had been poured the jugs of milk and molasses, and the whole stirred together and a broom left lying in the mess.

Mrs. Hyrne and Dinah worked all day at scooping it up and salvaging what they could. It was all they had; the washed peas and some rice and grist could be used. But the little boys complained at supper: "Ma, this hominy doesn't taste like it tasted before."

Dinah awaited John Croft's arrival that evening with dread. She intended to tell him the whole story and ask him to release her. It would be an ordeal for her and it would hurt him deeply; more so because she had just renewed her promise. But Morry was alive and Morry was coming back to her! That was all that mattered. She was in his arms again even as she thought of it. They would have life together. She was practical enough to know that the Bays had lost all their worldly goods. It added to her joy to think that the way would not be easy and that now she could make it less hard for him as they walked hand in hand.

Croft came exactly at nightfall and brought them some Army rations. "Looters got in here while I was trying to find you for the general's aide. I drove them out when I got back, but the damage was already done."

Mrs. Hyrne and Mrs. Cochet were so anxious to show gratitude, and the two older boys were so interested in the soldier, that it was nine o'clock before he and Dinah were left alone. He drew her over to the sofa and sat beside her.

"I know what a night you had last night, so I shall send you to bed soon. We have years ahead of us, lass." He put an arm around her. "I've been thinking of nothing else since you gave me your word."

He was making it so much harder. She said: "But, John, I must—"

"No, you mustn't." He drew her into his arms then. "You mustn't do or say anything except let me hold you close."

"But, John, I must tell you."

"You can tell me all in the years ahead when we are man and wife. All I ask is to sit quiet with you in my arms. It's all I've asked and dreamed of in the years past."

She gave a little moan and turned her face against his shoulder. Would it be kinder or more unkind to let him have this short happiness? He held her tenderly, kissing her forehead and her cheek. Then, true to what he had said, he released her.

"I must not be selfish. Go to bed and rest. I have been assigned as your regular guard and will be here tomorrow night again. After that we have the rest of our lives, lass."

She made one last try. "John!"

But they both heard heavy, uneven steps approaching. Somebody was coming into the house.

"I'll get rid of them," he said, and went quickly from the room.

As she followed him into the hall she heard him command: "Be off! This house is under protection of General Sherman."

But a tall man, with blue tunic unbuttoned and his cap drunkenly awry, lurched forward instead of retreating. She did not recognize him, not even when he laughed. His voice was mean.

"Ah!" he said. "My Irish friend from Charleston. Little Dinah!"

She whispered: "Leftenant Twigg!" The man did not seem dangerous, for he was holding unsteadily onto a chair.

Croft hesitated. "He is no leftenant. Is he a friend of yours?" She did not reply, and he added sharply: "If not, I'll put him out."

"He is not my friend," she said. There was loathing in her voice.

Twigg heard it. He repeated: "I am not your friend?" His voice grew sad with drunken self-pity. "It seems I am nobody's friend. Nor am I, as you call me, Leftenant Twigg any more. All the Yankees did for me, after I sold out Charleston to them, was to tell me to go back south or be drafted into their damned army."

Croft understood now that the man was a traitor. He hesitated no longer. His revolver was in his hand. He ordered: "Get out! You're drunk, and I'm guarding this house."

"It must be pleasant duty if a girl like Dinah helps you. But she's a Rebel." His lips drew back in a snarl of hate at the memory. "She's the damndest kind of Rebel, because she comes from Charleston. They despised me there. But now they're not so high and mighty. They're down. And I'm with the victors."

He let go his hold on the chair and lurched toward her. "And the victors take what they want!"

Croft stepped between them and she saw him raise his revolver.

But, although Twigg had lost everything else, his hand had not lost its cunning. Before the Englishman could squeeze the trigger, he drew and fired.

44

A LEAN, HARD-FACED captain of Regulars was the first outsider who reached them. A young orderly came in on his heels.

As the officer entered the door he said: "I heard a pistol shot in here."

His voice and his face grew harder as he saw the man in blue sprawled on the floor. He looked from Dinah, kneeling beside him, to the three pale women standing by. "Which one of you killed this soldier?"

The girl on the floor looked up at him. She could barely whisper. "Twas another soldier shot him. Is—is he dead?"

"Don't try to lie to me," he said harshly. "Nobody is here but you. I've been warned that you southern women lure our men into your houses in order to murder them."

He looked from her to Mrs. Hyrne, young and tall and handsome.

Mrs. Bay turned toward the stairs. He said: "Come back! Don't leave this room."

"I was going for brandy," she said. "Harriet Hyrne has a small flask saved for emergency."

Dinah had her hand now inside the bloody blue tunic. "I think he is still living, but he is bleeding to death. Will you, for the sake of God, get a doctor to him?"

He turned to the orderly. "Get a surgeon and an ambulance."

The boy saluted. "Yes, sir; but I wish to report—"

"Did you hear my orders? Ride as fast as you can!" The boy hurried out.

The two older little boys, in their flannel nightdrawers, were now on the stair looking over the banisters.

"William Hume," said Mrs. Hyrne, "look in the wardrobe and get your father's flask."

The child brought it and Dinah tried to force a few drops between Croft's lips. But he did not even know her now. His head lolled aside and he muttered faintly: "Twigg . . ."

The captain missed nothing. "Who is Twigg? What's he talking about?"

The girl told him simply: "Twigg is the man who shot him. He would have attacked me, but John Croft stepped between us."

He noted the use of the wounded man's name. It was some personal affair, he decided. There were some women willing to dicker with the invaders for what they could get out of it. The same type was likely to turn on a man and kill him.

The small woman in black was showing him a paper. It was an order of protection from his commander-in-chief. He said irritably: "Are you Mrs. Bay? Why didn't you show me this at once?"

"I was too distracted," she said. "I am Mrs. Bay."

"And this man was your guard?"

"Yes, he was," she said.

He questioned them sharply but fairly, as the three women held that frozen tableau. Dinah hardly heard him at all. She was trying again to make Croft swallow the brandy. But his teeth were locked now. She gave a low cry, set down the flask and put both hands over her face.

The officer, watching her shrewdly, could not believe she was acting. He had thought her guilty at first, but both her behavior and the order he had read were testimony of her innocence. He took her by an arm and pulled her to her feet.

"Sit down, miss. I'm going to see this matter through. Whether or not he's dead and whether or not you shot him, you won't help matters or help your case by weeping and fainting."

They were all so intent on the tragedy that none of them looked at the door. It was still open and two new figures had entered.

Mrs. Bay said earnestly: "Captain, this soldier is the fiancé of the young lady whom you accuse. They have been parted for years and have just found each other again."

"If you can prove that, it would help her," he admitted.

"I can prove it and can testify to her blameless character. What motive could she have to kill the man whom she was engaged to marry?"

A voice from the door struck as swiftly as a snake. "I can tell you that, Captain." It was Mel, with the same lieutenant who had escorted her to the house the day before.

The captain looked at her as she came forward. She was as

lovely as ever and her voice was low. But she made no impression on him. "If you have evidence, give it. If not, don't interfere."

"I have evidence. It is perfectly true that this girl was engaged to this soldier. For some reason she left him in Ireland and came to America. He followed her and found her when sent here as a guard. The lady of this house told me about it yesterday."

She was looking at Mrs. Hyrne. He asked shortly: "Is this true?"

"It is true," said the tall, slender young woman.

"Meanwhile, this immigrant lived for six years in the home of my fiancé and managed to estrange him from me."

She paused to touch her eyes with a small scented handkerchief. It was a mistake. The captain disliked scent and tears and was beginning to detect a personal grudge. He said: "Go on—if you have anything else to say."

"I have this to say: Captain Bay, who treated me cruelly because of her, has just been found in Fort Lafayette after being thought dead for a year. That girl heard it night before last. It gave her a motive to get rid of this humble man who loved her."

The girl she accused sat, as white as a sheet, in the chair where he had placed her. He looked from face to face and saw at once that the three women were on her side. One of them moved quickly to her and put both arms around her.

"I am Captain Bay's mother," she said. "This girl is as dear as a daughter to me. If my son loves her it is because she is good—and this woman is not." She looked directly into Mel's eyes.

"Stand aside, but do not leave," said the captain. "Here is the surgeon."

The medical man needed only a look. "The man is dead," he said. "He has been shot through the heart by someone who knew how to shoot." His voice was coldly professional.

"Then we will take these five women"—the captain's glance included Mel—"straight to the guardhouse in your ambulance. I intend to find out who shot him."

Mel gave a cry of protest and clutched her lieutenant's arm. He was infatuated enough to stammer: "But, captain, I—I was with this lady. She cannot be involved because it was all over when we came in."

He seemed to shrivel under the look of his superior officer. "You may go, lieutenant. I do not need your assistance. But I call your attention to the order that United States officers are not to mingle with the women of Columbia."

The girl in the chair spoke then. She could hardly speak, but she said, "I was alone with him. You need take only me. Mrs. Bay has an ill daughter upstairs and Mrs. Hyrne five small children. I was alone with John Croft when Twigg came in and shot him."

The other girl cried out at that. "Twigg? Is he in the city?"

The captain looked from one to the other. He had heard the wounded man whisper: "Twigg." He spoke to the girl in the chair. "At first you said 'another soldier.' Now you say 'Twigg came in and shot him.' "

"It was Twigg," she said, "but in uniform—the uniform of your army. He is a man I once knew. I knew him as a bad man."

"She's lying," said the dark girl. "Twigg is a traitor but a southern man. He could not be in the Union Army."

The orderly, afraid to interrupt, had been awaiting his chance. "Sir, I was riding behind you when we heard that shot. I was nearer this house and I saw a soldier run from it."

"Then why in the devil didn't you tell me before?"

"I started to, sir. But—but I had to go for the surgeon."

The officer looked hard at him, then turned to the woman who had her arms still around the girl in the chair. "If you know this man Twigg, describe him."

She did not hesitate. "He is very tall and his eyes are—are shifty. In Charleston he sold information to the enemy. He was about to be arrested when he escaped to a Union ship."

He looked for confirmation from one face to another. The two other women were silent. The blonde girl said: "He is tall." The dark girl nodded sulkily.

The captain looked back at his orderly. "Does that description fit the man you saw?"

"I saw him silhouetted against the light from the door. He ran across the garden and jumped the fence. He was in United States uniform and he was tall."

"I'll set a guard around this house for the night. So do not try to leave. If there's a Twigg in the Army here we'll have him before morning. If there is not, I'll have you all arrested."

Mel, in a fury, spent the night on the lower floor alone. Mrs.

Bay, Mrs. Hyrne and Mrs. Cochet had silently turned their backs on her as they gathered around Dinah and helped her up the stairs. Early next morning they saw the captain's orderly arrive. He informed them that Private Twigg had been caught, and that he was carrying a revolver with one empty chamber. He had been still drunk enough to involve himself by what he said. Their guard was dismissed and the women were no longer under suspicion.

But Dinah, their mainstay, had broken under the horror of it. She lay now in the same bed with Dorry, refusing to eat, unable to sleep. Day and night thoughts of Croft tormented her and she blamed herself for his death. Had she caused it, or was she a victim as he was? What train of events had been started when she was taken away to America—a train of events that must continue and complete its pattern?

She was still ill when the Union commander and his aides rode up to the house one day. Mrs. Bay went out to meet him on the piazza.

Sherman said: "We are resuming the march, madame. I have ordered sent to you some of the stores left at my headquarters. There is a ham, several flitches of bacon and a few other things."

She thought of the two sick girls and of the little boys who ate grist mixed with molasses because they had nothing else. She tried to choke down her hatred as she looked around her at what had been a beautiful city on a broad river. But the man had been kind to her and hers.

"I thank you, General Sherman. Your gift is a priceless one."

He held out his hand, and an aide handed him a silver chain from which hung a dozen or more keys. She had worn the same kind of chain around her waist once, with her house keys hanging from its ring.

"These are duplicate keys to the house which has been my headquarters. I am presenting them to you. The house is yours."

She had the silver chain in her hand. She looked from it to him. "Neither the house nor the keys are yours to give, General Sherman."

He spoke sternly. "I have the right to confiscate any and all property of a state in rebellion against the government."

She remembered, as if it were from a different world, his passionate love for the Union when she had known him before.

Morry had said that every man had a right to his own convictions. She had tried to drink that toast with her son, but the whisky had burned like fire. She put her hand to her throat, remembering. It had burned like the fire that had consumed this lovely city.

"I thank you again," she managed to say unsteadily. "But I must tell you that I will return these keys at once to their owners."

"As you wish," he said shortly. He turned to go.

But old Mr. Harris had heard the voices and came tottering out through the front door. Mrs. Hyrne followed him. "Pa," she implored, "please come back!"

He shook his head. "I have a duty to perform."

He removed from his head the black silk skullcap that he wore around the house. "First, I am in courtesy desirous of thanking General William Tecumseh Sherman for shelter and protection given my daughter's family."

Sherman, his soldier's instinct scenting danger to come, paused with one foot on the step and looked back at him.

"Secondly," said the old man, and he replaced the cap on his head, "I wish to tell you to your face that you are an arsonist, a blackguard and a thief."

"Pa!" screamed Mrs. Hyrne. She seized him by the arm.

"Let him speak," said Sherman. He was controlling himself, but Mrs. Bay saw that his eyes were flashing.

The old gentleman spoke. The ladies put their hands over their ears. Mrs. Cochet had, hearing the noise, run out on the piazza. The aides, finding themselves between the lines of fire, looked at each other in consternation.

They saw that their high-strung commander could barely control himself. But he waited until Mr. Harris had run out of invectives.

Then he flared back. "Sir, when I entered South Carolina I determined to ask no man his views. Those whom I met pursuing their avocations peacefully I would not molest. But if otherwise, I would shoot them down as I would a rattlesnake."

He stamped his foot on the step as he spoke, and his hair looked more red than gray. He raised an arm and clenched his fist.

"I would trample them as I would a viper!"

Then he turned and went down the steps, and his aides followed him.

"Oh, Pa," exclaimed Mrs. Hyrne reproachfully. "He had been kind to Cousin Clelia and to me."

"Stop Pa-ing me," he said. He shook off her arm and started back in the house with a more sprightly step.

In the doorway he turned and informed them: "I feel a darn sight better!"

45

IT WAS LATE April when Mrs. Bay and the girls and Hilton reached Charleston. To their joy and surprise they found Maurice there ahead of them. He looked a little thinner and a great deal older.

"Robin McRae arranged my parole. No use refusing to give it now," he told them. Dinah thought his eyes were sadder than she had ever seen them. "General Lee would not have surrendered had he seen any hope. It's over now and we've got to try—" but his voice broke there—"to look ahead instead of back."

But women are better haters than men. Mrs. Bay was still looking back. . . .

"Titus tells me that Rex and Melinda ran off as soon as you left, Mother. They are a good riddance. All the younger servants have work or will get it. We have to take care of the older ones as long as they live."

He was figuring how he could take care of them and of the three women. What had been a fortune had simply ceased to exist. He and his mother had put every cent they had in the Confederate bonds. Dorry's share he had not touched. But it had been almost entirely in cotton; and cotton had been either confiscated or burned. The rice plantations on Winyah Bay were so many acres of low ground, to be sold later for taxes.

But Mrs. Bay was not thinking of that as she looked back. She was thinking of the destruction she saw around her—of the burning of Columbia; of John Croft dead, and young Sedgwick Lewis; of her own son, safe but old and tired.

"Morry, you look ill! You've always been too thin, but I've never seen you as thin as this."

"I'm the lean kind, Mother, and strong in spite of it. But what have we done to Dinah?" His eyes were on her with anxiety and love. "She's down to witch's weight."

It made his heart ache to see this silent, white-faced girl. Even his slender sister, now recovering, looked stronger. He was alarmed too, for he could not know what had happened since he had spoken with the Englishman in Fort Lafayette. Mrs. Bay signaled him to be silent, and she told him about it later.

It puzzled him as it was puzzling Dinah. Where in the plan was the necessity for this man to die? But he never spoke of it to her. He told them what had befallen him after, half-drowned and only semiconscious, he had been picked up by a blockade runner from Savannah zigzagging to avoid Union warships on her way to Bermuda.

"They nearly ran me down. It was bright starlight and the watch happened to be looking overside to port. The first I knew of it was the noise of the steamer alongside and her wash smothering me. I heard somebody shout *'Man overboard!'* Then I was hauled in."

He would always remember that long and terrible fight against waves and wind. Something stronger than mortal will or physical strength had swept him to the point where his course and that of the blockade runner converged.

Dinah was thinking of how she had stood at the east window all that long night. Great as her love was it had not been able to help him. Coaxum's death, still unexplained, had occurred in the street beneath her even as she stood there. She loved Morry more than ever, but she felt numb with sadness.

He came to her that same day. "You and I have an appointment. Don't try to say no. I can throw you across my shoulder now, you're such a lightweight."

She smiled faintly. It was the first time she had smiled since her return.

"Do you mind when you took me in the buggy to Lowndes Grove and we fell out?"

He began to laugh. It brought back old and happy times. They had heard from Rolly and Roddy and both would soon be at the plantation again. Even now the road must be a tangle of wild-flowers and vines. He had no horse to drive her there, but he still had . . .

She was going on. "Betsy hurt my feelings something terrible. She said that, fat as I was then, I might have killed you when I fell on you."

"You didn't hurt me," he said, "although Rolly gave you credit for my black eye."

Her gray ones were wide and innocent. He explained to her.

"Ah," she cried, "as if you would ever have given me cause to, Morry!"

"I might at that. You don't know how often I was tempted. Now get your tippet or whatever you will wear. You'll need a wrap. You're going with me to a destination unknown."

They walked together across the street and out on the Southern wharf. He had always kept his boats there. A rowboat was moored underneath it. He hauled it out by the sodden rope and held it while she stepped in.

"It is so leaky and old and small that it was overlooked." His face hardened, "Overlooked by the vultures who are already gathering."

He was pushing off when they heard the shout. A man was running along the wharf.

"'Tis Captain Gaunt," said Dinah.

Maurice held the boat with his oars. Gaunt cried: "I had to catch you, Bay!" His cool voice was urgent. "I have to ask you two questions. First, where is Miss Manchester?"

Maurice said: "I'm sorry, but I neither know nor care."

Dinah saw Gaunt's expression. She told him kindly: "She is still in Columbia, I think. She was there when I left a few weeks ago."

His face was so hurt and hungry that she had not the heart to wish him to know what the other girl had done to her. He thanked her, and spoke again to Maurice. "Is she still engaged to you?"

"No!" said Maurice frankly. "I'm going to marry Dinah."

Gaunt smiled then and waved a hand. The tide was taking them out. Maurice called back: "But may God help you if you marry her, Gaunt!"

They heard him laugh. "I can handle her, without help from man or God!"

The rowboat was clear of the city wharves now and in the current from Town Creek. Maurice pulled purposefully around Castle Pinckney's marsh. Dinah remembered and cried out: "It is my dream come true!"

He looked at her under dark, raised brows as he bent for the stroke.

"I dreamed I was in a boat with you. I had been confused and troubled. John Croft had just told me that you were alive and I was going to tell him . . ."

He rested a moment on his oars. "You never told him, Dinah?"

"I tried, but he would not let me. He was happy and did not suspect, and he kept telling me there would be time enough to talk. Then—then Twigg came and killed him."

"I tried to tell him too," he said, "in Fort Lafayette. But it was at that exact moment the guard came and took him away." He looked out along the channel. "It seems as if it were planned. Neither you nor I could help what happened."

"'Tis what I would like to think," she said. "For I have been blaming myself."

"Dinah, so much is ahead of us—so much work for our hearts and hands—that we cannot afford morbid looking-back. I learned in my student days that hate was a self-destroyer. Something stronger than you or I prevented us both from telling Croft. I see now that it was well. It let a good man die happy. Can't you see that and stop blaming yourself?"

"Do you really believe it, Morry, or are you just comforting me?"

"I wish to comfort you, darling, but I believe it too. There is a pattern planned and we are used in shaping it. We can even help if we work with it. Old Uncle told me that long ago. This plan can be changed temporarily when a thread is broken or soiled: by awful events like war or by the violence of men like Twigg."

She repeated softly: " 'Better far a man should have been dead. . . .' "

"Better far. He destroys himself, but the whole design falls back into place. It is a thought that makes one feel very small and yet very important. Even this rowing of a leaky boat across the harbor has part in it"—he was teasing now—"although you still don't know why."

She was looking at him with relief in her eyes. "Ah, it was in the dream! All was clear and happy then, though I did not know where we were going. I knew that you knew, and it was enough for me."

He laughed at her. "What a wife you'll make! Yes; I know where I'm going."

Her heart had lightened strangely. She sat happily on the thwart and smiled at him as he faced her, swinging to stroke and lift. She did not recognize the creek where he had taken her and Dorry on a summer afternoon that seemed so long ago. They were approaching its mouth from a different way.

He jumped out and dragged the boat up on the shore, stepped alongside and lifted her. He held her tight against his heart for a moment before he set her down.

She looked around. It was early for the hot-hued gaillardias, but the feathery tamarisks swayed in bloom from pale pink to deep rose.

"'Tis the shipyard," she cried, delighted. "Shall we see Mr. Mullen?"

"We shall. I've come to see him about something that means a great deal to us both."

With his arm around her waist they went up the path together. The building sheds were not badly damaged and small boats were moored in the docks. Mr. Mullen was climbing out of one. He seemed to be wearing the same clothes that he had worn when they saw him last, and he still smoked the same pipe.

"'Tis Morry Bay!" he cried aloud. "I heard that ye were destroyed!"

"I'm too tough to kill, Mr. Mullen." He laughed without mirth. "We'll have to be tough to get through what is ahead."

The shipwright nodded. "Times will be hard, I'm thinking. But it is me luck that already men are calling for boats."

Dinah saw Maurice's eyes light. "Is that so? Who can buy them?"

"Fishermen, ferrymen, skippers who carry cargo in and out the waterways from sea island truck farms. They must take up their work again and at once, in order to live. Their boats were taken. They have no ready money, but they'll pay me as they can. I have work enough for years, but I'm short on skilled labor."

Maurice's voice was eager. "That's *my* luck! For I've come to ask you to give me that job you offered me when I was a boy."

Mr. Mullen smiled, then gripped his shoulder with a large, hard hand. "Do you mean it, lad?"

"I mean it more than I've ever meant anything else in my life."

"Then ye are hired," the Irishman said. He and Morry shook hands.

He turned to Dinah with twinkling eyes. "I mind when ye were last here I was bold enough to give the two of ye advice. The lad has done as I bade him. What of yourself, lass?"

She blushed as pink as the tamarisk bloom. Maurice drew her forward and close against him.

"Aye," she said, "Mr. Mullen. I took your advice myself."

On the return trip, Maurice's back was turned to the shattered skyline. Dinah saw it in every detail, but it did not daunt her. All she had ever wanted, all she wanted still, was to stay close beside him and share whatever came to him. Before, he had had so much more than she. She had felt that perhaps he did not need her. Now she could wait with the lamp lit when he came home from his task.

He was asking himself the same thing, from his standpoint rather than hers. He had had so much to give her and had longed to give it. Was he selfish to take her now when he had nothing at all? He fell silent as they neared the wharf. She watched his face and was troubled. He stood up and tied the painter to a ring, stepped over and sat beside her and took her in his arms. In the damp twilight under the lee of the wharf the boat creaked softly and bumped gently.

"Dinah, it's going to be hard. Do you love me enough to fight it through? When I think of what I could once have given you, sweetheart, I feel selfish to hold you. What have I got now?"

"You have work to do and a woman who loves you," she answered him promptly. "The two are enough for any man. For myself I am content. I never cared so much for the things you had. Don't you see it was those things that nearly kept us apart? All I ever wanted is what I have now, Morry: the right to be always at your side and to help you if you weary."

DATE DUE